UNANSWERED LIVES

UNANSWERED LIVES

Lindy Lieban

Copyright © 1998 by Lindy Lieban.

Library of Congress Control Number: 98-88476
ISBN: Hardcover   978-0-7388-0167-4
                Softcover   978-0-7388-0168-1

All rights reserved. No part of this book may be reproduced or transmitted in any form or by any means, electronic or mechanical, including photocopying, recording, or by any information storage and retrieval system, without permission in writing from the copyright owner.

This is a work of fiction. Names, characters, places and incidents either are the product of the author's imagination or are used fictitiously, and any resemblance to any actual persons, living or dead, events, or locales is entirely coincidental.

Any people depicted in stock imagery provided by Thinkstock are models, and such images are being used for illustrative purposes only.
Certain stock imagery © Thinkstock.

Print information available on the last page.

Rev. date: 06/01/2015

To order additional copies of this book, contact:
Xlibris
1-888-795-4274
www.Xlibris.com
Orders@Xlibris.com
569405

CONTENTS

Chapter One 9
Chapter Two 16
Chapter Three 21
Chapter Four 25
Chapter Five 30
Chapter Six 34
Chapter Seven 37
Chapter Eight 41
Chapter Nine 45
Chapter Ten 54
Chapter Eleven 58
Chapter Twelve 62
Chapter Thirteen 64
Chapter Fourteen 70
Chapter Fifteen 86
Chapter Sixteen 96
Chapter Seventeen 102
Chapter Eighteen 117
Chapter Ninteen 119
Chapter Twenty 124
Chapter Twenty-One 130
Chapter Twenty-Two 134
Chapter Twenty-Three 136
Chapter Twenty-Four 142
Chapter Twenty-Five 153
Chapter Twenty-Six 162
Chapter Twenty-Seven 164
Chapter Twenty-Eight 170

Chapter Twenty-Nine 175
Chapter Thirty 181
Chapter Thirty-One 195
Chapter Thirty-Two 205
Chapter Thirty-Three 229
Chapter Thirty-Four 239
Chapter Thirty-Five 247
Chapter Thirty-Six 275
Chapter Thirty-Seven 285
Chapter Thirty-Eight 293
Chapter Thirty-Nine 297
Chapter Forty 302
Chapter Forty-One 333
Chapter Forty-Two 356

CHAPTER ONE

Cara Covington's name was fancy but she wasn't. Her bones stuck out to greet people long before they heard her hello. Much like the rings of a tree tell age, the lines in her face told of pain, neglect and harshness. She was at the same time weathered and withered. Her long, skinny, yellowed fingers clutched the cigarette as she opened the car door.

The engine of the 1979 Pontiac Bonneville rattled almost as loudly as Cara's lungs. The black smoke coming from its exhaust made the tail pipe vibrate with exaggerated power. She picked up the insulated cup and took a long deep drink. Nothing soothed her as much as the taste of her fourth glass of whiskey at ten a.m. on a Sunday morning. Before backing out, she took a moment to eye an older gentleman pumping gas. He was bent, not so much with age as with life. Cara felt a connection.

Sighing deeply, she steered the Bonneville toward her trailer. As she drove past boarded up businesses and deserted little bars, she thought about how lifeless Sunday mornings were in Jacinto Corners. It was a town that thrived on what most people would call Bubba's Bests: bars, beer and brawls. Texas law prohibited denizens from buying, drinking or selling booze before noon on Sunday so the only place in Jacinto Corners that was lively until then was the washeteria. After a Saturday night, people not only aired their dirty laundry but shared it and showed it off!

As she pulled into the driveway, acrid smoke made her nostrils lift in defiance. Her old man, Buster, was burning tires again. She grabbed the packs of no name cigarettes off the front seat and opened the car door. She was greeted by Buster's dog, Old Blue. Cara wasn't an animal lover but Blue was tolerable. He stayed outside and was easy to ignore. He had only one habit that bothered her and that was sniffing her crotch when he said hello. She'd always thought it was his way of telling her that if you lie with the dogs then you end up with ticks. He was right most of the time so she'd just pat him on the head and go on her way.

The screen door didn't need opening. The hinges had long since rusted off and it hung to one side, much like the head of a baby nodding off to sleep. She dropped the cigarettes on the kitchen counter and looked around at her life. The trailer looked as worn and used as did she. Charlie came mewing, not out of affection but hunger.

"Damn cat! You eat better than we do and you want more?"

Sinking into the velour of the couch, Cara took a long drink from her insulated mug. She hated Sunday. It wasn't so much that she liked any other day better; it was just that Sunday meant another week would start all over tomorrow. The day made her feel she begat hopelessness, just as her parents before her and their parents before them. They all had known the sorrow.

Cara picked up the remote and punched at the worn, numberless buttons. Television would keep her company until Buster came stumbling in, sweaty and hungry. She sat staring at the television as if it could take her away from the vast nothingness that lived in her heart.

Coughing loudly at some ridiculous Gap commercial, she instinctively repositioned the wayward pin that closed a gaping hole in her blouse. She was normally a woman who put great care in putting herself together but on Sunday she didn't doll up until it was time for a trip to Liars and a night of being one.

She heard the screen door and Buster's thuds as he came into the kitchen. Buster coughed, lit a cigarette, opened a beer and farted into the already stagnant air. Laughing loudly, as if he had accomplished something, he said,

"Bet my farts smell sweeter than them tires I been burnin'!"

Cara and Buster had been together for a year. His social security disability check helped pay the bills and he was a low maintenance partner. He was satisfied tending his few head of cattle, working his small corn field and tinkering in the barn with machinery. A little domestic attention and occasional sex made him a happy man. She liked that he could hold more beer than a keg and was a friendly drunk, not obnoxious or mean. To her, Buster was a prize and a good man.

Any dreams Cara had of a better existence had long ago been devoured by the sharks of life. She had been attractive once but circumstance and the lack of it made her into what everyone knew she would become, haggard. She'd thought for awhile that she'd live to see her daughter, Sandy, break out of the mold but she'd lost hope when Sandy met Avery.

Sandy Covington-Anderson was a massive woman. Her pink stretch pants had been worn too often, were stained and had a tear in the back that showed her dingy underwear. She didn't mind the tear, since it was as much a part of her as were all the other holes in her life. She wore her clothes with as much pride as she wore her own skin.

Sandy moved the grocery basket slowly along the dairy aisle, not noticing that her son, Tommy, had disappeared. Her husband, Avery, looked for cheese that was cheap but didn't taste like it had been made with soured milk. She watched him as he bent over the shelves. She didn't mind that his stomach came bounding out from his belt, circled around to his back and jiggled with every movement. She saw beyond the filth of his clothes and the natural stench of sweat mixed with dirt. He was her man and she was his woman.

It was Tommy's eighth birthday and he was scouring the store for birthday gifts. He came running up excited and jabbering ninety to nothing. Sandy noticed the pinwheel in his hand.

"Hey, Mama, look what this here thing does when I blow on it!"

He pursed his lips and blew the foil pieces into a kaleidoscope of turning colors. He blew a little too long and spittle came from his mouth, ran down his shirtless chest and mixed with the caked-on dirt of poverty.

"Mama, ain't that pretty? Can I get it for my birthday?"

His excitement was evident in his frail, sunken chest as it heaved its bones forward in an effort to breathe and speak at the same time. His bare feet danced on the cool linoleum floor, leaving traces of his dirt as gray shadows on the wax.

He tried to show his mama the pinwheel again but saw the look that meant her answer was no and she better not have to say it. She gave him that look often and he knew better than to press the issue. He placed the pinwheel in the middle of the floor and turned to follow his parents.

Avery put the cheese in the basket and smiled a semi-toothless smile at Sandy. His eyes always twinkled when he looked at her.

"Hey darlin', what time did you say we had to be at your mama's? She's gettin' Tommy a cake, right? We ain't gotta worry with buyin' no cake. Sure was sweet of your mama to be doin' this."

Tommy chimed in.

"Mama? Granny ain't gonna forget, is she? 'Member last year when we came knockin' on the door and old Buster couldn't even get her to wake up? 'Member when you slapped me 'cause I said somethin' 'bout granny bein' drunk again?"

Sandy opened a bag of chips and shoved some into her mouth. Her words slid out with ease, as if the oil from the chips greased their exit from her mouth.

"Shut your trap, Tommy! Your granny was just ill, that's all. She was feelin' poorly. You're such a selfish little bastard! You need to get over thinkin' the world was made for you, little boy!"

Tommy felt the sting of her words and quickly made amends.

"Sorry, Mama. I wasn't meanin' to make you mad all over."

Tommy moved away, afraid that the hand of denial would be forced against his face. He loved his granny but he knew things about her, things no one ever talked about. He'd seen her pour herself from a bottle his whole life. He knew where she got her personality because he'd seen her without it at times.

Passing the beer aisle, Avery looked longingly at his wife.

"Darlin', you got any cash on you?"

Sandy pulled some bills from the inside of her bra and started counting the small stash. She resented that the state dictated what they could buy. She thought it a cruelty to keep people in circumstances that demanded occasional escape and then deny them the means to do it.

"I was savin' this for washin' clothes but lord knows we both need beer right now more than clean clothes. Get the cheapest, okay? It ain't the cost but the affect that counts."

Tommy watched as his mama counted the money again and then handed it to his dad. He often wished that he was grown up so he didn't have to ask for things. He didn't like that he had no say or control over his life. He hated that to be heard meant risking trouble.

"Hey, Daddy, with that much money I could get me the pinwheel and one of those cool cars I done seen on the toy rack!"

His daddy's reply made him wince.

"Tommy, me and your mama gotta do without 'cause of you! We can't be wastin' no damn money on toys and such! It's about time you learned, boy! Life don't come easy and if you shit in one hand and wish in the other, the one that stinks fills up the fastest!"

Hanging his head, Tommy apologized.

"Sorry, Daddy. Mama's right about me. Guess I'm just a selfish boy! Ain't nothin' special about no silly birthday. Ain't nothin' special about nothin', not even me!"

Cara took the cake out of the oven, removed the toothpick from her mouth, wiped off a bit of spit from the end and stuck it into the layers to see if they were baked through. She didn't care that the layers were uneven or that a roach had been left to bake in the bottom of the pan. It was the effort that counted and little Tommy would never notice the difference once the icing and candles were in place. She poured another glass of Jack Daniels from the gallon bottle and drank it down before wiping the drying jelly off the knife. Giggling, she thought the stain the jelly made on her shirt resembled a heart. She sure was glad her family didn't stand on ceremony. Hell, Tommy would be lucky if any of them were left standing at all by the end of the evening.

Opening the icing container, she had a coughing spell and dropped the just cleaned knife into the pot of bacon grease sitting on the counter. She needed another cigarette. Her lungs always rebelled when too much fresh air got in them.

Buster came walking in from the bedroom where he had been taking a nap. Cara looked at the indentations on his face from the pillow creases and was glad he had slept hard. She loved the sound of sleep in his voice when he asked,

"What time's Sandy, Avery, and that young un coming over?"

Using the other side of her blouse to wipe off the bacon grease, she said more to herself than him,

"I told them around seven. You know how they can eat and I figured they'd done snacked a while by that time. I bought two chickens for them chicken and dumplings but that's an appetizer for them two! By the way, you need to go slide that board under the cushions again or we'll be needin' a new couch after they leave!"

Tommy got out of the car before it came to a full stop and ran to the door. He knocked, peered in and called out.

"Hey, Granny? You in there?"

He smelled cake and the smile on his face looked like a summer slice of watermelon with a few of the seeds spat out.

"Hey, little birthday boy! Get yourself in here and give your granny a hug! Let's see, are you two today?"

He rolled his eyes at his granny's silliness. She knew he was eight or at least he thought she did. She was just messing with him and that meant she was in a good mood. He wrapped his arms around her thin body and he realized he'd seldom been that close to her. She smelled of a strange combination of cake, bacon, jelly, cigarettes, body odor, whiskey and exhaustion. He looked at the half iced cake sitting on the counter and the box of candles sitting next to it. He felt love in his heart for his granny. She hadn't forgotten.

Tommy sat at the kitchen table listening to his family laugh the laugh of liquor. Every once in awhile, he scooted his chair back and joined them in the living room. He tapped his granny on the arm and asked,

"Hey, Granny, anyone ready for me to blow out the candles and eat some cake?"

She looked at him but he couldn't help feel she didn't see him at all. His mama just kept hushing him up and telling him to go color in the book his granny got him for his birthday. He tried to tell her it wasn't that kind of book but she looked right through him, too.

He went back to the table and stared at the candles on the cake. He wondered if he scrunched his eyes up real tight and blew hard that maybe his wish would come true? He wanted to believe it was possible but his wishes never came true. He'd wished on the way to his grandma's that his mama would take him up on her lap, squeeze him real tight, and say,

"Happy Birthday, Tommy! I sure am glad you were born! And just because you are such a good boy, here's that pinwheel you wanted. Your daddy and I decided you were more important than beer. In fact, we decided you were the most important thing in the world to us."

He stared at the candles again. Nope, he wouldn't be getting any wishes. He was only eight but disappointment had been a word he had learned early and so he was careful about not disappointing himself.

CHAPTER TWO

The Texas moon hung full in the sky and Cara was already high enough to join it in its dance with the clouds. She reached to grab the thin black strap to her shirt but she kept grabbing shoulder blade instead.

"Damn! I don't know why they make this shit so hard to get into!"

Buster had a pillow over his head to block out her irritating rantings. His day had been spent working in the hot Texas sun and he cared nothing at all about spending a hot Texas night in a urine pit of a bar watching Cara rub all over strange men. He wasn't a jealous man. Cara was a good ride and he knew when he met her he would never own her. He just wished she would hurry and get her drunk ass out of the bedroom and turn off the light.

Cara slapped Charlie off the stack of dirty dishes in the sink and picked up a cigarette butt from the overflowing ashtray.

"This sure in the hell ain't gonna be the only butt smokin' tonight, old cat! Mama's ready to have her some fun!"

Charlie watched her as she stepped over the spilled cat food on the floor. Her inebriated legs had trouble maneuvering around the hard kernels. She glared at the cat for mocking her with his eyes.

"Charlie, quit lookin' at me. You know in some Asian countries they eat the likes of you! You just better watch that I don't make stew out of your ass!"

Cara moved the clothes off the coffee table in order to find her car keys. She tried to remember where she laid them after she had gone to get her cigarettes. Her laughter sounded like years of smoking, booze and swallowing the acidity of life. She wished she had put her keys on the counter before opening the whiskey. She reached into the couch corners to see if they had perhaps fallen between the cushions. All she found was a dirty pair of her underwear, a half eaten cookie and the black lace bra she'd wanted to wear with the blouse she had on. She thought about changing but was not about to have another wrestling match with her blouse straps. She didn't think it mattered anyway. She smiled and thought that a white bra would come off just as easy as a black one!

Liars was a typical East Texas dive set back off the highway. The paint on the outside was as flaked and worn as the patrons on the inside. It smelled like mold, lust, sweat, old wood and broken hopes, all wrapped into a crust of stale beer. The floors creaked from years of too much spilled life. Scuff marks told of people slipping through the cracks but inebriated patrons were too busy to notice their souls seeping into the dusty crevices as well. Beer, whiskey and country music made everyone fill with hope that the next guy had it worse. It was as it had to be.

Cara saw Roger sitting alone at a table, seemingly making love to a beer. She watched as he stroked the side of the bottle, rubbing his fingers along the smooth surface. She almost choked when he lovingly peeled back the label, as if to undress the rough surface waiting underneath. Yes, she thought, his attention to the bottle was much like peeling back a woman's panties to find the rough, hairy surface waiting to be touched by gentle fingers. He hit a chord deep inside her that made lust take over and her body twitch with excitement.

Taking the seat across from Roger, Cara dipped her bony right shoulder down to let the strap loose on her shirt. Roger looked up to see the white of her bra outline the wrinkled, but inviting, protrusion jutting out atop the lace. He reached over and ran his fingers just above the lace and then curved them slightly to cup and caress the softness. Cara took in a sharp breath, feeling wetness penetrate her too tight black Wranglers. Yes, tonight she would not cry in her beer, or anyone else's. Her life always went unanswered but she'd be damned if her desires would!

Roger had been an incredible lover but as Cara struggled once again with the straps to her shirt, she felt an emptiness inside. She watched Roger sleeping soundly on the bed beside her. She wondered why her search for life always left her feeling dead once the initial excitement was gone?

Cara finished dressing and kissed Roger lightly on the forehead. She felt a desperate need for Charlie's warm mewing and the sound of Old Blue's bark as she turned the Bonneville into the yard. More than anything though, she needed to hear the deep snores of Buster, mixed with his occasional loud farts. She needed to be home. She scribbled a quick note for Roger:

Thanks for an incredible evening darlin'. Sex was great, you were sweet, maybe we'll do it again sometime!

The night was clear and warm as she drove the ten miles back home. Her dances with temptation always put her in a reflective mood. She didn't think much about her life or how it happened to her except when the whiskey was wearing off and she was wearing the left overs of sex.

She had been one of thirteen children. There wasn't a middle to thirteen. There were only those older and those younger. Not even being child seven could be considered the middle. Her daddy was a farmer who spent as much time planting his personal seed as he did cotton, corn, and alfalfa. Their life was poor, rigid and dirty.

Cara had to quit school in the ninth grade. Her mama had gotten ill years earlier and she had to take over the duties of the house. She had six older brothers and three younger ones. There were things that were set out for women to do and other things left to men. The raising of babies, dishes, cleaning, and cooking were not things her brothers would ever do. The last three babies had been girls but they were too young to be of any help. Cara never had time to resent her lot in life. She was too busy with the cooking, cleaning and mending of other's lives. She wiped more dirty noses and dirty butts than she could count.

She met Henry when she was seventeen and married him. She

never loved Henry. He was a convenience, a way out of a life that knew no reward. He wasn't handsome, or charming, or rich. He was just there. They bought a little shack in the piney woods of East Texas. Henry worked the fields and did construction work when the weather was good. Cara went to work for a local grocer and worked in the vegetable section. She spent her time throwing out bad fruit and vegetables. Many was the day at work when she thought of throwing herself out with the rotten apples. Her job seemed to suit her. She often thought how Covington was a name much like Red Delicious, indicative of something grand but really nothing special. A name didn't keep a person from bruising, rotting in the warmth, developing worms or being unfit for the purpose for which she had been intended.

When Henry drank enough, he would mount Cara and ride her like a bronco in need of taming. She often compared sex with him to her daddy's nightly visits that started when she was nine. There was a difference. Her daddy had been needy but so apologetic and tender. He'd whispered to her the whole time he was atop her. He told her he was so sorry but it was just something he needed to do. It felt natural, like cleaning up his dirty clothes or washing his dirty dishes. With Henry it was like he was taking something rather than her giving something.

Cara pulled up to the trailer and placed her head on the steering wheel. Hot tears stung her face. She dealt with life through a bottle just as surely as her daughter, Sandy, dealt with it through food. She'd heard the sounds coming from Sandy's bedroom before Henry died and she knew. Her own guilt kept her from saying anything but she knew. She even remembered the awful scream that first night. The scream of a young girl whose future had been entered, cast in stone and then cast aside!

Cara opened the screen door and wished she hadn't gone home with Roger. She lit the back burner on the stove, drew the fire into the cigarette, inhaled deeply and left her memories right where they belonged. The back burner had been their home for so long and it was better to leave them there. She had no business dredging up the past when she needed all her strength to get through each day.

CHAPTER THREE

Avery rolled off Sandy, breathed deeply, and then drifted happily off to sleep. Sandy took the box of cookies off the night stand and shoved three into her mouth. The motion of her jaws reminded her of where her mouth had just been and she wanted to cry. She loved Avery but guilt kept her from savoring the bond of sex. Still feeling the wetness between her legs, her thoughts went to her first time.

She had been only eight. She'd cried both from the rough feel of being ripped and from a deeper pain she'd been too young to understand. She'd loved her daddy so much and knew in her heart he would never really do anything to hurt her. As she swallowed the cookies, she remembered his words afterwards.

"Little Darlin', you have so much more cushion than your mama. You feel like home. All nice and comfortable like an over stuffed couch!"

She'd never felt hate in her heart for her daddy. It seemed to her that he'd always been a desperate man searching for the love of family and looked to her for what he couldn't find in Cara. Her child's body accepted him with innocence and with no conditions. Any resentment and anger she felt was directed at her mother, not him.

Sandy heard Tommy coughing and struggled to get her four hundred pound frame out of the sunken mattress. She was damn glad to have a boy. She never told him that. She never wanted him for a minute to feel special. He would suffer fewer disappointments in life if he knew his place. She loved the boy and even wanted to spoil him but she knew better. She would never be able to give him anything but what he needed to survive and she would not coddle him into being too weak to take the punches of life.

Sandy made sure Tommy was okay and went to the kitchen to feed her emptiness. She never took all the food out at once in her late night feedings. If she ever looked at what she consumed, it would make her see the vastness of the holes she was filling. Two chickens, two boxes of brownies and half a box of cereal later, she thought about going to wake Avery with a gentle caress. The food hadn't filled all the spaces that felt empty.

She tried to slide quietly into bed but her girth caused the trailer to shake from one end to the other. Avery turned a sleepy head towards her.

"You okay, darlin'?"

She decided a lie was better than truth and told him she was fine. Her mother used booze to construct walls and she used food. They were both architects of their own designs but their buildings were made the same way. The roof was strong, the walls were in place, but there was no foundation. She watched as Avery slept soundly beside her and she wanted desperately to feel the safe warmth of knowing the future would be different. The loud, drunken voice of her mother played in her head. The same thing was always repeated.

"That which is, is. That which ain't will never be. The world is fucked and we don't got the balls to go against the game!"

Sandy squeezed the silent tears from her eyes and slept not to dream of tomorrows but to forget the todays. She knew she would wake up to the same damn world but for a while, in the dark of night, she was a princess, Avery her prince, and there was hope that Tommy could live life rather than have it live him.

Tommy tried to close his eyes to find sleep but the walls of his life were much too thin. He heard his parents in their bedroom and felt the rocking of the trailer each time he heard the grunts and the moans. His parents kept him awake many nights but tonight it was more his worried mind that kept sleep from him. He was only eight but he had things to think about. Fear often curled around him like the torn, dingy blanket that covered his bed. Tomorrow he would be reminded of what it was not to be in control of life.

The welfare lady, Ms. Callier, was coming to the house and he knew what that meant. He would have to get up early, clean his room, fluff up the clothes in his drawers to make them seem fuller, and above all tiptoe around his mama because she would be fit to be tied! School started in a week and this was the *big* visit. Ms. Callier didn't cut his parents any slack when it came to the before-school visit. She always said the same thing,

"The boy's only chance in life is to be educated. You don't want him growing up with the same deficiencies the two of you have!"

He never understood why but he always felt like she had slapped him when she said those words. She had an attitude, a distaste, that made him feel like he was less. As he drifted off to a slow sleep, he thought Ms. Callier was no better than the kids at school who made fun of him all the time.

Tommy awoke to the sound of something banging against the wall in the bathroom. He knew his mama was trying to clean the shower stall. He usually did it for her. She had trouble bending her large body into such a tiny area.

Tommy yanked his pajama top over his head. He inspected it to see if it had another night of wear in it. His mama had not washed clothes. The wash money had gone for other things. Looking at the stains on his pajama bottoms, he wondered where he could put them where Ms. Callier wouldn't see them. Tommy sometimes forgot himself and wet the bed at night. When his mama didn't do wash, he had to just let them air dry. Panic suddenly struck his heart. Oh gosh, he thought, what about the sheets? Would Ms. Callier unmake his bed and see the yellow stains that had run together with his body's dirt and made a ring of noticeable shame? He ran to the bed and quickly pulled the sheets and blanket up. Maybe if he did a real good job of making it, she wouldn't have the heart to undo all his hard work.

Tommy placed the old worn teddy bear his mama gave him on the pillow. He hugged it for luck and hope. He went to his closet and suddenly wished the doors were still on it. No matter how he placed things in it, it seemed like it was always a mess. He seldom thought about his life being a mess but sometimes other people made him think about it. He felt dirty many times in school. He saw the other kids with clean hair, shiny faces and really cool clothes. He knew no matter how hard he scrubbed, he never looked like the other kids. It seemed to him that as soon as the soap left his body, the dirt leapt from the water back onto him.

Placing the last toy into the closet, Tommy looked around his room and sighed. His room was like him. He could put things away, straighten things up, but he couldn't hide the stains on the carpet, get rid of the mold on the wallpaper, fix the tattered curtains, or put fresh paint on the furniture. He never wanted fancy but he sure would trade filth for fixed sometimes. He heard the voice of Ms. Callier, and his heart sank. He knew that tonight there would be lots of beer, loud battles and blame would be thrown around the room like a ball.

Tommy smoothed the cow lick down, pinned his shirt where the button was missing and prepared to go look at his world through welfare's eyes. He'd already grown tired of seeing the attitude of the people at the grocery store when his mama handed them her card. He hated how the other kids at school called him names because of the way he looked and dressed. He hated wanting things and knowing he couldn't have them. He wanted to be proud of who he was and people just wouldn't let him.

CHAPTER FOUR

Sandy watched as Ms. Callier opened the refrigerator door. She saw her back stiffen and knew it was because of the bottles of beer on the shelf.

"I am assuming these were *not* bought with food stamp money?"

Her voice had that superior tone that made the hairs on the back of Sandy's neck stand up.

"Ms. Callier, we ain't stupid and we ain't criminals!"

Tommy ran to the refrigerator to take out the orange juice to pour himself a glass.

"Look here, Ms. Callier! My mama cares about me gettin' my vitamin C. They taught us that in school. We got apples too! And know what? Look here, there's cheese and even bologna! My parents been takin' real good care of me!"

Celia Callier looked at Tommy. She wanted to like the child but she just saw a smaller version of his dad standing before her. She looked into the dullness of his blue eyes. She stared at the permanently stained neck rising just above the tatters of what was once a t-shirt collar and found her hands going to her own neck to feel its smoothness. She wanted to believe he would grow up different from what he was but she knew he wouldn't. She wanted to like him but found her opinion of his parents flowed over onto him. She wanted to reach out to hug him but was afraid he would rub off on her.

Sandy had to allow Ms. Callier free range of the house, including drawers, cabinets and closets. She hated the tsking, the stupid little negative shakes of her head but mostly she hated that there was no attempt to mask her disdain for them. Sandy wondered if the woman ever realized that her case load was human.

Sandy showed Ms Callier to the door and the moment she was out of sight, turned to Tommy.

"What the hell was all that foolish talk about them groceries? You think your daddy and I need you to defend what shit we bring into this house to eat?"

Tommy was shocked at her anger. He thought he was helping. He tried to explain.

"But Mama!"

"Shut up and get to your room!"

"But Mama, I was just...!"

The slap came seemingly from nowhere and Tommy didn't wait for a second. Picking himself up off the floor, he ran to his room.

His tears couldn't stain old teddy more than he already was. The old bear never minded anyway. Tommy held the softness close to his heart in order to ease the harsh reality of his life. In broken hearted sobs, he told teddy of his woes.

"I ...I wasn't m...m...meanin' no hhharm! I..I..I..know m...m..mama ain't r..r..really m..m..mad at m..mme! It's j..j..just that old M..Ms Callier."

With his heart still hiccuping with sobs, Tommy fell asleep. His arms were wrapped tightly around teddy's warmth and his body was curled in a fetal position. He awoke to the sound of his daddy's drunken voice.

"Boy! You get your ass in here!"

Tommy wasn't frightened. He knew whenever he tried to fix what was broken there would be a price to pay. He walked into the living room and saw the belt in his daddy's hands.

"Your mama told me you got to bein' a little smart mouth when that bitch was here today."

Tommy bent over without being told and took what his daddy gave. He figured it was better for his parents to take their anger out on him than on each other.

Tommy slipped his pajama bottoms over his sore behind, and thought of his granny. He understood why she drank and wished he could stay drunk too! He was so tired. It wasn't the whippings or the going to bed without supper that bothered him, it was the feeling that he'd somehow deserved what he got but didn't know why.

Avery hated having to whip Tommy but he wouldn't stand for Sandy or him to be disrespected in his own house. He'd promised himself that he'd have a hand in the raising of his son and if that meant having a heavy hand at times so be it. His thoughts turned to his own childhood as they often did when he drank.

Avery's mama was good at having babies but she wasn't very good at raising them. He always blamed his daddy for his mama being a baby factory. He'd often imagined his daddy begging for sex after one of his long trips on the road. One night he heard his mama's voice coming from the bedroom but the voice answering her wasn't his daddy's and it was his mama doing the begging!

"Just one more time, Frank! Please!"

His daddy's name was Arnold, so he'd tried to look through the keyhole. Before he could get a good look at what was gong on, his baby sister, Ariel, came out of her room crying. He was ten, and the oldest, so he took it upon himself to see to things when his mama was indisposed. He brought her back into the darkness of the room that resembled a mattress store. There wasn't room for head boards or frames, just mattresses placed on the floor all pushed together. The five youngest boys and three baby girls slept in the room. As Avery found an empty spot to soothe away Ariel's bad dream, he felt damn lucky to share his room with only his younger brother, Thomas, and the real baby, Carter. The mattress room was reserved for the kids that still wet the bed and the smell of ammonia was enough to knock a person on his ass.

Avery heard his mama's bedroom door open and saw a shadowy figure go down the hall to the living room. He saw the kitchen light go on and got up to see what the stranger was doing. The man was naked and stood in front of the refrigerator, swaying slightly. He turned once he sensed he was not alone. The man's eyes were glossed over from too much sex and too much booze. He had scars on his chest and neck from nights of sharp words and sharper knives. The tattoos gracing his arms and chest were the fantasies little boy's dreams were made of, women with big breasts and snakes around their waists. He took a beer from the fridge and sat naked at the kitchen table.

Avery puffed up, poured a glass of milk and sat across from a man he saw only as not his daddy.

"My daddy will be home in the mornin', ya know? He is a big man. He'll kick your ass if you're still here!"

The man sat sipping his beer in silence for a moment and then in a voice that could chill a ghost, said,

"Son, I was in the mood for a whore tonight but I ain't in no mood for some snot nosed brat threatening me with what tomorrow will bring. Time you learned, boy. A man fucks a whore, he don't spend the night with one!"

Avery didn't bother finishing his milk but got up feeling dirty being in the same house with his mother. He crept past the mattress room and back to his own to find Carter standing in his crib in need of changing and a bottle.

Avery sat in the rocker and rocked little Carter back to sleep, holding the bottle upright so air wouldn't get inside. He wiped the tears he didn't understand. He cried not so much because the man called his mama a whore but because he knew she was one. Why should he care what his mama was or wasn't? Why did it matter that the man who had just been riding her like a vintage Harley had no respect for her? Why did Avery know that the baby in his arms would never know a loving mother's arms, just as he hadn't? He didn't know why he cared about any of that shit. He was only ten and all he wanted to care about was whether he could play in little league or got picked to be on a team at recess. He wanted to romp and play. He knew he would never have what he wanted. More than anything he wanted to be a kid, not to take care of them all the time.

Avery placed little Carter back in his crib, then sat on the edge of his bed with his head in his hands. He heard his mama's voice coming from the hallway. She was begging, crying. He knew the man was leaving and that his mama didn't want him to go. He heard the front door slam and a car engine start. He was not prepared when his mama came into the room, a flimsy, torn robe wrapped around her naked body. She screamed at the top of her lungs.

"You little bastard! Now look what you've done!"

He didn't mind the slap across the face near as much as his mama's voice waking up all the babies.

CHAPTER FIVE

Tommy heard his mama's sobs as he peered through her slightly opened bedroom door. Knocking softly, he could see her stiffen and quickly wipe away her tears.

"Mama, you okay?"

She turned to face him, her eyes stained red with sorrow and her large frame seemingly made small and frail by her pain. Sitting next to her on the bed, he wasn't sure if she would tell him what was wrong or just ignore him. The phone rang before she said a word and she rose as if her four hundred pound body contained the weight of the world. Tommy didn't follow her right away but remained on the bed looking around his parent's bedroom. He saw his mama's flattened shoes sitting in the corner, looking as tired from the load they carried as did his daddy after a hard day of construction work in the heat of a Texas summer. The closet door couldn't shut because of laundry baskets long over flowing with unwashed clothes. Getting up to leave, he brushed a roach away from a half eaten doughnut on the dresser. His mama would never know it had shared her unfinished breakfast.

Walking down the hall, he could tell by his mama's voice that it was his granny on the phone. He always thought his mama sounded like a child when she talked to her mama. He listened to the conversation.

"I didn't plan this, Mama! It ain't what neither of us wanted to happen. Don't matter now anyhow. It's done. I been stuck my whole life. Another baby will just add more glue to the sorrows!"

Tommy sat on the couch, feeling her words pierce his heart. He didn't want to be a sorrow to anyone. At one time he thought it would be great to have a little brother or sister but he realized there was little room for him in his parent's lives, let alone someone else.

When Sandy hung up the phone, she turned to Tommy with a look of disgust dripping down her face.

"Guess you heard, Mr. Nosey! There's gonna be another mouth to feed around here soon." He knew she wasn't happy so he wasn't sure how to answer her or even if he should. Getting up from the couch, he put his skinny arms around her enormous waist and rested his head against the softness of her massive body.

"It's in here, ain't it? Can I hear it, Mama? Will it talk to me?"

He seldom saw his mama laugh but he felt the rolls of fat start to jiggle and felt the earthquake of laughter bounce his head against her body. He looked up into her face and saw that she was actually pretty when she smiled.

The tenderness was short lived, as she pushed him away to go back to her bedroom. He had long since learned to take such moments and file them away in his heart. To him it was like a memory treasure chest, a place he could go to unlock hopes, dreams and wishes. For him, all those things were the same. He wanted just one thing, to be loved.

Walking into his room, to give old teddy a hug, he had a sense that even less happiness would be living in his house. He hugged teddy and let his tears fall. He felt sorry for the new baby, for his mama, his daddy, and for himself too. Their trailer already felt like a casket and their life felt like a war. He doubted anyone would be happy about upping the body count!

Cara hung up the phone. She took a long draw from her cigarette, a drink of whiskey and stared out into the poverty that surrounded her. Thinking back to when Sandy was born, she remembered her as such a beautiful baby. The doctors feared there would be brain damage due to all the drinking Cara had done and at the moment she thought they might have been right. She always believed being conceived from sex rather than love was more a shame than anything. Resentment is easy when something so dang fun results in another nail in life's coffin.

Pouring another glass of whiskey, Cara thought how lucky she'd been to have the hysterectomy so young. Her hoarse giggle bounced off the hollowness of the walls in her life. She'd sure been a sex machine but no way had she been placed in a baby factory. She had always loved sex. She was sorry that her daughter had to pay the price for doing the Texas Two Step under the sheets at the wrong dance hall but she was so damn glad it wasn't her. Maybe if Sandy drank whiskey instead of eating, her innards would have quit on her too.

Cara watched through the screen door as Buster cleared a path to the shed. Her conversation with Sandy made her feel reflective and not even the whiskey was helping her forget. Her mind kept going back to when her only child was born.

She'd been in labor for hours before going to Henry. He'd been passed out on the couch and when she tried to wake him, he had back handed her across the room. She could still feel the scar where her head had hit the corner of the kitchen table. The doc said the only thing that saved her was her being so drunk. Her fall was more crumple than propulsion. All she knew was that the stitches they put in her head made her forget about the labor pains she was having!

For a time after Sandy was born, Cara thought she never wanted sex again. She'd made up her mind that if she ever did, it wouldn't be with Henry. She'd grown tired of being slammed against walls and his only apology sucking her tits a little longer when they had sex. He knew he wouldn't have trouble finding other holes to fill with his longing but she never dreamed he would turn to their own daughter.

Cara drained her glass and swallowed the guilt down with each gulp. There was nothing she could do about the past and nothing she could change. Life was breathing the air each day and anything more was considered a gift. There were no guarantees for any babies put on the earth except that they would breathe, cry, wet, poop and sleep. If they were lucky, they would have parents that cared when they did those things. She thought about the baby held within the great walls of her daughter and she couldn't be happy. It just wasn't right to be happy for a life being born to a slow death.

Cara called out to Buster. She needed to feel his warmth for a time. He couldn't get it up like he once could but her lips could make him come to life. She didn't mind that he was dripping with sweat and stank from the hot Texas sun. He was what she needed at the moment. For Cara, when whiskey couldn't make her forget, getting lost in passion could. She grabbed Buster as he came in. She loved the way the sweat had dripped down to the crotch of his overalls. Nothing had changed, nothing ever would. Cara smiled as she grabbed Buster's handful of life.

CHAPTER SIX

The old pick up sounded funny to Avery as he turned into the grass at the trailer. He thought maybe the old truck was just protesting being driven the same route every day. He knew he sure in the hell was tired of one day being just like all the rest. The only day he ever varied slightly from his schedule was on Sunday when he drove up to the rest home to see Mabel. He'd quit calling her mama when he turned fourteen. She and one of her men friends had gotten into a fight and he had tried to protect her. He was amazed when they both turned on him and beat him to a bloody pulp.

Kicking debris and clutter out of his path, he sighed heavily. He hated Texas summers. One hundred degree weather made him feel that the sun was trying to squeeze the juices right out of him. He dreaded getting up in the mornings and prayed for rain every night before bed. It wasn't just summer that squeezed the life out of him, it was breathing. He never felt like he'd breathed the same air as anyone else. It came into his nostrils the same way but the essence of it never made it to his insides. The only good thing to ever happen to him was Sandy.

Tommy came bounding out the screen door just as Avery was about to open it.

"Hey, Daddy! Mama needs some milk and told me I could ride my bike all the way to Granny's to get some. Mama's in the kitchen stirrin' the cream gravy."

He watched as Tommy's bare feet ran across grass and shell without noticing the difference. He thought it was a good thing to have tough soles on your feet and even better to have a tough soul on the inside. He felt a pang of envy at Tommy's freedom and youth. At least they tried to do for him what they could. Sure in the hell was more than he'd ever had.

Kissing the back of Sandy's neck, Avery rubbed the front of his filthy body into the warm folds of her back and butt. He felt just the slightest resistance to him and knew something was wrong.

"Rough day, darlin'? That young un cause you grief?"

He gently took her by the elbow and turned her so he could see her face.

"Baby, you been cryin'! What is it?"

The news of another baby hit him so hard he had difficulty remaining in a standing position. He reached up into the cabinet and took down the bottle of whiskey.

"Avery, you know how you get when you drink that stuff! I got some beers in the fridge."

His words were already anger filled.

"Fuck beer! Fuck every god damned thing in this hell hole of a life! Fuck you!"

Her tears became ones of returned venom immediately, as she whipped around to look him square in the eye.

"You bastard! You already did, that's how come I am havin' another baby! You can bet your ass it will be a cold day in hell before you do again, though!"

Avery walked out of the kitchen, kicked the screen door opened and plopped down on the porch, bottle in hand. He wished he was dead. He wanted to be dead. He felt like he had died years ago. He took a swig from the bottle and then thought of his baby brother, Carter. He remembered holding him because his mama wouldn't, caring for him because his mama just couldn't. He felt the same loneliness in his heart that he'd felt at ten. That feeling of being lost in the familiar.

He was not his mama. He worked damn hard to keep what little he had together. He loved his family and he would not let his anger get the best of him. It wasn't anyone's fault and though it sure wasn't what they asked for or needed, it was done.

He thought back to when she had told him about being pregnant with Tommy. Hell, they hadn't even been married then. She was sixteen and he had just celebrated his seventeenth birthday. They'd been kids and they'd managed to survive.

He walked back into the kitchen, put the bottle back on the shelf, took out a beer and went to have a good cry in the bedroom with his wife.

CHAPTER SEVEN

Tommy's granny sat in the kitchen with Sandy. The smoke from her cigarette curled around her head and made her seem like she was in a fog. Her hoarse cough and voice cut through the fog like a warning horn of impending danger.

"Ya know damn well you're gonna gain more weight! How healthy is that for you or the baby?"

Sandy looked at her mother, holding her cigarette in one hand, whiskey in the other.

"About as healthy as that smoke is for your lungs and that whiskey is for your liver, Mama. Ain't no use in even talkin' about it, 'cause there ain't no changin' it now. "

Tommy sat silent, eating his peanut butter and jelly sandwich. He knew better than to join in on any discussion his mama and granny were having. He had seen the anger and resentment that lived in each of them and he was scared of evoking the same in either. He tried to see the people sitting with him without staring at them. His granny's wrinkles, if stretched smooth, would be enough skin for four faces and his mama's fat made her face look like four instead of one. He wished he could see their hearts. He wondered if they beat differently. He'd heard a word on a show on television, generations. It was about a family get together and the gathering of different generations together. He kinda understood now, looking at his mama and her mama. Granny generated his mama and his mama generated him. Tommy busted out laughin' when he thought about what old Buster generated, big old farts. He knew the laughter was a big mistake the minute it broke the silence between mother and daughter.

"Tommy, Mama and I are havin' a grown up talk. Take your

sandwich and go sit on the porch to eat it."

His granny winked at him and raised her arm in the air so the loose, wrinkled flesh seemed to wave goodbye to him. He knew he would still hear them if he sat out on the front porch. He wasn't sure why, but he needed to hear what they said. He felt his granny's eyes on his back as he walked toward the screen door.

"I'm glad you told the young un to leave, Sandy, 'cause now I am free to say what I really think about this mess!"

Though her mama couldn't see, Sandy gripped the seat of the chair so hard, her knuckles were as white as if they had been bleached.

"Mama, I am warnin' you. This subject ain't up for discussion. I don't want to hear how I can go to the free clinic and get this taken care of. Let one damn word come out your drunk old mouth about killin' my baby and I swear I'll throw you out of this house! I ain't never asked you for nothin' and you ain't never give me nothin'. You ain't got no say here!"

Tommy threw the rest of his sandwich to the dog, Blue. He suddenly felt like throwing up. He couldn't believe his granny was really going to say anything about killing the baby. His eight year old mind raced with fear. The baby was inside his mama and if granny wanted to kill the baby, she must want his mama dead, too!

He had no idea what possessed him to burst back into the house, other than raw fear. Tears streamed down his face, both from hurt and anger. His voice was the most forceful it had ever been.

"Get out of here, you mean old witch! Ain't nobody gonna kill my mama, or her baby! You ain't nothin' but a drunk old slob, just like my daddy says! I hate you! I hate..!" He collapsed in tears on the kitchen floor, unable to utter any more words.

He felt his mama's arms around him and the warm softness of her girth as she held him next to her. She placed him on his bed and put old teddy next to him. He reached up, using just the tip of his dirty finger to wipe the tears from her eyes. His emotional outburst had made him tired and as he closed his eyes, he said,

"They said on television babies is from heaven. Mamas are too, ya know?"

Sandy sat for a few minutes watching her son sleep. She had never intended life to be the way it was. She had dreams of grander things when she was a child. She looked at Tommy's skinny little legs and remembered her's running through the corn fields as she yelled, "Olly, olly, oxen free!" She'd spend her summer days playing in the fields with her cousins, Marabeth, and Sarah Lou. She had been only Tommy's age when it all changed. She wondered what life would have been like for her if she had not fallen victim to her father's desires and her mother's drinking.

She had been a decent student. Hell, she had been a decent person until the summer of her eighth year. Sandy laughed as she thought of the movie with Marlon Brando where he had said, "I coulda been a contenda!"

She heard the screen door slam and knew that her mama left before she was asked to. As gently as she could, she rose from her son's bed and went to start dinner for Avery. She loved being his wife and loved him more than she had ever loved another living thing. They were two peas in a pod hung out in the Texas sun to shrivel up and die. Their parents had never given them nurturing care. They had survived on their own. She felt they would survive the latest turmoil as well.

She'd been surprised when Avery had come into the bedroom, eyes filled with tears and apologies. He'd held her close to him and told her that their baby would be born from love and not sex, as her mama thought. He'd told her that nothing mattered except what was in their hearts for each other. She wanted so much to believe him.

The tears coursed down her face as she took the reduced price hamburger out of its plastic wrapper. She squished the meat together and felt it glide between her fingers. Pieces got away and fell to the counter below. She tried to retrieve what had been dropped but doing so was near impossible. It was almost as if the meat had a mind of its own.

Buster raised a few cattle for slaughter. She wondered if the cows knew why they were so well fed? She paralleled her life with a cow's. Some things are just bred for certain things. The summer she turned eight had set her future in stone and left her no hope of being anything other than the lived-out expectations of her parents. Sometimes she felt just like the meat in her hands, fatty, once full of life, and hoping for greener pastures. It didn't matter that her pastures turned brown, that her hopes had been dashed and that life had slaughtered her like the cow she had become. She put a slice of potato in her mouth and thought about the rawness of life.

CHAPTER EIGHT

Sandy had a ritual for the first day of school after a long summer home with Tommy. She would put on her best clothes, nicest shoes, do her hair and makeup, and take the bus to the mall. She would have only enough money for lunch in the food court and a drink or two but for her it was a treat. She'd spend hours in all the little shops looking at things she'd never be able to afford and wouldn't have a place for if she could buy them. She'd left as soon as Tommy got on the bus and she arrived before the stores were opened. She saw a man walking hurriedly towards one of the opened food places.

"Scuse me. Do you know what time it is?"

Robert Laningham turned around to see a woman standing a full two feet away from him but, due to her size, almost hugging his elbow. Her shirt was one of huge flowered print. He thought manufacturers of larger women's fashions must want to telegraph their coming so their girth could be given a wide berth. In the split second before looking to his watch, he looked into eyes that interested him. They were filled with the blue of a life that had been less than kind but had an undeniable spark to them. He heard indeterminable seconds ticking away in the slightly green/gray circles just above the rounded full cheeks. He studied her greasy, stringy hair and thought it as dull as the sound of her massive legs placing the weight of her body onto the floor. The word "thud" came to his mind when he looked at her.

"It's ten after nine." He waited for her to respond. He recognized the shell that surrounded this stranger and felt a need to talk to her. He felt something with her that he'd not felt in ages, an automatic kinship.

"Thanks. It's my son's first day of school so I rode the bus into town just to spend some time doin' stuff I don't usually do. Guess I got here a little early. This sure is a great mall. Too expensive but sure does got some pretty things! I enjoy lookin' at things that make me feel frilly inside."

Robert took the opportunity.

"It is a great mall. I work at Macy's in the Men's Department. The stores don't open for another forty five minutes; might I buy you a cup of coffee or something? By the way, my name is Robert Laningham. What's yours?"

He saw panic in her eyes, and the desire to run away.

"My name's Sandy, Sandy Anderson. Thanks anyway but I can just find some place to sit until the stores open."

Robert looked into those blue eyes again and decided he had to put her at ease.

"Nice to meet you, Sandy, and listen, you'd be doing me a favor. I hate drinking alone."

There was something in his laughter that made Sandy want to trust him. She had no friends at all and sometimes wished she could talk to someone besides Avery, Tommy or her mama. Her discomfort with her size made her shy away from being out in public much and even when she was, she had Avery with her as a safety net.

Robert noticed a spark of adventure light the corners of her eyes and a slight blush come to the fullness of her cheeks. He saw a question on her lips. It blended with the 1970's pink Avon sample lipstick she wore. He smiled at her and invited her to ask with the relaxed look on his face. Her lips parted and she stammered,

"Robert...you ain't no slasher or rapist are you?"

His laugh echoed through the empty mall. He thought she was the cutest thing he'd seen in years.

"Slasher? No. Rapist? Never. Gay man? Yes."

Sandy hoped her mouth didn't fall open as wide as she felt it did before she accepted his invitation for coffee and conversation.

She'd never had anything against homosexuals but mainly because she'd never met one in her life or didn't know it if she had.

The forty-five minutes they talked seemed an eternity. When Robert left Sandy he knew he'd found a friend and knew he could help her. She left him with a smile in his heart. He saw it as surely as he could see the Texas sun shine through the sky lights of the mall. He walked into the Men's Department lighter of heart, full of hope and ready for the hours of life he would have to spend wanting things he could not have. He smiled as he thought of Sandy. Life for her too had been wanting everything she could not have. He wanted to change things for her and for himself. He coded his employee number into the register, humming an old Simon and Garfunkel tune.

"Time it was. Yes, and time it was. A time of innocence."

He knew that even though life had lived both of them, there was still hope they could both spend time living it!

The drone of the Montel Williams Show was in the background as Sandy did the breakfast dishes. She seldom watched the shows. The people on them always reminded her of her own family and that was not something of which she needed to be reminded. The hot soapy water turned her hands bright red as she repeatedly dipped deep into the sink for the silverware. It wasn't silver but it certainly had a lot of wear! She thought it representative of her entire life…used, a hand-me-down.

She looked out into the tiny space allotted her in the trailer park for yard and privacy. She suddenly felt way too large for the space she had been given. She felt it from the moment she'd met Robert in the mall. She had never taken time to sit with a stranger to talk. While she was not sure what in him made her want to know him, or what in her made the need so obvious but she was so glad. He called her every day now, just to talk. She found her hunger for food lessened and her hunger for life increased.

She stared out of the window and past her circumstance. She could see beyond what birthright had handed her and past the pain of existence. She saw things she had never seen before and dared to dream of happiness. A smile came across her lips, the corners curved up in a fullness that made her eyes crinkle at the edges. The aroma of the soapy water, mixed with the bubbles that had been placed in her heart, made her feel more complete than she had in all her twenty-five years.

The television intruded as she heard a daughter's raised voice, full of venom and blame, directed at a mother without a clue. Yes, she thought, it is much easier to blame than to take responsibility for oneself. Her thoughts were not original but ones Robert talked about when explaining her relationship with food. He made her see herself in a manner she had never seen before. He was brutal at times, even cruel. He told her that she used food, just as Cara used alcohol, to build a buffer between herself and life. He told her that she was still a child emotionally and that if she didn't break out of the tomb she had built, she would die having never lived.

Sandy picked up the last fork from the soapy water, ran the dish rag over it and placed it in the dish drainer. Going into the living room, she picked up the remote and turned off the life she had known. Putting on the tennis shoes Robert bought her, she ventured out of her world of safety in search of her dreams. Walking out into the sunlight, braving the honks of insensitive men yelling "get out of the way you cow!", she started her morning walk to the future. It was only a mile for now, and a slow one at that, but Robert promised her life is always one step at a time. She felt the shell crush beneath her weight and felt so good to be moving her massive body towards life, rather than away from it.

CHAPTER NINE

Cara felt Buster get out of their bed. The floor creaked under the weight of his naked bulk. Her head ached from a night of whiskey and wild dreams. The film of dehydration clung to her mouth like coating to southern fried chicken. Her hands were clammy and her body was covered in a fine mist of whiskey sweat. She smiled, thinking she wouldn't have to go to the kitchen to fix her morning drink because she could lick her arms and be satisfied.

Licking arms made her think about her daughter, Sandy, and the sexual deviant she'd adopted as a friend. Cara shifted her naked body under the sheet and adjusted the fan so it would blow directly on her. She never did cotton to perverts. Hell...incest, rape, those things were different from same sex carrying ons. She just didn't understand why Sandy liked this Robert homo so much! She would talk to her about it today when they all got together for their Sunday barbeque. She was angry at Sandy for inviting him. Most often, she didn't care what her daughter did, but this had folks talking and it needed to be nipped in the bud. She was sure Avery would agree out of fear for the safety of little Tommy.

She heard the toilet flush and knew that Buster would soon be headed out to busy himself in the yard. Getting out of bed, Cara looked at herself in the full length mirror on the closet door. She had the kind of breasts that defied gravity. She was her body. She'd never had any formal schooling, wasn't interested in anything but drinking and having a good time, and her body insured free drinks and lots of fun. Tracing around her right nipple, she suddenly understood why the change in Sandy bothered her so. She'd always felt superior to her daughter. She was better looking and a ton smarter as far as common sense. Robert was changing Sandy from the inside out and it was scary!

Lighting a cigarette, Cara let loose a throaty laugh. She just knew if she ever got a hold of Robert, his high horse ways would change as easily as his sexual orientation. She knew she was the answer to his problem. He had just never been with a woman who put the fu in fun! She would show him this afternoon how the other side lives. Yep, she would wow him with her potato salad and her firm breasts. He would forget all about bringing Sandy into the world all over again.

Taking a halter top out of the closet, Cara planned how she would be the center of attention. Sandy couldn't be allowed to venture too far from their world. No one who was born to it could leave. Damn it, there was little to feel good about as it was and her daughter was not about to make her grieve over her lot in life. No sir, she would either change the face of this threatening friendship or destroy it all together.

Slapping Buster on the ass, Cara poured some whiskey into her coffee. Lifting her cup to Buster, she said,

"Here's to bein' born to sorrow. Champagne dreams is another man's beer nightmare!"

Her laughter hit a chord of hysteria as she pranced with exaggeration back to the bedroom to adorn her only weapon. Education to her was knowing you don't know, and being satisfied with it.

Standing next to the barbeque pit, hand extended to Avery, Robert wondered for a moment why on earth he had accepted Sandy's invitation. Just one look at her beaming face at the screen door made him know why he did. He could not deny the change in her and it thrilled him to be a part of it. He could move beyond the protective, chest beating gorilla that was his friend's husband if it meant a chance to bring out the human in her. Sandy reminded him of his sister, Mavis, who everyone, including family, called Massive instead. She'd died a year and a half before of complications from diabetes and he saw Sandy as a tribute to her lost life.

He smiled at her as she came out to introduce him to Avery. He was glad when she asked him to help her in the kitchen.

Cara had never met Robert but from Sandy's description of him, she had a clear picture in her mind. She could just imagine the pink of his manicured nails and the pressed look of his button down shirt. Her preconceived ideas were fresh in her mind when Buster turned the car onto the grass yard of her daughter's trailer. The whiskey had poured freely and she was ready to be the loud, obnoxious, bigoted harlot it made her.

Cara's voice pierced his ears long before he ever saw her.

"Hey Sandy! Where you hidin' that homo you been tellin' me about?"

Robert saw the deep red come up from Sandy's collar, through the crevices of her chins and light her face like a flare in the fog. Placing his hand on hers, he said,

"Why hell, I'm in here. Ain't the kitchen where all Nancy boys belong?"

He saw a spark of wonder flicker in Sandy's eyes and knew she was reveling in his response to Cara's obvious play for attention. He'd been forewarned and was ready for whatever would be dished up for him.

Cara walked into the kitchen and as Robert reached his hand out to make introductions, she slid her hands around to his ass and gave it a squeeze.

"Hmm. Nice and firm, but then ya'll got to keep those buns a burnin' at all times!"

He knew her type. Hell...his mother was her type! She was coarse, crude, crunchy, but more than anything crazed with a need for things she never felt worthy of having. He reached down and grabbed at her halter top and with the very nails he knew she imagined traced the outline of her cleavage. His voice was deep and sexy.

"And I see that you, dear lady, have very ripe melons. Too bad

I prefer grapes to cantaloupes!"

Robert then reached his hand up to the chin just below Sandy's mouth and pushed upward.

"It is not good to stand with your mouth gaping open when there are so many holes in the screens. Flies are not appetizers even in Texas!"

Sandy's laughter came from deep within and radiated out until all of her folds were dancing in the delight of her friend. Even Cara was laughing, though she did mention the fact that she would have to watch that she didn't pee on herself.

"My tits are firm, but my bladder went south years ago!"

Sandy looked at her mother and thought that she saw a hint of acceptance. She was thinking maybe Robert was magic. If he could give as good as he got with the cartoon character Cara, then he was not only magic, he was amazing! She felt the tension go out of her as she placed the last of the lettuce and tomatoes on the plate. Looking out at Avery flipping the hamburgers, she thought that while hamburger could never be steak, perhaps with a little sauce strategically placed, it could taste like it. She was hamburger and Robert was steak but they had a common sauce to share... life.

Avery heard the laughter coming from the kitchen and he felt the rumble of jealousy churn the acid in his whale sized gut. He looked at Buster sitting in a lawn chair, beer in hand, and didn't want the image to be his future. He knew Sandy was changing and it scared him. He sat next to Buster and grabbed a beer out of the cooler.

"Pretty damn hot for September, ain't it?" Buster said. "We better get some rain soon or everything's going to shrivel up, including us!"

Avery looked at Buster as if he hadn't understood him. Who the hell cared that it was hot. It was September in Texas. It was always hot. He wanted to talk about the man standing in his kitchen filling his wife's head with thoughts of improvement. Looking out into the yard, he wanted to tell Buster that what he saw was never what he had planned for himself. Instead he said,

"Yep, hotter than cow shit in a microwave!"

Buster laughed so hard he spewed beer down the front of his overalls and the only way it could be distinguished from the sweat already soaking him was by its foam. The sight made Avery want to cry.

He heard voices in the living room and then heard the screen door open. Cara, Sandy and Robert were still laughing when they came out onto the porch. He looked at Robert but addressed his statement to Sandy.

"Sounded like you girls were having quite a time in there."

The look she shot him hurt to the core. Hell, a few weeks ago she would have joined in if he would have said something about a guy they saw as obviously light in the loafers. He was already seeing what he feared the most, a separation in likeness.

Avery hated that Sandy somehow saw Robert as better than him. It wasn't like he hadn't wanted things for himself. He had been a good student and had hoped to go on to college. It hadn't been his fault he had to be a parent to his siblings and then when Sandy got pregnant step up to be a man. Robert never had to worry about making some girl pregnant or having the responsibility of a wife and child.

He guzzled his beer and crushed the can between his oil darkened fingers and dirty nails. He opened the cooler to get another. He noticed Robert's thin, delicate, uncalloused hands and suddenly wanted to hide his own. He began to realize that sexual threat from another man was not nearly as dangerous as the threat of a better life. Sandy wouldn't run off with Robert but she could well run away from Avery, both intellectually and emotionally.

It was Buster who brought up the idea of a competition. He suggested a game of horseshoes but they all knew the premise behind the challenge. Robert made both Avery and Buster feel less a man, not because he was gay but because he was what he wanted to be. Avery knew he would have hell to pay for going along with the idea but he needed to feel good about himself and maybe he would if he beat Robert at something. He even took it a step further by adding a new rule to the game. Each man would have to down six beers in succession and then start the game. Hell, Robert weighed maybe 140 pounds; six beers and he would not be able to hold a horseshoe. Smiling as he popped the top to another one, Avery knew if there was one thing he could do, it was hold his beer. He offered one to Robert and announced,

"Let the games begin!"

Robert was the funniest drunk any of them had ever seen. The pink of his lips would not cooperate with the white of his straight teeth when he spoke. He worried about the tail of his crisp shirt coming out of his carefully creased Dockers and once when he moved his arm too far back to throw the horseshoe, he completely lost his balance. When trying to right himself, Robert placed his left shoe in a huge pile of dog shit and Avery thought he would scream with laughter. It seemed like justice to him. He'd stepped in shit all of his life and now Robert could understand what life smelled like when shit happened.

Sandy took the paper towel and wiped the dog poop off Robert's shoe.

"I am so sorry, Robert. I wish I had never had this ridiculous idea. What made me think that you would enjoy being around my family?"

If she could have, she would have dabbed the tears from her eyes with the paper cloth as well. She had never before felt so acutely that her life was indeed shit!

Robert knew what was in Sandy's heart and toeing a worn spot in the kitchen floor with his argyle socked foot, he placed his left hand on her shoulder.

"Sandy, it's okay. I'm used to it. Besides, it was kind of funny. I was shit faced and fell in it too! My presence here is different for Buster and Avery. Cara calls me a homo, but those two men out there see me as one of them, yet feel me as a homo. I am threatening to them, sweetie, in more ways than the obvious. Sandy, I am glad to be here. Please don't wish I wasn't."

The slam of the screen door, accompanied by a hoarse cough,

told them Cara was inside the house.

"Hey, you two!" Cara yelled. "There's more dog shit in the yard! Who wants to be a pooper scooper next?"

The grin on Robert's face was genuine.

"I have another foot but it's the one I put in my mouth frequently and I prefer to keep it shit free, Cara. I think we are ready to go back outside, though."

Sitting in the chair where plastic separated from stuffing and the cardboard back bared the stains of years, Cara studied Robert.

"Darlin', I just have to tell ya this. You are one hell of a waste of a good-lookin' man! You see these little puppies sittin' in this halter top? Well, they need tender lovin' care but, baby, they don't leave no mess on shoes!"

Leaning in close enough for her to feel the warmth of his breath, Robert flashed the white of his teeth in an enormous smile.

"And nice little puppies they are but, Cara, they don't howl or bark up the same trees I climb. And by the way, the men I date wear Hush Puppies but are not as light in the loafers as you might think. They are no different from the men with whom you fill your lonely moments."

"The hell you say, homo boy. They damn well better be!"

Buster dozed in the warmth of the sun as Avery continued to bristle at the laughter emanating from the kitchen. He knew he had been a jerk but he couldn't help it. He had always been a hero to Sandy and now he saw another man in her eyes. He always thought of gays as less than him. Robert's intelligence was proving him wrong. He wanted his life with Sandy to change but he wanted to be the one to change it for her. He had pooh poohed her thoughts of going back to school but education was now sitting in his kitchen with pooh on his shoe!

Avery sat back in the lawn chair. He wondered what twist of fate brought people to their place in life and what cruel injustice kept them there. For some reason, his thoughts turned to his childhood and the naked man in the kitchen that night. He felt his fate had been sealed that night when he was only ten.

He suddenly knew why Robert scared him. Robert had not let life beat him. He was a damn homosexual and a better man than Avery ever thought about being. Hell, judging from his laughter, he was even a better sport! Avery knew the difference for Sandy was that Avery's shoes belonged in dog shit, while Robert's belonged on argyle socked feet with toenails softened by pedicures. He may have kicked Robert's ass but it was Avery who sat alone on the porch with the bruises.

Avery was essentially sitting alone with his thoughts, as Buster sat snoring from both ends. He wanted to go inside and apologize to Robert. Hell, he was the last person on earth with the right to judge anyone. It was just his manhood that was in question. It had always been his manhood in question. As a kid, he had always been the man and with Sandy he had always been the man! Thanks to Robert, he questioned what a man was exactly. His head bobbed and his eyelids drooped from the beer he had consumed.

He was nodding off when he heard the screen door open. Robert effortlessly and quietly moved into the empty chair beside him.

"I don't want you to apologize, Avery. I understand completely and I wanted to come out here to tell you that."

Avery opened his right eye and then his left.

"What the hell makes you think I was thinkin' of apologizing and how could you possibly understand anything about me? You ain't lived my life. How's some fancy pants going to know why it's important that I show him up and then apologize after?"

"Because in some ways, I was you. Avery? Have you ever felt like life has played a really cruel joke on you by making you a part of it? Have you ever looked in the mirror and thought you were the result of a comedy of errors?"

Robert looked at Avery to watch the recognition happening in his eyes. He knew. No one had to tell him.

Avery looked at Robert and saw something he had not seen before, a human being.

"Yes. My mom was a whore and I always felt like one too."

"I know Avery, I lived the same life. Marta, my mom, used me to attract men. I was a gorgeous child, long lashes, big, wide, hungry eyes."

Robert's laugh seemed more hurt than humor.

"She put me on display to rev up their libido and their passion for loving! Hell, the first sexual experience I had as a gay was with one of her ex lovers!"

Avery sat in his beer silence. He was trying to understand the words he was hearing. Before he could stop himself, he was telling Robert his darkest secret.

"I know, Robert. It is one of the reasons I was so angry with you. The first sexual experience I ever had was with this lover of my mom's. He had all these cool tattoos. He told me I could touch them. When I did, he asked me to touch him in other places. Robert, I just wanted to make peace with the life I had. I wanted to belong in the world I lived in. I didn't even know why I felt a need to touch him or what the liquid was that shot out at me. I just knew it made me feel ashamed and excited at the same time. I was so confused!"

On a porch in East Texas that afternoon, on a hot Sunday, there came an incredible understanding between lives so different, yet the same. Avery confessed his darkest hour and Robert relived his noir entry into the life of the gay. Life was their common denominator and beer their truth serum.

Robert was pleased with the outcome of the day. He didn't understand why Sandy had been so nervous about him meeting her family. He only wished little Tommy had been there, instead of spending the weekend with Avery's sister, Jane. He wanted to see the entire family dynamics at work. He smiled as he thought about Cara. What a hoot she was.

CHAPTER TEN

It was Sunday so Robert knew that Maurice would be home. He and Maurice were no longer lovers but they continued to share the three bedroom condo. It wasn't that bad. Maurice was a flight attendant with Southwest Airlines, so was home only occasionally. They were both mature adults and the arrangement was convenient to both of them.

He met Maurice at a gay bar in the Montrose seven years ago. The chemistry was instant and they spent a passionate weekend at a downtown Houston hotel. They quickly decided move in together. The sex was great, explosive. Their mutual love of finer things made an amazingly comfortable living environment. The condo was filled with fine art work, wonderful music and furniture that would be the envy of any cultured soul.

Images of Maurice's taut body played tricks on Robert's mind. He had not been with anyone in three years. It was a conscious choice. Maurice let his voracious sexual appetite dictate his behavior. He worked many business flights and ended up being the boy toy for too many strangers. AIDS became a real issue in the relationship. Maurice swore he never had unprotected sex but Robert knew better. He was sure Maurice was in the Hall of Fame in the Mile High Club and there wasn't room in an airline bathroom for condoms.

Robert knew that sex, or the lack of it, was becoming a problem for him. Hell, he had even been turned on by a few women lately! Granted, they were rather androgynous, nondescript types but it worried him. It was the reason he threw himself into his friendship with Sandy. He was not at all attracted to her but knew she would need much of his idle time.

Smiling, he thought about Cara. He knew the drinking was a buffer, the overt sexual play and the loud bravado a complete sham used to hide her quiet suffering but he liked the hell out of her. She oozed with quick wit and no one who could think quickly on her feet was stupid.

He pulled into his driveway and saw a strange car parked behind Maurice's. His disappointment was visible. He wanted some time to catch up on things with Maurice. He planned to cook some of his special pesto sauce, open a bottle of wine and have an intimate conversation.

"Hi honey, I'm home!"

He knew it would make Maurice and whoever else scramble and/or stop whatever they were doing. He wasn't prepared for the person he saw sitting on the living room couch with a carefully poised cup of tea in hand. He knew Maurice was deriving great joy from his confusion.

"Robert, I would like you to meet Ms. Callier. She is a social worker. She is your friend Sandy's caseworker."

Offering his hand to her, Robert said,

"Pleased to meet you, Ms. Callier. What might I do for you?"

"Well, Mr. Laningham, as you know it is my job to oversee the Anderson family. I watch for possible problems and I am not very comfortable with the current situation."

"Wait just a minute, Ms. Callier. By the current situation, do you mean my friendship with Sandy? If that is what you have questions about, you have no right what so ever to dictate who their friends are or who mine are either."

"Mr. Laningham, I am doing my job. You make no secret of your sexual preference. Do I need to remind you that Tommy Anderson is only eight years old?"

Robert was feeling the darkness of real anger shadow his words. It was something he battled any time he looked stupidity in the face. With restraint, he answered Ms. Callier.

"Ms Callier, I am a gay man not a pedophile! Perhaps you didn't learn the difference in the correspondence course you took to procure your college degree. How dare you! Ms. Callier, I suggest you do go quietly into that dark night!"

Robert slammed the door behind Ms. Callier. He was seething inside. It was the kind of anger that made him want to hit something or someone. The tears came without control as his narrow shoulders gave in to the quake of anger's passion. He felt the warmth of Maurice's arms encircle his shoulders.

"Let's talk about this."

Maurice's voice was soft, sympathetic and soothing. With a gentle arm, Robert felt himself being propelled back into the living room. He slumped onto the couch and put his head in his hands. He knew Maurice had gone into the kitchen to open some wine. He heard the squeak of the cork sliding against the glass of the moistened neck and then a slight pop of a penetrated vacuum. He picked up a tissue to dab sorrow from his eyes. Taking the long stemmed glass from Maurice's outstretched hand, his voice was almost a sob.

"Oh God, Maurice! I thought I was over feeling apologetic for being me. Why did I let that stupid bitch upset me so?"

His eyes looked searchingly at Maurice. He needed reassurance that the world was different than he was seeing it at the moment. He could tell that Maurice was trying to find the words. He decided he was being unfair to ask answers from someone who was part of the question.

"She upset me because I was stupid to believe anything had really changed. That ridiculous woman made me see that in the eyes of the world I am a perversion that most people would like to sweep under the damp, dusky darkness of a black hole. She really thinks I have befriended Sandy to get to Tommy! Doesn't she understand that such a thought makes me want to throw up? Doesn't she know that I am as capable of love as any human? No. I am more capable of loving. I had to accept myself, so that makes it easier for me to accept others! I am a person of heart, soul and mind, Maurice!"

The hands that stroked his face were at the same time familiar and strange. The fingers were ones he had felt for a time as a lover but somehow had been transformed into the essence of friendship. Maurice had attached his heart to his body some time between their initial meeting and the present. It was part of what Ms. Callier could not see.

The Ms. Calliers of the world saw him as a disease but people like her were the germs that made him one. He would have to call Sandy and tell her about his visitor. He would give her the option to end the friendship. The last thing he wanted was to cause her more problems.

He slumped further into the comfort of Maurice. He felt the weight of who he was take on the heaviness of what others thought he was. Why was it people couldn't understand that the real key to life was in the living of it? Why couldn't people see that the beauty lies in the difference, not the sameness. Why did Ms. Callier fear him so? Why did he now fear himself because of her? Why?

CHAPTER ELEVEN

Tommy put the last of his clothes in the sack. He couldn't get rid of the sinking feeling in his stomach. He wasn't ready to go home. It wasn't that his Aunt Jane was that different from his mom, it was that her husband Bob made her different. They lived in a real house and had nice things. The pall of darkness didn't lurk in the corners like it did at his house.

He picked up the Tonka truck his aunt had bought him. She said it was a combination belated birthday, happy you are here present. He'd never owned such a large truck. He hadn't dared ask for it. The twenty-five dollar price seemed more like a million to him! He'd watched as she wrote the check and thought it strange that her hand wasn't shaking the whole time.

His Uncle Bob worked at a chemical plant. He heard his dad say that Bob had just been at the right place at the right time. Tommy thought that seemed right. His family was never in the right place at the right time. Life was always leaving when they arrived and their grasping handshakes seemed to meet with the empty air life left behind.

Tommy looked around his cousin, Mark's, room. Everything matched and had a brightness that showed in his cousin's face. It seemed to him that laughter and love made things fresh in the house. There was a crispness to the feel of everything. He hated himself for wishing the room was his and that his aunt and uncle were his parents but the thoughts were in his heart anyway.

The sound of his aunt's voice intensified his shame.

"Hey there, sweetie. Are you ready to go?"

He wanted to scream "No! Please don't bring me back there!" His voice was as small as he felt his future would be.

"Yes, Aunt Jane. Everything is in my sack. The truck won't fit but I can carry it in my hand."

She opened the front door for him and he looked back with longing as she closed the bedroom door. He felt tears light the corners of his eyes but he squeezed them back. He'd heard someone say once that home is where the heart is. He didn't know where his heart was so did it mean he didn't have a home either? He knew he didn't have a home like the one in which he'd spent the weekend. He didn't have a home in the heart of his parents like his cousin, Mark, did. No one in the trailer had a home in themselves. Their hearts were kept in darkness. Life for them was spent feeling their way through the corridors of a maze of lostness.

Taking strong hold on the truck, he heard the front door shut behind him. He stepped out into the dusk of a warm Sunday evening with his sack of clothes, his new truck and with a pang of loneliness he didn't understand. His Aunt Jane bent and kissed him on the cheek. Her words brought him comfort.

"Tommy, please know that I love you. I understand why you enjoy coming to stay with Bob and me. It's okay to want things to be better. When you play with this truck, imagine that it can take you away when you need to go. Your imagination can take you to wonderful places."

Buckling his seatbelt, Tommy decided then and there that he would not merely have things one day, he would be something! He wanted crispness in his life. He felt the same pain in his heart he did when he sat at his desk and heard the other kids talk about what they were going to do over the weekend. While they talked of baseball practice, water parks, and family outings, he would think about surviving well enough to get back to school on Monday without losing too much of himself.

Sandy lay in the darkened room and reflected on the day. Tommy had recoiled from her touch. She couldn't get the look on his face out of her mind. He had stiffened and the white of his knuckles evidenced his anger as he clutched the toy truck his aunt bought him. She knew at that moment that he didn't want to be where he was. He didn't want to be home.

She lay rubbing her abdomen. She carried a new life in the darkness of her womb. Would this new baby hate its life too? Did she hate her own life? Had she ever even considered the possibility of making it anything better?

She and Robert spent many hours talking about expectations and disappointments. She'd known disappointment her entire life but had grown to accept it. Robert explained that Tommy's resentment stemmed from not having any say in his own life. He made her see that what lived in his soul was the same thing that had lived in her's as a child. He wasn't sexually abused but was abused by circumstance just the same. Her sorrow was as much for herself as it was for her son.

The sound of the phone startled her. Her hello sounded far away and foreign. The voice on the other end sounded apologetic and confused.

"Sandy? Did I wake you?"

"No, Robert, I was lying here thinking. Is something wrong? It's almost midnight."

"Well, yes, or maybe. Sandy, I'm not sure really. Your social worker, Ms. Callier was here when I got home. She said some pretty stupid things about our friendship and Tommy. I got angry and asked her to leave. I'm so sorry but she made me insane, Sandy! Her sick innuendos pushed me over the edge!"

"What the hell? She came to see you? That bitch!! Oh Robert, I'm so damn sorry! She had no right!"

"Sandy?"

"Yes, Robert?"

"There is something else. I was so upset and Maurice was so sweet, so understanding. I ended up in bed with him."

The silence on the other end of the phone scared him. He was afraid that there would be a difference between intellectualizing about his being gay and the reality of it.

"Are you still there?"

Her voice came back to him like a wave of loving compassion.

"You needed him and he was there. Hell, we're all human. I was just thinking that's how this new life ended up inside of me! You ain't worried you might be pregnant are you?"

Her laughter made the tension melt right out of him. His own laughter danced on the miles between them. He was not prepared for her next question but found real joy in the attitude.

"So tell me, girlfriend, how was it?"

"I love you, Sandy. Please know that when it feels like no one else in the world does, I do. I knew the minute I saw you that you were deeply special. I also knew that you had never seen it in yourself. You couldn't show it to others because you didn't even know it was there but it shined right on me like a beacon!"

"Talk to you about all this in the morning?...and hey, Robert? I hope you are calling from the same bed Maurice is in. Sometimes sex is about being, not having."

He hung up the phone, astounded by the profound words of his backward friend.

He thought of the Beatles song, "Let It Be". Yes, let it be, let us be, let you be.

Nestling closer to a snoring Maurice, he thought of words to another song, Doris

Day's "Que Sera Sera"...what will be, will be. Yes, he thought, and what is, just is.

Letting sleep take over worry, Robert knew the warmth of friendship had surrounded him this night. Not even the Ms. Calliers of the world could make him shudder from cold reality when the solace of caring was his cover of night.

CHAPTER TWELVE

Celia Callier gathered her robe around her and moved towards the kitchen to get some Sleepy Time tea. Her mind would not shut down. Her thoughts and guilt played ping pong between synapses.

She had worked long and hard to get where she was and she did the state's bidding as asked. She did her job well, sometimes too well. She replayed the words that had come out of her own mouth and was appalled. She would never forget the hurt and anger in Robert's eyes.

The cup warmed her cold hands. She stared at her reflection in the toaster. The person staring back was not what others saw. Her reflection revealed her secret. She spoke what she saw.

"Celia Callier is a lesbian. She has always been a lesbian."

She had not given in to her urges until high school. Her first lover was one of her teachers, Ms. Cantell, who taught her about equations and balance. Celia smiled, sipping the tea. Twenty years later she could still hear her teacher's words.

"If you look like a woman, men will want you. However, if you look like a man, everyone will know you want women. Be soft on the outside and quiet on the inside."

Not even her parents had known her heart. It was important to keep up appearances. She was a bureaucrat who dictated the right way for others to live. Her denial of self made it possible.

Tonight she had denied herself at the expense of another. Sleepy Time tea was not going to erase the vile taste of betrayal. Her mind would not bring peace to her heart. She knew sleep would evade her still.

The phone felt cold in her hands as she dialed the number.

The voice on the other end sent chills up her spine.

"Louisa? You will never guess who this is."

"Hello, Celia. It has been a long time."

"Louisa, I...well...I. I know it's late, but would you mind if I came over for a while?"

Celia's fingers were shaking as she buttoned her blouse. Tonight she had seen herself through Robert's eyes. She let the door hit her in the ass as she shut it. Smiling to herself, she said,

"That was for you, Robert! I sincerely hope you ended up in loving arms tonight, too!"

CHAPTER THIRTEEN

Buster sat at the bar twirling his beer bottle. He saw the flash of Cara's red Roper jeans out on the dance floor and wished he was at home. Sunday night at Liars had become a tradition, one he didn't like.

He wasn't sure why he always agreed to go to Sandy's for Sunday dinners. He knew that after an afternoon of family and whiskey Cara would be hungry for men and dancing. It was his duty to bring her even though he might not be responsible for bringing her home. He figured it was about a fifty-fifty thing.

Turning his back to the dance floor, he thought about Bessie Mae. They had been sweethearts since grade school, married at sixteen and together for thirty-five years until her death two years ago. She had been the only woman he ever loved or would ever love and he missed her as much as his own breath.

His thoughts were interrupted by loud cheers. He turned towards the commotion to see Cara in the middle of the dance floor without her halter top. She was writhing seductively to a Clint Black tune and cupping her breasts in an open invitation. She never noticed Buster leaving.

He hated that he felt a twinge of guilt as he started the Chevy dually and backed out. He usually hung around until she made her pick for the night. Hell, why should he care how she got home or if she got home? It wasn't like they were married or even in love with each other. Their's was a union of convenience. She washed his clothes, cooked his meals and some nights offered him warmth. He'd always thought of her as kind of like a pet, nice to have around but real low maintenance, emotionally speaking.

The sound of the crushed concrete under the weight of the

truck tires made Buster feel lonely. He sat in the truck just staring at the trailer for a while. It didn't look like a home to him. It wasn't a home to him. For him it was the place he would live out his days until he was reunited with Bessie Mae. Sometimes he felt Cara was looking forward to the reunion more than him.

Placing his keys on the counter, Buster looked around at the disarray that was his life. He called out Bessie's name but the cat was the only one that appeared out of the shadows. The soft mewing and warmth against his legs almost made him want to cry. He bent his large frame to pet Charlie. His words were as soft as its fur.

"She makes you 'bout as lonely as she makes me sometimes. I know why you stay. I wish like hell I knew why I did!"

Cara looked around the bar for Buster and figured he must be in the bathroom. She couldn't believe how much fun the place was without the usual crowd of desirable men. Hell, not one man had even touched her during her topless dance. She felt only a little slighted. Not even she could drink enough whiskey to make most of the men in the joint seem attractive.

She decided she needed to go to the bathroom too and stumbled her way across the hardwood floors to the back. Her red Ropers were the tightest pair of jeans she owned and getting them down far enough as to not pee on herself was quite a task. She sat and stared at the dingy walls of the stall. The messages written and scratched into the painted steel served as personal ads for the love lorn.

Hearing the door open, she lifted her feet off the floor. It was a game she played in order to make people think they were alone in the room. She loved the things other women said either to themselves or someone else. Their drunken stupidity always made her feel less drunken and less stupid. She recognized one of the voices as being Candy's, the waitress.

"Boy I think Cara done run Buster off with that little show of her's tonight! You'd think that drunken slut would realize what a damn good man she's got there!"

Cara physically winced and crouched further onto the toilet, her skinny butt almost sinking to water level. She didn't recognize the voice of the other woman but her words were just as biting.

"Ya know, she don't even know what all them men really say about her. They call her CC and anyone with a brain knows what they mean by that! As for Buster, I would take hold of that man in a minute if he'd ever look my way. She might have made that possible tonight!"

Cara heard the door shut with a thud but it felt like her heart hitting the porcelain sides of the commode. She wished she could pass off the statements as catty jealousy but Candy was beautiful and young. She wasn't being jealous; she was being honest! There was a sick feeling in Cara's stomach and she wished with all her heart she didn't have to walk back out into the place. She had to hurry and find Buster. She wanted to go home.

Walking out of the bathroom, the sea of faces all seemed to be laughing at her. In a panic she searched the crowd for Buster. She knew that he would never leave without her. He always waited until he was sure she had a ride home before taking off. Walking up to the bar, it was Arnie, the owner, who recognized the question in her eyes and pointed to the door.

As Cara dialed her own phone number, the words from a song played in her mind.

"Here's a quarter. Call someone who cares!" She hoped she was!

Buster woke earlier than usual. His back ached from a night of tossing and turning. He raised up on his right elbow and watched Cara sleeping. Her snoring sounded almost soft, as if she was singing herself a lullaby. He eased himself out of bed with extra care. He hadn't asked what had happened at the club and she hadn't offered any explanation.

His first thought when he got her call was that she had either been in an accident or beaten up by some cowboy type. He had been surprised to see her standing outside the club intact but looking contrite, red faced and amazingly sober. His thoughts of Bessie Mae had caused him to make a comparison between the two women. Bessie had been a God fearing woman. Cara on the other hand, was God's worst fear.

Buster couldn't fault Cara for what she was anymore than he could blame her for what she wasn't. He had known what she was like long before he became a part of her life. He wasn't nearly as base and dumb as everyone thought he was. He just chose to sit back and filter life through his own senses and make his own judgments. His beer drinking and loud bodily noises were used to mask a much deeper vein of sensitivity. He, after all, lived amid the harshness of life and gentle giants usually don't survive a fall.

He wasn't sure why he felt a need to make the coffee, fry the bacon and turn the eggs with perfection but acts of kindness need no reason or explanation. The pervasive feeling that the woman asleep down the hall had experienced some sort of assault and needed his special attention made him feel important to her. He'd lived with Cara for a year and it was the first time he had ever felt like more than a monthly income. He knew how strong she liked her coffee, how crispy she wanted her bacon and just how runny she wanted her eggs. He just wished he knew what it was that could make her happy and whether the thing that would lived inside him?

He heard her deep cough coming from the bedroom and knew she was ready for her coffee and aspirin. He smiled as he thought about her slant on hangover medicine. She told him once that the docs said too much drinking can lead to a heart attack but that aspirin decreases the risk of one. She'd smiled at him and said that she figured that meant her life was pretty damned balanced. He knew that at its best her life was like a teeter totter and at its worst a runaway roller coaster. She never fooled him with her cockiness or bravado.

He stood at the bedroom door for a moment to watch her. Her

eyes were still shut against the morning. He placed the coffee on the night stand and bent to kiss her gently on the forehead. She opened her eyes to him and he swore he was looking into a heart he had never seen. He wasn't at all prepared for what she said.

"Hey darlin, this is one morning I don't need coffee and aspirin nearly as bad as I need you. Think ya could lay here with me awhile and hold onto me so I don't slip completely through the cracks?"

He had lain with Cara in his arms more times than he could count but for the first time since he had known her, he really felt her. And to his great surprise, she felt good!

It was the drinking. Cara knew that was her problem. Life inside a whiskey bottle felt safer than the life outside it. She was super woman under the influence. She could leap her monumental problems without letting them touch her heart or rip through the little sanity left in her mind.

She sat up in bed repositioning Buster's arms around her. She had heard truths about herself last night. While she knew they would have an impact for a moment, the Cara inside knew she would be back at Liars repeating her shame. A flash of memory brought forth her taunting topless dance for a room full of strangers. She knew that even the men in the room with which she'd had sex remained unknowns to her. They were lucky if she remembered the feel of them inside her, let alone who they were. She tried never to put a face to sex.

Tears were not a part of her life anymore. She could no more cry for herself than she could another living soul. Her tears had been spent on dirty, stained pillows as a child. She had cried them all out in the wee hours of so many mornings after her father would get up from her bed as if nothing had happened. Those hours of feeling sore, bruised and ripped apart made her feel like nothing. The danger had always been in listening to the voice in her nine-year-old mind that told her she deserved something more. Every time she would listen, her father would come take from her what she didn't have to give.

She took a long drag off her cigarette and remembered thinking that her mother must have surely died from the violent taking of her soul each night. There were so many times Cara wanted to die, too. In some ways, each night as she felt the weight of her father over her, she did die. He killed her a little more each time. She had heard her older brothers refer to sex as getting a piece. It seemed appropriate to her. By the time she was sixteen, she had no pieces of herself left.

Turning to look at Buster, Cara wanted to be different for him. She wanted to give him the kind of love he needed. He was nothing but kind to her. He picked up the broken parts and put them back together time and time again. She wished she could be more like his wife, Bessie Mae. Bessie had died two years ago but Cara had died long before that. Looking at life through whiskey colored eyes made seeing its reality easier, tolerable almost.

She knew no matter what she remembered about her past, nothing in her future could change it. She was uneducated but she wasn't stupid. As surely as the Texas sun would greet another day, she would climb in a whiskey bottle to forget her past and become it at the same time.

She was Cara Covington and she was alone in the world. A bottle of Jack Daniels was her only friend and a drunken state her only hope of survival. The distortions caused by the contents of the glass were not nearly as painful as the reality seen through the clear blue of her sober eyes.

Pulling her robe around her, Cara moved down the hall to where she kept comfort. Hell, it was after nine a.m. She'd let the real world invade much too long already! God, would those first swigs be welcomed. With a head full of whiskey there was no room for pain and with a head full of pain, she sure needed her whiskey!

CHAPTER FOURTEEN

The red digital numbers on Maurice's alarm clock flashed in Robert's eyes as he slowly opened them. He had heard the thunder and rain during the night but had no idea they had lost power. He stretched his legs under the covers and turned on his side to look at Maurice.

He felt awkward watching the rise and fall of Maurice's smooth chest. He wanted to reach out and touch him but felt that the tenderness which had brought them together the night before had ebbed. He knew that they would go back to being just friends and roommates. He eased his way out of bed and turned at the door whispering his thanks.

The coffee was still brewing when Sandy called. He laughed at her excitement and need to hear details.

"I am not the kiss and tell type! You are just sooo bad, girl!"

He really wanted to turn the conversation around. He didn't feel comfortable talking about Maurice and their evening together. It wasn't that he didn't feel comfortable talking about it with Sandy, it was that he didn't feel comfortable with the whole thing. He could not dismiss the need that made landing in Maurice's arms so easy. He'd always had a problem with confusing sex with love and it frightened him.

He asked Sandy if she was upset with him about the Ms. Callier ordeal. He was so relieved when she said she was the one that should apologize for dragging him into such a mess. He heard Maurice stirring in his bedroom and he excused himself by telling Sandy he needed to shower for work. He wasn't ready to face Maurice just yet.

As soon as he placed the receiver on the base, the phone rang again. He picked it up at the same time Maurice answered the phone in his room. He knew the call was not for him but something told him to listen anyway. He didn't want to believe what he was hearing. Words, words of endearment, promise, and change. He hung up the receiver with shaking hands. Maurice was taking a lover and moving him in! He felt like someone had punched him in the stomach.

The warmth of the shower washed over him and he wished the steam could peel the night of sex off his body. Why had he let it happen? Why had he been pulled in by Maurice's charms? He owed Celia Callier a very swift kick in the ass. He bent to turn the shower off and realized that it wasn't Ms. Callier who needed a kick or Maurice either. He had been ready for romance long before Ms. Callier shook his world. Looking in the mirror, he saw Sandy's face staring back. He answered the reflection as much for his own peace of mind as for practice for when he and Sandy next spoke of the incident.

"I know, Sandy, I made my own bed, slept in it and I can't complain if the sheets turned out to be dirty."

Robert was in his closet trying to decide whether to wear the red Tommy Hilfiger tie or the soft blue Dior, when he heard Maurice calling his name.

"I'm in here Maurice. Maybe you can help me decide which tie to put on with this suit."

He noticed that when Maurice entered the huge walk-in closet, his robe was opened and his skin was still moist from his morning shower. He tried to avert his eyes and ignore the feelings the sight and smell of him stirred.

"Wear the blue, Robert. Red is such a manly power cliche!"

The temptation was to do the opposite of what Maurice suggested but he knew he was right. He didn't want to give any indication that he knew anything about what Maurice obviously wanted to keep secret. His anger was at himself, not Maurice. He was the one who had been needy. Hell, if Maurice was in a serious relationship and on the verge of giving up half of his bed to someone, then he certainly wasn't the one starved for attention! He couldn't help but wonder when Maurice had planned to tell him about the planned change.

Suddenly, he felt a chill go up his back. He turned and saw tears streaming down Maurice's face.

"My gosh, Maurice, what in the world is wrong? Are you in pain or something?"

"Yes, Robert, but not the physical kind. We need to talk."

Robert followed Maurice into the kitchen and waited for his revelations about the future and his apologies for what had happened between them. He thought he knew what Maurice was going to say but nothing prepared him for what ended up being laid out on the table.

"Robert, I've met someone. We have been seeing each other for about a year now. We're deeply in love and want to move in together."

Reaching across the table, Maurice took Robert's hands in his. The tears took a different route down his cheeks as he lowered his eyes and his head.

"I'm moving out. Charles is very wealthy and has a wonderful estate in Colorado. I'm quitting my job and giving him all of me that he needs. The moving van will be here this afternoon around two and I have a flight to Denver at four."

Robert sat too stunned to speak. He had assumed that the other man was one of Maurice's usual pick ups. Some business man who'd left his wife to find himself. He never thought for a moment about Maurice moving out and establishing a life someplace else.

Suddenly the night before made more sense than he wanted it to. It had been a goodbye, a farewell, an "I am moving on", roll in the sack. He felt raped. Even though it had been consensual, he had no idea of the real circumstance. He was in shock and all words failed him other than the ones he meant most.

"I'm happy for you, Maurice. I wish you all the happiness in the world. I will miss you."

Robert went back to his room, took off the blue tie and donned the red. He needed all the manly power he could muster, cliche or not!

Sandy had just finished her morning walk when she got the call from Robert. She knew something really earth shaking must have happened if he called her from work. He sounded desperate and asked if she would meet him for lunch. It was already ten fifteen and she would have to hurry if she was going to make it in time to meet him at the mall for lunch at noon. The buses ran every fifteen minutes but she had not even showered yet.

She couldn't get rid of the sinking feeling in her stomach. She wished that he had been able to give her a clue as to what was wrong. Her imagination ran rampant. Her thoughts ranged from possible problems due to Ms. Callier's visit, all the way down the line to illness. What she didn't understand was why he hadn't mentioned anything earlier when they spoke. She didn't want to borrow trouble but she couldn't deny the obvious upset in Robert's voice.

The mall was crowded and the cafeteria already had a line of people snaking their way out the door. She finally saw Robert and instantly engulfed him in a huge hug. It didn't matter what was troubling him; she knew he needed the warmth of her friendship and acceptance. She found out soon enough that at least his sense humor was intact.

"Oh honey, red is definitely your color! Girlfriend, was that actually a hip bone I felt? See, I was right from the beginning. You aren't a blob, just a well padded skeletal frame!"

Robert picked a table that allowed them a little privacy and before she could even finish placing her plates from tray to table, he blurted out his news.

"Maurice is in love and is moving to Denver! He's leaving this afternoon at four and didn't even ask me to come to the airport to say goodbye."

Sandy looked at Robert and tears welled up in her eyes. The

pain he felt was as thick as the no-fat Ranch dressing on her salad. She went to him and hugged him again but this time it was more an embrace of receiving than giving. She wanted to draw the pain from him and take it in as her own.

"Oh God, Robert, I'm so sorry! I just don't know what else to say. Why don't I shut up and you tell me how this all came about."

"What bothers me, I mean besides sleeping with him last night, is that he didn't share such a monumental thing with me. I mean, it has an impact on me, Sandy, not just emotionally either. Do you have any idea how much a month we pay for the condo? Our mortgage is $950 a month and that doesn't include utilities! I'm not only going to be alone, I'm going to be broke!"

Robert stirred his tea and Sandy could see the wheels turning in his head. She had come to know him well. She watched him stew and felt a love that she had never known. It was an "outside her family" love and unlike the love of her family, it was healthy. She leaned in to listen as Robert readied himself to speak.

"Sandy, I was brainstorming on the way into work. It's part of the reason I called you. How much does Avery make a week? I know that's personal but there is a reason I'm asking. Maurice's leaving is going to put me in a real bind. I may even lose the condo."

She could tell he had other questions to ask but she also knew they weren't ones with which he felt comfortable. She wanted to make him feel at ease.

"Robert, you can ask me anything. The best way to do it is to take a breath and let the words fall out of your mouth!"

"Sandy, how would you like to be like the Jeffersons?"

"The Jeffersons? Who the hell are they? Are they your neighbors?"

Robert's laughter rang out loud and sincere.

"Sandy, they're a television family from years ago! They moved on up! What I want to know is if you, Avery and Tommy would consider moving into the condo with me. We could do up a contract and a terms of living agreement. You don't have to answer now and I know you must speak to Avery but please think about it. You're the only family I have now!"

Sandy left Robert with a promise that she would think about what he proposed. Her mind was swirling with the magnitude of his idea. She had never been to Robert's home but common sense told her it was paradise compared to what she was used to. She saw the bus round the corner and smiled as she remembered her first vision of how Robert lived. It had been so stereotypical. Red crushed velvet had come to her mind the most, like an Elvis painting, or those bullfight scenes with rhinestones and glitter!

The bus was crowded and she felt hemmed in and claustrophobic. She wanted to have the freedom of thought but crying babies and the drone of Spanish kept interfering with the clarity of her thinking. She had not had any time to consider the enormity of what Robert proposed.

She was not even sure how to broach the subject with Avery. Her thoughts had not long been on Avery, when a vision of Cara popped into her mind. Oh good God! Her mother would have more to say about this than a politician on the floor of the House during a filibuster! Her head ached from the top of its crown all the way through her teeth and into her neck! She had to have time to think and the bus just wasn't the place to do it.

By the time she walked the half mile from the bus stop to her trailer, her head was clearer. As she approached the trailer, with its green slime stains and damp, sagging insulation jutting out from beneath its buckled frame, she realized that she really wanted what Robert had offered. She had never enjoyed the way she lived but merely accepted it as her lot in life.

Robert had been hope to her from the moment she met him. She was awed by the generosity of his friendship. She also loved the thought of being able to help him out of his current circumstance. He had often talked of how spacious his condo was and how nice the area in which he lived. It would mean better schools for Tommy and a chance to escape the threat of gangs as well. Even at eight, he had come home on more than one occasion talking about the bad kids. Hell, just last week a fourteen year old had been shot and killed at a convenience store a block from Tommy's elementary school!

The more she thought about moving, the more excited she became. She had watched an Oprah show once where a psychologist said that if faced with a big decision, it is a good idea to put it to paper. She found a notepad and pencil and started making an outline. The first consideration would be finances, then environment and then emotional impact on their family. With the possible exception of Avery and Cara, she felt family issues would be the most positive consideration of all.

By the time she heard Tommy's school bus out front, she had written down three pages of pros and cons to present to Avery. She felt confident that she had ample ammunition to diffuse any argument he could possibly throw at her. She fixed Tommy a peanut butter and jelly sandwich and told him to watch his afternoon cartoons while she went to take a shower. She smiled at herself in the bathroom mirror, if logic didn't work on Avery, perhaps a little loving would!

She knew as she stepped into the warmth of the shower that Robert would be proud of her. She was making a stand and trying to facilitate her own happiness. She knew that she would meet tremendous opposition but she had prepared herself. She let the water run soothingly over her and said a small prayer.

"Dear God, please open Avery's ears, if not his heart, to our future and if not for me, then for Tommy and this new baby!"

Avery was in need of a cold beer and a hot shower. His day at work had been crap. He had to take crap, listen to crap and now after eight hours of it, he felt like crap. With his luck, the beer would be hot and his shower would be cold. It was just the way things happened in his life.

The old pick-up seemed to echo Avery's longing for peace as it chugged and churned down the same path it took every day. Sometimes it seemed both him and his truck wanted to veer off the road and go exploring. There were big houses with well paved driveways that he wanted to pull into. He wished he lived the life of the people with well manicured yards, buffed fingernails and tailored clothing. It seemed to him their lives were made to fit them. His life fit him as well but he didn't feel he fit his life.

He often thought of people who took their unstained existence for granted and wondered how they could be blind to the incredible gift. Longing was something that beat inside him as surely as the oxygen rich red blood that pulsed through his heart. He had seen the hunger in Tommy's eyes and understood it. He had lived the same starvation for twenty-six years.

It hurt him that his path had been paved by uneducated, lazy people. If a ditch didn't swallow a vehicle, then it made a decent passageway. If stains on the walls didn't rot the boards, then why do anything to cover them? If that which was broken still had use, then why try to fix it?

Avery was tired. He loved Sandy and Tommy but he didn't love himself or his life. He thought about Sandy and realized that his greatest fear when she met Robert had been that she would realize that the life she had known with him was so much less than most people lived.

He thought back to the day they first saw the trailer they were renting. He smiled as he remembered the excitement in her eyes. She had raced from room to room with the glow of ideas in her head. She talked about cheap material for curtains and little touches to make it their's. His thoughts had centered only on the things that he wanted to give this woman/child some day.

His disappointment was in himself. He had given Sandy the world...his world! It was the same one she had grown up in and it hurt him more than he could ever tell her. It wasn't that she ever complained, it was more her silence about things. He understood. He too lived with quiet suffering.

The truck instinctively turned into the entrance to the trailer park. Avery felt his heart lurch forward in his chest, as he pressed on the clutch to slow his speed. He drove by the rows of poverty with their telltale signs of less than life. It seemed to him that just as a telegraph sent messages in code, so too did these homes of the homeless. The same words were transmitted by each one...Help!

Avery veered as he pulled into his own patch of grass. He had to avoid Tommy's rusted old bike. His life was paved with terra firma rather than concrete. Hell, it made sense to him. There had never been anything concrete about his existence. Well, perhaps one thing had been assured. He was Avery Anderson and that meant that he was destined to live on the fringe of the world, not in it. He was dirty and had been dirty from conception. Tears threatened the corners of his eyes and he used his shirt sleeve to wipe them away.

Sandy popped the top from a Shiner Bock and took the iced glass from the freezer. Robert had slipped her ten dollars and told her to treat Avery to something other than beer that tasted like horse piss. She wanted to be at the door with it when Avery walked in. She could see him out in the yard with Tommy.

Avery looked tired to her. The kind of tired when the weight on a person's shoulders exceeds the ability to shrug things off. She knew the thought of another mouth to feed worried him tremendously. There was so little money now and babies were so expensive. She took a deep breath and held tight to the list she had made for reasons to move in with Robert.

She saw him walking towards the porch and opened the door in welcome. Her right hand held the beer and her left contained the list. She protectively tucked the list into her pocket. She didn't want to mention a thing to him about Robert until he was relaxed and the grime of his day lay in the bottom of the tub.

Her hug was one of real love. She often thought about their relationship. Regardless of what they had been through, no matter the hardship, it was something that was as solid as all the emotional mountains they had been forced to climb. The one person she had always been able to count on was Avery. She hoped beyond hope that she could count on him now.

Avery looked at the glass of beer and shocked her with his tone of voice.

"What the hell, woman! I break my back trying to make rent and put food on the table and you go out and waste money on some foo foo beer! Tommy just told me he needs some kind of damned special paints for art class in school and we ain't even got enough toilet paper to last the month! Damn it, Sandy, I like Robert and all but he's starting to make you into someone I don't know!"

She looked at Avery through tears. She couldn't allow herself to take on his mood, not this time. There was too much at stake and she had to be the bigger person for now.

"It didn't cost that much, darlin'. Besides it was a gift, so it didn't cost nothin'. You look so tired. Tell ya what, you go on and take a hot shower and when ya get done we can talk."

She always wanted his beer to be cold and his shower to be hot. She was no different from him in that way. If there was one really important discovery that Robert had helped her make it was that the unanswered needs and wants of people sometimes come out as anger and blame. She wasn't going to blame Avery for his wants, his needs or his anger. Tonight she wanted to love him and show him a way out of hell and into life. Tonight she wanted to be the one to fix things. She wanted to bring a smile of relief to his lips and freedom to his sagging shoulders.

The water felt like silk against Avery's tense body. He stood under the stream and wished he could become it. He felt guilty about jumping on Sandy the minute he walked in the door but nine dollars for beer could have bought Tommy the paint set he needed for school.

He hated the smell of Ivory soap. It wasn't because its odor was foul but because it was the cheapest that could be bought and all he could afford. He took the wash cloth and placed it over his eyes. He needed an excuse for the intense redness. Sandy could understand soap or beer but she would never understand tears. She had seen him cry but until now there had always been a reason. The tears that he shed now were generic and genuine.

Never in all his years had he felt so helpless. Never had he wanted to give up, give in and give out. He was scaring himself and knew that his mood would throw Sandy into panic. He held the soap dish tightly with his right hand. He had to get a grip, figuratively and actually.

He thought about what he heard on the news at lunch. The Noble Prize for Medicine was awarded and the guy who won got like three million dollars. Avery thought to himself why doesn't someone discover a cure for poverty, hopelessness and despair? Hell, the cause of most heart attacks, cancer and other diseases was stress. Award a prize to someone who found answers, not treated the symptoms!

Thoughts of disease and stress made him wonder where in the hell he would come up with fifty dollars for his portion of his annual physical? He thought about the dollar a glass beer and thought he should have hated the taste. He saw the beer as the life he didn't have and for him its taste was bitter. It wasn't that he didn't like it, it was that he couldn't afford to like it!

He let out a yell as the water suddenly turned cold against his skin. The cold water just confirmed the fact that he'd stayed too long at the fair and the price of being poor had just become too much. His body shivered under the cold of the water but it was his heart that quaked under the weight of his burden.

He stepped out of the shower and reached for the already damp towel. He'd smelled Sandy's bath on her skin and wished he could smell the linen closet of one of the houses he had passed on the way home. He bet the only towels they ever shared were ones to wipe away the evidence of sex. Hell, right now, he couldn't even afford to use toilet paper for that! He and Sandy were forced to wear their sex. It hurt him so much that everyone would soon see it in her well- rounded belly.

The underwear he pulled over his girth was stained and had holes. Somehow to Avery it didn't matter anymore. He was very close to taking on one more burden. He wanted out. He would never leave Sandy but there were other ways. He wondered if death would hurt less than his life?

Avery poured another beer. Sandy was stirring the chives into the mashed potatoes and he could tell that she was lost in her own thoughts. He assumed she was brooding about his mini tirade over the beer. Placing his glass on the kitchen table, he went to her and placed his arms around her from behind. His head rested against her back and his body communicated his apology.

The strong ale taste of the beer was a truth serum because he wanted to tell her how he had been feeling. He needed her to know that his dissatisfaction was not with her but with his inability to make things happen the way he wanted them to. Like a wayward Catholic sitting in a confessional for the first time in years, Avery's words spilled forth.

"Forgive me, Sandy. I've been going through some shit that makes me wish my life was written on a blackboard so I could use one of those big black erasers and wipe the shit off my face!"

He felt Sandy shift her weight to turn and face him. He stepped back so he would be able to see the questions in her eyes. He was surprised to witness hope sparkling in the deepest part of their blue and the sprinkle of understanding formed on their lids. He felt the warmth of her voice wash over him just as the water in the shower had only moments before.

"I know, Avery. My heart has listened to the sound of life dangling before us for nine years . I've seen the grit go from your clothes straight to your soul. Sandpaper is useful but if used on the same spot over and over, it tends to wear down the surface it rubs against. Soon the sandpaper takes on more of the components of what it chafes than is left on the surface itself."

Avery just nodded in agreement. She knew without his telling her. It was obvious to him she had been feeling the same way. He held her close in a gentle embrace and whispered into her hair.

"I am so sorry, Sandy. I wanted so much more for you. Damn it! I wanted more for me!"

"There can be more, Avery. It's at our fingertips. Let me open you another beer. We need to talk. We have a way out. We have a real chance to change things. We can set out on an adventure together and discover how the real world lives."

He sat with his head tilted to the right side, fear and hope battling in the corners of his mind. He flinched a little when he felt Sandy's hands on his. He stopped breathing a moment when he heard her next words drop to the kitchen table.

"Maurice moved out on Robert and he proposed a wild idea. He wants you, me and Tommy to move in with him!"

He didn't care about knocking over his beer as he pulled his hands from Sandy's. He didn't care that he heard the words "what the fuck are you talking about" yelling out from his mind. At that moment he just didn't care about anything. The only thing he heard coming from his wife was that he was not good enough to take care of his own family. She was telling him another man, a homosexual to boot, had more to offer her than did he.

He left Sandy at the table and walked out onto the porch. He needed to think out all the rage in his heart. The Texas moon even seemed to mock him. He walked into the yard and picked up the old tire resting against the tallest pine tree. He hurled it into the air and screamed in agony.

"Damn you, life! Damn you to the same hell you've made me suffer. Fuck you for fucking me!"

The grass felt cool to Avery's tear stained face. Life kept slapping him and he had no more cheeks to turn. He couldn't take anymore.

The truck started with the first crank. He backed out of the rut that had been made by his repetitive existence. He knew if he ever came back to this place, he would not be driving into the same indentations of time and space. He knew his life would never be the same.

Sandy called Robert at work. She needed listening ears and a caring heart. She knew from the sound of his occasional sniff that he had been crying too. She asked Robert about Maurice's exit.

She was not prepared for the halting, gasping sobs of words she heard.

"The hell...of...it...the thing is... Oh God, Sandy, he took my heart and the damn furniture! It's ironic really. If I would have come home, instead of having lunch with you, I could have stopped the movers!"

Sandy tried to console Robert but her heart was hanging in her chest by a thread and Avery was the only needle that could mend it. It was Robert who ended the conversation abruptly.

"Sandy, we're having a one day sale and the store is just crazy. I need to get back to work. I love you, darling. I should be home by ten. Call me then?"

She put the receiver back on its base and heard as well as felt the click of lost communication. She wanted to crawl into a hole but there was only one that her frame would fit, her own life.

The sound of the phone made her jump. Cara's voice was loud, drunk and accusatory.

"Well hell, I didn't think you'd be home! I figured you'd already moved in with homo boy livin the life of Riley! You know it ain't gonna make a bit of difference where you live. You can mask what you are but you ain't never gonna be able to mask who you are."

"Mama, I am not in the mood for this. I feel like I've been fighting with everyone and I'm tired. Can I ask you something? Why are you so mad at me for wantin' to be better than I am?"

"Cause, Sandy. You ain't never gonna be anything but poor white trash. That's all any of us can be. I'm scared for you. Ain't you had enough disappointments in life?"

"Yes, Mama, I've had a million disappointments. They all started with you and the night you didn't stop daddy. You put the garbage in my room 'cause you couldn't stand the stench of it in your own. You made me trash, Mama, and it's time I crawled out of the dump!"

Sandy listened to the click and the dial tone for what seemed an eternity. In one day she'd managed to alienate her husband and her mother. The pull of what could be against the cement wall of what was caused a tension on her arms that stretched her bones. The night fell silent around her except for the sound of the eighteen wheelers whizzing past the trailer park. Sleep came to her as she made her decision. She would do for Tommy what no one had done for her. She would make his life better. She would move in with Robert with or without Avery.

Sandy tried to sleep but the emptiness of the bed only reminded her of the fullness of her mind. The things she wanted, mixed with what she didn't have, swirled around in her head. She stared at the brown water stains on the ceiling and thought they matched the dingy feel of her entire life.

Rolling over on her right side she looked at the clock hoping time was spinning in reverse. She thought about what her mama had said. White trash was pretty much an accurate description of how she'd felt all her life. It was something that lived in the eyes of a person and in the dirt under their fingernails. Cara was a carrier, as were she and Avery. Trying to improve most often meant putting a coat of paint on a sod house. It wasn't that they started out less than anyone else, it was that they had been made less by everyone else.

Sandy had never understood why all the anger of her past had been directed at Cara and all her forgiveness given to her dad. He was the one who had raped her but it had always felt like her mama was the one committing the act. No matter how much she wanted to rage against what had happened to her, she was incensed about why it happened.

Her own mama permitted the taking of her innocence, trust and childhood. Sandy choked back the tears as she sat up to let the emotion drain from her head to her heart. She looked towards the window and saw the tattered curtains as another reminder of what had never been. Holes in a heart never served to block out the darkness of the mind and memory.

Sandy heard the front door open and the familiar sound of Avery's steps shake the trailer. She wanted to squash down the anger inside before he made his way to the bedroom. She heard him in the hallway and then silence fell around the house as if life was suddenly a slow motion film without sound.

She quietly got of bed and walked down the hall. The sobs were almost inaudible as she passed Tommy's room. She stood at the doorway and saw Avery kneeling beside his son's bed. He looked like a child of ten saying his prayers before the dust of sleep was sprinkled over the night. She knew in her heart that for the moment, he was that child.

Kneeling quietly beside him, Sandy took Avery's right hand in hers and shared his tears. There were decisions to be made and futures to be decided. The raping of their souls had been the lesson of their childhood but they both knew they didn't want Tommy to be a victim of their lacking.

CHAPTER FIFTEEN

Cara drove along the back roads. The night was moonless and she got drunk all over again from the whiskey contained in each of her exhaled breaths. She felt more in command of a vehicle intoxicated than she did when she was sober. Shoot, her shaking alone made it impossible to steer if it had been more than eight hours since her last drink! She laughed loudly to herself as she thought she would only pass a sobriety test if she was inebriated!

The green of the East Texas trees flashed by in the headlights and an occasional armadillo or racoon would try to avoid their intrusive illumination. The times between fun and sleep were the only times Cara really gave herself time to think about life. For her, it was a time of purgatory. She only did well in an unconscious state. When she was drunk, she didn't care if she existed. When she was asleep, she didn't know she existed.

She had to drink more than usual thanks to her conversation with Sandy. Her thoughts kept drifting to her daughter even when she tried to think about the new stud she'd met. Yep, she thought, that girl of mine always did get in the way of pleasant moments. Cara always had trouble understanding why Sandy blamed her for the past. It wasn't like Sandy had ever gone hungry or slept out in the cold as a child!

When Cara turned on to the back road to her trailer the chill of reality hit her. She turned up the heater in the car to stop the sudden quaking of her body. With total memory and full impact, she remembered the first time her own daddy had raped her. The incredible wave of repulsion hit her and made her grab the steering wheel hard enough to leave finger indentations in the plastic. It was as if the violation happened at that moment.

Cara ignored the police car parked on the shoulder as she sped by at ninety miles an hour. She heard but did not heed the whining of its siren in the still air of a Texas morning. She could only think of home and sleep. She needed out of her thoughts and away from the jail that had kept her prisoner.

When Cara finally pulled over and rolled down her window, she was sobbing uncontrollably. When the officer approached, a screeching voice came from the darkness of her soul.

"I WAS RAPED!"

The truth hit home but only Cara knew that the words were over forty years old!

Sandy's heart stopped when the phone roused her from the sleep of an emotional night. She grabbed for the receiver in the darkness as if another ring would drive her insane. Her hello was sleepy, scared and angry all at the same time.

"Mrs. Anderson, this is Cindy Banks at East Texas General Hospital. Your mother was brought into our emergency room by a Harris County Sheriff's officer. She is asking for you. Could you please come down to be with her?"

Sandy started to ask if Cara had been in accident but before her words could make their way out of her mouth she heard a dial tone. She woke Avery to tell him she had to go to the hospital. He bolted upright thinking she was having a miscarriage.

"Oh God, are you bleeding?!"

"No, darlin', I'm fine. It's Mama. She's at East Texas General. They didn't tell me what was wrong, just to come down there. I'll need you to get Tommy to school. It's three a.m. and I likely won't be back for awhile."

She knew by the way that Avery kissed her goodbye that he was relieved that whatever was wrong had not been visited on them directly. Sandy felt like the chill in the air was being generated from her own heart. She couldn't help but be a little angry at Cara. It wasn't the first time she had gotten a call in the middle of the night. Her mama was known for terrorizing trees or telephone poles while driving home in a drunken state. Whatever she hit was usually in worse shape than she.

Sandy pulled into the Emergency Room parking lot and wrapped her sweater around her to ward off the brisk, biting air. She went to the nurse's desk and said she was looking for Cara Covington.

"Oh, you must be Mrs. Anderson. They have moved her to the psych ward but that officer over there would like to speak with you."

Sandy's head turned in the direction the nurse was pointing to and saw a familiar face staring back at her. The officer's name was Morris Foley. He and Sandy had gone to school together and he had been the arresting officer on two of Cara's DWI cases.

"Sorry, Sandy. I think your mom has really gone off the deep end this time. She keeps screaming that she's been raped and no one can make no sense out of what she's saying. She keeps talking about how she is just a little girl and that ain't nobody should steal from a little girl!"

Sandy stood in front of Morris and tried to imagine what her world looked like to him. It was something she did when she could make no sense of her own life. She wanted to see things through someone else's eyes to see if there was any understanding. She had felt transparent her entire life and for once wished she actually was.

Sensing that she was off some place else or in shock, Morris took Sandy by the elbow and helped her to a chair. He had always felt sorry for her and hated that he had to tell her he was duty bound to make a report on what had happened.

"Sandy, I have to write this up. I know your mom has had problems with DWIs before and that she will likely lose her license this time but I gotta do it. Sorry, but it's my job."

Sandy looked at Morris as if he were stupid.

"Hell yes you have to report it! If my mama's been raped then a god damned felony has been committed and it sure in the hell is your job to report it!"

"Sandy, I don't think you understand. There was no rape. They checked her. There was no evidence of seminal fluids. Your mama's just losing it. That's why they took her up to the psych ward."

Sorrow covered Sandy like a patchwork blanket of shame, guilt and anger. It didn't really matter if the tests proved negative. She knew that Cara Covington had been raped repeatedly by life. Hell, even if what she was going through now was merely the DTs, it meant she raped herself! That was how it was in the trash heap. There was always more garbage inside than out.

Cara tried to moisten her lips. They were cracked from dehydration and her mouth felt like the lint found in the dryer screen. The straps chaffed Cara's wrists, while the need of a drink made her entire body strain against them.

The nurse was way too cheerful as she opened the mini blinds to let the morning sun stream through. Her smile made Cara want to throw up.

"Get the hell out of my room! I don't need your damn fake smile or pretend caring!"

"A little grumpy this morning aren't we, Mrs. Covington? Here, drink this juice. It will put the sunshine of Florida in your veins."

Cara felt helpless as the nurse sat on the edge of the bed and held the glass up to her lips.

"I ain't no god damned baby! Undo these straps and let me hold my own fucking glass!"

"Now, Mrs. Covington, you know I can't do such a thing. The doctor would have me on bed pan duty for a month if I did. I'm tellin' you, it would be a lot easier on you if you just cooperate."

Cara was about to sip some juice just to spit it at the recalcitrant smurf when the doctor came into the room.

"Mrs. Covington, I am Dr. Moreland. Do you know why you are here?"

"Sure doc, you saw me at Liars and decided to bring me here for a night of kinky sex! I've been handcuffed plenty of times, doc, but you're the first to use wrist and leg restraints! Tell me, sweetie, was it good for you?"

"Anger is a normal reaction, Mrs. Covington. By all means, please feel free to vent all you like. I am here to listen."

His invitation left Cara feeling cold and silent. She knew how detox worked and would play their game for a day and then sign herself out like before. She wondered why people who had degrees thought people who didn't were stupid. She wouldn't let this guy inside her outside walls, what made him think she would let him explore the ones in her mind?

"Mrs Covington, the officer that found you last night said you were yelling about being raped. Would you like to talk to me about the incident?"

An evil smile crossed Cara's lips as they parted to extract venom from her ready tongue.

"Sure, doc. I would love to talk about it with you. You just slide yourself over to the side of this bed and I'll not only tell you but show you!"

Sitting up as far as the wrist straps would allow, Cara let loose the anger inside.

"Get the hell out of my room! I may be poor. I may be uneducated. I may even be a drunk but I ain't no god damned attraction in your freak show! You and all the others like you live off the flesh and hearts of others. You call yourselves healers and all any of you are are lying cannibals!"

Without fanfare, Cara started shrieking in a voice that would make a sane man crazy and an insane one suffer a cerebral hemorrhage . Her fervor escalated as she rocked and chanted.

"Cara, Cara, come suck my dick. Daddy's pockets are full so take your pick. A toy in one, money in the other. I'll give you both if you don't tell mother!"

The nurse fumbled with the syringe as she hurriedly filled it with halidol. Trying to find a vein was no problem as Cara's clenched fists made each arm look like a road map to her private hell. Dr.

Moreland patted Cara on the arm and said he would be back when she was feeling better.

Stupor is a wonderful land. Cara thought everyone should visit once in awhile. The world is there but it has no feel. Hell, she thought, whiskey did the same thing and was sure in the hell cheaper than a hospital stay! The pillow felt like a cloud and the silence of an empty room like heaven. All was right with the world for the moment.

Sandy approached Dr. Moreland with the uneasiness of a student who has been sent to the principal's office. She hated having to talk to educated people. They always made her feel like she had been raised in a pig pen. She saw the narrowing of the eyes as they made their assessment of her weight, clothes, demeanor and lacking. They never turned their heads so that their eyes met hers. They looked past her or through her. She always felt they were afraid she would somehow rub off on them.

"Mrs. Anderson? I am Dr. Moreland. I am in charge of your mother's care. She has suffered a serious psychotic episode and I think she should be committed for the long term. I was wondering if you might be able to answer a few questions for me?"

Sandy trusted doctors about as much as she trusted lawyers. She knew that her mama would want to sign herself out after her seventy-two hours were up and knew if she said the wrong thing that wouldn't happen.

"Dr. Moreland, I don't know anything about what happened. All I know is I got a call saying to come down here last night and I came. May I see my mama now?"

"No, Mrs. Anderson, she was in a very agitated state a moment ago and we had to give her something to calm her down. Are you sure you can't enlighten me on what brought all this on?"

Sandy was not educated but neither was she stupid. She shifted her weight in the chair and contorted her face in a look of childish wonder.

"The hell you say, Doc! You mean they actually make something that can keep my mama calm and I never knew about it? Well, don't that beat all! All them years of putting up with that drunk bitch and I could have given her something that would have actually shut her mouth?"

She was about to expound on Cara's drinking escapades but a nurse came running and whisked Dr. Moreland away. She had done well, she thought. Everyone knew her mama had a drinking problem but unless she agreed to treatment there wasn't a way in the world to keep her in the hospital. Being crazy was a whole other ball game. Hell, if they thought she was a threat to herself or others, then they could keep her indefinitely. Sandy knew that from watching doctor television shows.

She smiled as the attendant unlocked the door to the psych ward to let her out. Yep, she thought, who says a person can't learn from watching television! All these people in their tidy little uniforms thought they were the ones that could help Cara. Sandy knew different. She knew what she had to do and would go straight home and start making some calls.

Avery sat at the kitchen table staring at the clock on the wall. He noticed the build up of grease on the scratched surface of the plastic covering the face. He couldn't help but feel the grime that seemed to permeate his own pores. Dust collected on his life just as it did on the surfaces surrounding him in the kitchen. He wished that a good cleaner, a rag and gentle pressure could make clean his life. Wouldn't things be simple if people's surfaces were plastic? He smiled to himself as he envisioned the people he knew that were seemingly like that. They were the people who wore hand washables or dry clean onlys. Their material was of finer quality and their lives high maintenance. Everything about them was crisp and clean. They had problems but they were always outside problems, not inside ones. It seemed to Avery their holes were not in their hearts, or their minds, or their souls, just on the surface of their lives and easily patched with dinner at a great restaurant or shopping spree at a local mall.

He'd watched Tommy as he boarded the bus for school. Actually, he had watched Tommy in context with all the other trailer kids. They looked like ripped pockets of people whose pants were too tight and had come apart at the seams. Avery wondered if it was just circumstance or if society wanted to keep the leppers together and recognizable. He was sure that when their bus pulled up at school all the plastic kids scurried inside to be safe from the sudden onslaught of dirt, grease and grime.

Avery put his cup in the sink and wished Sandy would get back from the hospital. He didn't like the feel of the house without her. He had been thinking about how the trailer and his life felt even more dilapidated when she wasn't there. A twinge of guilt circled his head and shot to his heart as he felt almost glad that Cara had gotten herself in trouble again. He knew that with Cara's current situation Sandy would be too busy to think more about moving in with Robert.

"Oh shit! Robert! I was supposed to call him and tell him about Cara."

He took the piece of paper Sandy had left by the coffee pot and dialed the number.

"Hello, Robert? This is Avery Anderson, Sandy's husband."

He felt stupid for the words the minute they left his mouth. How many people did Robert know with the name Avery Anderson? Why on earth did he always say things that made him appear more uneducated than he really was?

"Hi, Avery. Is something wrong with Sandy? You sound flustered."

Avery suppressed a laugh as he thought flustered was a word only a man like Robert would use. He immediately envisioned a frail man waving his arms in the air with feminine orchestration!

"Sandy is fine. It's Cara. They have her at East Texas General. Sandy should be home any minute. She wanted me to call and let you know."

"Oh God!! Was it an accident?"

Avery bit his tongue before answering. He wanted to say, "Hell yes, it was an accident. Cara has been an accident since the day she was born!"

"I don't know what happened, Robert. I won't know until I talk to Sandy. I'll have her call you, okay?"

"Oh yes, Avery. Please have her call me at work. She has my number. Oh, this is just so upsetting! Poor Cara, and of course, my heart is breaking for all of you. I hope it isn't too serious."

"Thanks, Robert, and I'll tell Sandy to call you as soon as she comes in. Bye."

"Bye, Avery, and my prayers are with you."

The phone went cold in Avery's hand as he placed the receiver back on the base. He couldn't dislike Robert. He almost understood what Sandy saw in him. There was a real warmth to him, an acceptance and sincerity that made the person receiving his kindness seem more real.

There was a reason Avery felt uncomfortable with Robert at times. He had a secret that few people knew. It was something that haunted him at night when the sound of the crickets sounded like the voice of God chiding him for what he did. He'd blocked out the memory for the most part, but Robert had brought it to the forefront again. His thoughts were interrupted by the sound of the old truck pulling into the gravel. He went to the screen door and watched Sandy as she got out of the truck. He sighed at the sight of her. He was safe now.

The wood supports groaned with anguish as Sandy slumped into the too thin cushions of the couch. She looked as worn as the soft velour and as faded as the flower print that once represented life in its glorious bloom. Avery settled in beside her and took her right hand in his.

"Is it real bad? Did she kill someone this time?"

"It wasn't a wreck, Avery. Morris Foley was up there waiting on me and said she went speeding by him. He said when he pulled her over she said she'd been raped! Only thing is, they can't find no evidence of it happening. They think she's lost her mind finally. They have her up on the psych ward."

"Has she, Sandy? Has she finally snapped? How'd she look?"

"I didn't see her, Avery. They gave her something to calm her down. I know what I gotta do, Avery, and it makes me want to run away and hide. I think I know what's wrong with Mama. I think the past has come back to haunt her. It's the only thing that makes sense."

Sandy wasn't sure why but the feel of Avery's hand on hers repulsed her. The night had dredged up the sewer of her soul. She didn't have to see her mama to know what was hurting her. She knew what was living inside her mama because she was the shame of Cara repeating itself. When it came to pain, her and her mama were joined at the heart.

Sandy looked to see if Avery had any clue as to what she was talking about. She was not prepared for the tears running down his face.

"I swear, Sandy, it's the first time I've seen disgust in your eyes for what we are. I've always seen it in other people's eyes when they look at us, but I ain't ever seen it on your face!"

"I'm tired, Avery. I need some sleep and you need to go on to your doctor's appointment. You gotta pass that physical so don't be making your blood pressure get all crazy. It's a good thing they took blood last week or you'd be showin' all of them just how much beer you drink in a night."

She knew it was a mean thing to say but she found no comfort in her life and couldn't find an ounce to give to any one else at the moment. Alcohol, abuse, incest, anger, she was swimming in a sea of it. Why on earth were people afraid of sharks? Ha! At least if a shark attacks a person it can only kill them once!

Avery picked up the car keys from the coffee table and kissed Sandy goodbye. He felt heavier than his three-hundred and fifty pounds. He carried an anvil of want on his shoulders and the heaviness of not having in his belly. The morning was bright and sunny but his mood was damp and cold. He hated life almost more than he hated himself.

CHAPTER SIXTEEN

Avery drove across the huge suspension bridge and marveled at the sunlight bouncing off the yellow of the suspension wires. Man was capable of making such beautiful things to bridge the gaps between one side of the road to another. He wondered why engineers couldn't build the same thing for people? A sadness lived in Avery and it lived in every person he had ever shared his life with.

He often watched the other guys at work and thought that even the women looked like the face he saw in the mirror every morning. There was just something about people who let life etch itself out in them rather than them etching out a life. The leather of the skin looked stretched and worn no matter how ample. There were no graceful lines or well defined edges, just crevices and protrusions of wanton despair.

The smell of chemical plants had the odor of money to most people in the area but for Avery it was just another place he wasn't good enough to be. The plants smelled like shit to him, just like life in general. He watched the shine of the other cars as he pulled up to a red light. It all made sense. All the people who had things were shiny. Their faces shone, their homes shone, their kids shone and their cars shone. The things in his life were black holes with no light and no shine.

Avery turned onto a road that was seemingly paved with money. It was a street of doctors offices where more was spent on the landscaping than he made in a year. He saw a car backing out and steered the truck towards the space. He didn't see the handicap sign until he had pulled in. His anger was immediate. He wanted to cry out to the world that he might not have a handicap sticker but he was riddled with crippling ailments.

Avery hated the doctor's office. He always felt like he had to sit on his hands to try to hide the dirt under his nails. He felt like a child in a store where there were signs every place saying DO NOT TOUCH! He felt that if he picked up one of the magazines to read, the receptionist would throw it in the trash after he left. It was the same way when the nurse would call him back into the examining room. She would step way away and try to pinch her nose shut without the use of her hands. He was startled when they called his name.

Avery watched as the nurse opened the door as widely as possible and put his patient chart up to her nose as he walked by. He looked at her name tag to see if it said bitch on it. A beautiful woman but bitch just the same. He wondered how such people could sit on the pot and then think that their shit didn't stink!

Dr. Stewart was a no nonsense physician specializing in industrial medicine. His practice was dedicated to drug testing and routine yearly physicals. He occasionally had to refer someone to their primary care physician but seldom within the confines of his job did he have to give a patient bad news. Today would be a first for him.

He heard the nurse talking to the patient in examine room 3 and stood outside the door to listen. He hoped to get a fix on the voice. He wanted to have some vision of the man he was about to destroy with bad news.

He looked at Avery as he entered the examining room. He walked in expecting to see a man of slight build and most likely an engineer type. The man sitting shirtless before him fit none of the profiles he had read about. Even the name when he said it seemed to be wrong.

"Mr. Anderson? I'm Doctor Stewart. I need to talk to you about the results of your blood test."

Avery's first thought was that they had found some kind of drug in his system and he was about to lose his job. He never did drugs but he had heard of the tests coming back positive for use even when a person didn't use. He felt the red of anger creep up the back of his neck. That was the way of his life. Find the worst possible day to get bad news and then heap it on with a shovel!

Avery saw something in the doctor's face he had trouble understanding. He thought it looked like pity but as he studied the expression, it looked more like pain. He suddenly felt terror rip through his heart. Oh God, he thought, I have cancer and this guy has to tell me! His mind was flooded with thoughts of Sandy, Tommy and the new baby. What would they do?

He stopped his thoughts in order to focus on what the doctor was about to say.

"Mr. Anderson, Avery?"

He jolted upright as the doctor stretched out the long, thin fingers of his right hand and placed them on Avery's twitching right knee.

"Your blood test came back positive for the HIV virus. I am sorry. There is no other way of saying it."

The world that Avery thought he knew crumbled before him like an eggshell meeting the business end of a hammer. He didn't hear another word the doctor said. He could see the moving lips but no audible words were coming out. He wanted to throw up the words he had just heard! How, why, when, where?

Avery took the literature the doctor handed him and walked out of the examining room as if he were going to the refrigerator in the middle of the night. He was in a sleep, numb state and wasn't sure the walls, ceilings and floor could contain him as he drifted in and out of reality.

He tried to unlock the door to his truck and couldn't see that the key was turned the wrong way. His life had just been turned upside down and he'd become a bottom feeder who had a great distaste for the sand he dredged up with his voluminous mouth.

He wished someone was there to drive him home but he was a poor man and owned an old truck that didn't shine. He didn't care who heard him as he gripped the steering wheel and cried out to no one!

"I'VE BEEN RAPED!"

Avery started the truck, wishing it would blow up. Life had been a cesspool he had been forced to swim in and now he would drown in his own shit. His mind raced with pictures of the AIDS patients he had seen on television. The vision of them with sores all over their bodies made his skin crawl . The yellow tinge of death colored their skin as if an artist had dipped them in it.

He tried to imagine himself as an emaciated skeleton and found it difficult as he felt the touch of the steering wheel on his huge stomach. He wondered what effect the drugs would have on him and how he could even afford to buy them. He tried to imagine not wanting to kiss, touch, or make love to Sandy. He thought for a split second that if she had the virus too then it wouldn't matter. The tears rolled from his eyes. He wanted her spared even if it meant them never being together again. A smile of irony formed on his lips like the cross bones on a bottle of poison. This is your life, Avery Anderson.

The drive home was a blur. Nothing was in focus and Avery's grip on the steering wheel was an attempt to get a grip on life. Memories played Russian roulette with his brain. The secrets of his past were clicking in place until the empty chambers of his heart were pierced by the blow of total recall. Avery drove into the past as if he were living it all over again.

The first time he'd gone exploring played over and over in his mind. He had only known the man's first name, John. He was sure it was just a name the guy made up to coincide with his profession. Avery was sixteen and had to prove something to himself. He'd always been haunted by the memory of touching the naked tattooed man.

The Montrose was not an area in which Avery had spent much time but he knew enough to know he was in the right place. It was a time in his life when sexual curiosity was not nearly as much a factor as making a connection to his mom. It was just before he met Sandy and he felt a darkness in his soul calling out to be filled with something, anything. He searched not for what his mother was able to give her men but what men could give her that made her love them so. He looked for understanding. He wanted the experience of being loveable.

He would gas up his 1980 Camaro and cruise Westheimer. He remembered the thrill of seeing the men standing in the shadows on the sidewalks, some hand in hand, others looking out toward the street and the passing cars with anticipation. Invariably, at one red light or another someone would approach his car and his search would be over.

Sometimes they would end up in his car in some dark corner of a park and other times in some seedy motel room rented out by the hour. There was never money exchanged, only the misery of lost souls looking for something they'd never had in the first place. The experiences always left him emptier and yet fulfilled. He somehow felt confirmed by the absolute anonymity of raw passion. He had been breast fed on the power of the flesh. With each pick-up he felt he was telling his mom that she had been a good teacher when it came to loneliness and being invisible.

Avery shuddered, not from revulsion of his memories but from the realization that his mom, and not some willing stranger, had given him HIV. He knew, and had always known, he was not gay. He simply wanted to have what he never got, the warmth of his mother's love. He couldn't help laughing as he thought Cara's psychiatrists would have a field day with his revelations!

He approached the bridge again and tears ran down his face and formed a pool in the crevice of his first chin. He had spent his life searching and not finding. Sandy and Tommy were the only good things that had ever happened to him and now there was a chance he would be the cause of their death. He thought about making things simple. One hard turn on the wheel and he could go over the edge. The bay would receive him and wrap him in it's cold, murky waters. What made him most sad was that even suicide would not save him from the destruction that was now his life.

As Avery moved the truck off the bridge, he was amazed that he had crossed it. The old adage was true, he guessed. People cross bridges when they get to them. Many times he had tried to cross bridges in life but usually ended up moving backwards for lack of the price of the toll.

Avery exited and took the long way home. He looked out at the cows standing together in a field. How strange they looked in the vast empty pasture that abutted the huge hardware and lumber store. To Avery it seemed significant. Sort of the past and present coming together to make the future. He wondered if the cows were happy the owner of the land didn't sell out to progress or if they resented looking out at cars, people and a building that sold things to do more building?

Avery knew people sold out all the time. They gave up pieces of themselves to facilitate the living of life. He knew that he had been used as chattel in the transaction of life. His mother sold him out the moment she opened her legs to receive the sperm that would create him. The picture of a determined sperm swimming upstream to get to nowhere came to mind. That was what was inside his mother...nowhere and nothing. There was nothing to love and nothing to hate.

CHAPTER SEVENTEEN

Avery wasn't sure what made him turn into Robert's subdivision but pulling into the driveway made him know it was the right thing to do. Robert's yard was just as he had pictured it, well manicured and immaculate. His hand shook as he reached for the door bell. The sound was almost soothing as he heard Robert yell,

"Hold on! Be right there!"

Robert opened the door and could not disguise the look of shock on his face or the sound of shrill surprise in his voice,

"Oh good heavens! Avery! Is it Cara? Oh God! Is Sandy okay?"

Avery found himself falling into Robert's arms, crushing him with a hug and sobbing like a child. He could not speak. He could not explain. He was amazed at how Robert's arms felt so strong. He knew the thinness of them couldn't possibly support him and yet they were.

He felt himself being guided to a chaise lounge, the softness of the carpet barely giving way under his feet. He sat with his head in his hands and his shoulders convulsed with sadness. He was aware that Robert had disappeared but was helpless to look up to see where he was.

Robert opened the cabinet and took down the 12 year old Scotch. He poured a more than generous sip in each glass. His long, thin fingers wrapped around them with such care. He didn't know what was wrong but he knew that if it brought Avery to him then it was devastating. He also knew that whatever sadness and pain had visited him lately, he would be strong for the near apparition sitting in his living room.

Robert reached out and took Avery's right hand and gently

placed the glass in it. He placed his left arm around Avery's shoulder and whispered,

"It's okay, Avery. You are safe and I am here. Take a sip and tell me. We can figure this out no matter what is wrong."

Avery put the glass to his lips and drank in the warmth of the liquor. He almost choked on the good quality of the booze. He turned towards Robert and with tears glistening in his eyes he again hugged him. He put his lips to Robert's right ear and said,

"I have HIV and I probably gave it to Sandy, Tommy and the new baby too!"

Robert felt as if someone had taken a wrecking ball and hit him full force. He thought for a moment he had heard wrong but knew he hadn't. He could only think to hold the huge bulk of Avery in his arms and join him in sobbing. He cried for Avery, Sandy, Tommy, Cara and every dear friend he had known with the same fate. He sobbed for himself and for Maurice because he knew how lucky they had been. He straightened himself on the small couch, took another sip and said,

"Talk to me, Avery. You know that you can, otherwise you would not have come here. You have my understanding, my heart for support and my hand for comfort. It can take as long as it takes."

Avery downed the rest of the Scotch and held out his glass for more. He had never told anyone about his life before Sandy. He had never owned the memories but pretended they were memories from some movie he'd thought up in his head. Telling someone else meant coming to grips with what he had done and the pain was that he *had* done this to himself. He decided if he was going to speak out loud about his past then he needed to anesthesize the present.

Avery poured it all out from the tattooed man at ten, to his visits to the Montrose area. He found himself going into more detail than what would have been necessary. Perhaps the compulsion to tell all came from his need to impress upon Robert that he was not gay or maybe because he knew that Robert would understand.

He appreciated Robert's silence and when he finally came to the end of the story, he was so thankful for the look on Robert's face. He was not prepared when Robert took his right hand and stroked the side of his face and said,

"You poor child. I am so very sorry for your visit to hell and even sorrier that your mother abandoned you there. We have to go home, Avery. We always have to go home but this time, I will go with you. We will tell Sandy together. It won't be okay, Avery, but life seldom is."

Robert patted Avery's knee and told him he would be right back. He excused himself from the room by saying he had to go get his coat and car keys. He rose from the couch and left Avery sitting there swirling the liquor around in his glass in an absent-minded, almost disconnected fashion.

It seemed to Robert that the cold dampness of Texas December had suddenly penetrated the walls of his house. He turned the thermostat to seventy degrees as he walked down the hall to his bedroom. He looked at the phone sitting on his night stand and toyed with the idea of calling Sandy to tell her he would be bringing Avery home. He decided against it. Just Avery's being with him would alarm her. She would want to know what in the world he was doing there and why he needed a ride home. The news that awaited her was not something someone should hear over the phone and Robert wasn't good at lying. He was particularly bad at hiding intense emotion.

Robert walked into his closet and caught himself debating whether to wear his black wool jacket or his lined trench coat. For a fleeting moment he actually thought about the wool coat not matching his faded jeans. He stopped himself and grabbed the jacket off the hanger. For some reason he had one of Cara's pet names for him running through his mind and whispered to himself.

"Good God, Robert, a life is hanging in the balance and you

want to make Calvin Klein proud! You can be such a Nancy boy sometimes!"

Before turning off the light in his bedroom, he looked over at a picture of Maurice he kept on his dresser. Through tears, he blew a kiss toward the portrait and then left it to be in the darkness of a gray December afternoon. Shutting the bedroom door, he took a deep breath and walked back down the hall to be Avery's strength.

He was surprised to see Avery standing looking at all the pictures poised on the mantle.

"Is this your mother?"

Robert knew that the silver frame with soft pink roses Avery was looking at did indeed contain a picture of his mother, but he went to stand by him anyway as if he needed to confirm it.

"Yes. That was taken four years ago. It was done by a professional in front of her summer home in Maine."

"Summer home? You mean she has separate houses for the seasons?"

Robert could not suppress his laughter. He wanted to hug Avery for his inviting innocence.

"Well, yes...sort of. She spends winters in Florida and summers in Maine. The Florida house was a settlement from husband number five and the Maine house was provided by number six. She finally learned that hanging out in fancier bars and better hotels got her more than black eyes and unpaid bills. She still got the black eyes mind you but she could afford to hide them behind Gucci sunglasses!"

Robert placed his left hand on Avery's back. He knew that even if Avery didn't know who Gucci was, he made and felt the connection.

"Come on, Avery, let's get you home and into those loving arms of that wonderful lady you're married to. I have a feeling we are all going to have a very long night."

Avery could not believe how clean Robert's car was. It still had the new car smell and yet had to be at least two years old. He wondered how people kept the stench of life off their things, off themselves? It was something he had never been able to do. He smelled like his life, looked like his life and now was his life. He stared out the passenger side window as the car started its backward motion down the driveway. He made a decision as he looked at the rows of well kept houses. He would tell Sandy to move in with Robert and start a new life without him. She had been a part of his misery for way too long and deserved better. At that moment, Avery ceased seeing the world through his eyes and started seeing it through the eyes of a dying man.

Robert tried to watch the road and Avery at the same time. He would occasionally pat Avery's knee or touch his shoulder. How strange life is, he thought. Under any other circumstance, Avery would knock him into next week for touching him with such familiarity. In fact, he doubted Avery would ever willingly ride in a car alone with him. At least now he understood why Avery had acted so macho when he first met him. Avery was guarding secrets he felt Robert would instinctively know. It all made so much sense. He just wished life did.

Sandy heard the drone of the diesel engine of Tommy's bus and felt anger in her heart. Avery had been gone for hours and she knew he had not gone to work after his doctor's appointment. She had been listening when he called and told his boss there had been a family emergency. She was sure he was at Liars getting drunk. He often went on benders during the Christmas season. The month was a constant reminder to him of what he didn't have and couldn't get. Actually, they both noticed Tommy's eyes light up when he would see a commercial for some toy he wanted. Neither of them could stand the look on their son's face when he would turn to them with childish excitement and then realize he was being drawn in by insane hope and hype. He would always stop the words before they came out of his mouth. He had swallowed more I wants than any child should have to.

She heard the screen door fly open and Tommy's excited voice call out from the livingroom...

"Hey, Mama! Guess what? You'll never guess in a million years!"

She tried hard not to dampen his excitement but the mud on his shoes made her yell anyway.

"Damn it, Tommy! How many times do I have to tell you that when you don't wipe your feet its like not wiping your butt! It makes me have to clean up your shit. Now go take those shoes off and then you can talk to me!"

She noticed the look on Tommy's face and thought how like Avery he was. He was easily crushed by life but never completely beaten down. She knew he would come back in with an apology and another guess what.

Sure enough, within in moments he was back in the kitchen telling her to guess what had happened to him in school. She guessed three times and was purposely silly with her guesses to diffuse the anger she had directed toward him. She loved the look on his face when she begged for mercy and for him to tell her.

"I'm going to be a shepherd, Mama! They picked me to be in the Christmas play at school! Ain't that neat?"

He was explaining that he would wear a sheet and have a stick when they heard a car pull into the driveway.

Sandy was both happy and surprised to look out the living room window and see Robert's car sitting outside. She could tell there was someone with him but couldn't see the man's face. She opened the screen door with a welcoming smile and then realized it was Avery with Robert.

Her first thought was that he had been involved in an accident. She felt the anger rise in her throat and just as she was about to spew venom, she saw the look on both of their faces. Something fell inside her and terror gripped her lungs. She couldn't speak at all and as she stepped back to let them inside, she felt as if the grim reaper had just entered her house. She watched in silence as Avery went towards the kitchen.

Robert motioned to her and took her into the hallway.

"Sandy, I think it would be a good idea to have Tommy go visit a friend down the street."

She didn't ask why; she didn't need to. She went back into the living room but Tommy was no longer watching cartoons. She could hear him in the kitchen telling Avery about the Christmas play. She went in with as much calm as she could muster and suggested to Tommy that his daddy was tired and that he go play with George for awhile. She promised he could tell his daddy all about the play later.

Tommy was happy to go play before doing his homework. He didn't wait around for his mom to change her mind. When she heard the screen door slam, she turned to Robert and Avery.

"What the hell is it? Did someone call you from the hospital, Avery? Is Mama dead?"

It was Robert's voice she heard, not Avery's.

"Sandy? Do you by chance have a bottle of whiskey? I think it would be a good idea if we all went into the living room and sat down to talk."

Sandy moved the half-empty sack of flour and crusted tin of cinnamon out of the way to take down the bottle of Jack Daniels. She had a feeling that Jack would be everyone's best friend tonight. She looked for three matching glasses and suddenly felt stupid for caring if the glasses were all the same or not. She walked into the living room holding the Jack Daniels, two juice glasses and one of Tommy's Flinstone jelly glasses. She poured three drinks and gave Avery the Fred glass. He always said he was a lot like Fred.

She sat in the old worn recliner across from where Avery sat on the couch. She tried to read his face. She could tell he had been crying but couldn't tell if his tears had been from his heart or his head. Again, it was Robert's voice she heard.

"Sandy, I'm not sure Avery is able to talk just yet. I'll start talking and if he wants to tell you for himself then he can stop me."

The pain she saw on Robert's face scared her more than she had ever been scared in her life. She both wanted to know and didn't. Robert made the decision for her.

"Avery got some bad news at the doctor's today. He is sick, Sandy, real sick."

Sandy just sat in the recliner. She took a huge gulp of her whiskey and tried to be matter of fact.

"Hey, cancer is cured every day. I just heard on the news this morning how it ain't always a death sentence anymore. It's gonna be okay. We'll get through this, Avery."

She had never seen such darkness in Avery's eyes as he lifted his head to speak. For her it was like looking into a void that had swallowed her husband whole.

"It ain't cancer, Sandy."

His voice had the slur of several shots of straight whiskey around the edges but strangely it sounded far too sober and somber.

"Okay, Avery. Whatever it is, we'll get through it. I thought from the looks of you two someone had died. Whew! What a relief."

Robert went to Sandy and knelt in front of the recliner. He took both her hands in his and looked straight into her eyes.

"Sandy, listen to me carefully. Avery needs us to be strong right now. He needs us to not run and hide or go into denial but stand with him at every twist and turn. I love you but you have to take hold. Sandy, Avery tested positive for the HIV virus."

Sandy's eyes stared straight through Robert, straight through Avery and right into the future. The sound from her mouth started out as a low guttural moan and peaked to a voluminous wail. It seemed every thought she ever had and every experience she'd ever known raced through her mind in tornadic upheaval. She was alive, dead and hanging in the balance.

She pushed Robert away from her chair in order to stand and he rose to steady her. Just as he was going to suggest that she sit back down, he saw her mouth twist, her eyes water and saw her lurch forward vomiting with such force that even the screen door was spattered. He was helpless to do anything but place his left hand on her back as again and again her stomach released its anguish on the worn carpet.

Doubled over, with Robert's loving hand rubbing her back, it was Avery's gentle touch to her face with a towel that finally stopped her retching. Avery placed both his arms around her and guided her to the couch to sit next to him. They sat holding each other in silence while Robert went to the kitchen to get a mop and bucket.

As he watched the water churn the soap into bubbles, Robert wished more than anything it had been him instead of Avery. He had no family, not a real one anyway, and besides, it would prove his mother right. She had always told him he would be condemned to hell for going against nature. She never said whose nature and Robert found that humorous. It was her nature to be a bitch and he always thought she told him he would go to hell because she wanted company. What a manipulative, controlling woman she had been and likely still was. Robert smiled to himself as he thought about the conversation they had when he told her he was gay. He stood at the sink picturing the pink dress she wore. It was a sheath type with tiny white dots. He remembered the clustered pearl earrings she wore and how when she spoke it looked like she was a badly dyed Easter egg. He thought of her in terms of pastels but the words from her mouth didn't match her outfit.

"What do you mean you're gay? You do it to men? That's disgusting and had I known you would have grown up to be a damn pervert I would have aborted you without a second thought!"

Robert heard the sobbing coming from the living room and left the memories for another time. He took the bucket and tried to find a place where the throw up wasn't. He wasn't sure the filthy string mop would be at all effective in cleaning up the mess. He saw Sandy make a move to come help and said,

"No. You sit with Avery. I have this covered. Well, you had it covered actually but I'll take care of it."

He knew it was a feeble attempt at humor but he felt so damn helpless. Occasionally, between mopping and dipping, he would glance at his friends. He thought they looked much like deflated dolls in search of a bicycle pump. Their bodies seemed to flatten against each other, neither really supporting the other.

He heard the screen door open and then saw Tommy stop dead in his tracks.

"George . . . His mom fixed dinner and I had to come back home. What happened, Mama?"

Without permission and without a thought, Robert turned to Tommy and said,

"Guess what? You're coming to stay at my house tonight! We're going to have a boys night out. Hey, we can stop and get some fried chicken, rent a movie and have a grand time!"

Tommy's excited jumping made the trailer thunder with life and for just those moments things seemed normal. Robert saw Sandy's face and knew she was glad for his offer. She and Avery could not deal with explanations to an eight year old right now. Robert told Tommy to put his things together while he finished cleaning up. To soothe any fears about the vomit, he told Tommy his mom had gotten a little sick. He explained that pregnant women often do.

Once Tommy was out of the room, Robert took total command.

"I am going to keep Tommy at my house until you two have a chance to talk and plan. Don't worry about school. I'll make sure he gets to and from school every day. I'll drop by tomorrow while he's in classes and pick up some more clothes for him."

He half expected Avery to protest but saw only heartfelt appreciation and even love in his eyes. He walked over to them and bent into their grief.

"We will get through this. It will hurt. We will get angry, frustrated and depressed but life will go on. I love you both and I am with you both on this."

Sandy held onto Tommy as if it was the last time she would ever see him. Perhaps it was that she felt it was the last time he would ever see her. She knew in her heart she would never be the same again. Nothing would ever be the same again.

As soon as Sandy heard Robert's car pull away, she turned to Avery. Her question was simple.

"How?"

Avery stroked the side of her face as his mind looked for the answer. It was the one question he dreaded the asking. How could he explain a time in his life that he'd never understood himself. How could he talk to his wife, his love, about picking up strange men and doing unspeakable things with them? Would she ever understand the terrible longing in his heart to find what it was that made his mother love everyone but him?

He took her hands in his and started to speak but her words came first.

"Did you sleep with another woman, Avery? Did you get crazy one night and go do drugs? I know you ain't never had a blood transfusion."

The fact that gay sex never even entered her mind stung him as if a wasp had landed on his penis. He could not think of a more tender place to have exposed to the outside world and that was what he was about to do.

He saw the question dancing in her eyes and knew that the truth was all he could tell her. Somehow her acceptance of Robert gave him hope that she would be able to understand what he would have to tell her. His voice didn't even sound like his own.

"Sandy, you know the hell I grew up in. For me, life was confusing and love was something I thought just happened on television or in the movies. When I was sixteen I started making trips into Houston. I guess you could say I went exploring."

Avery stopped to assess whether or not Sandy was even listening. He watched her breasts as they moved with each breath. He memorized the pain in her face and the anger in her eyes. He knew she had already determined that it had been an affair that had brought the monster to her door and weakness that had let it inside. He had seen the jealousy on her face when he would notice the skinny little heroin addict that lived in trailer 4215 C. He knew she was convinced that he had gotten paid in sex the day he'd taken the girl into town when her car wouldn't start. He stroked her pudgy fingers as he inhaled enough courage to continue.

"Anyway, I would end up in the Montrose area searching for

men to hold me like my mother held them. I wanted to know what they gave her that made her want them more than she wanted us kids. I would listen night after night to the moans and her promises to them. I thought they were magic. I would see her hang on their every word as if they held the secret to life. I wanted to know that secret, Sandy. I wanted my mother to hold me and promise her life to me, too."

As Avery spoke, Sandy was to the right of him with her knees turned toward him and touching his. The sudden push of her arms against his chest as she started to rise off the couch literally took his breath away. He tried to grab her arms to make her sit back down to listen but she jerked free and disappeared down the hall. He could hear her in the bathroom throwing up again but he couldn't move to go help her. He felt like he would never be able to help her understand what had been in his heart all those years ago. The look on her face as she pushed against him was burning a hole in his heart and mind. He saw his reflection in her eyes and it was of a slimy monster. She wasn't wrong. That's what he was to himself, too.

Avery grabbed the bottle of Jack Daniels off the coffee table and poured another drink. He knew that rather than make him drunk, it would clear his head. Sometimes in life when a person discovers that the bottom you reach is not bottom but quicksand, there are no more wrong decisions to make. He knew the whiskey wouldn't hurt and it would loosen the strangle hold of shame on his mind and heart.

He heard the toilet flush and wondered if Sandy's love for him was swirling in the water along with the contents of her stomach. Tears stung his eyes as he thought about seeing a different woman walk back into the living room. He knew that if he lost Sandy and Tommy's love over this then life meant nothing at all. He was prepared to let them go but he was not prepared to lose them.

He looked up and saw Sandy grasping the door jam as if to steady herself.

"Are you okay? Here, let me help you."

He rose to help her back to the couch but she held her right hand up as if to stop his approach.

"Avery, I gotta call the hospital. I need to check on Mama. I just need to center my thoughts on another catastrophe for a second. I need to take my mind out of this trailer and out of the shit hole it's fallen in."

Her words hurt but he understood what she meant. He knew that when life is nothing but a sewer, it's always important to know just which rat pissed where. At least with Cara and all her problems Sandy was working in familiar territory. She could count on Cara's chaos, in a strange way. What he had revealed to her was something she had no way of anticipating. She needed to touch base with the problems that she knew as her reality.

He could hear her in the kitchen talking to the nurse.

"I see. I see. So she'll be gettin' out tomorrow at noon. Okay, I'll be there to get her. Thanks."

Avery could only see her back. She was sitting at the kitchen table. He heard the beeps of the phone as she dialed another number, then her voice.

"Hello? Uncle Billy? This is Sandy."

He knew Uncle Billy was like the family historian for the dysfunctional annals of Cara's childhood. He stopped listening to the conversation because he didn't have the strength to hear Sandy's questions. He knew she was asking about incest, abuse and things that just touched too close to home. He loved Sandy for thinking that such a call would help her take Cara out of the depths of despair but felt such sorrow at knowing it wouldn't. There was no hope for Cara, just as there was no hope for him. He wondered what made Sandy different. She had known the same page in the book of life and except for her problem with food, she was a creature of loving kindness. He wondered if she used her fat to cushion the sharpness. Maybe she insulated herself to avoid being harsh, broken and lethal to herself like Cara.

He was deep in thought when he felt her sit next to him on the couch. He opened his eyes and saw a glimmer of hope sparkle in her eyes. Yes, he thought, she needed to find a straw to grasp in the great sea of despair that had been her life and to weather the great storm he had sent her way. Looking at her, he suddenly remembered Buster. Why had nobody heard from him through Cara's ordeal?

"Hey Sandy, I was just thinkin' about your mama and wondered how come we ain't heard from Buster."

"He came by, Avery, while you where at the doc's. He dropped off his key to the trailer and told me Cara could have the place. He said he couldn't take it no more and that loving Cara sullied the memories of him loving Bessie Mae for so long. He was cryin'."

"Oh Sandy! Your mama's gonna be heart broken! How could he run out on her now?"

His statement was heart felt and innocent but it caused both of them to raise their heads and meet eye to eye. The moment of discovery and forgiveness was at hand. Avery had unwittingly given Sandy a cue to say whether she would stay or go.

He held his breath while he waited for her to respond to his question about Buster. He knew it would be the answer to his question too. He searched her eyes for the answer he wanted.

"Life's a funny thing, Avery, and love is even funnier. Buster did what he had to do and I guess I'll do the same. If I hate you for what you did, then I gotta hate Mama too. If I hate Mama, then I gotta hate myself and Tommy, too. I love Tommy, Avery, and so I guess I'll just back up and start with a new load of sorrow in my heart."

Silence sat on the couch between them and they both knew that time would take care of the space and new distance. Sandy was the first to speak again.

"Me and Tommy got to get tested, Avery. Oh God! The baby, Avery! What about the baby?"

Avery had not even thought about the life that Sandy carried inside. It hit him like nothing had hit him all day. How was it that his past had somehow come in to affect his future? How fair was that? Wasn't it enough that he had already ruined so many lives?

Sandy and Avery went to bed spent and exhausted. The sandman would get no change from the dollars of life tonight. They shared a mattress, shared a life but at least for one night they would sleep worlds apart. He knew that slumber would bring them together again. In their unconscious states, their bodies would naturally gravitate one towards the other but it was the morning he feared. Sometimes the mind takes control of what the heart claims.

CHAPTER EIGHTEEN

Robert looked in on Tommy before heading to bed himself. He felt a little guilty about making Tommy sleep on the spare room floor. Robert had laughed when Tommy had asked to sleep with him in what he called the big bed. He knew that Tommy sensed the incredible desperation at home, even if he didn't know the cause. It was just that any semblance of impropriety made him feel uncomfortable. Considering the circumstances under which Avery was now confessing, he felt it was better for Tommy to have a room to himself. After all, he was only a yell down the hall. The boy would be fine.

Robert took off his watch and placed it in the tulip dish Maurice had purchased for him at a little antique store in Old Town Spring. A smile lit the corner of his mouth as he remembered the spontaneous stop at a bed and breakfast en-route home. Their stay and joy had lasted two days and they had actually dared to walk arm and arm down to breakfast. He needed to call Maurice. He would want to know what was happening with Avery. They had not talked at all since his sudden departure. It dawned on him, as he picked up the receiver to call, that if Maurice's lover answered the phone he would feel the bite of loneliness hollow out the remaining portion of his heart. He placed the receiver back on the cradle and told himself he would call in the morning.

The sheets felt cold against his bare back. He'd thought about getting up to put on a pajama top but he never slept well with material bunching up around him. The buttons would always end up sideways during the night digging into the bones in his chest. He scrunched up his pillow and shivered until his body warmth transferred to the sheets. He knew that there was another cold bed in the world tonight. He drifted off to sleep with a vision of Avery and Sandy turned away from each other but sharing the same nightmare.

Robert awoke to the darkness of his room and looked at the clock.

"Oh man, it's only one o'clock. Nature is an unreasonable partner sometimes!"

He swung his legs over the side of the bed and hit something as he did. He almost screamed but stopped himself as he realized it was Tommy lying beside his bed on the floor. He had no idea how long the boy had been there but Tommy's soft peaceful breathing told Robert it had been long enough to feel safe again. He thought for a moment about putting him back to bed but decided not to disturb his sleep. He understood that Tommy just needed to be close enough to someone to scare away the unseen monsters.

Robert went into the bathroom down the hall rather than his own. He didn't want to wake the boy. He stood in front of the toilet and waited for the stream to start flowing. He found it so irritating to be awakened with such an urgency and then to have to wait for the first trickle. He knew that going back to sleep was going to be difficult, specially with the sound of little Tommy's breathing as a reminder of the day's events.

Robert returned to his room and as his eyes adjusted to the dark once again, he saw that Tommy had kicked away the blanket. Robert bent to him and placed the blanket back over Tommy's body. In a soft whisper, Robert wished his little friend a night of loving dreams. Somehow he knew as he crawled back into bed, the sheets would not feel nearly as cold this time.

Maybe he needed someone to scare away all the monsters too.

CHAPTER NINTEEN

Cara asked the lab technician what time it was. She was so sick and tired of them drawing blood, waking her to give her stuff to sleep and taking her blood pressure. It seemed to her that they were all hands and no brains.

Cara laid her head back on the pillow. There was only one thing she wanted, to be in her own bed with Buster. She had thought many times about how his loud snoring and farts were a sight better to hear at night than the screams she heard from down the hall. Cara hated the hospital and thought it gut busting funny that the docs thought tying a person up in hell made them get rid of their demons.

For her, the place had created new ones and they were more scary than any of the ones in her real life. She would see Dr. Moreland in her nightmares for a long time to come. The scar on his right cheek had become the place she fixed her eyes when she spoke with him. She knew it made him uncomfortable because he would often put his pen up to it and trace the line when she would feed him some bull shit story. It took a lot of control for her not to laugh because it looked like a second mouth to her.

She'd always thought people who thought they could solve the miseries of others were just too scared to look at their own. Dr. Moreland was a good example. He had a twitch in his right eye that the coke bottle glasses magnified rather than hid. And when he spoke, his right leg would swing as many times forward as each syllable his words contained. She was willing to bet the bones in his closet rattled every time someone walked by him!

Cara turned over on her right side so she could look at the bars on the window. She stretched out in the bed and quietly said to the night.

"Yeah doc, I blow this joint tomorrow and come the evening I'll be back on the outside looking in. Guess what, you four eyed shadow of a human? You'll still be behind these bars eating up the bull shit these people feed you with a spoon!"

It wasn't that Cara had anything against education. She just hated when people confused wisdom with crap and thought their toilet was so high it made them a god. She had nothing against smart people but she didn't cotton to smart asses at all! Some of these people were so stupid they didn't know the difference between being fucked and getting fucked! She felt sorry for them all.

Cara turned away from the window and thought about Buster. She knew they hadn't let anyone in to see her but she thought it was strange that no one mentioned him to her. The nurse with the identity crisis that put a "we" before everything she said, had said Sandy had been around to see her but had no word about Buster.

Cara smiled to the ceiling. Boy was she going to ride Buster like a bull when she got home. Even the thought made Cara wet and squirmy. She found herself touching the patch of hair to see if it was still there. She laughed as she thought the damn attendants never walked in when she thought they should. She was willing to bet they wouldn't go run for Dr. Moreland if she offered them a piece of Cara cake! No sirree!

The medication started to take hold and Cara felt her eyes drooping. One more night, she told herself. One more night of crisp, sterile, sexless sheets and disposable pillows. Tomorrow she would be home in the filth that made her feel comfortable. The dry mouth she would feel would not be caused by drugs but too much whiskey, and the taste of Buster's wad would be her final shot of the night. Licking her lips, Cara let her eyes close and her body give into the doc's answer for peace. Yep, she thought as she drifted off, a doc's bible is his prescription pad.

Jack Moreland spent many of his nights and early mornings in the hospital. He would drink coffee with the nurses or sit in his office looking over patient files. He had no home and had no life. He had been an idealist from the start.

He picked up Cara Covington's file and started to draw up her release papers. In his heart he knew he was doing the wrong thing but he was bound by law to let her go if she didn't agree to treatment. She was combative and not at all amenable to being helped. Most of his patients were like Cara and it made him burn with a quiet anger. He had gone into psychiatry because he truly thought he could help people. It wasn't long before he learned that the people who needed help the most wanted it the least. He'd often felt that he was banging his head against a wall and all he got for his effort was a headache and dents. He found himself being sucked into a black hole and knew if he didn't change he would be needing more help than his patients. As he had done a million times, before signing her release papers, he went to her room and watched her sleep. He sat quietly and wondered about the horrors her heart had suffered. The feelings he had were always the same, lonely, sad and helpless.

Cara Covington was the future he had seen in his own wife. His sweet Pattie had lived with monsters in her heart. His specialty was psychiatry, not cardiology. He tried but was unsuccessful at saving her. He wanted to touch her mind but couldn't even touch her heart. Sometimes Jack thought the memory of her left him colder than the damp ground into which she'd put herself.

When he looked at the lump that was Cara Covington lying beneath the sheets, he saw sorrow. He looked at the face and saw lines of demarcation. The ones over her brow were from the abuse of an uncaring mother. Then there were the deep skin ones. The ones she had given herself. It was as if the whiskey that ran through her veins colored her skin and rotted the flesh. He looked at the thin fingers clutching the sheet to her chin. The digits where slim, almost graceful but the yellow tinge of them coupled with the chipped nail polish made them evidence of what lived inside of this woman.

As he sat and watched her, he almost felt compelled to reach out and take her hand in his. All things look at peace when sleeping and even the Cara Covingtons of the world seem tamed by slumber. He was tired, lonely and felt the pain of not being able to help her. That which drove him to do his job, also drove him to not want to do it. He helped so few and nothing he ever did helped the guilt that lived in his heart. He watched as she stirred and knew that soon her mind would be awake to the world but that her heart would stay closed to it.

Cara woke with a start. She could feel eyes boring into her soul as if to take it from her. Looking up, she saw Dr. Moreland sitting in the chair in the corner near the window.

"Were ya waitin' for me to roll over and take the sheet with me, Doc? Is that why you guys always make us wear hospital gowns with no back so you can see something you never get?"

"Feeling a little agitated this morning, Mrs. Covington?"

"Hell, Doc, I was born agitated. I just get kinda pissed when I wake up and see some species of the insect family watching me sleep. You got the papers ready for me to be released from this cracker factory? You guys are givin' them little elves a bad name!"

"Yes, they're ready. I have to tell you, Cara, I think you are making a huge mistake. Nothing will be resolved by your leaving and I expect to see you back in here within the month. Are you sure you won't let us help you?"

"Doc, I'll make ya a deal. You let me push a broom stick up your tight, judgmental ass and I'll let you screw me with all your bull shit mumbo jumbo!"

Cara never thought she had seen a redder face or veins that looked more like worms crawling under a person's skin. She thought the scar on his face was going to have heat bubbles from the anger she'd placed in the old doc's furnace. She didn't give a shit. The man deserved her rage and venom. She had always been a poisonous snake and never pretended to be otherwise. He rose to leave and she wanted one last whack at his ego.

"Hey, Doc Moreland, ever hear the phrase physician heal thy self? Well, maybe if you took some of the loads of money you make here and invest in a plastic surgeon and contacts, one of your crazy patients will want to fuck you!"

Cara had never heard a hydraulic door slam but Doctor Moreland made the son of a bitch resonate all through the corridor. Cara ripped off the hospital gown and decided she would sit naked until they brought her back her regular clothes. She was through with these people and she swore to herself she would drive her car into a tree before anyone ever brought her back to a place like this.

CHAPTER TWENTY

Avery heard Sandy in the bathroom and desperately wanted to do what he had done so many times before, sneak up behind her and show her what dreams of her had done to him during the night. It wasn't about sex but about the special bond the two shared. He felt like he had lost the only place he ever fit, Sandy's heart. She hadn't given him an eviction notice but he knew it would never be the same. He raised up on his right elbow and said to himself, "Yep, Avery, you can never go home again."

Sandy flushed the toilet and used a clean towel to finish wiping her mouth. She hated using two to wipe away the vomit from her chin but she was afraid the smell of the one she used before would just make her get sick all over again. Hell, what did it matter? She was just making more work for herself and not putting anyone else out.

She looked in the mirror and saw a stranger looking back from the glass. She had the same dark circles under her eyes, the same greasy, stringy hair, the same pockmarked skin but there was a deadness to her. She felt as if a murder had been committed in her home and she was the victim. She pulled in close to the glass and practiced what she would say to Avery.

"Avery, I love you. I have always loved you and probably always will but me and Tommy gotta spend some time away. I ain't deserting you. I just need time to think."

It wasn't until the last words had come out of her mouth that she caught sight of Avery's reflection in the mirror, turning away from the bathroom door.

She went to their bedroom but he wasn't there. When she opened the door to Tommy's room, she found Avery with his huge body curled up on Tommy's bed clutching one of Tommy's stuffed bears. He was rocking back and forth like a child and sobbing with quiet anguish. Her heart shattered into splinters on the floor. She knelt beside him and wrapped her arms around him and rocked with him, her tears running down his bare back. She spoke then with her heart and not her mind.

"Avery, my sweet Avery. It's gonna be okay. I ain't going anywhere in life without you. I didn't mean what I said in there. I just feel so alone and mixed up. Oh God, Avery, what the hell are we going to do?"

When Avery turned to her, the look in his eyes frightened her. There was something hollow glaring at her from deep within his soul. He stroked her face and touched her tears with gentle fingers. His mouth contorted in the way it did when his brain was moving faster than his intelligence could handle. HIV was too much to handle, too much to comprehend.

Sandy suggested they either go back into their bedroom or into the living room. Her knees were aching from the weight of her on them. Her heart had gained a lifetime in the past twenty-four hours and it felt too heavy in her chest.

Avery heard the bed creak under him as he moved to get up. The worn Winnie the Pooh sheets bunched under the mass of his thighs and came up with him. Trying to fling the sheets off, he knocked Tommy's cowboy lamp off the night stand. It was a 1960's lamp with a plastic bow legged cowboy on the base. The cowboy had a lasso and on the other side of the base, a plastic cow stood as if grazing in a pasture. Suddenly, Avery felt rage well up in his throat.

"God damned piece of shit! That's all any of it is and ever was! Shit, shit, SHIT!"

"Avery, calm down. It ain't broken. Here, let me put it back on the stand."

She was surprised when Avery took the lamp from her hands and threw it across the room.

"I don't want that piece of shit in here! It was the only damn thing my mama ever bought me and she only did it to buy my silence about all the bruises her and that other drunk mother fucker put on me that night I tried to help her! The lying, fucking whore was worried about my dad beating the shit out of her when he got home, so she went to some garage sale and bought me a fucking used lamp. I was too stupid to know, back then. I thought for two seconds that she actually cared about me. I was proud to have that lamp, Sandy. It lit up my heart, as well as my nights!"

Sandy put her arms around Avery, leaving the lamp where he had thrown it. They walked in silence down the hallway into the living room. Sandy went to the kitchen to make some coffee while Avery sat on the couch staring off into space, picking at the lint that peeked through a worn space on the arm rest.

"Avery, you need to call work to tell them you won't be in today and I need to go to the hospital to pick up Mama. Robert said he would come by before work to pick up some more clothes for Tommy. I ain't done wash this week but I think he has two pair of jeans in his top drawer and get him a couple of shirts and some underwear. I'm going to drop Mama by her house and come straight home. She'll ask a million questions but I'll just tell her you're sick and I gotta get back home. Avery, are you listening to me?"

Avery nodded but she wasn't at all sure he'd heard a word she had said. She went into the bedroom to get dressed and wondered how she was going to survive. She had known sorrow for most of her life but all of this was more than she could take. Cara had to be told about Buster too and she knew that while Cara would have a who gives a shit attitude about his leaving, she would be very hurt.

Avery was sitting in the same position as he had been when she left him. She felt anger well up immediately. Just like a man, she thought. The world is crumbling down around them and he is too stunned to grab the mortar to start patching holes. She was convinced the story about the little Dutch boy was a lie. It was much more likely that when the dam sprung a leak he stuck his dick in the hole and said, "Screw it!"

"Damn it, Avery! I can't carry this alone. You have to take hold for a minute and help me!"

Picking up the truck keys from the counter, she turned before opening the door.

"Avery, I love you. I'll be back as soon as I can. If Robert gets here before I get back, tell him I'll give him a call later."

Avery heard the door shut and sat staring at the clothes Sandy had put on the table. He looked at the worn knees in Tommy's jeans and the fray around the belt loops. He felt as if his family had figured out the cloning mystery years ago. Their genes not only had worn knees but had come unraveled long before they got any use from them. He hoped he and Sandy had made Tommy out of stronger material but he doubted it.

Avery had to look up the number for Baker Diesel and Heavy Equipment. He seldom called in sick and never had any other reason to call, so the digits weren't ones he had committed to memory. He heard the perky little voice of Mary Canter, the receptionist, slash, secretary, slash, office hot mama. For a fleeting moment he thought how her voice on the phone sounded as uplifted as her tits. The men he worked with always teased that her knockers would be great in the military, always standing at attention! He asked Mary if Joe was around.

Avery felt a wave of nausea creep into the lining of his stomach. Joe Magill thought only wimps and weasels called in sick. He knew telling Joe he wouldn't be in for a second day was going to have repercussions. He heard Joe's rough cough and hoarse voice in the background.

"Who the hell is it, Mary? I gotta a god damned Mack engine half way hoisted to heaven out there and four fucking employees holding the chains until I get back!"

"It's Avery Anderson, Joe. I think he's calling to tell ya he's sick again."

Their conversation made Avery feel like he wasn't there. Of course, to them he wasn't. People like him didn't exist unless they saw him standing in front of them; sometimes not even then. Joe's voice was irritated and cliche.

"Yeah, Avery? It's your dime but it's my time!"

"Joe, I was just calling to let you know I won't be in today. I think this must be the flu instead of a cold. I'll come in tomorrow even if I have to drag my ass around work using one of the god damned cranes!"

He felt stupid trying to assure Joe that he wasn't faking. He hated that his life was ruled by forces that saw him as a slab of meat and that he had to beg the butcher to cut him a break. He almost laughed when Joe said,

"Yeah right, Avery. Like our fucking cranes could tote your heavy ass."

Avery didn't know if Joe slammed the phone down because a dial tone sounds the same no matter how the receiver is placed back on the cradle. Avery hung up the phone and was pouring another cup of coffee when he heard a knock at the door.

Avery was glad to see Robert standing on the stoop. He noticed that the smile on Robert's face looked painted on and that the dark circles under his eyes were more telling of the truth. He was sure that worry had been their friend's bed mate. Avery wasn't sure why, but he suddenly spoke words he'd never intended to...

"Sandy ain't going to survive this. Damn funny if you think about it. I'm the one who is terminally ill but it's going to kill her!"

Robert put his hand on Avery's shoulder. Ever since Avery had told him the news the world had a surreal feel to it. If anyone would have told him a few months before that he would be trying to bring comfort to a big East Texas ox of a man, he would have laughed until his stomach hurt. His stomach hurt now, but it sure wasn't from laughter.

Robert, like Sandy, wanted to bring Avery back to action. He sat next to him on the couch and tried to sound upbeat and excited.

"Hey, Avery, I have a plan. Cara's coming home today, right? I was thinking, since I work until nine anyway and Tommy has to come here after school, why don't you, me and Cara go have a few drinks at Liars after I get off work? Come on. It'll be fun. We can welcome the old broad home!"

Robert saw a sparkle in Avery's eyes. He knew his suggestion would be tempting. He saw the excitement leave as quickly as it appeared.

"I can't do that, Robert. I can't go out drinking and leave Sandy here with all the sorrow. I ain't sure I'm ready to be around Cara, anyway. I don't think Sandy's going to tell her yet but it would be hard to look at her and act like nothing's wrong."

"Listen, Avery, going to Liars is just what you need and Sandy would understand. I really think an evening of normalcy would be just what the doctor ordered. I tell you what. I'll call Sandy on my dinner break and see what she thinks. I won't tell her I discussed it with you and maybe she will suggest it to you herself."

Avery agreed to Robert's plan and went into the kitchen to get a plastic bag for Tommy's clothes. Hugging Robert goodbye felt as natural to him as hugging one of his own brothers, if there had been any of them that he loved enough to hug. He shut the door and turned on the television. The Montel Williams show was on. Avery slumped into the couch as he heard Montel say, in his melodramatic whisper, that today he would be talking to teens who were HIV positive. Avery didn't have the energy to get up to change the channel and didn't have the heart to listen.

CHAPTER TWENTY-ONE

Sandy pulled into the parking lot of East Texas General and wished she was going in for a stay. People like her never got vacations unless it involved childbirth or major surgery. Her baby wasn't due for months but she needed a rest now.

She punched the button in the elevator for the fifth floor and then put her hand on the door to keep it opened for a woman who was running through the lobby. The woman pushed the button for the third floor and moved towards the back. Sandy stood with her body toward the doors. She saw that the woman had been crying and felt the cold steel of the doors would preempt any warm exchange between the two. She just couldn't care about someone else's tears right now.

Sandy watched as the woman exited on the third floor and collapsed into the arms of a man. The pediatric ward was on the third floor and both the woman and the man looked like young parents. She wanted to feel sad that they must be suffering a tragic loss but her heart was just too full of her own tragedy.

The elevator doors opened to the fifth floor and the smell of slow death hit Sandy as if to suck her in. She knew and had always known that the line between sanity and this place was merely a step away. She had always refused to cross that line but felt now that she was being pushed over it.

The nurse's station was a hub of activity and Sandy stood for a full five minutes before anyone even saw she was there. One of the floor nurses finally told her that Dr. Moreland wanted to speak with her before releasing Cara. She took off down the hall and Sandy didn't know whether to follow or wait there. Half way down the hall, the nurse turned and impatiently waved Sandy forward.

"Wait in here. Dr. Moreland will be here in a few minutes."

Twenty minutes later, Dr. Moreland entered the room. Sandy was agitated. A minute to her right now was a lifetime and twenty minutes was more lifetime than she had left to live! It rankled her that she never seemed to be as important as anyone else.

"Mrs. Anderson, I have no choice but to release your mother but I am telling you again it is against my better judgment. I feel sure that she will be back in this hospital within the month and that she will be lucky if it is only the psych ward to which she is admitted. My only hope is that when something happens it is only herself she destroys. If this sounds like a lecture, it is. Your mother has a problem with alcohol and it will only end up in devastation."

Sandy glared at him. Who the hell was he to know anything about a life that left a lacking that could only be filled from the outside in? She was in no mood for people who looked down their noses at the rest of the world and didn't see their own snot covering their perspective! She was too tired to argue with him.

"Doctor Moreland, is my mama ready to go?"

"Yes, take these papers to the lock down station and they will bring her out. I'm sorry for you, Mrs. Anderson. Your mother is going to be a stick for your back as long as she doesn't consent to getting help."

He offered his hand but Sandy had already turned and was half way out the door. She was pissed at the world and couldn't walk fast enough to get this part of the future over.

Sandy looked through the thick glass window at Cara walking towards the door. She suddenly felt overcome with sadness. She was going through the most horrible pain of her life and all she wanted was the warm hug of comfort from her mama and instead was watching a woman whose hugs were restricted to strange men in the throes of passion or a whiskey bottle. As soon as she heard the attendant put the key in the door, Sandy's shoulders slumped and so did her heart.

Sandy opened her arms to Cara but watched the rail thin body of her mother turn to the gate keeper instead.

"Hey, all you tight assed fuckers! Cara Covington is leaving the building!"

The harsh laughter that followed rang as truth in Sandy's ears.

"Shit Sandy, I sure in the hell wish you smoked! Damn do I need a cigarette and a shot! I tried to get that fucker Dr. Moreland to give me some needles and that *I don't care shit* he pumped into me but it was a no go. I told him he needed to give the drunks in here what they want, a shot of whiskey and a good lay. That's the answer to the question, fat girl. Give a person what they crave and life is good for everyone!"

Sandy's blood was boiling. She tried with everything she was not to let her anger blow out of her mouth but the battle was lost the minute Cara opened her mouth.

"Shut the fuck up you stupid bitch! No one hears your fake bravado but me and I could give a shit!"

Sandy felt like the look on her Mama's face. She had no idea where the words had come from. She covered her mouth as if she could retrieve what she had just let out but it was way too late.

They walked in silence down the hall and to the elevators. The cold steel doors shut and Sandy felt like she was sharing space with an alien. She no more wanted to communicate or look at Cara than she had the woman with the teary eyes. Part of her wanted to run back up to the fifth floor and beg Dr. Moreland to help her.

The parking lot seemed like a marathon walk. Even the vision of it seemed to stretch to eternity. When they got to the truck, she opened the passenger side door for Cara. Sandy's mind was racing with excuses she would have had for her outburst. She wasn't ready to tell her mom about Avery. She decided on her tactics and thought that even fat foxes have wiles.

"Mama, sorry about that outburst back there. It's just that I have been so worried about you and I got some bad news to tell you."

Cara almost seemed human to her for a moment. She thought she actually saw a look of concern cross her face. It wasn't until

Cara opened her mouth to speak that Sandy saw the concern was not for her but was a self-involved reaction.

"I just spent two days in hell and the only words out of my daughter's mouth are to call me a bitch and to say what I done been through don't matter to anyone! If that's all the thanks I get for living my life the only way I know how, then fuck you and this piece of shit of a horse you rode in on!"

Sandy didn't want to be vindictive but Cara left her no choice.

"Yep, Mama, you're the saint and people like me and Buster just suck from you the gifts of life and then leave!"

Cara sat in the seat and felt her heart hit the speed bumps as each one was crossed. The fear in her eyes showed the pain in her heart that couldn't be muted.

Sandy looked at her mother as she came to the stop sign leading out of the parking lot but something inside her would not stop the attack.

"Yep, your saintly ways have led Buster to fuck the brains out of little Candy Washington, the barmaid at Liars. The talk around town is that when they do manage to crawl out of bed for a minute, everything they do is a lead up to the next round! Oh, by the way, Mama, here are the keys to your trailer. Buster said you can have it all. Funny, you ain't got nothing!"

Sandy had never been able to shut Cara up before, but then she had always walked on eggshells around her and had never spoken the truth. The drive to Cara's trailer was spent in palpable silence. Cara barely waited for the truck to come to a stop before jumping out. She defiantly turned on the porch and shot the finger at Sandy.

CHAPTER TWENTY-TWO

Cara's keys still fit the lock but her heart didn't seem to fit the house. Her hands were shaking as she turned the knob to silence and loneliness. God, she needed a drink and a smoke. She hoped Buster had left her enough whiskey and hadn't smoked the eight packs of cigarettes she'd bought last week.

The color of the whiskey seemed pale in the dimly lit kitchen and the cigarette started a coughing spell that made her pee her pants. It struck her that unless she went out to find someone to sleep with, she was as wet as she'd be for a time.

Cara walked into the various rooms of the trailer to see if the sound of aloneness could be heard as well as felt. The bathroom smelled of wet, dirty towels as she ran her fingers into the sides of her lace panties to remove them. The tub had brown mold at the bottom near the drain but she ran the warm water without sponging the grime out first. What did it matter if scum was growing in her tub when it had been growing in her life for years?

The porcelain felt hard against her tail bone but the water felt calming and kind. She thought about Sandy's outburst and knew that within days her daughter would be crawling back begging for forgiveness. She didn't really care if she ever talked to Sandy again. She didn't care if she ever talked to anyone again. Jack Daniels was the only friend that she could depend on. Whiskey was dependable in a way that people never could be.

Cara watched the steam rise off her hand as she reached for the glass of whiskey. She took another huge gulp and wondered why it didn't feel as good going down as it used to. She put the glass back down on the place for the soap and watched the bubbles shoot out from the bottom. Taking the sponge from the side of the tub, she ran it the length of her right leg up to her pubic hair. She closed her eyes and thought of how Buster's large hands felt on her freshly shaven skin.

The razor actually felt good against the stubbled hair on her legs. There was something really sensual about the slide of the blade on the soap. Cara pointed her foot and ran the razor carefully along her shin. She placed the shaven leg back into the water and watched as the soap floated away from her leg and towards the side of the tub. Not even that which cleansed her wanted to remain too close to her right now.

The tears came and fell with the same silence that filled her life. Her wet, frothy shoulders slumped and quaked as she cried and rinsed, rinsed and cried. Everyone thought she was such a bitch, hard and uncaring. She cared but it was too painful to continually expose a soft heart to a world that saw it as a bubble to be burst! Lifting herself from the water, she whispered into the only clean towel she could find.

"Don't no one see? My words ain't the way I communicate the truth, my actions are! When I say fuck you to someone it ain't them I mean, it's me. I'm the one whose been fucked in life and I don't know how to crawl out of the dirty sheets!"

The towel around Cara's body did nothing to warm her. She went to the bedroom with intent to put on her Liars best but took out her gown and robe instead. She wasn't in the mood for Liars. When whiskey doesn't do its job and thoughts of sex lead only to Buster, then home is where a body belongs. Funny, she thought, those two things were the very reason I don't got no home now.

It was four in the afternoon but Cara climbed into her bed and pulled the covers up around her chin. The pillows smelled of Buster, she smelled of soap and her life smelled of shit. She placed the sheet over her head to block out the daylight and closed her heart to herself.

CHAPTER TWENTY-THREE

Sandy felt awful about talking to her mama the way she had. She knew how much her words had hurt and how shocking it was for her mama to hear them. A tiredness came over her that made it difficult to steer the truck towards home. It just wasn't fair. Just because a body doesn't have the same lung capacity as someone else it doesn't mean they need less air to breathe. How come it was that the ones who have less always get less? Hell, if anyone else had suffered the pain she had, they would take a vacation to the Bahamas to reward themselves. Her reward was to go face the next catastrophe and try to survive it.

As she approached the entrance to the trailer park, she wanted to drive right past. Given the choice, anyone would pass up the gate to hell. It was different for her though. All the lacking that had lived in her mama as a wife and parent, made her feel the responsibility of it all the more. For every meal her mama never cooked, she had cooked three and eaten five. That was the way of it.

Sandy pulled into the yard and sat looking at the trailer for a moment. Inside that aluminum box lay her past, present and future and it sure wasn't a treasure chest. She barely found the strength to climb the steps to the porch. She could hear the television and knew it was likely that Avery was still sitting in the same position he had been in when she left. She couldn't be angry anymore. She was just too tired.

She opened the door and smelled something wonderful emanating from the kitchen. There were candles lit on the small, rickety coffee table and two plates were set on the side that faced the couch. Avery was nowhere to be seen and as she placed her purse on the counter she noticed the kitchen had been cleaned. Thinking she was in the wrong trailer, she started to pick up her purse and go back out the door!

Avery came up from behind her and whirled her around. He bowed in an exaggerated manner and said,

"Madame, my wife is away for the day. You are a vision of loveliness and I am in the mood for a dance!"

Sandy didn't know whether to laugh or cry. He didn't give her an opportunity to decide, as he scooped her into his arms and waltzed her to the couch. He effortlessly let her down on the couch, placed a soft kiss on her neck and smiled into her eyes.

"I love you, Sandy Anderson. I have no life without you in it."

She laughed as he waltzed his way into the kitchen and took a plate from the refrigerator. She laughed louder when he threw the stained dish towel over his shoulder and lifted the plate up towards the ceiling on his huge hand. He swished and swayed like a waiter dodging busy tables and placed the plate on the coffee table between the candles. It was perfect! It didn't matter that the candles were hurricane candles and not fancy tapers or that the serving dish was Corelle ware. The wonderful attention was just what she needed. The pasta they ate could have been cooked longer and the sauce was too salty, but the mood was perfect.

Avery cleared away the dishes and came back to sit next to her on the couch. He kissed her lips with tenderness and passion. He felt her body respond and his own react. He was surprised when he felt her pull away.

He saw in her eyes question and worry. He understood. He rose and went to the kitchen counter and came back with a box.

"Robert made a side trip before coming over to pick up Tommy's clothes. He even checked the expiration date before buying them for us. He said we still needed to be inside each other, even if it meant having a thin layer of protection around our hearts. He's a good man, Sandy."

Once again he placed his lips against hers. Her response surprised him as she opened her mouth to him and he felt her tongue searching for his. His right hand reached under her blouse and found the softness of her breasts. It was easy for his fingers to caress both at the same time. His head bent and laid soft kisses along her neck and sucked at her breasts through her shirt.

Sandy was the one to get up from the couch and take Avery's hand to lead him to the bedroom. The urgency of merging with him, feeling close to him again, was overwhelming. Almost as soon as they slid into the sheets, he slid inside her. The passion was animalistic at first and then the most tender coming together they had ever known. They both knew they were coming home to each other and, to them, they had the best house on the block.

Sandy was in the shower when Tommy came home from school. Avery was actually excited to see him get off the bus and run towards the house. He met him at the door and engulfed him in a hug.

"Dang, Daddy, you're going to crush the life out of me!"

His laughter sounded like music to Avery's ears, the feel of him more special than anything Avery could imagine.

"Where's Mama? I got to tell her how funny Uncle Robert is. You should see how he cooks breakfast! He looks like one of them cartoon guys who tries to do too many things and ends up burning everything. It's so funny."

Tommy's animated gestures made Avery laugh. He watched as Tommy explained how Robert tried to be cool and break two eggs together and ended up with one on the floor and the other thrown half way across the kitchen. Tommy's hands came together in a spastic motion and then missed each other. He loved that Robert tried to entertain Tommy and make him feel comfortable. Robert was good at that.

Sandy heard Tommy and Avery in the living room but she took her time in the bathroom. There were thoughts in her head that she didn't want showing. She had been overcome with sadness as the warmth of the water washed over her. She was keeping something from everyone. She needed to keep her emotions in check. She opened the bathroom door to the sound of the phone ringing.

"Sandy? It's Robert." Avery's voice had a lightness to it.

She picked up the phone and rubbed a little shampoo out of her ear before placing the receiver to it.

"Hey there! Thanks for picking up Tommy's clothes. Yes, he just got off the bus."

She thought she heard hesitation in Robert's voice, as if he was trying to judge her mood.

"Avery made me a romantic lunch. Was that your doing?"

The surprise in Robert's voice told her it truly hadn't been.

"No. He made you lunch? How cute. Was it any good? Hey Sandy, I have to get back to work soon. Listen, I was thinking it might be cool for me and Avery to go to Liars tonight to welcome Cara home. No doubt she'll be there and we could surprise her. I think something familiar would be good for Avery."

Sandy shifted her wait and felt her neck muscles tense. The mention of her mama made her feel uncomfortable. She didn't care if Avery went but she wasn't sure he could stand to be around Cara right now. Still, she agreed that Robert would pick Avery up at nine thirty and promised he would have him back before midnight. Tommy was tugging at her because he wanted to talk to Robert too. Sandy explained that Robert was in a hurry and had to hang up.

Avery was on the other side of her and appeared almost happy when he asked,

"What did Robert have to say?"

"He wants to take you out to Liars to surprise Mama with a welcome home. I told him if you felt like going, it's fine with me. Me and Tommy can have a night at home together."

Sandy couldn't quite figure out the look on Avery's face. He looked guilty about something but she assumed it had to do with leaving her at home to go party with Robert. Actually, she thought the idea was a good one. She'd spent so much time and energy worrying about everyone. An evening of relative quiet would be welcomed. By the time Robert came to pick Avery up, Tommy would be sound asleep and maybe she could figure out what to do about the problem she was having.

Tommy jabbered on and on at dinner about Robert. He would stop every once in awhile to look at the people at the table with him to make sure they were his parents. He didn't understand why they weren't yelling at him to shut up or to not talk with his mouth full. He noticed that there were no empty beer bottles lined up by his daddy's plate and that there was so little food on his mama's plate that he actually had more than her. He didn't know what happened but he knew something had.

Kicking his feet under the table, while chewing a huge piece of the hamburger, he decided to enjoy the change. It was the first time he felt like a member of the family. He thought if some magic person had put a spell on their house then it might only last a day. He wanted to cram as much of himself into the moment as possible. That was his thinking when he turned to his mama and let loose a glob of hamburger from his mouth with his words.

"Hey, Mama? Whoops! I'm sorry. I thought my tongue had hold of that."

He instinctively recoiled for fear he would be slapped but no hand struck out. To him, no reaction was almost as scary as if there had been one. He was starting to think maybe it wasn't magic but that aliens had taken over his parents' bodies. He decided right then and there, if his grandma came over and was wearing a dress he was running all the way back to Robert's by himself!

Avery went in to take his shower. He'd felt almost normal for a time during the day. Making love with Sandy had been an incredible release. It had been pure passion but he wondered if next time would be different. He would be on medication soon. He wondered how sexy he would be or feel when he started taking AZT. He wondered *if* he would start taking it! The medication itself posed a huge question in his mind. He knew that the regime was exacting and that the chemicals were toxic. The words weren't his.

He'd heard some doctor say them on the Montel Williams show. She said that being HIV positive came with physical, as well as mental, dilemmas. Avery had thought it a stupid comment and had felt like saying DUH?

Avery looked in the mirror as he put the thick foam on his face to shave and wondered what he would look like with a beard? He patted the lather into a full growth facsimile around his chin to see if he would look distinguished or stupid. Hmm, he thought. On the up side, a beard would hide the multiple chins he sported but on the down side, it would make his cheeks look like he was storing Texas pecans for winter. Fat was fat and poor was poor and distinguished he would never be.

Sandy knew when she heard the knock on the door that she should set every clock in the house to nine-thirty. Robert was the most reliable and prompt person Sandy had ever met. If he said nine-thirty then he didn't mean a minute earlier or later. There was another thing about him that Sandy admired and loved. Robert was one of the kindest souls she'd ever met. It wasn't so much the things he did, it was who he was in total. It didn't surprise her a bit when he asked if Tommy was asleep yet and whether he could go in and say goodnight. It also didn't surprise her that he came in with a new pair of jeans and a shirt for Tommy to wear to school in the morning. His excuse had been that he wasn't sure the kiddo had clothes, since he was technically supposed to be staying the night in the same place his clothes had been taken. Sandy knew he just wanted Tommy to have something new.

She thought it was funny how some people take shit in life and make it into something useful like fertilizer and others just spread it around to stink up other's lives. Their mamas had been the former and pride made the three of them struggle to be better than what their mamas made them. She was glad at least one of them was making progress and she still had hope for her and Avery.

Robert kissed Sandy's cheek and thanked her again for what was to be a boys night out. Avery pinched her butt and said,

"Bye, baby. I love you and we won't be too late."

CHAPTER TWENTY-FOUR

Robert drove with the same careful calculation with which he ironed and creased his pants! Avery wanted to take his left foot and place it over Robert's on the gas pedal. As the second pick up truck whizzed around them, he finally mentioned that the speed limit was forty-five miles an hour.

"Hey, Robert, the cops don't pull you over for doin' forty-five but they might for going three miles an hour!"

He waited for Robert to accelerate but the car continued to go slow enough for Avery to read detailed signs along the way. Feeling a little playful, Avery said,

"Hey look, that piece of china in McNamara's display window has a chip in it! I think I'll go in tomorrow and ask them to give me a marked down price for it!"

Robert's laughter made Avery feel great. He hadn't been sure how he would feel about actually going out drinking with Robert. It was one thing to end up liking someone he thought he wouldn't but for him go out in public with an openly gay man was another step entirely. It was hard to think of Robert as a buddy. He wasn't the kind of buddy Avery had ever had. He doubted Robert had ever been in a duck blind at three in the morning, or gone cow tipping, or ever held a match to his butt after farting. No, he wasn't the bubba boy type and bubbas had always been Avery's choice for companionship.

They pulled into the parking lot of Liars and were surprised when they didn't see Cara's Pontiac parked in front. Avery spoke as the knowledgeable son-in-law.

"Hmm. We both know it's way too early for her to have given

up for the night, so maybe she's just waiting for the place to be rocking for her grand entrance."

Robert was fascinated by the decor of the tiny club. It smelled of hormones, beer, want, and really cheap perfume. The ear splitting country music at first made Robert feel he was suffering from a cerebral hemorrhage. The vision of his brains leaking out from his ears seemed to fit the place. The wood floor was filthy and the tables looked like things even Goodwill would discard. There was little lighting and Robert thought that was a good thing. Some of the faces in the place were the stuff of which nightmares were made and so far he had only seen the barmaids! He and Avery sat at the bar and ordered a beer. Avery yelled so loud that Robert actually jumped.

"So what do you think of Cara's closet?"

He yelled back at Avery to be heard but the music stopped just as he yelled the first sentence.

"It's loud and dirty, just like the patrons! I love it!"

The I love it part was a stunned whisper. He felt eyes on him and knew what a gold fish in a baggie felt like. He slapped Avery on the back and started laughing. His gesture was meant to be like Foghorn Leghorn in the cartoons when he says, "That's a joke, son!" He sure hoped the people that heard him watched cartoons!

Robert knew he was being very judgmental but sometimes the truth of things in East Texas would sit hard on the mind of any reasonable person. What he loved about the people was that they never pretended to be anything other than what they were. They took pride in the fact that they still called blacks, niggers; gay men, fags; women, whores; and themselves, right. He had always said that it was better for a person to know the enemy than to try and guess who to fight.

He was deep in thought when he heard Avery's name being called out from somewhere in the middle of the room.

Avery almost knocked over his beer trying to move his massive body around to see who had called him. A man sitting at a table with four other men was waving his arms to motion Avery over.

Avery leaned in close and said,

"Oh shit! That's George Mason. I work with him and I'm supposed to be home with the flu! Oh man, of all the people to run into! He's sure to tell my boss he saw me. Come on, I gotta do something to make this better. When we go over, don't be obvious. Know what I mean?"

Robert knew exactly what Avery meant. It wasn't as if he was going to go swishing over and suddenly break into show tunes! Hell, he didn't even act that way in a gay bar. He got up from his stool and followed Avery to the table where the men were sitting.

"So the doc told you beer was good for what ails ya, huh Avery?"

The sarcastic laughter matched the knowing looks that shot around the table from man to man. It was sort of the nudge nudge wink wink thing. George was a tattooed wonder. He had arms the size of hindquarters, a neck that looked like it had once been two feet long and then suddenly compressed, and a booming voice that sounded like thunder itself. He was definitely the leader of the pack.

Avery introduced Robert to the group and the two grabbed chairs and sat. George took the responsibility for further introductions. He called off the names of the other four men: Harry, Spike, Leo, and Sponge. Robert felt something strange with each handshake. It was a pervasive feeling that he should go scrub his hands after touching these men. He was acutely aware that George was the only one that Avery knew.

George explained that Sponge had just moved to Texas from Mississippi and was new to the group. His voice had a weird tone of affection when he spoke of the other three.

"I been knowin' Harry, Spike and Leo since back in the days when bein' a white male meant something! Man, the times we used to have! We meet here once a week to drink beer and talk over the nigger and spic problem we have in this town."

Spike chimed in.

"Hey, speakin' of that, did ya'll see where them people got fired in Houston for speaking Messican at work? I laughed my ass off when they showed them ignorant fucks all pumped up about not being allowed to speak their native language. Ain't there a law against dumpin' grease in public areas? Those taco heads are lucky we even let them into Texas!"

Robert thought he was going to get physically sick right on the table. He was sitting in a hornets nest of skin headed, brain dead, hate mongering bastards. He looked at Avery with the eyes of a terrified fawn. He'd been watching the one named Leo and thought he'd seen him someplace before. His instincts told him there was a reason he and Avery had been called over to the table and even more reason to find an excuse to leave quickly. He was trying to get Avery's attention when the sound of Leo's voice sent chills up his back.

"Hey, Robert, you sure look familiar to me. Have we ever met before? You from around this area?"

Robert prayed that his voice wouldn't crack when he answered. He knew these men could smell fear even if they couldn't spell it. He certainly couldn't say that he had just been thinking that Leo looked familiar to him too. He felt relief wash over him when he heard Avery say,

"Nah, old Robert here is a college boy. He grew up in Houston and moved when they gave him a manager's position at the mall."

The men just nodded and each picked up their beers and took huge gulps. He could not get rid of the fear in the pit of his stomach. He got up from the table and tried to sound as macho as any whore-loving man would.

"Man, I gotta take a piss. Be back as soon as I empty this hollow leg."

He kicked himself all the way to the bathroom. How stupid was that? That sounded as macho as if Pee Wee Herman had said it. He opened the door to the bathroom and was glad no one was in there with him. He turned on the water without touching the faucet handles and splashed cold water on his face. He was doing deep breathing exercises and patting his face dry when he heard the door open. It was Leo.

"Must be catching. I had a powerful urge to piss myself the minute you left!"

Robert acted like he was drying his hands but could see Leo standing at the urinal. The memory of a monstrous night at one of Houston's most elite gay bars came flooding back. Leo's profile made him remember. He had a large nose that looked like a cookie that had been melted on the tray, big and all over the place. It was a nose Robert had seen before and it sat on a monsters face. The man and a few of his friends had given gay bashing a new meaning in Houston. He felt strange saying anything to Leo while the bastard was still peeing but he had to get out of there.

"Man, nothing like taking a load off. See ya back outside."

He hurried back into the club and tried to get Avery's attention. He didn't want to go back to the table and didn't want to stay at Liars another minute. Avery had his back turned to him and it was George who saw him.

"Hey, your little friend is out of the boy's room. Looks like he needs something. Maybe he peed himself!"

The laughter was of a juvenile pitch as Avery got up to go see what Robert wanted. He was a little irritated as he approached because the last thing he needed was for Robert to be acting like a Nancy boy!

In a harsh whisper, Avery said,

"Robert, this isn't the time or the place to be attracting that kind of attention to yourself!"

"Avery, it's about that Leo guy. I thought I'd seen him when George introduced him and I just remembered from where."

Robert felt like he couldn't get the words out fast enough and leaned into Avery as he spoke.

"A few years ago there was a rash of gay bashings in Montrose. It was rumored in the gay community that the Jacinto Corners Control League was behind them. Men would infiltrate gay bars and then follow people out of the club and beat the holy shit out of them. Avery, I saw Leo at some of those clubs and trust me, he wasn't dancing with drag queens!"

By the time they saw Leo standing at the bar two feet away from them it was too late. They smiled and nodded in his direction. They watched as he put money on the bar, took his cold beer and walked back to the table. Avery and Robert saw him sit down and lean in to talk to the others.

"Okay, let's be calm about this. Maybe he didn't hear you but let's assume he did. You go out to the car right now and I'll go to the table and say we have to leave because you're sick."

Robert didn't have to be told twice. He was out the door before Avery made it back to the table. Avery walked up to the men shaking his head.

"Well guys, it seems like the smoke and beer is more than college boy can stand. He's feeling like shit and needs to go home. George, I'll see you at work in the morning. Spike, Leo, Harry, Sponge, I hope we meet again. Ya'll have fun."

Avery hoped it didn't sound as much like a lie as it was. He felt a little guilty about seemingly detaching himself from Robert by calling him college boy but he thought it sounded better than calling him by name at the moment. He doubted it mattered anyway. There seemed to be a shield between him and the others. He heard it in George's parting words.

"I hope your *little friend* feels better real soon. Now don't ya'll go and get in any trouble on the way home!"

Avery climbed into the passenger side and could see that Robert was visibly shaken. He knew exactly how he felt. Sometimes in life a person finds himself feeling dirtied by circumstances and the filth seeps so deep into the skin that feeling clean again takes awhile.

Robert didn't speak until they were out of the parking lot and a mile down the road.

"What'd they say when you left, Avery? Do you think they know? If you ask me, they knew before they ever called you over to the table. The neolithic, neo Nazi bastards!"

Avery wanted to make Robert feel safe but he thought what he said was probably true. He knew that ignorant men were not always stupid. He was almost positive that the truth about Robert had been told before they ever sat down at the table. Leo probably had a better memory than he deserved and he was sure it was reserved for logging incidences when his hatred was exercised. He didn't tell Robert the whole truth about the attitude he met when he went back to the table.

"Oh just the usual macho goodbye. You know."

Robert shot back,

"Yeah, right. Avery you may have lied to them but you can't lie to me. I'm sure they found a not so subtle way to let you know they knew."

Avery noticed that Robert was actually driving the speed limit and wanted to lighten the mood in the car.

"Hey, could you slow down a little? I can't see what's on sale at Kroger's this week!"

Robert laughed and felt some of the tension leave his shoulders. He hated how the evening had turned out. It made him furious that men like them got to him but he knew the difference between people who hate and the ones who act on their hatred. It was why he couldn't stop looking in the rearview mirror as he drove. It was a moonless Texas night and the road felt lonely and so did he. He could tell that Avery saw a part of himself in those men and he knew it was bothering him.

"Avery, I don't hate those people. I mean, I hate what they stand for and I hate their violence against others, but I don't hate *them*. I guess because I have been different than others most of my whole life, I am adamant about a person's right to be who they are. It's just that when a person hurts someone else because they don't agree with them it ceases to be their freedom they are exercising but an infringement on someone else's. I don't care if those people hate me but I do care if they want me to hate myself! Does that make any sense? "

Avery nodded. He thought it made perfect sense. Even though

he'd been prejudiced himself at times, he'd never actively set out to hurt people. He was about to explain his views to Robert when Robert screamed.

"Oh shit! Avery, I think they're behind us. Don't turn around but there is a pick up so close to my bumper that the people in it could suck on the tailpipe. What do I do?"

"Don't panic, Robert. Slow down and see if they pass."

It was difficult for Robert to take his foot off the accelerator. His leg was shaking from the knee down and had no feel to it. He slowed the speed of the car without stepping on the brake. He didn't want to alert them or give them an opportunity to actually hit his car.

The truck switched lanes and passed at lightning speed in the right hand lane. Both men sighed so deeply they sounded like a leak in a propane tank. Robert applied the brake in order to make the turn onto the long road that lead to Avery's trailer. They'd watched the truck go past their turn so they both felt relaxed. The two were discussing how strong Sandy was when the vehicle behind them started honking and flashing its lights.

Before they even had time to react, the truck that had passed them earlier was back at their side and then directly in front of them. Another truck was behind them and moved to the left of them. It was the third truck that made the box complete by coming up from behind. Robert looked at Avery with real terror in his eyes and was not comforted by what he saw staring back at him. He had no choice but to slow and then stop the car. Robert asked Avery if his door was locked and liked his answer.

"Hell yes, it's locked! I locked it when we got in at the club!"

Only three men got out of the trucks. The absence of George and Leo was conspicuous and noted. Sponge carried a baseball bat and struck terror in Avery's and Robert's hearts. The first two blows were to the hood of the car and then there was the sound of breaking glass from the back of the car. Robert screamed but knew the only person who heard him and cared was in just as much trouble as he. Sponge yelled as he brought the bat back with full force at the driver's side window.

"Let the games begin, you fucking queers!"

He and Avery had the same thought at the same time. They exited the passenger side of the car just as Sponge swung and shattered the window. Glass flew and Robert felt jagged pain in the bakc of his neck and warm liquid splash into his shirt. He felt a rush of adrenaline and pounced on Harry with the force of a crazed man. He couldn't see Avery but heard grunts, heavy breathing and the sound of fists against flesh coming from the back of the car.

Avery was glad to be a large man as he used his sheer size to ward off Spike. He rammed the man to the ground and landed a few punches to the face before Spike picked up a rock and split Avery's skull.

Blood gushed. Avery felt dizzy and slumped to the ground, vaguely wondering how Robert was fairing.

Just as Robert thought he was getting the best of Harry, he felt the first blow of the baseball bat. Sponge was behind him and the blow sent him reeling into the ditch head over heels. He heard Sponge ask Harry,

"Hey, you want a crack at the mother fucker? Man, he tore your nose up pretty good."

The second blow came to his right leg and then the third to the back of his head. The last thing he remembered was hearing Spike's voice.

"That's enough boys, George and Leo said to hurt 'em, not kill 'em. We need to get out of here before anyone comes driving by. There's just one more thing."

Spike took a billy club and a hand scrawled note from the glove compartment. He went to the ditch where Robert lay unconscious and rolled him over on his back. He undid Robert's jeans and pulled them down. Rolling him onto his stomach, he pinned the note to Robert's torn shirt and shoved the billy club up his ass. Harry asked what the note said.

"Oh, it's just a little note that Leo put together. It says, How do you like that queer boy? Now ya done been fucked by the JCCL!"

Avery woke up to flashing lights and someone screaming.

"Charlie, there's another one over here in the ditch. Oh God! Look what they've done to this poor boy!"

Avery tried to get up but the paramedic held him firmly to the ground. He wanted to see about Robert. He had to know if he was dead or alive.

"My friend . . .Robert . . .how is he?"

The paramedic told Avery to relax because the more he moved the more blood he lost. The word blood made Avery grow cold with fear. He was HIV positive and he had to tell these people. God, he'd hit a man tonight and had been carrying the most dangerous weapon of any of them!

He was telling the paramedic about having the virus when he saw the flash of a camera go off, not once but four times. He started crying. Robert must be dead and they're taking crime scene photos. He couldn't stop the tears. His heart was left on a lonely, dark, Jacinto Corners road as they hoisted him into the back of the ambulance.

Mike Long had been a paramedic for fifteen years. He thought he'd seen it all, but Robert lying in the ditch like they found him broke his heart and made him sick. It always pissed him off that so many times when he was called out to a scene the injuries were preventable, but seldom did he see things done with malicious intent. Morris secured the brace around Robert's neck and asked his partner Charlie Whitcomb if he was finished putting on the leg brace.

They were ready to transport and Mike handed the IV bag to Officer Morris Foley. He had been the one to identify the first victim. He helped them lift the Gurney into the ambulance and told them he would meet them at the hospital after stopping by to tell Sandy Anderson she needed to go to the hospital. He wanted to cry for Sandy. She was going to take this really hard. He couldn't believe it when the paramedics instructed him not to touch the victims because one had admitted having the HIV virus. Morris shook his head as he got into his cruiser.

CHAPTER TWENTY-FIVE

Sandy heard Tommy in the bathroom and went to see what had awakened him. As he rubbed his eyes, he asked if his Uncle Robert had come by yet. Sandy thought it was so cute the way he looked up to Robert. She was glad Tommy liked him and even gladder that he was such a good friend to her.

The silence in the house was welcomed. Sandy went to the shelves under the kitchen bar and took out the pregnancy book Celia Callier had given her months ago. She needed to see if there was anything in it about the pains she'd been having. She hadn't said a word to anyone about them and they were happening much more frequently of late. She had just settled onto the couch when someone knocked at the door.

Her heart sank when she turned on the porch light and saw Morris Foley standing there. She opened the door and started talking before he could open his mouth to speak.

"Morris, if my mama is in trouble again I don't want to know. I ain't got time to get her out of any more messes or hold her hand while she screws up her life!"

Morris took Sandy's hand in his.

"Sandy, it ain't your mama. It's Avery. He and a guy he was with got beat up real bad. You need to get to the hospital."

She reeled back and fell before she could catch herself. Morris rushed inside and helped her up. She was incoherent and he knew then he would have to drive her to the hospital himself. The only thing coming out of her mouth that made sense was the name Tommy. He knew she had a son named Tommy so he walked down the hall checking the bedrooms. He opened the door to the middle bedroom and saw Tommy lying in a peaceful sleep. He walked back into the living room and asked Sandy where he could find a phone. He followed the direction of her finger. He looked up Cara's number and called. He really didn't think she'd be home but he had to try. Even Cara qualified as an adult, in desperate circumstances.

Cara was in a deep sleep when the phone rang and she instinctively hit the other side of the bed for Buster to answer it. Feeling only emptiness, she remembered she was alone. She would certainly have some choice words for the son of a bitch calling at eleven at night when she'd just gotten out of the hospital. She dropped the phone twice before she managed to get the receiver up to her ear.

"Yeah. You best talk fast because I'm mean when someone wakes me up."

Morris wanted to say, Hell, you're mean when you're asleep, Cara, but he got straight to the point.

"Cara, this is Morris Foley. I'm at Sandy's and she needs you to come over to stay with Tommy. Avery and his friend Robert were pretty badly beaten up tonight."

Cara was suddenly wide awake. She sat up in bed and rather than ask a million questions told Morris she would be right there. She went to her closet and took out a pair of Wranglers and one of Buster's button down shirts he'd left. She threw on her tennis shoes, picked up her keys and was out the door.

She was trembling as she started the Pontiac and knew this time it wasn't from booze. Somehow her earlier conversation with Sandy made her see herself in a different light. She was pissed as hell but she knew there was a lot of truth to what Sandy said. She *was* self involved and had seldom been there for her daughter. She knew how to be there as a mom and she wanted to show Sandy that she could.

It seemed the five minute drive to Sandy's took an eternity. The cruiser sitting in front of the house made her feel strange for only a moment as she passed by and looked into the very back seat she'd been in only days earlier. She flung opened the screen door and went to Sandy.

The hug was awkward but not forced. She asked Morris the condition of Avery and Robert. He said he really didn't know but that the beatings had been severe.

"Got any idea who the fuck did this to them? What in the hell were Robert and Avery doing out together anyway?"

It was Sandy's voice she heard.

"You know very well what they were doing together. They were at Liars with you for your welcome home."

Cara looked at Sandy and saw the anger dancing in her eyes. This was another thing she was being blamed for.

"Sandy, darlin', I didn't go to Liars tonight. I been sleepin' in the bed since this afternoon!"

Morris called into the substation and told them he was escorting someone to East Texas General.

"Let's go, Sandy. I gotta get a report from Avery if he's able to talk."

The door shut and Cara felt the thud in her heart. She tried to imagine someone beating on Robert. It made no sense to her. He was a twig of a guy and couldn't be intimidating if he wanted to. She took the afghan off the back of the couch and laid her head on a throw pillow that smelled of the drool that comes from someone sleeping with their mouth opened. She lit a cigarette and closed her eyes as she inhaled the smoke deep into her lungs. There was little that Cara understood about the world when she was sober. It was a much more difficult place to live in.

Morris unlocked the passenger door and helped Sandy into the seat. As he walked around the front of the car he looked at her slumped over as if she was about to break. It was strange to see her as someone who looked small and deflated. She'd been overweight for as long as he'd known her and that had been more years than he cared to think about. He wondered about Avery having HIV but it wasn't his place to ask. He often found out things about people that few others knew. Part of being a policeman was the integrity of the badge and he carried a deep respect for what that meant. He would know about Avery but Sandy wouldn't be aware he did.

Morris waited until he was away from the trailer to turn on the red and blues. He didn't need his siren but he knew people would get out his way when they saw flashing lights.

It only took fifteen minutes to get to East Texas General. Morris helped Sandy from the car and held her elbow as they walked through the automatic doors into the emergency room. He told Sandy to sit down for a minute and he'd go find out where they had taken Avery.

He was gone only moments. He bent to Sandy and tried to sound as comforting as possible.

"Sandy, Avery is in surgery. It seems Avery has a head injury and they're inserting a shunt in his head to take the pressure off his brain. The nurse said to take you to the second floor waiting room and the doctor will talk to you as soon as he can."

Morris couldn't even tell if she heard him and then saw her mouth open.

"And Robert? What about Robert?"

As he helped her to her feet again, two solitary tears ran down her cheeks. The sight made him want to cry. Sandy was a nice woman and she didn't deserve the terrible pain she was repeatedly forced to endure.

Morris brought Sandy a diet Pepsi and sat down next to her to drink the coffee that looked more like the black water from a trailer's storage tank. He thought about Christmas and what he'd bought his three old daughter, Sarah. He'd enjoyed going shopping even though it was the first Christmas since his divorce. Thoughts of Sarah made him remember the look of little Tommy sleeping peacefully, unaware that life around him was crumbling to pieces. He'd imagined his ex-wife, Becky, having to tell little Sarah bad news about her daddy and he felt so sad for Tommy.

Morris didn't know much about Avery but he did know he had a clean record and worked hard to provide for his family. He hoped that Christmas for them would mean that two lives would be saved. He thought perhaps that was what Christmas was really about anyway. He was thinking about Sarah opening the doll house he'd bought her when he felt Sandy's hand on his upper right arm.

"Morris? Why do people think people like us don't matter?"

He looked at Sandy's face and knew she expected him to have some kind of answer.

His voice was soft when he spoke.

"Sandy, my belief is that we represent their fear. We are what they could have become or might become if circumstances change in their lives. You know, sort of by the grace of God thing. You see, we are sort of a mirror whose image is what they don't want to reflect so they can't look at us. If they don't look, we don't exist."

"But we do exist, Morris. We live and breathe just like everyone else. We have wants and needs and hopes. We have children and spouses we love. We matter, Morris, even if only to ourselves and each other. We matter!"

He patted her leg and nodded in agreement. He was about to ask her how she met Robert when Dr. Albeji walked up.

"Mrs Anderson?"

He offered Sandy a hand that felt like the finest of silk. Even the fingernails seemed soft and for some reason Sandy didn't want to let go of the feel. The hand was the one that moments ago was busy saving Avery's life.

"Your husband is out of surgery. He suffered a severe blow to the head and there was major blood loss. I inserted a shunt into the right side of his head to reduce the swelling of his brain. The next twenty four hours should tell us if there are visible signs of permanent brain damage. The fact that he is HIV positive is a secondary concern for the moment but is a factor since his immune system is weakened by the virus. He is in ICU right now and will remain there tonight. You may go in and see him but he won't know you're there."

"Yes he will." Sandy released the doctor's hand and rose to go to Avery.

Sandy tried to prepare herself for how Avery would look when she saw him. She had seen enough episodes of ER to know that tubes and machines were par for the course but those were actors and she wasn't married to any of them. She went to the nurse's station and saw the closed circuit monitor. She thought all the patients looked the same on the screens, each one clinging to life by a tube. A tiny slip of a nurse took her to Avery's room.

Sandy stood to Avery's side and before the nurse left, she asked her if she knew anything about Robert.

"Mr. Laningham was life flighted into a Houston hospital, Mrs. Anderson. His injuries were fairly severe and we just didn't have the facilities to give him proper care here. I'm sorry I can't tell you more."

Silent tears coursed down Sandy's face as she bent to whisper to Avery.

"Hey, Avery Anderson. I've known you close to my whole life and I ain't ready to die so you gotta get better. It's almost Christmas, Avery, and right now all I want is to hear your laughter again, to have your arms around me, to eat some of your lousy pasta and to watch how you can down a beer faster than anyone I know. I don't want nothin' but the chance to love you as much as I always have. Hell, Avery, wasn't HIV bad enough for you? Did you have to go and get beat up too?"

The little nurse came in again and said if Sandy was going to stay she could stay in the waiting room and have visits with Avery for fifteen minutes every hour. She said there were coffee and snack machines on the floor and somewhat edible food in the cafeteria on the first floor. Sandy thanked her and decided she would try the cafeteria.

Sandy picked out a turkey sandwich that didn't show obvious signs of mold, a bag of chips and a diet Pepsi. She looked around for a vacant table and saw a familiar face. It was the woman she'd seen in the elevator earlier in the day when she had picked up

Cara. Unlike earlier, she wanted to hear this woman's sorrow, if only to make herself seem less lonely.

"Excuse me. This place is more crowded than I thought. Would you mind if I sat with you?"

The woman looked up and had the age of pain in her eyes. She was beautiful and perhaps twenty-four years old. Her hair was long, full and a mass of curls. She said not a word but motioned for Sandy to sit.

"My name is Sandy Anderson. My husband is in ICU on the second floor."

The woman turned her eyes to Sandy but was looking way beyond the person she saw. When she spoke she sounded like a robot on automatic pilot.

"I'm Virginia Copeland. My three month old son is on the third floor. He's just been diagnosed with leukemia. We thought he just had a really bad cold. I swear that's all we thought it was. Tyler is our first baby. We didn't know. I swear. We didn't know he was sick."

Sandy put her sandwich down. The obvious guilt this young woman felt ripped at her heart. She felt the words but wasn't sure how to say them.

"Life ain't your fault. We got no say in things. All we can do is swim and hope we don't drown or get eaten by the sharks."

Virginia looked up at the simple woman sitting at the table with her. She couldn't help but think she was someone, that only days before, she would have turned her nose up to. Her clothes were not bought from the Galleria but K Mart, her education was nil and Virginia would have been sure she could not possibly have anything in common with her. She was glad for the company and asked,

"Do you have children?"

"Yes, a son, Tommy, he's eight years old. We're expecting another in about six months. I know this don't sound right but I would trade the life of this baby for my husband's right now."

Virginia contemplated choosing the life of her child over her life or Ron's, her husband.

"I wouldn't. A baby is a new beginning and has everything to look forward to. A baby is magic. They see the world through different eyes and feel like it is their's to discover. I love seeing that in Tyler."

Sandy agreed but wasn't sure she had known it until recently.

"Yes, everything is new and wonderful to them. They ain't had time to be ruined by the truth of life."

Soon the two women were sitting together laughing over the antics of their children. Most doctors would have seen it as hysteria and most psychologists would have seen it as denial but Sandy and Virginia saw it as comfort. They recognized it as a bond of familiarity. They shared grief but needed to hang on to life.

Sandy was thankful to Virginia for seeing her. She knew that under different circumstances, Virginia would have passed her by as if she were invisible. Sandy's thoughts were interrupted by Virginia.

"They are talking about bone marrow donors. If we could find a match, it would give Tyler a forty/ sixty chance of survival." Her words were merely informational and she did not really expect any response.

Sandy took hold of the words and showed them the door to her heart. She knew the importance of life, even if the world didn't think she did.

"Virginia, I don't know much about such things but I would be glad to take a test to see if my blood would work. I can't think of anything better than helping out a baby."

She saw tears well in Virginia's eyes as she spoke.

"That would be a great gift, Sandy, but it doesn't involve being a blood donor. It is a complicated procedure where they tap into the bone of the donor and extract the marrow. It is a painful procedure and the chances of finding a match is not all that great."

Virginia told her Tyler's oncologist was searching the data bases for a donor. Tyler was not expected to live more than three weeks if one wasn't found, so he was a priority.

Sandy was listening to Virginia and reality hit full force. She had just offered a stranger her blood without a thought that it could be poisoned by the HIV virus. A feeling of horror struck at her heart and must have shown on her face.

"Sandy? Are you okay? You look like you just saw a ghost."

Sandy thought for a moment. Even if she knew what to say, she certainly didn't know how to say it. Sandy stammered and then blurted out.

"Virginia . . . I . . . well . . . I guess . . . I don't know what I was thinking. I just realized wanting to help Tyler and being able to are two different things."

"Oh Sandy, I understand. You just got caught up in the moment. People say things in the heat of things, you know?"

Sandy wanted this woman to understand but didn't want her to know.

"No, Virginia, you don't understand. I would get tested for being a donor if I could. It don't matter that it hurts or anything like that. It ain't that I don't want to do it; it's that I can't do it. Sandy couldn't say the words. She couldn't tell this woman she might be HIV positive. Why had she said anything at all? Why had she let her heart speak before her mind thought?

It was Virginia's right hand that took Sandy's this time and her look, as well as her words, were kind.

"Sandy, it was a very selfless thing you were ready to do. You needn't worry that you hurt me and you needn't explain. The fact that you would be willing to do such a thing is all that matters. Thank you. Thank you for sitting here with me, for listening to me and for wanting to help me out of this misery when you have so much of your own. I am glad I met you, Sandy Anderson, and now I must go back upstairs. I hope your husband is going to be okay and maybe we can talk again soon."

Sandy sat feeling more alone than she ever had. The enormity of the world was sitting on her shoulders. She wrapped the rest of her sandwich in a napkin, rose from her chair and picked up her drink. Nothing tasted right anymore and the hunger she felt could never be fed with food.

CHAPTER TWENTY-SIX

Cara was sound asleep when she heard the whimpering. She was in a half sleep, half awake state when she walked down the hall towards the sound.

"I'm here, Sandy. Mama's here. Don't you fret now. Mama will take care of everything."

She met Tommy half way down the hall, crying. He stopped when he saw her and said,

"Grandma, what are you doing here? Where's my mama? I had the most awfulest dream!"

Cara put her arms around Tommy and guided him back to bed. She felt his hesitation to lay back down and wondered what monsters had visited him. She went over to turn on the light and saw the reason for his hesitancy. He'd wet the bed and it had woken him from the hell in which he had been sleeping. She fumbled in the drawer for a clean pair of underwear for him and told him to put them on.

Without a word, Cara steered him out of his room and to the comfort of Sandy's bed. She lay with him and stroked his forehead until his eyes grew heavy. He yawned twice, snuggled deep into the familiar smell of the covers and fell asleep.

Cara went back to Tommy's room to remove the soiled sheets. Without warning, the tears came and she collapsed onto the bed sobbing uncontrollably. Changing Tommy's sheets brought back memories of removing Sandy's sheets from her bed when she was eight. She wished it had been urine she'd seen and smelled. How she longed that instead of blood and semen she'd had the acrid smell of ammonia hit her nostrils.

She had never known such pain and until that moment had

never realized Sandy's. She picked up the sheets and carried them to the hamper in the bathroom. She wished she could simply put herself in a washer and be cleansed from all the stains she had suffered and caused. There was a sadness in Cara at that moment, a grief, that no artist could draw, no actor could portray and no writer could express.

Cara's mind raced as she walked back to the living room. It was hell to come to grips with life when there was nothing left to hold onto. She'd felt alone her entire life and now she really was by herself with herself and she didn't like the feeling. The couch felt cold and lumpy as she lay back down to rest.

CHAPTER TWENTY-SEVEN

Sandy went back upstairs and was surprised when she walked into Avery's room to see his eyes opened. For a fleeting moment she thought he was dead but then saw his long brown lashes touch his cheeks as he blinked.

"Hey there. Welcome to the land of the living. Don't try to talk, just rest."

Sandy placed her hands over Avery's heart and moved her fingers in a circle as if to touch it through his skin. He closed his eyes again and she felt the rise and fall of his chest. She leaned in to him and spoke her heart.

"Avery, I know you can hear me. I've had quite a night tonight. I learned some things about the world and about myself. Moments count, Avery, and I done had the best ones of my life with you. We ain't got no guarantees and ain't nothing going to get better unless we make it better for ourselves. We gotta make it better, Avery. We gotta quit looking at the hole our parents dug us and bein' sorry we're in it. You gotta help me find a way out, Avery. You just gotta hang on!"

Sandy pulled the only chair in the room up to the side of the bed. She had five more minutes before the nurses would shoo her out of the room. She needed to be connected to Avery. She needed to feel him by her side as much as he needed to feel her by his. There was a certain amount of comfort in listening to his labored breathing, a solace in the beeps of the machines. They were the sounds of life and that's exactly what she needed to hear.

Morris Foley went back on shift when the doctor told him Avery Anderson would not be giving any statements tonight. It was almost time for shift change and he was writing up his report for the night. He sat at the long table in the muster room and wondered how Sandy was holding up. He hadn't told her that the JCCL had been involved in the brutal attack. He didn't tell her that they already had suspects because of the company Robert and Avery kept at Liars. He hadn't even told Sandy about the note pinned to Robert's shirt. Some things are better left unsaid until circumstances allow for understanding.

Morris finished his report and handed it in to the desk sergeant. He walked into the locker room to change into his street clothes and the din from the room full of officers coming off duty with the ones coming on was deafening. He opened his locker and watched as Bob Minter tucked his shirt into his pants. He was taken aback by Bob's words.

"Don't be watching me like that, Morris. The guys in here will think you're a fucking queer like those two bastards that got beat up tonight. The way I hear it, they got what they deserved. The AIDs spreading perverts!"

Morris felt every muscle in his body tense, his fists clench and his teeth grind down hard enough to crack walnuts. He knew better than to say anything because it would be lost on the ears and hearts in the room. He also knew that everyone in town would soon know, not only about the incident but that Avery Anderson was HIV positive. Hell, even if HIV was never mentioned, being with a known gay man would ruin him in the town forever. Sometimes Morris hated his environment and hated himself for his continued silence.

Sandy called Bradcliff Memorial and asked for the nurses station in the intensive care unit. The head nurse in the ER unit had told her Robert had been life flighted there because they dealt with multiple trauma cases. She'd said Robert had been in critical condition with a suspected spinal chord injury.

She felt sick as she heard the phone ringing. She wondered if the nurse who answered would tell her anything at all about Robert's condition. After all, she wasn't family. It seemed like an eternity before she heard a voice on the other end.

"My name is Sandy Anderson, I'm calling about Robert Laningham. He was life flighted there from East Texas General. He and my husband were badly beaten up tonight."

Sandy felt panic because there was not an immediate response.

"Oh yes, Mr. Laningham. He's no longer here. Ms. Anderson, are you a relative?"

Sandy felt her heart drop to her shoes. Her body started trembling and real terror gripped at her chest. She wasn't a liar but this time would be an exception.

"Yes, I am his younger sister."

The waiting room seemed darker, the air colder, and the world a dimmer place as Sandy waited for the nurse's response.

"Mr Laningham was moved to a room an hour ago. He underwent surgery for a badly fractured right leg, a cracked vertebrae in his back, and repair of a skull fracture. He was kept in ICU until he regained consciousness and his vital signs stabilized. He is in guarded but stable condition. I can give you his room number if you'd like."

Sandy was amazed at what the nurse was telling her. It seemed ironic to her that Robert had fared better than Avery. She guessed it was true that the bigger they are the harder they fall. She jotted Robert's room number down and asked if she could be transferred directly. The nurse suggested she wait until morning, because Robert was heavily sedated and needed to rest as much as possible. Sandy thanked the nurse and hung up the phone.

She felt a little guilty because part of her wanted to dance around the waiting room with glee. She looked at the clock and saw that she still had another half hour before time to see Avery again. She wanted to tell him the good news about Robert. She sat down and picked up a copy of Reader's Digest off the table in front of her.

Robert opened his eyes to the stark white of his hospital room. He tried to feel the areas that had been damaged. He wanted to take an assessment of all his parts. He still had a head, two arms, two legs, his penis and balls but wasn't so sure about his heart. Morphine is an amazing thing. It makes reality tolerable.

A nurse came into the room just as Robert was trying to learn to navigate around the back brace and found he couldn't. He mouthed words to the gorgeous man in the starched whites pumping the blood pressure cup.

"You're adorable! I still have a penis. I checked!"

The smile on Robert's face made Clevis Monroe laugh. He was used to patients saying almost anything when under the influence of drugs. Morphine made their minds relax and their hearts speak.

"You're pretty hot stuff yourself."

The white of his teeth looked like a beacon of hope to Robert. His black skin looked like satin and his arms held the healing warmth of hands that knew how to make pain go away. Robert grasped Clevis' hand as it came up to check the bandage on his head.

"Hey, want to blow this joint and then blow me?"

Clevis withdrew his hand gently and smiled once again at his cute but incorrigible patient.

"Hey, are you trying to get me in trouble? That might just upset my wife more than a little."

Robert laughed and then gasped from the pain it caused. He felt like someone had taken an allen wrench and twisted each bone in his back. He wanted his lungs to be outside his body so they could expand without touching anything. He drifted into the morphine and let it take him to a place of no pain.

Clevis listened to Robert's heart and knew it would end up the most damaged part of him. He'd requested Robert as a patient. He'd been at the nurse's station when they'd called from

ICU for a room. He had a sense about Robert before he ever arrived.

He lingered a moment when he saw Robert drift with the wave that the morphine swept him up in. He quietly whispered to him.

"Your healing will be slow but I sense you're strong and centered. I recognize that in people like you. You may have been beaten to within an inch of your life. You may be broken and maimed but you survived. You're going to be fine, Robert Laningham. Oh, and by the way, sweet man, not all male nurses are gay."

Clevis left room 313, glad once again for the choices he'd made in life. The joys of being a nurse far outweighed the stigmas. He placed Robert's chart on the counter and told the charge nurse he was going on break to have coffee with his wife.

Sandy woke with a start. She was disoriented at first, not realizing where she was, and then remembered. It was three a.m. and she was angry that the nurse had not come to wake her. She stormed out of the waiting room and headed for the nurses station. She spoke to the first nurse she saw.

"I missed a visit with my husband! Why didn't someone come wake me? My husband's layin' there half dead and you can't send someone to the waiting room to get me?"

The nurse was smiling, which pissed Sandy off even more. The nurse guided her towards Avery's door and said,

"This is why we didn't wake you, Mrs. Anderson."

Leading Sandy around to the side of the bed, the nurse gently touched Avery's arm and his eyes shot opened. Turning back to Sandy, she said,

"You see, he asked us not to!"

Her heart felt like it was going to burst as she looked into Avery's blackened but beautiful eyes for the first time that night. They were the eyes she recognized, not the half dead ones she'd seen before. There was a new pain in them but they were Avery eyes, her Avery eyes. Her tears dotted the white sheets and snot ran from her nose but neither she nor Avery seemed to mind much.

Avery's voice was a mere whisper as she bent to hear him. Sandy thought it was the most amazing and wonderful sound she'd ever heard.

"Go home, Sandy. Go home to Tommy and get some rest."

It was as if those few words totally exhausted him and he once again closed his eyes and drifted off to a place of healing. The nurse told her Avery was right and that she would be of little use to him if she ended up in the hospital as well. Sandy had to admit she was more exhausted than she had ever been.

It suddenly occurred to her that she had no way of getting home. She couldn't call Cara because that would mean getting Tommy out of bed. The only other people she knew she could depend on were Avery and Robert. It was then she thought about Buster. She knew he was staying with Candy and since Liars didn't close until two the chances of him being up were pretty good. She wondered to herself just how up he would be! She laughed at herself for thinking about such a base thing under the current circumstances. She picked up the phone book to look up Candy's number.

CHAPTER TWENTY-EIGHT

Buster watched as Candy danced naked in front of him. He'd felt doubt all day about his life and what he was doing. He couldn't explain it even to himself but it gnawed at him and made him edgy. He noticed that Candy was pouting because he hadn't already attacked her gyrating body.

"Buster, what's wrong? You ain't in the mood for sweet Candy? Don't you want to lick the sugar and suck the yummies tonight?"

Normally Candy's baby talk made him feel special but for whatever reason, tonight it rankled him. It made him feel like an old man grasping for youth. He felt stupid and foolish. He felt his muscles stiffen as Candy came up to him, her lips in an exaggerated pout. She felt his resistance too and her anger was immediate. He was glad when the phone interrupted what he knew would be a childish outburst from her.

He thought Candy was going to throw the phone at him when she said,

"Buster it's for you. It's Sandy Anderson, that bitch Cara's daughter!"

Buster's first thought was that Cara was dead. It was the only reason he could think of for Sandy calling him. He was afraid to pick up the phone, afraid to hear the words he'd dreaded for a long time. It had been why he left. He could no longer watch as Cara slowly killed herself.

He took a huge gulp of air and said hello.

"Buster, this is Sandy. I feel terrible about calling you but I ain't got no one else. Mama's . . ."

Buster felt his body go weak when he heard Sandy say it. He felt the world come crashing down and his response surprised him. There were tears in his eyes and his voice.

"Did she finally do it, Sandy? Did she find the peace she's been after all these years? Why? Why wouldn't she listen to me?"

Sandy screamed into the phone.

"Buster! What the hell are you talkin' about? I was going to tell you that Mama's at my house with Tommy 'cause Avery and Robert were beaten up real bad tonight and are in the hospital! Morris Foley brought me up here to East Texas General and I don't have no way home."

Buster felt the kind of relief a man feels when he discovers the hole in his favorite pair of boots can be patched. It makes a difference to a man if a thing is new and exciting or old and comfortable. Candy was exciting, but Cara was comfortable. He let relief settle in and then thought to ask about Avery and Robert.

"Oh good God, Sandy! Were they fightin' each other or someone else? Are they okay?"

"Buster, I'll tell you about it when you get here. I'm gonna go up and see Avery one more time and then I'll be waitin' for you outside the east entrance."

Buster drove to the hospital with his mind on everything but the road. He'd never liked turmoil and confusion. He was a simple man who'd always lived a simple existence. He never expected more from life than what he put into it. He wondered if he should shoot the person responsible for making Cara a part of his life. He sure never asked for or expected the shit he'd put up with since meeting her!

He pulled into the drive at East Texas General and saw Sandy standing on the curb with her jacket pulled up around her ears. He'd always felt sorry for her but never as sorry as he did at that moment. He couldn't really say they had a relationship because Sandy always kept a certain distance from Cara and an even greater distance from Cara's men. He wasn't sure about the things that had happened in their past but he was sure that removing herself from her mama seemed to put a cap on it ever happening again.

He watched as she crawled into the passenger seat. Her eyes were wild with lack of sleep and worry. He hair was matted to her head. He was sure that as pitiful as she looked, she felt much worse. He wanted to make her feel better but had never been good at such things.

"How's Avery?"

Sandy looked over at Buster and thought her mama was a fool. Buster was the only man Cara had ever been with that Sandy could even tolerate being around. He was a good man and cared the best way he could. It had dawned on her while she was waiting for him that never before would she have ever considered calling one of her mama's boyfriends to help her with anything. Hell, half the time she had barely known their names, let alone whether they were good in a crisis! She sighed deeply and started to explain about Avery and Robert.

Buster listened without interrupting. He knew that Sandy's strength was minimal and he didn't want to ask a bunch of questions. He figured in time the whole thing would make sense and sort it self out.

When they turned into the yard at the trailer, Sandy asked Buster if he would like to come in for a cup of coffee. She knew that he would have reservations about Cara being there but also had a sense he wanted to see her. He turned off the engine.

"That would be nice."

The front door was unlocked. Sandy had called Cara from the hospital to tell her she was on her way home. She expected to walk in to find her mama sitting on the couch with a cigarette in one hand and a drink in the other but she wasn't in the living room. Sandy told Buster to have a seat, put her purse on the counter and went to find Cara.

She panicked a bit when she opened the door to Tommy's room and saw that his bed was empty. She knocked quietly on the bathroom door and then opened it when she heard no response.

Then she heard soft snoring coming from her own bedroom. As her eyes adjusted to the darkness, she saw her mama lying asleep with her right arm over Tommy in protective warmth. Her eyes filled with tears and her heart filled with the closest thing to love she'd ever felt for her mama. She carefully shut the door and walked back down the hall to where Buster was waiting.

She and Buster drank two cups of coffee each. Sandy could tell as they talked there was something he'd wanted to ask her. She was exhausted but gave him an opening anyway.

"Buster, I noticed you look puzzled. You got a question about something?"

He shifted his weight around so that rather than looking directly at her, he looked to her side. It was if he was including her in his vision but ready for a reaction that was contrary to what he wanted to hear.

"Sandy, I was wondering if I could have the keys to my trailer back. It's really late and the trailer's a lot closer than driving all the way back to the other place."

Sandy felt glad. Even if he didn't stay, for at least a night something would be like it was before the nightmare started. She went to the counter in the kitchen and removed the keys from Cara's key ring.

"Here ya go, and Buster? Before you go, there's something I want you to see."

She motioned for him to follow her down the hall. She gently opened the door to her bedroom to show him Tommy and Cara sleeping. She saw a softness in his heart for the woman lying on the bed. She knew he was reconsidering his choice to leave Cara and thought seeing the potential for love in her might help him with his decision. Shutting the door once again, she followed Buster back down the hall.

"Thanks for coming to pick me up. I won't tell Mama you're at the trailer, in case you decide going back is a mistake. I'll hide her keys and make her think she misplaced them. If you're there, it will be a nice surprise and if not then just leave the keys in the mail box out front. Night, Buster, and thanks again."

Sandy shut and locked the door and went to lie on the couch. The afghan felt warm, the couch soft and her eyes heavier than they had ever been. She heard Buster start the engine of his truck but heard no more after.

CHAPTER TWENTY-NINE

Tommy woke and nudged his grandma.

"Grandma, it's nine and I missed the bus. We gotta get up now."

Cara opened one eye and started to scream she didn't give a shit about any god damned bus but stopped herself. It wasn't his fault she'd slept so little. She raised her head off the pillow and looked at her grandson. It was something she didn't remember ever really doing, not even on the day he was born. She looked at his blonde hair and the blue of his eyes. He had his head tilted to the right side and was looking at her in a way that his whole face looked like a question mark. She realized that he was likely looking at her for the first time too. She smiled and offered a suggestion she thought he would like.

"Well, since ya done missed the bus how about we spend the day not doin' the things we're supposed to? I could sure use a day of stayin' in and watching cartoons. How about you?"

Tommy jumped up and bounced on the bed.

"How cool! I ain't never stayed home to watch television! Boy, Grandma, I never know'd you was nice!"

Sandy felt like she'd been asleep for fifteen minutes when she heard the commotion coming from down the hall. She tried but just could not keep her eyes opened. It felt to her as if her head melted into the pillow when she laid it back down.

Cara got up and went into the kitchen to make coffee. She was surprised to see Sandy on the couch. She hadn't heard her come in and felt a little guilty about being in her bed when she knew how tired she must have been. Tommy came running in yelling for

Fruit Loops and Cara quickly put her finger to her mouth to tell him to hush. She turned his head towards the couch so he could see that his mama was sleeping. Tommy tugged on the tail of her shirt and whispered,

"Hey, Grandma, how we gonna watch cartoons if Mama is on the couch?"

Cara hated to wake Sandy but knew she would sleep better in her own bed. She gently shook her and told her to go to her room. Sandy mumbled something about being too old to be sent to her room, got up and lumbered down the hall.

Tommy immediately turned on the television and jumped on the couch. He put his feet on the coffee table and his thumb in his mouth. Cara watched him as she poured the milk in his cereal. She'd never noticed him do that and figured he was feeling insecure about things. She thought there had to be a reason why the holes in a person's body substituted for happiness and security when their minds and hearts didn't feel any. She'd been pouring whiskey in her mouth and men between her legs for as long as she could remember. Sandy had filled her holes with food. She thought kids probably poured dreams, wishes and imagination into theirs.

Cara brought Tommy his cereal, lit a cigarette and sat next to him. He was explaining some cartoon called the X Men when there was a knock on the front door. Cara tried to get to the door before whoever it was knocked again. It was too early in the morning to be alive, let alone have company. She opened the blinds just enough to see out and saw Morris Foley standing on the porch. She threw open the door and yelled,

"I didn't do it!"

Her laughter sounded hoarse and guttural. She noticed her humor was lost on Morris. She thought he took his job and himself way too seriously. She asked him in and told him she would have to go wake Sandy.

Cara walked into Sandy's bedroom and tried to think of the best way to wake her daughter.

At first her voice was a gentle whisper saying only,

"Sandy."

Sandy didn't budge so she leaned over to shake and speak at the same time.

"Sandy, wake up. Morris Foley is here. He wants to talk to you."

Sandy shot up in bed, looking terror stricken. Cara knew her immediate thoughts were that either Avery or Robert had taken a turn for the worse.

"They're fine, Sandy. I think Morris just got back from talkin' to Avery. He looks like a hound on the trail of a coon. You know, the animal kind."

"Mama, yes, I do know and that's the only kind of coon there is. People don't call blacks that anymore."

Cara rolled her eyes. She wasn't going to start an argument over coons, animal or human. Sandy walked toward the bathroom and Cara decided to make the bed so she and Tommy could watch the little television in there while Sandy talked to Morris. She finished pulling up the bedspread and Tommy came bounding in saying his mama was talking grown up talk.

He jumped and landed right in the middle of the bed. Before she could stop herself, her hand shot out and popped him on the behind. He turned around, shocked and confused.

"Boy, didn't you just see me make that bed? You best learn to respect the hard work of others!"

Cara saw the tears in the corners of his eyes and the anger that held them there.

"You should be more like my mama. She says it's dumb to make a bed 'cause it just gets messed up again. I guess that makes you dumb, Grandma."

Tommy got off the bed and stomped to his room. Cara laughed when she heard his door slam. He might have thought she should be more like Sandy but he was more like his Grandma than Cara had ever realized. What a pistol he was and why hadn't she seen it before? Cara sat on the edge of the bed and said the reason out loud.

"You didn't see it, Cara Covington, because the view from a whiskey bottle made everything the color of piss. You never cared about a god damned thing except where your next drink and lay would come from. Your life has been cigarettes, semen and whiskey. How in the hell do you think you'd see anything through the fog when you *were* the fog?"

Cara needed to go home. This self discovery shit was killing her. She walked into the living room and saw Sandy sobbing. She was sorry for her but knew nothing she'd say would make it better.

"Sandy, I'm goin' on home for awhile. Give me a call when you're ready to go back up to see Avery or just send Tommy on down to the trailer. Morris, I'd like to say it was nice seeing ya but it never is."

Cara started out the door and then remembered her keys. She went back into the kitchen to look for them and was greeted by the terse voice of her overwrought daughter.

"Mama, what the hell are you looking for? I thought you were leaving."

"Well, Sandy, driving home is hard without keys. I put the son of a bitches on this god damned counter and now they're gone!"

"I have them, Mama. Buster brought me home this morning. He asked for the keys to the trailer. He was tired and didn't feel much like driving. I wasn't goin' to tell you, in case he decided to be gone before you got home. Here and thanks for staying with Tommy."

Tommy heard his grandma leave and walked down the hall to stand just out of sight behind the living room door. He heard his mama crying but could barely hear what she was saying. He moved forward enough to barely see beyond the door jam. He wondered if his daddy had done something wrong. He went back to his room wishing there was no such thing as grown-up talk.

Morris took another sip of coffee and continued reconstructing what he thought happened at Liars and afterward. He said he was certain of who had beaten Robert and Avery but there were complications.

Sandy had heard enough. She held her right hand in front of Morris' face to halt his words. She felt a rage inside that made her want to walk out the door, shotgun in hand, ammunition at her side and a list of names she was sure she already knew.

"Shut up, Morris. Just shut the fuck up! When did you become a cow? There's nothing but bullshit coming from your mouth. You must like the taste because your damn good at pumpin' it out!"

Morris was shocked by Sandy's outburst. He moved a little closer to the end of the couch in case she decided to strike out. He knew she was exhausted but she had no call to treat him like he was the enemy.

"Sandy, I ain't against you on this. It's Avery that said he wouldn't identify the guys that did this to him. Our only hope will be Robert and he is so whacked on drugs he don't even know what's happened. It hasn't sunk in yet. Shit, the poor bastard had a two foot club stuck up his ass, a broken back, and head injury. I wasn't telling you we aren't going after the JCCL, just that we have to build a case."

Sandy looked straight into Morris' eyes and was as honest as she dared to be.

"Yeah, right, Morris. I'm sure your fuckin' JCCL buddies on the force will be sure to make a thorough investigation. Thanks for nothing. I'm tired and need to get some rest."

Morris felt more than just Sandy's door close on him. He knew there would be a lot of doors closed to him on this case. He hated to admit it but much of what Sandy said was true. For the first time in his life, Morris was ashamed of being a police officer.

Tommy came into the living room after the policeman left. He tried to crawl onto his mama's lap to ask her why the officer needed to talk to her but she pushed him away. He started to speak and she smacked him in the mouth. Her words were like dull knives that tore at him rather than cut him.

"God damn it, Tommy, I got enough to worry about right now without you climbing all over me! Go get ready to go to your grandma's! I ain't goin' to tell you again!"

CHAPTER THIRTY

Cara tested the door and it was unlocked. She'd parked her Bonneville at a friend's house down the block. If Buster was there, she didn't want him to hear her pull up. She wanted to sneak in on him and then surprise him. She opened the door as quietly as she could and peeked in to see if Buster was in the living room. She turned to look toward the kitchen and saw no sign of him. Feeling a little disappointed, she walked in and put her purse down on what was once his recliner. She checked the rooms in the rest of the trailer and there was no sign of Buster anywhere.

Cara sat on the toilet reading an old copy of The Enquirer. She'd not been able to take a decent shit in days and felt more than ever she was full of it. That was one thing she could say about whiskey, it kept more than her tongue loose. She was in the middle of a story about Elizabeth Taylor when she heard the front door open and pounding noises. She grabbed toilet paper and tried to wipe in a hurry when she heard what sounded like things being knocked over. Cara thought how perfect it was that she would be caught with her pants down when a robber slash rapist came calling!

She looked around the bathroom for a weapon and took the huge can of hair spray off the shelf and carefully opened the bathroom door. She listened to see what part of the house the noise came from and realized the person was in her bedroom. She walked down the hall, her finger perched on the nozzle and the hole away from her own eyes. She went into the room, saw that the closet door was pulled opened and heard someone rifling through things. She decided to wait until they came out and then hit them full force.

She saw the man's butt first as he bent over to pick something up off the closet floor. He backed out of the closet, turned and she pushed on the nozzle. She was surprised to see Buster looking at her like she was insane. He picked up another shirt from the bed and said,

"Hey there, darlin, that can is empty. You really shouldn't use so much in your hair if you plan to use it as a weapon."

Cara laughed and took the shirt he had in his hand and put it back on the bed. She put her arms around Buster's neck and said,

"I think it should be clear to you now that I am the most dangerous weapon in this house and the only thief, too."

She wanted to ask if he was home for good or just stopping over until he found another place to stay. She figured after almost spraying him with hair spray she'd better wait on that question. He hung up the last of his clothes, shut the closet door and asked if they could talk.

"Hell yes, we can talk. I been doin' that since I was about a year old and ain't never stopped!"

The look on his face was serious when he interrupted her.

"Cara, you know damn well what I mean. We got shit to talk about, important shit. Hell, you didn't even recognize my ass! I don't trust you in a bedroom so let's go to the living room."

Cara walked down the hall like a child who was being forced into a nine by twelve room to be tortured by lecture. She imagined a stark scene where instead of water torture, people picked word and truth torture. She could only imagine what Buster was going to say and she knew he'd be right. As they passed the bathroom she felt a need for humor.

"Hey Buster? If you really want to know a room you can't trust me in it's this one. I go in full of piss and vinegar and come out full of shit!"

He didn't laugh and she didn't stoop to her normal tickle of his ample waist to make him. She'd felt his determination to get things out in the open and knew she was in for some honesty. Damn, she thought to herself, if people in her life kept it up she wouldn't have any delusions or lies to hang onto at all about herself.

He sat in his recliner and she sat down on the couch. She wanted a drink but picked up a cigarette instead. She looked over at Buster and noticed he looked different. It suddenly dawned on her why she hadn't recognized his ass. His butt was wearing Levis and not overalls. That young thing he'd been with must have drug his buns and him down to the mall to buy new clothes. She was starting to get angry when she heard him say,

"Cara, the night they took you to the hospital, I left because I felt guilt and fear. I realized I was partly responsible for you bein' put away like you were. I ain't the one that started you drinkin' but I sure in the hell never stopped you. I laughed at you for making a fool of yourself and played your game when you'd go off with other men. I told myself it wasn't my business. Cara, the night they took you to East Texas General, I knew I couldn't watch you die anymore. I guess in a way that's why I headed straight for youth, life and Candy."

The mention of Candy's name made Cara bristle. She felt the hairs on the back of her neck stand up like they do on a growling dog. She had to bite her tongue not to come out with some vengeful joke about candy that looked as sweet as sugar but tasted like ungutted fish lying out in the hot Texas sun. She had a lot to say about Candy but it would wait for another time.

Buster looked at Cara's face and knew exactly what she was thinking. He could tell by the downward turn of the corners of her mouth and the evil spark that danced in her eyes that her brain was chomping on Candy. He smiled in spite of his resolve not to and her response was immediate.

"Having a sweet tooth attack? Got a sudden hankering for a Baby Ruth, a spice drop, or maybe a Buttered Finger?"

Buster couldn't hold it in any longer. His laughter filled the room and he rose from the chair to go sit beside the hot tempered Cara. He knew sitting near her was risking being hit but he'd really missed the feisty old broad. He put his left arm around her shoulders and decided to ease her mind about the Candy thing once and for all.

"Darlin', Candy is for kids and not an old fart like me. I need someone that's old enough to know who Bob Wills is and yet young enough to bob at my will!"

It was Cara that couldn't contain her laughter this time. She collapsed into Buster's lap a helpless heap of laughter. When she raised her face to look up at him, he truly saw the potential for beauty there. Her eyes sparkled with clarity, her hair fell in her face in almost childlike fashion and her lips looked soft in a smile. He longed to kiss her at that moment but knew the air wasn't clear enough between them yet. He had more to say. He lifted her head in his hands and with gentle command said,

"Cara, here's the deal. I want you to get help. I want you to start going to A.A. meetings and no more lies, Liars or lays outside this house. I thought it didn't matter to me what you did but it does. I thought I didn't care, but I do."

The silence in the room made Buster feel uncomfortable. He wondered if his demands were too many too soon. He knew there was no other way he would stay, but was afraid Cara wouldn't think him worth the sacrifice. He could see her thoughts dart back and forth in her head. Her eyes moved as if she was watching a tennis match. The ball was in her court and he sat waiting for her return volley. Her mouth would open as if to speak and then the wrinkles in her forehead would deepen as she pondered what he had said. He finally heard the little grunt that preceded words that were hard for her to say.

"Buster, the night they took me to the hospital, something happened inside me. I cracked or something. I ain't felt the same since. You know how when you go lookin' for something and then you find it? Ya know how it makes you feel relief inside? Well, that night something found me that I wasn't lookin' for and it weren't no relief. The truth found me, Buster, and it was like a bolt of lightning coming straight from God."

Cara drew her legs in and crossed them with her skinny knees jutting out as if to add emphasis to what she was saying. She faced Buster squarely as she continued.

I ain't going to be nothin' but Cara 'till the day I die, but I been thinkin' lately I ain't even sure who that is exactly. I been living in a whiskey bottle in more ways than one, Buster. Ya see, I'd fill up with Jack Daniels and then feel like the empty bottle. I had to go out and find something to fill the hole left in me by Jack. Sex is different for a woman, Buster. When your heart don't feel like your own, it's a wonderful thing to have something else come inside ya to make it beat so ya know it's there! It weren't the men, Buster, it was the feeling they brung me. Merry Christmas, Buster, you got a deal. I'm tired of the loneliness Jack brings me."

Buster sat looking at the woman he'd lived with for the past year and was struck by how little he'd known about her. For the first time in years, he felt his heart open up and engulf the beauty of a moment. He knew the road would be one with more pot holes than he cared to navigate but he felt a beginning.

He kissed Cara long and deep. He loved the feel of the familiar pressure rather than the urgent pressure he'd felt with Candy. Cara was the rug of warmth with worn spots, while Candy had the feel of wire and tight knit mesh. He much preferred the feel of Cara at his age. She looked up at him and asked,

"Is it safe to be in the bedroom now? Tommy'll be knocking at the door here any minute!"

They both knew as they walked down the hall that they had just put fresh sheets on their bed.

Tommy was mad at his mama. He sat in his room with his toy soldiers and killed everything in sight that wasn't dressed in green. He picked up a figure with a flame thrower melted into his hands and said,

"I am a god damned part of this war, Colonel, and I fully expect to be briefed on what's going on! I don't mind puttin' my ass out there on the line but I sure want to know whether it's worth it!"

He'd heard the words in some movie he'd watched one night with his daddy. He wondered where his daddy was and how come no one told him anything. He wondered why adults thought kids didn't have brains. He had brains. He heard his mind tell him things all the time. It told him something was bad wrong right now and he felt alone and scared. It told him when he grew up and had kids he would like them and tell them things. It told him not to hate his mama but just stay mad at her for a little while.

Tommy put the plastic figure among the ranks to see how he compared. He looked at each figure, as if to study their makeup. There was the grunt who was always cowering down hoping someone besides him got shot. That was his dad. Then there was the guy with the grimace on his face who ran up the hill firing away the whole time at nothing. That was his mom. The ones that really had the control were always in the back, looking like they wondered how they got there. That was his grandma to a tee! All he wanted to be was the radio operator so that someone, anyone would communicate with him! He wanted to scream as he put the toys back into the drawer.

"I'm Tommy everybody!!! I'm just like you, 'cept I ain't had time to grow as much! I want to know where my daddy is!"

Tommy heard his mama calling him. He yelled back that he would be there in a minute and put the rest of his soldiers away. His mama was standing in the living room with her purse on her shoulder and the phone in her right hand.

"Mama, I'm sendin' Tommy down right now. He'll be on his bike, so look for him. I gotta get to the hospital to talk to Avery. I'll probably be back in a few hours unless they put Avery in a room where I can spend more than fifteen minutes with him."

Tommy stomped his foot while tugging on his mama's shirt.

"Mama, I can't ride my bike to grandma's, the tires is flat!"

He hated the look in his mama's eyes when she glared at him as if he were nothing but a nuisance. He wished he had a flame thrower melted into his hands. Boy, would he show her!

"Get in the god damned truck, Tommy! I'll go out of my way

to make sure you get to Mama's! God forbid you use those skinny legs of yours to get yourself the fuck to mama's trailer!"

Tommy didn't understand what he'd done that was so bad, but then, he seldom did. He crouched down in his seat and felt smaller than he was. He wished he was a cartoon character so he could be erased and then put back in another time with different people. He was tired of being. His mama, daddy, grandma, and teacher all said he was being bad, being loud, being rude, being wrong, being awful. He disagreed with them all. He wasn't being anything but what he was, Tommy Anderson. He was the soldier that joined the army to be all that he could be but no one was letting him! He wished someone had told him they lie on television!

Sandy literally pounced into the front seat. She was pissed off and didn't care who got in the way of her stream! She couldn't wait to get to the hospital to ask Avery just what he thought he was doing by not pressing charges! He would know real pain when he felt the sting of her tongue like a cowboy's bullwhip!

Tommy had never seen his mama drive the truck eighty miles an hour to get someplace that was only five miles away. He saw all the same farm houses go by but they looked to him like a video put on fast forward.

Sandy pulled into the yard of her mama's trailer and barely waited until Tommy got out to throw the truck into reverse. She screamed out the window, as she started the truck forward.

"Tell your grandma I'll pick you up later."

Tommy shook his head as he watched the gravel and dust of the road spurt out from the truck tires. He wondered what later meant, later that afternoon or later that same year?

He walked towards the screen door and tilted his head in the same direction it hung. He wondered whose house he'd be walking into now. Sometimes it wasn't so much the place he was, but the people he was with, that made him feel to home. With his family, he was never quite sure who would be who at any given moment and it made him want to live in a mirror. He always knew just who it was looking back at him then.

Tommy pushed back the screen door since it really wouldn't open. He knocked on the door and waited to see if someone he knew answered. He heard laughter and then a happy voice say,

"Come on in, Tommy!"

He was glad to hear a voice that wasn't yelling but he never depended on anything. In his family the people didn't sometimes feel like a nut and at other times not. They either were nuts or becoming nuts! He kept waiting for the sweet chocolate covering but all he got was people going nuts, scratching nuts or cracking other nuts.

He put his book bag on the floor beside the couch and sat down with a sigh. He looked at his grandma in the kitchen putting together lunch and then heard the toilet flush. He turned his head toward the hall and saw Buster walking toward the bathroom naked. He giggled because Buster's butt looked like it was broken and one half moved separate from the other. He got up and went to stand next to his grandma. He wanted to know about his daddy and thought he'd chance asking her.

"Grandma, where's my daddy? How come mama's bein' so mean?"

Cara stopped putting the mayonnaise on the bread and looked at her grandson. She put the knife down and took Tommy into the living room. She sat on the couch with him and tried to think of what to say.

"Has your mama told you anything about your daddy?"

She watched Tommy's head as it jerked back and forth in exaggerated negativity. She could hear the anger rattling around in his mind. Cara knew Sandy would be pissed but the boy had a right to know that his daddy was in the hospital.

"Tommy, your daddy and Robert had themselves a little trouble last night. Some mean guys beat them up pretty bad and they had to go to the hospital. They're gonna be okay but they have to stay there awhile."

She searched his face to see worry but all she saw was anger. His blonde eyebrows arched with defiance and his eyes sparked with a killer's twinkle. Cara felt true wonder at the words that came from his mouth.

"I guess mama didn't tell me cause she knew I would go find those men and ask them why they'd do such a thing! Don't people know nothin', Grandma? Those bad men didn't just beat up Daddy and Robert, they beat up our whole family! Mama's so mad and upset, she acts like I done something wrong and that made me mad at her! She was bein' so mean before we came over here, I wished I had a bazooka in my hands like my army men and could make her go away. When she comes home I'll 'pologize and give her a hug."

Cara looked at her grandson and really saw him from the inside out. There was something different in Tommy. He wasn't like them. She wondered if he was different because Sandy and Avery really loved each other. She wondered if the foundation upon which a shack is built is more important than the material the walls are made from. She felt jealous of the little eight year old sitting on her couch. He was far wiser than she and had a better grasp of reality, to boot. She patted him on the knee and suggested they eat a sandwich and watch cartoons.

Buster walked into the living room to see Cara and Tommy sitting together laughing at the antics of the Animaniacs and felt a closeness to them both. He and Cara had taken a shower together after a lusty romp in the sheets and she'd talked about what had happened to Avery and Robert. He couldn't agree with Robert's lifestyle but he couldn't hate him for it, either. He was proud of Cara for being there for her daughter. He liked the woman without the whiskey, even though he had never realized he loved the woman with it.

Sandy went straight to ICU and the charge nurse said they would be transferring Avery to a room within the hour. The swelling in his brain had stopped and the doctor was confident that the shunt was doing its job. She told Sandy she could stay with him right up until the time they moved him.

Sandy felt the anger come from a place so deep she thought it would take surgery to remove it. The sound of the machines made her wish *she* had a little life support. Avery looked worse than he had before she left the hospital earlier. The bruising made him look purple and misshapen. She couldn't believe that the bandaged part of his head probably held even deeper bruising. Some of her anger dissipated as he tried to smile at her. When she saw him wince as she brushed a kiss against his cheek, it was quickly restored.

"Avery, Morris tells me you won't give him a statement about who done this to you and Robert. I'm thinking you have brain damage from the blow to your head. He knows you know, Avery. Hell, he fuckin' knows exactly who did it but he needs you to say it. This is a god damned small town and Liars ain't exactly the Astrodome when it comes to crowds."

She wanted to understand but she was blinded by a long held hatred. Her father had been a sympathizer with the JCCL, not a member in standing but one in heart. She remembered how he hated being poor because it meant he lived closer to the wrong side of the tracks than God intended. The worst beating she'd ever gotten was a time he'd come home early and saw her playing in a neighbor's yard with a group of black kids. He told her if she wanted to play with dirty apes she should get a job at the zoo. She was only seven but reared against him in defiance and said:

"Playin' with apes is a damn sight better than playin' in the sewer with your shit!"

All she remembered after was the look on his face as he picked her up and threw her against the wall. Twelve stitches and three weeks later she turned eight and he proved who really had the control. She was jolted from her thoughts by Avery's hoarse whisper.

"Sandy, you know these people. I ain't gonna start shit with them. I'm gonna be okay and the nurse told me today Robert's gonna be fine too. It'll be okay. We don't need to make those fuckers mad!"

Sandy looked at Avery's face and saw fear. It was the kind of fear that freezes a rabbit in the headlights of an oncoming car. The rabbit knows it can't win against the car and just stands in the road to be splattered all over the blacktop. It was a look she'd never seen in Avery before.

"You're scared of the chicken bastards! You're goin' to let them beat the shit out of you and get away with it!"

His anger was swift and unexpected.

"Sandy! One of them was a guy I work with! Not one of the ones who beat me up but he sure in the fuck was behind it. I'm HIV the fuck positive and was out drinkin' with a known gay guy. Why don't you just drive your fuckin' ass back home, pick up Tommy and burn the fuckin' trailer down with the two of you in it!"

"Oh Avery, you're being ridiculous! Them people are not above the law and besides people know who they are."

Avery tried to sit up but couldn't. He was pissed at Sandy. She didn't know shit about the JCCL. His struggle to get up set off the heart monitor alarm. A nurse came running in, took one look at Avery's red agitated face and asked Sandy to leave. Before she could get out of the room, a young intern was through the door and checking Avery's heart beat.

Sandy thought they were all insane. She wasn't the cause of his rapid heart beat. The bastards who tried to beat the life out of him were the monsters sitting on his chest! She walked down to the cafeteria to think and cool off.

She let the ice dispenser fill her cup until it ran over. She knew the heat of the tea would melt away most of it anyway. Taking the cup to the cashier, she saw Virginia Copeland wandering around looking for a table. Sandy was glad to see a friendly face. They found a table together and both started to speak at the same time.

Sandy was determined to speak first. She didn't feel like talking about Avery at the moment and had already heard Virginia's question. She wanted to know about Tyler anyway.

"How's he doin', Virginia? Did the doctor's find a donor?"

She could tell by Virginia's face they hadn't been successful yet. Sandy felt a sadness for this woman she couldn't explain. She remembered how she had treated Tommy before coming to see Avery and felt a sadness for herself, too. She listened as Virginia drew in a sharp breath and then spoke.

"No, not yet. We called my brother in Denver five days ago and he's flying in tonight to be tested. He is in the Air Force and has been stationed in Denver for the last three years. They are giving him a special leave to do this. He's a career man, you know, one of those lifers. I hadn't spoken to him in six years when I called him last week. We had a disagreement when my father died and I disowned him. Funny how little all that matters to me now."

Sandy watched as huge tears poured from Virginia's eyes. She thought they must have been the biggest tears she'd ever seen. Sandy felt helpless to do anything but get up and put her ample arms around the tiny shoulders of this grief stricken stranger. She felt only slightly embarrassed that the shirt she had on was stained with the morning's jelly or that her body odor was reaching pungent levels. She figured comfort was comfort and sometimes that's all a body needed. Virginia patted her and then released herself from Sandy's grip.

"So how's your husband? Is he still in ICU?"

Sandy stirred the ice around in her glass with her straw. She didn't want her anger to show in her words when she answered.

"They're getting ready to move him into a room. He looks like shit but he didn't look all that good before he got here!"

She looked up to judge Virginia's reaction to her little joke and saw the laughter dance out of her eyes and fall onto the table like a piece of food blown out of a mouth with a sneeze. They both laughed so hard they had to hold their sides. Sandy was glad for the laughter. In a very strange way she felt connected to this woman.

They lived in opposite worlds but for now shared a space in the same one.

Neither of them were paying attention when the nurse came up. She was to Virginia's right and her face said everything.

"Mrs. Copeland, we need you to come back to Tyler's room right away."

Sandy looked in Virginia's eyes and saw a veil of protection cover the iris. Sandy actually witnessed a mother's heart preparing itself to be childless. She knew she wouldn't be seeing Virginia in the cafeteria anymore. No one had to say it to anyone. Tyler was dead. Virginia's reunion tonight with her brother would be one not to test the marrow of any bones but to test the marrow of their souls.

Sandy had to leave. She had to get up and find a place to be alone. She almost ran to the women's bathroom and hurriedly shut herself into the handicapped stall. She slumped against the wall and wailed for all the life that wasn't. The cold steel of the supports stabled her but were not giving and felt hard to her hands. They kept her from falling to the floor but felt too much like harsh reality. She longed for arms and the beating of another heart.

Her sobbing rang off the tiles and porcelain as if she were in a recording studio. The pitch of her grief left the confines of the bathroom and touched the corridors outside. She wanted the world to share the grief of a child lost to death and mourn the mother who died with him. Sandy gripped the steel rails and brought forth her plea.

"OH GOD! BRING TYLER BACK AND TAKE ME! YOU DAMNED ME LONG AGO AND NOW I DAMN YOU FOR WHAT YOU'VE DONE!"

It was one of the hospital volunteers who found Sandy in a heap on the bathroom floor. She'd noticed blood coming from under the stall and crawled under the door. She pulled the emergency chord and knew that help was only seconds away. She watched as they carried her out of the bathroom and felt a sadness she didn't quite understand.

Sandy awoke to the harsh light of an operating room. There were doctors and nurses all around and she honestly thought the hand of God had come down to do as she'd asked. One of the doctors came up so that she could see him. His words sounded muffled.

"Mrs. Anderson, I'm Dr. Sethler. Do you remember what happened?"

Sandy felt her lips moving but couldn't hear her own answer.

"Yes, poor Tyler died."

Dr. Sethler looked at one of the nurses and shrugged. He wasn't used to people naming their babies so early on in a pregnancy and Tyler seemed a strange name for such a tiny baby girl. He grasped Sandy's right hand,

"We're almost finished here. We gave you a local so you wouldn't have to stay in recovery for so long. We need to keep you here overnight, but we've arranged to put you in a room with your husband. It isn't standard practice, but with what the two of you have just been through we thought it best."

Sandy felt a tiredness in her bones and thought how sweet it was that they would let her get some rest in the hospital. She drifted off to sleep wondering just what it was the doctor was finishing up.

Avery got the news just after they'd transferred him into the room. He tried to turn his head toward the bed where Sandy would be lying but the thing on his head made it impossible. Hot tears streamed from his eyes and burned the stitches in his skull as they made their way to his pillow. It seemed as if the tears acted as acid from his heart and his incision was a passageway for them to burn anger into his mind. He was filled with more rage than he ever thought possible. They had killed his baby girl and he meant both his wife and his unborn daughter. He was going to bring the mother fuckers down. He wanted them dead! He didn't care what he had to do, he was declaring war!

CHAPTER THIRTY-ONE

Buster answered the phone so Cara and Tommy wouldn't be disturbed. He just loved watching the two of them sitting together watching such silliness and laughing with their hearts. He felt a chill go up his spine when the voice on the other end of the phone said it was East Texas General calling. He motioned for Cara and knew she saw the deep concern in his face.

"It's East Texas. They asked to talk to you."

She took the receiver from Buster but was almost afraid to hold it to her ear. She knew it wasn't about Avery because it would have been Sandy calling, not some hospital personnel. She said hello but kept her eyes on Tommy the whole time she spoke. The conversation was short and as she hung up the receiver she bent low to the counter and let out gasping words . . .

"Oh dear God, my poor baby girl!"

It was Tommy's voice she heard first.

"You're silly, Grandma. My mama ain't no baby anymore, she's gonna have one! Don't you know nothin'?"

Buster told Tommy to go outside and check the mail and then to go to the shed to get food for old Blue. Tommy started to object because cartoons weren't over but thought better of it. Buster was a big man and he didn't really know him all that well. Once Tommy was outside, Buster went to Cara and put his arms around her. With her head against the warmth of his chest she managed to tell him the news.

"Sandy lost the baby, Buster. Some woman found her in a heap in one of the bathrooms in the hospital. I need a god damned drink. Oh God, this is going to kill her. That baby was the hope she was holdin' on to."

As if on a mission, Cara freed herself from Buster's grip and headed toward the cabinet. She took down the bottle of JD and a glass. Feeling Buster's eyes on her, she stepped back from the counter and tried to light a cigarette with fingers too shaky to manipulate the lighter. She felt Buster's hands around hers and then felt the lighter being taken from her grasp. He lit the cigarette held in her trembling lips. He poured a generous amount of JD in a glass and held it out for her. His only words hit Cara like nothing before.

"This might help you, Cara, but is it going to help Sandy?"

Cara stared at the glass. The saliva in her mouth curled around her tongue as if to wet her taste buds for the feel of that first sip. Her mind was yelling at her to pick up the glass and drink in the wonderful elixir of the land of forget but her heart kept beating out pictures of Sandy lying in a hospital bed. It was Tommy's voice that jolted her from her battle.

"Old Blue growled at me, Grandma. Alls I did was try to move his head so's I could fill his bowl. I guess sometimes even dogs do things they don't really mean. Old Blue 'pologized to me by licking my hand. I need to 'pologize to Mama."

Cara hugged Tommy as if through him she could touch Sandy.

"I do too, Tommy. I do to!"

Buster poured the JD back into the bottle and handed Cara her car keys. He kissed her gently on the lips and said,

"Bring back a pizza for dinner and while you're out running errands, pick this boy up something special."

He walked Cara to the door, whispering about what to bring Tommy and told her to give him a call from the hospital as soon as she could. Words seemed to be tumbling out of his mouth because his next sentence stunned even him.

"I love you, Cara."

Avery heard a commotion out in the hall and then heard the door to his room being opened. It irritated him no end that they had put this contraption on his head so he couldn't move it. He didn't care that his brain could swell if his head was moved. He wanted to look at Sandy as she was wheeled in. He wanted to touch her. He needed to take his fingers and trace along the place that had held their little girl. The guilt he felt was overwhelming. He had been so angry when he'd found out about the pregnancy. He'd seen the baby as just another obstacle placed in his way to make his life suck.

He wished he could take it all back. He wished he could go back and change it all.

He stuck his arm out as they moved the Gurney between the beds to transfer Sandy. He felt her hand encircle his and squeeze it tight. His body quaked with sorrow and his pillow was soaked from tears. He motioned for the nurse and asked that she call Morris Foley. He was ready to talk.

Cara pushed the elevator button again. She'd nearly run three red lights on her way and never once used a signal to maneuver the Pontiac in the traffic. She hated how when something was important time seemed to throw road blocks at every turn. She let her emotions get the best of her.

"God damned piece of shit elevators!"

A woman standing at the door waiting with her young daughter looked at Cara and said,

"God hears you and will make his place in hell for you."

Cara knew better than to open her mouth but it was as if she had no control.

"The fuck you say? Guess what lady? God does hear me. He and I made a pact a long time ago. He agreed to make my life shit and my heaven an endless supply of toilet paper!"

The woman covered her daughter's ears and walked away. What a strange gesture she thought, cover her ears and cover her brain. Cara wondered how much rejoicing the woman would do if the person she'd come to see was dead. It never made any sense to her that religious people grieved. If they lived lives to get to heaven then why did death make them sad? The elevator doors opened and Cara pushed the second floor button.

She walked down the hall looking at room numbers. She finally found room 234 and stood outside the door for a moment. She took as much air into her lungs as she could and pushed the door opened.

"Hey, someone told me half my family mistook this for the Hilton!"

She stopped just inside the door. Avery's face looked like a balloon that couldn't decide what color it wanted to be. Sandy lay in the far bed so lifeless she looked like she was a practicing to be a CPR dummy. Cara's breath caught in an audible squeak. She was trying desperately to squeeze back the tears. She didn't want to disturb Sandy, so she stepped around Avery's bed to just look at her. She turned with huge tears in her eyes and looked at Avery. She saw that his tears matched hers.

Cara carefully engulfed him in a hug. In the eight years that Sandy and he had been together, she never once remembered touching him. Oh, she had done the Texas Two Step with him on the dance floor of Liars and slapped him on the back when he'd won at their drinking contests, but she'd never touched him. She was starting to realize all the life she'd missed because she'd been married to JD for so long. She nestled against Avery's huge chest and let the tears choke her. She cried for Sandy, her dead granddaughter, Tommy, Avery and herself. She cried for Sandy's father, who'd been so wrong to hurt his daughter instead of loving her. It dawned on Cara that she was no different; he'd just kept it in the family. She'd been just as confused and guilty of heaping pain on her daughter.

She raised her head when she heard Sandy moan. Cara went to her and took her Sandy's left hand in hers. She said words that sounded so foreign, and to anyone who knew her, fake.

"Mama's here, sweet girl. I'm right here."

She couldn't make sense of what Sandy was saying. She kept muttering that Tyler was dead. Cara turned to look at Avery but he'd drifted off. She couldn't imagine why Sandy had named the baby Tyler. It seemed an off the wall name but then to have two children, one named Thomas and the other Tyler seemed kinda nice.

A nurse came into the room and Cara asked a question of her. She whispered it to her so that neither of the broken people that lay between her could hear.

"Do babies that die have birth certificates?"

The nurse told her birth certificates were only issued for live births but death certificates were always issued. Cara asked if it would be possible to see it. The nurse told her she would contact Dr. Sethler and have him come talk to her.

It was not five minutes later that Dr. Sethler walked in. He held his index finger up to his mouth and motioned for Cara to come outside in the hall. As soon as Cara closed the door behind her, he extended his right hand and introduced himself.

"I'm Dr. Sethler. I delivered your daughter's baby and took care of her. Janet told me you wanted to see the death certificate. She was partially mistaken. We issue death certificates for potentially viable babies born who die. Your daughter's child didn't really fall into that category but when I heard her say the child's name, I bent the rules a little. I thought it could be something for her to hang on to. You know, to make the baby's death mean something."

Cara couldn't stop the tears and found it difficult to bring her voice up through them.

"May I see it, doctor?"

He opened the metal casing that held Sandy's file and pulled out the sheet. He handed it to Cara.

"This isn't an official document. I was going to give it to your daughter but maybe you can do that."

Cara looked at him and tried to understand the matter of fact attitude he had. She didn't understand anyone or anything. He turned to go and she thanked him and added,

"It's official, doc. My granddaughter, Tyler, is officially dead."

It don't matter if the state didn't recognize her as a person, her family did."

Cara had to go find a phone. She needed to call Buster and tell him she would be there awhile. She longed to have the warmth of his voice wrap around her. She stared at her reflection in the silver casing of the pay phone and wondered why she'd been spared? She'd ignored life most of the time and when she had noticed it, she mooned it and raised her middle finger to it. She wondered if that might not be the secret, defy the living of life and it hangs on like the skin a person is born into.

She was surprised to hear Tommy's voice.

"Tommy, this is Grandma. Where's Buster?"

"He's takin' a poop, Grandma. Did you find me something, Grandma? I sure can't wait for that pizza!"

Cara was torn between staying with Avery and Sandy or going home to Tommy. Everyone had such ease ignoring him and that had to stop before it was too late. Hearing his voice made it easy.

"Tell Buster I'll be home in forty-five minutes. Hey, Tommy, what do you like on your pizza?"

"Pepper's roni, Grandma. I'll tell him. Oh, Grandma? Where is the freshener? Buster's poop stinks like my daddy's!"

Cara laughed and told Tommy they kept freshener in the bathroom but if he needed some outside the bathroom then he could look under the kitchen sink. She figured the best thing she could do for both Sandy and Avery was to make Tommy as comfortable as possible. She wouldn't tell him about Sandy and the baby. She would just tell him his mama had to stay with his daddy.

Cara went to the nurses station and asked if she could leave a note for her kids. Her words were simple.

> Avery and Sandy,
> I went home to be with Tommy. You two have each other and he only has me. I think you two are the luckier ones.
> Love, Cara

She handed the note to the nurse and walked toward the elevators. The doors opened immediately and standing to the right side was the bible thumping woman and her daughter. The woman had been crying. Cara didn't know what possessed her but she put her arms around the woman and whispered in her ear.

"You need to start your life now. Waiting for God to give you directions takes too long. He ain't a director and life ain't no play! Don't cover your daughter's ears and don't cover your own. Listen to life! It's yelling at you!"

Cara walked out of the hospital a person on a mission. She would not only get a pizza and gift for Tommy but would rent a Disney movie she'd always wanted to see. Tonight would not be about death and missed chances but life and chances yet realized.

Cara stopped by Country Inn Pizza and ordered a large pepperoni with double cheese. She'd already gone by Walmart and the video store so the pizza would still be warm when she got home. She had a new pair of pajamas for Tommy, a set of construction site trucks, a pinwheel and some flash cards for math and spelling. She'd made a decision that Tommy was the only hope for the family and couldn't grow up to be as stupid as his kin. There isn't always smarts in an active brain, she thought but she knew it was better to be touched in the mind rather than tetched in the head.

She pulled into the yard and took the pizza out of the car deciding she'd let Tommy get the packages. She walked into the trailer to see Buster wearing an apron, Tommy putting the finishing touches on a neatly laid table and the cat looking at both of them as if the world had gone mad.

"Excuse me, I must have the wrong trailer. I'm the third pig and done been lookin' for my two brothers for near half an hour! This ain't my sty so I guess I best give this pizza to old Blue!"

Tommy squealed and Buster just shook his head at her silliness. She put the pizza on the counter and looked in the refrigerator to see if they'd left her a cold Coke. She hadn't even managed to back her butt out of the refrigerator door before Tommy was asking what she'd brought him. She popped the top on the can and told him to hurry on outside and get the packages out of the car. She took the opportunity to talk to Buster about Sandy and Avery.

"She don't even know what's happened yet. They got her so sedated she couldn't find her own ass and you know how sedated that is. It's just sad, Buster. The saddest thing I ever saw. She named the baby Tyler. Can you believe that? You ever hear of a body naming a baby five months before you even know if it's gonna have a face?"

Buster didn't know what to say and was glad when Tommy came running in all excited. He only pouted a little when his grandma told him he'd have to wait until after supper to get into the sacks. Cara was glad someone invented paper plates, plastic utensils and cardboard pizzas. She wanted time to spend with Tommy explaining why his mama wouldn't be home until tomorrow.

By eight o'clock, Tommy was yawning and turning into a grouch. Cara decided that she'd give him time to enjoy his new things before telling him about Sandy. It wasn't that she was going to tell him what happened, it was that she didn't want him asking a bunch of questions.

"Tommy, you need to find a corner for those trucks so I don't come in here in the morning and kill myself fallin' all over them. You're gonna sleep in the middle bedroom just like you do at home and tomorrow you gotta get up for school, so get to doin' what I asked."

Tommy looked up at her and words shot out of his mouth before he could stop them.

"You ain't the boss of me! Where's my mama?"

The minute the words left his mouth he wished he hadn't said them. His grandma had been nice to him and he didn't want to ruin it.

"Thomas Avery Anderson! I know you're tired but you got no

call to talk to me like that. You're mama has to stay at the hospital with your daddy! This is my god damned house and you are my god damned grandson and that's all that needs be said! Get your ass in that bedroom now!"

Tommy hung his head and started out of the room. He turned at the door leading to the hall and walked half way back into the living room.

"I'm sorry, Grandma. Mama says I get a sickness called the meanness. She says it grows in my heart and then spills out when I get full of shit. She says I 'herited it from you. Anyways, I'm sorry."

Buster looked like he was about to explode with laughter and Cara shot him a look that would stop a giant in his tracks. She told Tommy to go on to bed and that they'd talk about the meanness in the morning. Once she heard his bedroom door shut, she went to sit in Buster's lap. She felt bone weary and missed the numb feeling whiskey had always provided. She told Buster that she was almost ready for bed herself. He smiled and rubbed her slumping shoulders. She leaned against him and said,

"I'm gonna drive in to Houston tomorrow to go see Robert. He needs to know about Sandy. I want you to go pick up Sandy from the hospital if I ain't back when they release her and bring her here."

Buster nodded, placed his hand on her face and spoke in hushed tones.

"I'm proud of you Cara Covington. Proud to see ya bein' what I knew ya had inside ya. You're a fine figure of a woman when you let yourself."

Cara was surprised to wake up to the sound of Tommy rattling around in the kitchen. She drug herself to a sitting position and looked at the clock. She blinked and looked again because she swore she'd read six on the screen. She grabbed her robe and wondered what in the hell time the kid had to be at school if he got up so damned early. She went to pee and as was her practice sat without shutting the door. She was surprised to see Tommy peek around the door at her.

"Hey boy, didn't your mama teach you no manners? It ain't polite to watch someone take a piss!"

Tommy looked at her and smiled. She knew he had something to say.

"It ain't polite to pee with the door opened neither. I thought my cereal was making a funny noise 'till I heard you in here coughing!"

Cara couldn't help herself, she laughed and peed, peed and laughed. She shooed him out and tried to stop laughing long enough to stop the steady flow. She wiped, washed her hands and then took a brush to her hair. She went out into the hall and closed the door to her bedroom so Buster could sleep. They'd spent half the night talking and the other half communicating.

She came up behind Tommy who was perched on a bar stool shoving huge spoons of cereal into his mouth.

"Slow down, Tommy, you're gonna be like that old cat and cough up things your throat don't want. How come you didn't make my coffee? Hell, up at six, fixin' your own breakfast, I may just keep you here and teach ya how to be my slave!"

Tommy rolled his eyes and fluttered his long eye lashes. He thought his grandma was just plain silly.

"Grandma, I can't be your slave. I ain't dark enough. I saw this picture in a book and all them slaves were as dark as night. They had big old muscles and were real shiny lookin'!"

Cara tried to remember if she knew what a slave was when she was eight. She sniffed the coffee grounds as she spooned them and hoped the odor would be enough to open her eyes. She needed as much caffeine as her body could manage to make that drive into Houston.

CHAPTER THIRTY-TWO

Robert woke with a start. He felt the nurse remove the IV needle from his arm and tried to stop her. The few times the drip bag had run dry, glimpses of reality touched his memory and the terror in his heart showed on the monitors and made the nurses come running. He needed the morphine to help the memories become tolerable.

He knew he was in bad shape because the doctors and nurses always spoke in hushed tones around him. The morphine made their words sound like they were spoken in slow motion and then placed in an echo chamber. His head spun constantly, his back felt like someone had hung his spine outside his body and the pain in his abdomen radiated hot poker-like stabs into his lower back.

Robert remembered a name: Sponge. He wasn't sure if it was a name, really. For all he knew it could have been something the doctor had asked for while cleaning him up but it stuck in his mind nonetheless. He remembered that what had happened to him had happened to Avery too but where was Avery? He couldn't imagine Sandy not coming in to see him. One of the nurses said she'd tried to contact his mother but she was on vacation in the Bahamas.

Closing his eyes, Robert savored the last remnants of the morphine coursing through his veins. The nurse said a Dr. Cantu would be in to see him soon and that he should rest. He thought it ironic for her to take away the lovely, lifeless sleep of the drug and then tell him to rest.

His sleep was deep but only death could have kept the memories out of his head. In his dream there were trucks everywhere, behind, in front, on the side. They were like ants at a picnic and he felt like the food. In a fluttering image, he saw a baseball bat. It was a surreal, almost a computer graphic type action swing, as he saw the bat come toward him. He tried to duck but the forces of reality precluded him from doing so and he was jolted out of the dream.

Robert lay motionless, sweat dripping from his body. He felt an uncontrollable quivering from deep within his body but nothing on his outside moved. He remembered! He knew what had happened and why he was there. The tears and terror mixed and danced from his eyes. Oh God! Avery! What about Avery?

He could almost taste the wet grass and mud from the ditch he'd landed in. The cold feel of the water that remained after torrential rains felt like coolant running through his veins. He even remembered the stench from the dead raccoon that was on the upgrade not two feet away from his head. He remembered.

In a fit of rage, Robert tried to wrestle free from all the things that held him to the bed. He had to get up and find Avery and Sandy. He had to tell them that he remembered Sponge, Harry and Spike! The very name Spike made him want to drive one into the heart of the son of a bitch.

Dr. Cantu came into the room just when Robert was at his most agitated state. He came to the side of the bed and placed his hand over Robert's upper body. His words were plain and simple.

"Mr. Laningham, you have a spinal injury and a skull fracture. You are immobilized for a reason and your thrashing about is not helping anything. Calm down and talk to me.

Robert looked at the man standing above him. From his demeanor, Robert assumed the man was a shrink or psychologist. For some reason the thought of telling this man his deepest thoughts and feelings seemed hilarious. Robert felt like an actor in a badly cast movie.

Robert decided to play a little.

"Well, doc, it all started when I was a little boy. My mom made me wear Catholic school girl uniforms and she was Baptist.

She beat me once because I said the bible could be a monopoly board piece if they changed it from King James to St James."

Dr. Cantu listened patiently, never once smiling. Robert knew what his problem was. The doctor was guilty of buying into himself way too much. He'd seen the phenomenon a million times; people who took the paper their degrees were written on and used them as skin. They often forgot that paper was porous and was supposed to let real life seep in.

Dr. Cantu cleared his throat and pulled up a chair with ugly green upholstery clinging to its equally ugly aluminum casing. He had no pad in his hand and Robert wasn't perched on the proverbial couch but the scene played out as a classic anyway. The doctor's words were impatience masked with patient enunciation.

"Mr. Laningham, it is quite normal for a person who has experienced a trauma such as you did to mask feelings with humor. If you are not ready to discuss the events that lead up to your injuries, then I can respect the fact that you need more time."

Robert had to stifle the incredible need to laugh. He heard the doc's actual accent but in his head it played out as sounding like Colnel Klink from the television series "Hogan's Heroes." He had the words rattling around in his brain from the series. Ve have vays to make you talk! Robert steadied his brain and put his humor in check so that he could respond to Dr. Cantu.

"Dr. Cantu, I know why I'm here. I know hatred. I saw it in my mother's eyes and thought for years it was directed at me. I was fifteen when I realized it was self hate she felt. I have forgiven her and myself. I allowed her to hate me, doc. The problem was hers and not mine and so too are the problems of the men who did this to me.

"I don't need you to get through this doc; I need me. You see, I like me. I have always liked me. It's not my responsibility to make others like me. That's why I'll exact a revenge that they will not understand or see. The sweetest revenge is action, doc, not violent action but action of the heart. I have a plan."

The doctor shook his head in the condescending way people

do when they think someone is full of bull shit but don't have the balls or heart to tell them outright. His words dripped with patronizing honey as he rose to leave.

"You are a strong person, indeed, Robert. I'm glad this horrific ordeal hasn't destroyed your sense of self. I can't help but think perhaps you're masking a few things but that's normal at this stage. I'll come in and talk to you again when you aren't quite so ready to dismiss reality in favor of physical healing."

Robert watched Dr. Cantu as he rose to leave. He felt sure the doctor was not one Robert would have chosen for himself. The one thing Robert hated most about being in the hospital was other people controlling his life. They fed him whether he was hungry or not, gave him medication to sleep, controlled who he saw and spoke to and even regulated his bodily functions.

Dr. Cantu's last statement more than irritated Robert. Who the hell was he to presume anything about a patient he'd never even seen? How did he know what Robert was feeling about what happened to him?

Lying back on the pillow, Robert stared at the ceiling. He pictured Avery's face just before the baseball bat hit the window. It occurred to him that never before had someone unrelated to his lifestyle been threatened or hurt because of him. Avery was his only heterosexual male friend. Hell, Avery was his only real friend since Maurice left.

The thought of Maurice made him wonder if he'd been notified. Robert had him listed as next of kin. He'd put Maurice's Denver number in his address book just days before the trip to Liars. He wondered if Maurice cried at the thought of him lying in a hospital bed all broken. Robert smiled an evil smile. He hoped Maurice had broken down and wailed right in front of his new boyfriend!

Robert was enjoying a painless nap when there was a knock on his door. Nurses never knocked and the doctors knocked while opening the door so it had to be a non-hospital person.

"Come in."

"Hey, homo boy! I heard you flirted with a baseball bat and got more than its woody!"

Robert was glad to be called homo boy, glad for the off color humor and more glad to see Cara than he ever thought possible!

"Hey, white trash slut! Boy, is it good to see you!"

Cara approached the head of the bed so Robert could see her. She bent to him and gave him the lightest hug. He didn't know why exactly but Cara had a different feel to her. Her face had a softness lying between the wrinkles, and her breath smelled sweet even if her words weren't.

He couldn't help himself. A choking sob came from deep within his chest before he could stop it. He felt her arms around him and the shaking of her silent sobbing. He hadn't expected such incredible emotion to come to the surface but Cara was his connection to what had happened. She was the link to Avery, Sandy and home.

"Ah shit, homo boy, ya got me spreading my mascara around my eyes like a god damned raccoon. Now how the hell am I goin' to get one of these rich doctors to fall in love with me just usin' my charm?"

Robert laughed so hard it hurt him as much as the original beating. He was glad, really glad, to see Cara's wrinkled, whiskey-worn face looking down at him. He grasped her hand and asked about Avery.

"I'm so pissed at Sandy for not calling me! I've been half out of my mind worrying about Avery! Of course, I've been half out of mind thanks to morphine anyway!"

His laughter was short lived when he saw Cara's expression. He'd never seen her eyes so filled with sorrow or concern. He recognized the look of a caring mother, but had never seen it on Cara's face. He could tell she was hesitant to speak.

"Cara, is Avery dead? Did those bastards kill him?"

He watched her eyes as she tried to look everywhere in the room but at him. He squeezed her hand as if to somehow squeeze out the truth.

"No, Robert, Avery ain't dead. He's got a fuckin' tube in his head but he ain't dead. It's little Tyler. She died, Robert. Died before ever havin' a chance at life. Her death will kill Sandy for sure."

Robert was confused. He didn't know who Tyler was or what she had to do with Sandy. He started to ask but Cara just kept on talking.

"They found Sandy in one of the bathroom stalls in the hospital. The doc said something about the placenta breaking or bein' torn or something. No matter really, 'cause in the end the baby was dead the only way a life can be, permanently."

Tears rolled down Cara's face and tried to navigate around the wrinkles because gravity said they had to. Robert thought it was the saddest face he'd ever seen. For some reason he thought of those velvet clown faces with all the make up and loud clothes but with a sorrow in the eyes that belied all the gaiety. He understood what she meant but he had to be sure.

"Sandy lost the baby?"

Cara turned to him and nodded yes. She didn't trust herself to speak because emotion that wasn't thinned with whiskey scared the hell out of her. Seeing Robert so badly beaten and having seen Avery and Sandy lying in heaps of ruin was just too much for her. She took something out of her purse and handed it to Robert.

"Here, homo boy, read this before we start flooding the place."

Robert opened the card. It was a child's card with a picture of a baseball player holding a bat, only it had been altered. Instead of a regular uniform, the player was wearing a shirt with a confederate flag design. Between the player's legs was drawn a tiny penis with balls the size of gnats. He opened the card to see all the writing blacked out and different words scrawled in primitive handwriting. The words read:

Just wanted you to know that men with small dicks always carry big bats. I knew there was a reason I never seen you play baseball, homo boy! You've got bigger balls than the Bulls! Love Cara

Cara had an evil gleam in her eyes and Robert didn't even care that she was probably causing permanent injury to him by making him laugh. She moved in close to him again, since the threat of over-exposed emotion had been diffused.

Robert looked up into her face, a million questions darting through his mind. Cara knew he wanted answers but she also knew he wasn't ready to hear the truth. Just as Robert looked like he was going to speak, a nurse came through the door and said she had to prepare Robert for the removal of his back brace. She mumbled something about Robert having to start physical therapy and then told Cara she would have to leave.

Cara hugged Robert and told him she would be back in a few days. She asked if he thought they would let him out before Christmas and laughed at his answer.

"Yeah, I told them I had to be home for Christmas because Santa comes down my chimney and I hear he doesn't play baseball!"

Cara walked back toward the parking garage and felt old for the first time in her life. She'd seldom thought about being fifty and certainly never admitted to it but her legs suddenly felt like they'd been around half a century. She wasn't cut out for this nurturing stuff. She did better with tight jeans and just plain being tight.

At least with Robert there were moments of humor. She knew it would be a cold day in hell before Sandy's and Avery's hearts felt light enough to laugh again. Thinking about Sandy made her want to be home and she still had to fight the Houston traffic.

The city scared her. It was a place she didn't belong. She felt dwarfed by all the buildings, by the clothes the people wore, and by their attitudes when they looked her way. To them, she had country bumpkin written on her forehead. She'd seen people staring at her mouth to see if she was missing teeth. She always felt she needed to carry her birth certificate and Sandy's to prove she didn't marry her cousin or brother.

Cara was so relieved to get back on her side of town. It always amazed her that the city was twenty minutes away by car but another world away in her mind. It wasn't quite noon and she hoped Sandy had already been released and was at home with Buster. She wasn't in the mood for another hospital; she'd smelled enough Clorox and Lysol. She turned into the yard and saw that Buster's truck had been used since she left.

Buster came out of the house when he heard Cara's car. He wanted to warn her about Sandy. He'd never felt so helpless in his life. He'd tried to make her feel welcomed and even offered her lunch but she just sat on the couch crying or looking like she was about to cry.

He kissed Cara and said he would be out back working in the barn. Cara sighed and bunched up her shoulders as if readying to tackle a blocking dummy. She wished she'd spent less time at Liars and more time watching television so she'd know how to handle situations like the one she found herself in.

Sandy was sitting on the couch when Cara walked into the trailer. She set her purse on the counter and went to sit next to her daughter. Sandy's eyes looked like marbles that had been left out in the sun too long, all cloudy and smeared. It was her mouth that moved but her eyes that spoke.

"Hi, Mama. Buster told me you went to see Robert. How is he?"

Cara wondered if she should answer the direct question or skip to the meat of the tomato and make sauce out of things. She was good at sauce.

"He's gonna be okay. How about you, little girl? Darlin, I'm so sorry and if I could take it away I would but I can't, no one can. You need to concentrate on gettin' Avery back to health and there is Tommy to worry about. What a pistol that boy is!"

Her laughter was interrupted by Sandy's cold stare. Cara felt it penetrate her skin and burn through her veins. She tried to place her hand on Sandy's arm but hit only the place it would have been if Sandy had accepted the gesture.

"Mama, don't tell me to suck it up and go on with life. We ain't takin' about not havin' a date to the prom or my husband havin' an affair. We're talkin' about a livin', breathing, human being who lived not only inside my body but inside my heart! What the hell? How could you ever understand?"

Cara felt close to tears herself. She understood more than Sandy knew. There were things that she'd locked away so many years ago the memories had turned to dust in her heart, or so she'd thought. There had been demons and shames that J.D. had drowned for her. She was finding the more days she spent away from J.D., the more the memories floated to the top. She extended the bony fingers of her right hand to Sandy.

"Listen to me, little girl. I got somethin' to tell you ain't no one ever been told by me. This ain't easy, so just hush and let me talk. I must have been close to thirteen when it happened. Yeah, thirteen 'cause I remember six months before it happened I had my first period and Daddy done beat the hell out of me 'cause I screamed that he'd made me bleed all over again. I didn't understand what was happening to me. Anyways, like I said, a few months after that first one I quit havin' my cycle and I didn't think nothin' about it. Daddy had asked me about my periods on several occasions and asked me how come he didn't see no Kotex in the garbage. One night Daddy came in more drunk than usual and got real violent with me. I don't mean the regular beatings. I mean picking me up and throwing me across the room and shit, kickin' me in the stomach and stuff. It felt like he was never gonna stop. I was hunkering down in a corner and all of a sudden I felt something warm start seeping between my legs. I'll never forget the smile on Daddy's face, like he'd done what he set out to do or something. After I heard the front door slam I got up to go to the bathroom 'cause it felt like I was peeing my pants but had to poop at the same time. I was sittin' on the pot and suddenly a cramping hit me that felt like my insides were being ripped right out. I remember looking in the pot to see if some animal had crawled inside and was trying to kill me from the inside out. The baby weren't no more than about four months along but it looked close enough to one for me know what it was."

Cara had to stop for a moment. The trembling of her body made speech almost impossible. She was visiting a place she'd never dared go. She looked over at Sandy and saw that she was too stunned to do anything but wipe the tears from her face with the sleeve of her blouse. Taking a deep breath, Cara continued.

"None of my older brothers were around at the time. It was mostly the babies and me in the house and an old nigger maid my daddy hired to do the cookin' when mama took ill. Her name was Ella Mae and she had the only voice in that house that I actually loved to listen to. I cleaned myself up as much as I could and I went to the kitchen where Ella Mae was stirring milk gravy. I remember the smell of the biscuits in the oven as we sit here. Ella Mae got an old sheet, fished that baby out of the toilet and me and her went out back and buried it as if it were a dead dog. So I know your pain, darlin', I really do."

Sandy put her warmth around her mama for the first time since she was a little girl. They collapsed into a hug of support and emptied their hearts onto each other. Buster walked in to see the two embraced and sobbing, and walked back out the door. He wasn't good with overflowing emotions.

Cara straightened up and sat back on the couch as if life had been drained from her. She knew whiskey had filled that place in her for way too many years. She felt something had died inside and yet been reborn as freedom. It was Sandy who spoke first.

"Mama? It ain't just the pain of the baby. There's something you need to know and you can't be asking too many questions 'cause I don't got many answers."

Cara tried to imagine what else Sandy had hidden in her heart. She didn't think there could be space left for any secrets. As was her way, she thought she needed to lighten the air in the room.

"Should I go grab a roll of toilet paper before you get started? I don't think your sleeve can hold much more snot!"

Her little joke didn't get the response she'd hoped it would. She turned to Sandy and waited for her to speak.

"Mama, when I lost the baby, one of the tests they did on me was an HIV test."

She saw Cara's mouth open to speak and she put her hand into the air to stop her.

"No, you don't say anything until I say what I have to. I ain't got no energy, Mama, and Tommy'll be gettin' off that bus in a half hour."

Cara nodded and settled into the couch with her right side against the cushions.

"Just before all this shit happened with the beating and all, Avery had his yearly physical for work. They found something out that made a huge difference to him, Tommy and me. He tested positive for the HIV virus, Mama. It don't matter how he got it, just that he did."

Cara leapt off the couch. She couldn't believe what she'd just heard or Sandy's dismissal of it with such ease!

"The hell it don't matter! He brought death home to my daughter and grandson and it don't matter?"

Sandy's face reddened. Why had she thought the woman sitting next to her had changed? She should've known the world could take the whiskey out of Cara but never Cara out of herself! She was sorry she'd trusted the brief moment of closeness.

"Sit down, Mama, and stop yelling. We don't even know if me and Tommy have the virus and plus your stupidity is showing. HIV ain't AIDS and it ain't death, not right away, anyhow. Don't you open your yap about this to Tommy or Avery, either one! I'm sorry I even told your sorry ass!"

Cara knew Sandy saw her shock and fear as anger but she didn't care. She felt cheated in a way she couldn't begin to explain. The past few days of her life had been spent seeing things she'd been too drunk to notice. She'd just started knowing herself and her relationship to the world around her. She'd made her grandson laugh and then made him dinner. The world had been good and now there was the threat of it all being taken away from her.

They both heard the diesel engine of the bus at the same time and shot each other almost the exact same look. Silent expression said they would finish the conversation another time.

Tommy came bounding into the house, his book bag beating against his back and an enormous smile on his face. He practically flew to Sandy for a hug.

"Buster told me you was here, Mama! Man oh man, did I ever miss you! I been hopin' all day that you'd be home from seein' Daddy. I made ya somethin' real special in school."

He slung his back pack around and fished in the front pocket, bringing out a green piece of construction paper. It was folded and with great care he unfolded it and placed it on the coffee table in front of his mama and grandma.

In his picture, he was holding what looked like a doll but was obviously a baby. It showed him sitting on a couch with his mama on one side and his daddy on the other. The most amazing thing was that in the picture his parents were thin, smiling and a part of something that was much bigger than them. In the corner of the room he'd drawn a Christmas tree and his grandma and Buster were placing presents under it. He'd written everyone's name except for the baby's. He had an arrow pointing towards the child in his arms with the words *my baby* written at the end of the arrow.

Sandy felt her heart break all over again. She knew it was time to tell him about the little sister who came but couldn't stay. She wondered how to explain it without scaring him too much about death. She looked at her mama and Cara came through in buying her time to think.

"Hey, that's a beautiful picture, Tommy. I bet the artist is hungry for a snack and a Coke! Come on with grandma and see if Buster left any of those Oreo cookies in the jar."

Sandy got up from the couch and walked toward the bathroom. She turned around because she hadn't taken the maxi pads out the sack she'd brought home from the hospital. She was bleeding pretty heavily but the doctor had said she would. She went into the bathroom and took down her jeans. Sitting on the toilet, she felt some of the clots being passed as she peed. It seemed appropriate that chunks of her were landing in the toilet. She fully expected to see her heart land in the reddish-water. She attached the pad to her underwear, pulled up her jeans and flushed, thinking about the story her mama had told her. She knew a toilet would never look the same to her, but then, she felt nothing would ever look or feel the same.

Sandy went toward the kitchen where her mama and Tommy were engaged in a conversation about multiplication tables. She stroked Tommy's hair as she stood behind him and spoke to her mama.

"I'm feeling really tired, Mama. I'm going to go lay down for a time. If I'm still sleepin' when dinner's ready don't bother waking me, okay?"

Cara nodded and hoped Sandy did sleep through dinner because sleep was the only way her mind would turn off the pain. She watched Tommy as he finished the last Oreo cookie. He looked like he'd outlined his mouth in chocolate and his lips had dots of creme filling protruding like white moles. Even with his messy mouth, he was an attractive child. She noticed that he had her bone structure, slight and willowy. He'd be a real heart breaker as far as the girls were concerned. Suddenly projecting into the future made Cara sadder yet. She'd worried the boy had no future because what he was born into and now she worried he didn't because of what he'd been born out of. There was a softness in her voice when she spoke to him.

"You go on in the bathroom and wash your face and hands. I'll let you go help Buster in the barn until dinner if you promise that you'll not give me grief when I tell you to take your bath and do your homework."

Tommy stuck out his hand in stiff arm fashion and said,

"You got a deal, Grandma. Buster's got neat stuff in that old barn. I saw a rat family the other day. They were hidin' under some of that wood Buster uses to start his tire fires. Pretty cool, huh?"

Cara looked in on Sandy before going out to see what Buster and Tommy were up to. She watched as her daughter slept and was reminded of her youth. She stood at the door with loneliness as company. She imagined the horrors Sandy suffered from having a mother who had taken on whiskey as a lover. The nights that Henry had gone in to be with Sandy, she'd either been at some club, or out with some man and always too drunk to care. There was no forgiveness in her heart for that. There never would be.

Sandy woke to the feel of a small hand stroking the side of her face. She opened her right eye and saw Tommy's face looking back at her with the soft love only a child can show. She stretched and shuddered to shake off the effects of sleep. Tommy's voice was angelic when he spoke.

"Hey there, Mama. Guess what? I made Grandma save you the biggest piece of pie 'cause you looked like you needed somethin' sweet to make you feel better."

Sandy felt tears straining against her eyes and pushed them back. Her heart spoke to what Tommy had just said.

"I don't need pie when I got you! I'm real sorry about bein' so mean when I left out of here yesterday."

She searched Tommy's face for forgiveness and was awed by his look and his words.

"Mama, life's a funny thing sometimes. You know how sometimes I come home and I act like I'm mad at you? Well, mostly I'm mad at the kids who talk about my clothes and call me Trailer Trash Tommy. See, it ain't you that made me mad but seems like you're the one I scream at. I figure if I fight with the ones that done made me mad, then I'll be in trouble with everyone at school but if I fight with you then I'll just be in trouble with you and Daddy. Ya'll like me better, Mama, so the trouble don't seem as bad."

Sandy drew Tommy close to her and hugged him as if he was brand new to her. She knew by the look in his eyes that he was confused by the display but pleased. She had to tell him about the baby.

"Tommy, that sure was a beautiful picture you drew of our family. It's somethin' I'll keep forever. I know grandma told you I stayed in the hospital to be with Daddy but that was just part of the reason I had to stay. Tommy, the baby inside me, your little sister, got real sick."

Tommy looked at her with concern and patted her stomach. His question was innocent and sweet.

"My sister? Mama, did the doctor's give her medicine? Does she hate cough syrup as much as I do?"

Sandy placed a gentle kiss to his forehead and smiled at him. She was so glad to have his warmth next to her. It really was what she needed, a reason to live. She took a few deep breaths and continued.

"Sometimes cough medicine doesn't work on sickness, Tommy. Your little sister was bad sick. The doctors couldn't help her, sweetheart."

Sandy pulled Tommy into her, cupped his face in her hands and asked,

"Tommy, do you know what it means when a person dies?"

Tommy freed his head from Sandy's grasp. He sat back on the bed and pondered her question.

His answer sounded a little angry.

"Yeah, I know. It means someone was killt. Did someone kill our baby, Mama? Was it those bad men that hurt daddy? Are they going to hurt us too, Mama?"

Sandy stroked his hair and wished she was better at explaining things.

"No, Tommy, those men didn't hurt the baby. It's just that sometimes a baby has things that are wrong with it and it can't make it to the bein' born stage."

Tommy's eyebrows bunched together and he tilted his head.

"Do you miss the baby, Mama?"

"Yes, Tommy, very much. A baby is a very special thing to

have inside."

He bent towards Sandy's stomach and gently kissed it. He laid his head on her and rubbed his cheek against her shirt. She thought he might be crying so she asked him if he was okay.

"Yeah, Mama, I'm okay. I just wanted to see if I could kiss you and make you all better. I ain't allowed to get up in the cabinet to get any cough syrup for you."

Sandy hugged Tommy to her. She wondered why she had never seen how truly wonderful and caring he was. She had promised herself to be a better mother than Cara and had fallen into the same trap of neglect. She hoped it wasn't too late to be reborn as Tommy's mother.

Cara went looking for Tommy and heard voices coming from the room Sandy was in. She opened the door and started to yell at him for disturbing her but saw them hugging each other on the bed. She wasn't prepared for Tommy's words.

"Grandma, my little sister died. Did you know that?"

Cara looked at Sandy and then back at Tommy. She had no idea Sandy was planning on telling him so soon.

"Yes, Tommy, I knew about Tyler. Now don't you be keepin' your mama up and besides it's time for your bath."

Sandy stared at her mother. Why had she said she knew about Tyler? How on earth could she have known about Tyler? She waited for Tommy to leave the room and then patted the empty space next to her. Cara went to sit and thought Sandy just wanted comfort after the news she'd just told Tommy.

"Mama, who told you about Tyler?"

Cara was confused by her question. She knew the hospital had called right after it happened. She wondered if maybe Sandy wasn't suffering from some kind of post stress or something.

"What do you mean who told me? Sandy, the hospital called when it happened. I talked to your doctor not ten minutes after you were put in the room with Avery. He showed me the death certificate and everything!"

Now it was Sandy who was confused. She wasn't talking about

her baby, she was talking about Tyler.

"Mama, I know all that but Tyler died before I had the miscarriage. I was with Virginia when the nurse came to get her. No one knew about me and Virginia bein' friends in misery."

Cara had had enough of talking in circles. She told Sandy exactly what the doctor told her about the miscarriage and her naming the baby Tyler.

Sandy was stunned. She hadn't even known the sex of the baby, let alone had a name for it.

"I didn't name the baby, Tyler, Mama. That was Virginia's little boy's name. He died while she and I were in the cafeteria talkin'. After she left, I went in the bathroom to be alone with my grief for her and that's all I remember."

Cara thought it strange that in a moment when Sandy was grieving over the death of another woman's child, her own was dying inside her. The sound of Tommy's voice singing in the tub made her smile. It was the sound of life and just what Cara needed to hear.

"Tommy took it pretty well, didn't he? I think he was more worried about you than anything else. Guess that's natural. He's only eight and you're his mama. He didn't know the baby yet. You all right, little girl?"

Sandy had the kind of sadness that makes a person numb. It wasn't her mama she wanted to talk to but Virginia. She'd thought and thought about how she'd told Virginia that she would trade the life of her baby for Avery's. The guilt she felt came up into her throat and crushed her windpipe. She felt strangled by her own words. What had she been thinking? She asked Cara to bring her a phone book.

"I need to call Virginia, Mama. I have to tell her I'm so sorry."

Cara left and came back with a phone book. Before handing it to Sandy, she decided to butt in just a little.

"Darlin', are you sure this is a good idea? I mean, talkin' to sorrow don't make you anything but more sorrowful. Why don't you wait 'till you're back on your feet and stronger."

Sandy knew her mama meant well but if a body shared sorrow then there was the strength of two hearts to try to mend it. She wanted to offer her's to Virginia and needed to feel Virginia's as well. She hoped Virginia remembered her. Before picking up the phone, Sandy called to Cara as she was walking out the door.

"Hey, Mama? Thank you for bein' there for Tommy and me. I'm real proud of you, Mama. You're tolerable without the whiskey."

Cara smiled at Sandy. The devil danced in her eyes and laughter played on her lips.

"Shit, Sandy, who'd ever think I'd actually want a divorce from Jack Daniels? I ain't sayin' I ain't still in love with him, ya know? I may even want to slip him some tongue every once in awhile but I'll do my damnedest to keep him from fuckin' me! You need me to shut this door?"

Sandy felt a slight twinkle in her eye as she nodded yes.

Cara went back to the living room and sat on the couch to read a copy of the Enquirer she'd picked up when she'd gone out for cigarettes earlier. The tabloid was a comfort to her because it made her feel like her's wasn't the only life whose sewer overflowed with all the shit dropped in it. She looked at Buster who was half dozing and half watching re-runs of the Beverley Hillbillies. She put the magazine down and went over to sit in his lap. He and Tommy were her comfort and balance in life for now. As she stroked his face, she asked if he would help her with something.

"Hey, darlin'? I need you to take me on up to the hospital tomorrow to see Avery."

He was surprised by her request because Cara seldom liked being a passenger. He'd always thought of that old Bonneville as the penis Cara wished she'd been born with!

"Sure, Honey, ain't the Bonneville runnin' right? You need me to take a look at it?"

"The Bonneville's just fine. I gotta drive Sandy's truck back here. It shouldn't be left in that parking lot too long even though there ain't a thing on it worth the stealing of."

Just as she was about to tell Buster what Sandy had told her about Tyler, Tommy came into the living room. He smelled of soap and his pajamas clung to the places he hadn't dried well enough. His hair was wet and he had puffs of soap around and in his ears.

"Boy? Ain't you learned how to use a towel? Go back in that bathroom and bring me the towel you used!"

Cara went back to the couch and waited for Tommy to return. He came in holding a towel and she grabbed it and him at the same time. She put him on her lap and started scrubbing at his ears.

He wriggled and dodged until he couldn't take anymore.

"Grandma, stop! Them ears are 'tached to my head, ya know! My teacher done asked me if I had sprouts growin' in 'em cause sometimes I don't hear her so good!"

Cara rubbed more gently and couldn't help smiling at the picture his words conjured in her head.

"More likely your smart ass attitude blocking your ears than anything else! Yep, your attitude along with about eight years of soap build up! There, done. Now get yourself off to bed."

Tommy laughed and pecked at his grandma's cheek before saying goodnight. He went towards Buster and wasn't sure about hugging him. He decided to play it safe.

"Night, Buster, and thanks for lettin' me help you work on the tractor today. Grease is so cool!"

Buster patted Tommy on the head. He and Bessie Mae had never had children and he'd never known quite how to act around them. He liked Tommy but he felt funny about being too familiar with him. The awkward moment was interrupted by Sandy's entrance into the room. Tommy ran to her without another thought of Buster.

"Hey, Mama! I was just gonna come in and kiss you goodnight!"

Sandy tried to bend to meet Tommy's lips but the pain in her abdomen prevented her from making it very far. She bent her knees and moved her body down so that he could give her a kiss.

"Night, baby. I'll see you in the mornin'."

Cara patted the couch for Sandy to come sit beside her. She was worried about her daughter. She looked awful in a way that was worse than the ordeal she'd been through. It was like the life had gone completely out of her.

Sandy sat and the weight of her made the cushion Cara was sitting on rise up from the imbalance. Cara felt like she was going to fall right into Sandy so she repositioned herself by tucking her legs beneath her cross ways. She put her left hand on Sandy's leg and asked about her phone call.

"Did you get in touch with your friend?"

A veil of grief covered Sandy's eyes that made it impossible to tell if she planned to answer. Her eyes seemed fixed on something out in the distance that could only be seen by her. It was clear that her mind followed the path of her eyes. She answered in a voice that was not her own but some recorded message left for people to inform them she wasn't home.

"Virginia's maid answered. She said they were all at the funeral home. Tyler's being buried tomorrow at Forrest Lane Cemetery. I'm gonna go."

Cara bit her lip. She knew if she said what she was thinking, Sandy would come unglued. The more she looked at her daughter, the more she felt compelled to speak.

"Sandy, do you think it's a good idea for you to be goin' anywhere? I mean, you just went through a physical thing that nearly ripped your insides out. It can't be good for you to be standin' at no grave sight for an hour or more."

She thought if she appealed to Sandy's sense of physical well being, maybe she wouldn't have to get into the emotional shit. She knew Sandy wanted to be there for her friend but she also knew she had selfish reasons for going. She wanted to be in a place of sorrow so she could feel normal again. What Cara worried about was that Sandy would get so down that there would be no bringing her back up. She thought it was a really bad idea to go but she could tell by the look on her daughter's face, it wasn't up for discussion. Cara suddenly felt overwhelmingly tired and rose off the couch feeling every bit of her fifty years. She turned to Sandy and bent to kiss her.

"You do what you need to do, darlin'. I'm as beat as a dirty rug. I'm goin' to bed. Buster? You comin'?"

Buster rose from the recliner and the leather sighed as his weight was lifted from it. The sound made Sandy smile. She felt the same way. She said good night to them both and sat on the couch just staring at the indentations Buster's butt had left in the chair. She thought how life was like the chair. A person makes an impression and then leaves. It just didn't seem fair.

A loud banging noise startled Cara out of a deep sleep. She looked at the clock and saw that it was only five thirty. She would spank Tommy for getting up so god damned early and waking the whole house! She gathered her robe around her and started for the kitchen determined to keep her anger no matter how cute he looked eating his cereal!

She came to the hallway door and opened it to see Sandy standing at the kitchen counter rolling out biscuit dough. The dust of the flour looked like a cloud around her daughter and the smell of yeast like the odor of a life fermenting in pain. She started to retreat and go back to bed but decided an early morning cup of coffee with her daughter might be worth losing a little sleep.

Sandy turned toward her with an apologetic look on her face.

"Sorry, Mama, did I wake you? I was looking for a cookie sheet and two pots fell out the cabinet. I'm making biscuits."

Cara went to the coffee pot and poured until her cup almost overflowed. She felt proud because her hands shook a little less violently with each passing day. She managed to get the cup to the table without spilling more than three drops on the floor. She lit a cigarette, took a sip of coffee to make her morning throat a little less like gravel and then spoke.

"I thought you were Tommy. The little shit got up early yesterday mornin' and fixed his breakfast. I was comin' in here to spank him for gettin' up even earlier today. Should I spank you instead?"

Sandy laughed at the thought. She took a glass down from the cabinet and started to poke out the biscuits from the dough. She placed twelve on the sheet, placed the biscuits in the oven, picked up her coffee and went to join Cara at the kitchen table.

"Hell, Mama, you had to stop spanking me by the time I was ten! I outweighed you by then and you weren't nothin' but hilarious when you'd chase me around with that belt in your hand. I swear, when you'd come in drunk and want to tan me for not doin' dishes or something, I thought you should be on one of them comedy shows! You got more bruises runnin' into things and falling over stuff than you could have ever given me if you had caught me!"

They both laughed at the memories. It was funny to them because it was true that Cara always hurt herself more and never actually got even one strike off to Sandy. Cara liked that not all the memories she'd given her daughter were thorns in her heart and cement to her spirit. There was no denying she'd weighed Sandy's life down with a heaviness that no diet could ever fix but there was a little comfort in knowing a few pebbles of laughter were included in the mix.

They were still laughing when Tommy appeared at the hallway door rubbing his eyes. He stood with the palms of his hands making circular motions in his eyes for a full minute before he spoke.

"Ya'll woke me up! I was sleepin' sooo good and ya'll laughed too loud!"

Cara could tell he wasn't in a good mood but couldn't resist needling him a little.

"Well, little boy, I saw you sleepin' so sound and I told your mama we needed to wake your ass up so you could get all the grouch out before school."

Tommy continued rubbing his right eye and went to his mother's side. He put his elbows on the table with his head perched atop his hands. It was obvious he wanted to say something back to his grandma but his mind wasn't working yet.

Sandy went to the refrigerator to get some milk for Tommy. She checked the biscuits and started cracking eggs into a bowl. She beat the eggs and then took the bacon out of the wrapper. It felt cold, slimy and disgusting to her. She placed it in the heated pan and thought regardless of how gross a thing feels on the outside, sometimes the essence of it is truly wonderful. She was realizing that her mama and bacon had something in common.

Tommy ate with the slowness of a snail. He preferred the sweetness of cereal to the gummy texture of scrambled eggs. He also hated that his mama told him to eat while still wearing his pajamas. It made him mad that he couldn't do things the way he wanted. He was listening to his mama and grandma talk about what they had to do in the day. When he thought they weren't looking he would move his mouth in an exaggerated mimic. He made himself a promise. When he grew up he wouldn't eat eggs for breakfast and would wear only his underwear to the breakfast table.

Cara poured the rest of her coffee into the sink and went back to her room to wake up Buster. She needed to tell him there had been a change of plans and that she would bring Sandy to the hospital. Sandy needed the truck to go to the funeral. She still didn't think the idea of her going was a good one but she also knew there wasn't a thing she could do to stop her.

Buster was snoring like a chain saw going against a piece of petrified wood. She crawled into bed next to him and slid her hand down between his legs. As if they were separate from his sleeping mind, his legs parted to grant full access. She was sorely tempted to take the opened invitation and seal it with a really juicy kiss to the place that mattered but there wasn't time. She gently shook Buster and then hit him when his eyes flew open fully awake.

"You faker!! You was just wantin' me to come in here and play with your bat and balls! I ain't got no time for games and you know it. You heard me and Sandy in there talkin', didn't ya?"

Buster laughed. He liked that he could now have with Cara the things he'd longed for. There was a playfulness to their relationship that he loved. He'd had that with Candy a little but there hadn't been anything deeper. He thought it sounded unlikely, even ridiculous but with Cara there was a deepness, a substance.

Cara jumped off the bed and grabbed a bra, panties, jeans and a tee shirt out of a drawer. She turned to Buster, opened her robe and said,

"Ain't none of this fake and to punish you for tryin' to fool me, I think I'll take my vibrator into the tub with me!"

Buster rolled over and moved the sheet away. He exposed himself, laughed and said,

"That's okay, darlin', it's been on vibrate all mornin' long. I got Energizers in it so it will still be goin' and goin' and goin' when you come home!"

He laughed loudly when Cara turned on her heels in mock embarrassment and took her bony ass out of the room. There was a part of him that felt happy for all the sorrow visited on them of late. It brought him a Cara he never thought he'd have, and for him, that was a real good thing.

CHAPTER THIRTY-THREE

Cara pulled into the parking lot of East Texas General and asked Sandy if she was coming up to see Avery for a minute. She was not at all sure of what it was she saw in her daughter's eyes when she answered.

"No, Mama. Tell him I'll be by later. There is enough pain in my heart right now and I just can't look at Avery."

She hesitated before getting out of the car, turned and spoke again.

"Mama, I said something terrible the night Tyler died. I told Virginia I would gladly trade the life of my baby if Avery would live. I said that to a woman who's son was dyin', Mama! If I look at Avery right now and then go to Tyler's funeral, I'll crawl right into the grave with the little guy!"

Cara wiped the tears from her eyes and reached across the console to hug her daughter. She'd had no idea what the sadness had been beyond the pain in Sandy's eyes. She understood.

Cara sat in the car for a moment and watched her daughter walk away from the Bonneville. She saw a different person from the one she'd always seen. She'd always thought, because of Sandy's size, that she was weak. The woman she was looking at through the windshield was anything but weak. She realized Sandy's being overweight had more to do with building walls than patching holes.

Cara got out of the car and walked towards the entrance to the hospital. She hoped Avery understood about Sandy not being with her. She felt a fear fill her as the swoosh of the automatic doors sucked the air from her. It dawned on her she would be talking to

Avery without Sandy as a safety net and she knew she would be thinking HIV the whole time. She talked to herself in the elevator like a mother instructing a child on proper behavior.

"Now, Cara, don't go sayin' nothin' about what Sandy told you. Avery didn't bring home the homo disease as a gift; he didn't know he had it. He's bad sick and this ain't the time to bring it up."

She hoped seeing him again all broken and maimed would make it easier to keep quiet about what was killing her inside. She just didn't know what she would do if Sandy and Tommy had the virus too. She turned down the corridor towards Avery's room and wiped tears from her eyes. She stood outside his door, squared her shoulders and knocked lightly and pushed the door opened.

Avery was sitting up in bed. Someone had told Cara the contraption on Avery's head was called a halo. She thought it a strange name and even stranger that anyone in her family would ever be able to say they actually wore a halo. The first words out of his mouth were about Sandy.

"Is Sandy okay, Cara? I mean . . . I know she ain't okay but is she? Why ain't she with you? She blames me, don't she?"

Cara thought okay was a word she'd never use in the present situation, not with Sandy, not with any of them. Nothing in their life was okay but she also knew it never had been. She wanted to be careful when she explained why Sandy wasn't there. She didn't want to make Avery feel worse than he already did.

"Sandy went to a funeral, Avery. Seems she met a woman here the first night you was brought in and the woman's baby died. She told me to tell you she'd be by later."

Cara could tell that Avery was irritated. His face always turned a bright red when he got upset. He had one of those huge faces, with ruddy patches and a pocked look to it. It was the kind of face that hid any nice looking features. His eyes sparked with blame when he spoke.

"You let her go to a funeral? What the hell for? Good gosh, Cara, ain't she been through enough in the past week?"

It was her turn to get angry. She walked closer to the head of the bed and leaned forward slightly.

"You just listen to me, Avery Anderson. Sandy is a grown woman and you know god damned well she has a mind of her own. For your information, I told her I didn't think it was a good idea for her to go! Don't you dare lay any guilt on me for what Sandy's been through in the last week! I sure in the hell ain't the one who brought the threat of AIDS into her house!"

Cara's hand flew to her mouth as if she could retrieve the words from the air. She had a horrified look on her face that was matched by the look on Avery's.

"I'm sorry, Avery. I didn't mean it like that. Please, I didn't mean to bring it up to you when you're so sick and all."

Avery's eyes looked right through Cara. He looked like a man who'd been stricken blind by suggestion. A wall of darkness had been erected and it was as if the visit was over. She reached out to him and touched his hand but his skin had the feel of a dead fish lying on a bed of ice. Desperate for him to know she hadn't meant the words the way they'd come out, she decided to talk whether he listened or not.

"Avery Anderson, I've known you for most your life. We ain't always agreed on things and we ain't always gotten along but I've welcomed you as my son-in-law since the day you married Sandy. We've had a common bond, you and me, and I don't just mean my daughter and grandson. You and me are the soles of the feet; we get harder with wear. The corns and callouses just get deeper and the skin gets crusty and abrasive. I was just lucky, Avery. I ain't never put a sock of protection on my old feet either and I sure in the hell have worn a lot of shoes that didn't belong to me!"

Avery's face looked like it had been chiseled in stone. She didn't know the particulars about how he got the virus but she'd bet it was from sticking his other head in a place it didn't belong . She patted his hand and started for the door. Just as she reached for the cold steel handle, he spoke.

"Cara, I've known lots of shame in my life. I hated that people knew about my mama and what she was. I wanted to die once when a boy in school offered me a piece of gum and quickly drew his hand away 'cause he said my hand smelled like shit. I remember putting my fingers up to my nose and realizin' he'd been right. He called me shit boy every day after that and got everyone else to too. I remember the way Mr. Robertson would stare at me when I'd go in to his corner store to buy bread or something. I felt like hangin' around to see if he sprayed Lysol all over things after I left but I was too afraid to watch in case he did. This is going to be like going' back in time for me. People ain't gonna want to touch my hand or anything my hand touched. I'm shit boy all over again and the worst of it all is I made Sandy and Tommy a part of it."

Cara released her hold on the door and came back around to the head of the bed. She put her arms around him the best she could and tried to place a kiss on his cheek between the bars of the halo. Her words to him were simple.

"Avery, there have always been people who think they are better than others. It ain't got nothin' to do with baby diaper hands, clean clothes, or a decent house. They think they are better 'cause they ain't been dealt a hand in life that comes back up, slaps them in the face, yanks on their privates and then rips out their heart. Me, you, your mama, and Sandy all drew cards that were too damned crumpled to be a part of the deck in the first place. It don't got to be that way for little Tommy. I been thinkin' a lot on that lately. We need to put our hope in Tommy. It ain't about havin' things, it's about havin' the opportunity to be somethin'."

Cara saw the worst pain in Avery's eyes she'd ever seen in a person. The tears that brimmed at the base of his lower lid looked like droplets of soul seeping out of their host. He started to speak and then pursed his lips together like a person does who has trouble speaking for all the emotion in his mouth.

"Don't ya see, Cara? That's just it. What if I gave Tommy a virus that will kill him? You and my mama might have been fucked up parents but the bullshit and the beatings sure didn't kill anyone!"

Cara wasn't so sure about the truth of his last statement. Many was the time she'd seen Sandy die inside. Sandy's may have been a different kind of death than a person with an illness but she knew damn well she'd passed on a disease to her.

"Yes, Avery, I did. I killed the spirit of my own daughter. I let the shit of my life overflow into her mind and heart. Good God, Avery, I let Sandy's daddy do the same things to her my daddy done to me! I was either out someplace gettin' drunk or layin' out on the living room couch passed out from bein' drunk. I brought my child disease, devastation and death. I did it and what's worse, I knew I was doin' it. You didn't know you was sick, Avery. I knew I was."

Avery wondered who the woman was in his room because the Cara he knew would never admit to the things this woman was. He wondered if the screws on the halo were too tight and affecting his hearing. He almost liked the woman standing before him.

Just as he was about to tell Cara how much her words meant to him, the door to his room opened and the nurse he called Sour Puss came in. She was blunt and always seemed irritated that people got sick or hurt. She placed the blood pressure cuff on Avery's right arm and stared at Cara in a way only another woman could. When she spoke, her words were spewed in a manner that made anyone within ear shot want to grab a tissue to wipe away the residue.

"Oh, by the way, they told me at the desk the little friend that was with you the night you got hurt is being transferred back today. He'll be on this floor but we don't cotton to conjugal visits, understand?"

Before Avery could even formulate an answer in his head, Cara was locked, loaded and ready for battle. She had the look of a mother lioness poised to pounce and kill the enemy. He'd seen her prelude to eruption before and was glad to be just an observer.

"Bitch, you want to back your fat ass up and repeat what you just said? I don't give a good god damn what kind of shit your toilet has in it but when you come in here and try to spread it on my family then you done made a big mistake! My son-in-law is your patient. He ain't your friend, your lover, or your kin so you got no right to stick your ugly ass in his face and make him smell your shit! Get the fuck out of his room and don't you dare come back. You ain't good enough to care for this man. You ain't good enough to care for anyone!"

Sour puss looked stunned, angry and homicidal all within the space of the few seconds it took Cara to skin her alive. She started to speak but walked towards the door instead. As she reached for the handle, she turned to Cara. Her voice had a low hissing sound when she spoke.

"I recognize you now. You're the crazy bitch the cops brought in one night when I was comin' on duty. You listen to me, you drunkin' little whore, you ain't good enough to wipe my fat ass! I ain't scared of you! You're the type that was born nothin', ain't nothin' and will die nothin'. Ain't nobody cares what you and your homo son here thinks, does, or feels!"

She opened the door, turned back toward Avery and said,

"Oh, by the way, Leo, my husband, says to tell ya you were damn lucky this time!"

Cara was shaking so badly she groped around to find the arm of a chair to steady herself. She had never wanted to hit someone so much in her entire life. She was not used to dealing with life as a sober person and had no idea what to do with the intensity of it all. She wanted to hurt that woman for hurting her family. She'd never really felt that way before.

Cara turned to Avery and felt her heart break into a million pieces. He'd taken a pillow from behind his head and sat sobbing into it. The halo's top moved like a satellite dish looking for a signal. She went to him but knew there was nothing inside her to make his incredible pain go away. She wanted a drink more than she'd wanted anything in her life. She wanted to get drunk, get naked and screw the world away. She took the pillow from Avery's face and bent right down to him on eye level.

"Look at me, Avery Anderson. You got nothin' to be ashamed

of, boy. You know that woman don't know shit about anything. It don't matter what her kind or anyone else in this place thinks. You hold that alien head of yours up and be proud that your heart ain't filled with the hate of the world. You be the friend to Robert that you are and be glad to call him yours. Them people talk shit because they speak out their asses!"

Avery laughed in spite of his pain. The thought of Sour Puss talking out her ass reminded him of the Jim Carey movie, Ace Ventura. He looked at Cara and said words he'd not planned to say and never thought he'd feel.

"I don't think we've met. I'm Avery Anderson and I'm damn proud to know ya. I think I could grow to love ya, Cara Covington!"

Cara slapped at Avery's leg in a oh, go on fashion. His affectionate words both embarrassed her and made her feel vulnerable to reciprocation. Hell, that's all she needed, to love her son-in-law! She was crazier sober than she'd ever been drunk!

Sandy pulled into the parking lot of the Restful Peace Funeral Home. Her old pick up was a contrast to all the cars parked in the spaces and she knew she would be a sharp contrast to the people inside. They would likely see her as an outsider but her pain on the inside made her a kindred spirit to Virginia and that's who she was there for. She straightened the six year old polyester blend her dress was made from. She felt like a fish out of water even in her own clothes. She bent to pull up the knee highs she wore and noticed the heel on her right shoe had been half eaten away by time, her weight and the cheapness of the material from which it had been made. Had it been any other time in her life, she would have turned to get back in the truck to leave but this was not about her insecurity; it was about being who her heart told her she had to be.

The entrance into the chapel was crowded with people signing the guest book. She waited her turn and then signed her name. The organ music was soft and sad but the sight of the tiny coffin in front of the podium made her actually reel with more sadness than she thought possible. She felt fingers grasp her elbow and turned to see Virginia's kind, loving face staring back at her. It was more than Sandy could stand and she let loose the aching moan that threatened to choke her. The two women joined their sorrow in a hug that melded understanding with love and pain with seemingly insurmountable sorrow. It was Virginia that released the grip first. She walked with Sandy down the aisle and seated her in a pew directly behind the family. She walked to the entrance of the first pew and bent to whisper something to a woman who was immaculately dressed, perfectly coiffed and bejeweled tastefully. As Virginia took her place between her husband and the woman, the classy lady turned to Sandy and offered her hand.

"I am Virginia's mother, Clarrisa. Ginny told me so much about you. Thank you so much for bringing my daughter a little laughter and comfort on those last days of Tyler's life."

She turned back toward the front of the chapel and dabbed at her eyes with a monogrammed handkerchief.

Sandy listened as the preacher talked about the short life of little Tyler Copeland. He spoke of a valiant battle by a little boy who should have been playing with rattles and listening to songs from Sesame Street. Sandy fished in her purse for a Kleenex as she pictured Tommy at Tyler's age. She was appalled at how little she remembered of him being a baby. She wiped the tears from her cheeks and was surprised when she saw Virginia rise and go toward the podium. She had no idea that Virginia planned to eulogize her own son. Sandy sat amazed by her incredible strength.

There was a quiet in the chapel like Sandy had never heard before. She noticed the shaking of Virginia's fingers and thought she could actually hear the bones in her hands rattling against each other. Her voice was surprisingly strong as she spoke.

"Tyler was more than my son. He was my heart, my life and my friend. Even when I'd been up with him all night long, the look of him, the feel of him, the sound of him, was everything I'd dreamed. His smile lit my days and nights. His cry called out to me and filled my heart with the need to love him. When he got sick, the last thing I ever thought about was not having him with me. Tyler showed me that sometimes a lifetime is lived in seconds and that every heart beat from beginning to end is magic. There is something I want all of you to know. The sadness I feel with Tyler's death is not from having lost him but from having had him and now to have him no more. It is a selfish pain, a selfish sorrow. He was never mine to keep and the parting was inevitable but it's not *his* loss I grieve but my own. Tyler's suffering has ended and for that I am grateful. The suffering I feel is for that place in my soul that he touched. He left his tiny finger prints all over inside me. They are there for good, even though he touched me for only a short time. Life is not about death but about living. Tyler Copeland lived and I will not, and cannot, be sad about that."

Virginia walked up to the tiny coffin, ran her fingers lovingly over the top and placed a yellow rose bud on the shiny wood. In a voice only audible to those in the first few rows, she said goodbye to her son.

"There, my little yellow rose. I saw the beauty in your budding though you didn't live long enough for me to see you blossom. I'm glad you touched me, Tyler, and I am so glad I got to touch you. Thank you."

Sandy's body convulsed with sobs as she tried desperately to regain control of her emotions. She wanted to run away and stay at the same time. Virginia was speaking words she needed to hear but couldn't listen to. Her heart felt like it was exploding into the pew and seeping into the wood to be with all the other sorrow spilled into it. Just when Sandy was about to get up to get some fresh air, she felt a hand on her shoulder gently forcing her back to a sitting position. It was Virginia's mother and her voice sounded like the voice of an angel.

"My poor child, don't be afraid of what your heart tells you to feel. There are times in life when recognizing and expressing deep pain is the only way to ever feel joy again. Don't run from it, Sandy, let it in with a joyous embrace and know that from your deepest sorrow comes your greatest happiness. If a person feels no sorrow for a tragedy, how then will they ever feel joy for the magic in life?"

Sandy could find no words, there were none. She just bent her head down and let the tremendous waves of compassion, worry, pain, and devastation wash over her. She looked up to see them preparing to move the casket out of the chapel and into the hearse. As they came past her, she put her hand out to touch death. It was something she'd never done. Death needed to be real to her and little Tyler, lying lifeless in that tiny coffin had done that for her. The shiny wood felt smooth and soothing at the same time it felt cold and ungiving. She whispered as they passed.

"Goodbye, little Tyler."

Sandy decided she couldn't bear going to the grave site. She went into one of the bathrooms at the funeral home to put on a fresh pad before driving back to the hospital. She felt strange seeing the blood that had run out of her while people said their goodbyes to baby Tyler. Her body was still saying goodbye to the baby she'd lost. Coming to say farewell to Tyler had made her heart open to letting her child go too. She felt a sense of peace come over her. She knew Virginia had been right. Life and its moments counted and she had a husband and son to feel alive for and to be alive with.

The traffic going back towards the hospital was terrible. She thought everyone who worked must have decided to go out to lunch. She turned on her right hand blinker to change lanes and then saw what was backing traffic up, the telltale headlights and police escort of a funeral, Tyler's funeral. She liked the thought of Tyler stopping traffic one last time. She hoped people took a moment to notice that death was passing them so they wouldn't let life pass them by too.

Sandy turned slowly into the parking lot of the hospital, her eyes fixed on the slow procession as it moved on through the next light and down the street. She said the words one more time before finding a place to park.

"Goodbye, Tyler, and thanks for making me see my own grief."

CHAPTER THIRTY-FOUR

The nurse came into Robert's room and told him she had some good news for him. He would be transferred to East Texas General for the remainder of his hospital stay. She explained that the insurance company deemed it unnecessary for him to stay in a special care facility any longer since he was recovering nicely from his injuries.

Robert was happy about being closer to home but thought it wasn't his best interest the insurance company was considering but their own. He knew that the teaching hospitals in Houston were a damn sight more expensive than any backwoods, small town, glorified clinic type hospital.

The nurse told him that after the doctor came in to see him, he would be loaded into an ambulance and taken to Jacinto Corners. He wondered if Avery was still in the hospital? Cara hadn't been very specific about Avery's injuries. They both had been caught up in the sadness of Sandy losing the baby. He thought how good it would be to put his arms around his dear Sandy. He thought how lucky he was to have them as his family now. He bristled at the thought of the card he'd received from his mother. It had simply said,

"Sorry to hear about your accident. I guess when you live in hell, the fire is bound to burn your ass occasionally!"

Then there was the little note from Maurice. He couldn't even think of the letter without tears stinging his eyes. It was a cruelty he had not thought Maurice capable of. It was a typewritten piece of shit that asked him to remove Maurice as next of kin on any and all documents of importance. He would remove him off things! Oh buddy, would he remove him! He had a feeling it was typed by Maurice's new love and only signed by him. They were the ones in hell because Maurice was surely screwing the devil!

Robert took some deep breaths to calm himself. He didn't want to elevate his blood pressure and take a chance on the docs changing their mind about his transfer. He needed to be home with the people he cared about. He needed to be cared for too.

Sandy went straight to Avery's room and heard laughter coming from within. She was surprised to see Cara still there when she opened the door and even more surprised to see Robert sitting in a wheelchair beside Avery's bed. She stood for a moment just staring because Robert had on the same head gear Avery did and they looked like two misplaced Martians who'd come down to party with her even more alien mother!

Robert was the first to speak and the joy he felt at seeing her was evident in his voice.

"Oh my God! It's my Sandy! The only woman in the world I would fall in love with if I could fall in love with a woman!"

Sandy hugged Robert, or the part she could get to, for a full five minutes before releasing him. He felt like life and he was just what she needed. She tried to move back to see his face but her hair caught in the screws at the top of his halo. She tried to get her hair loose but it was impossible for her to see which way the hair was wrapped around. Cara stepped forward and started unwinding the strands for her. Sandy didn't understand why they were all laughing so hard. It was Avery who finally calmed down enough to explain.

"Darlin', your mama and I were just telling Robert how it's all over the hospital that he and I are lovers. If that bitch of a nurse Sour Puss walked in here right now she would think that you were trying to hurt Robert in a jealous rage!"

Sandy thought the humor must have lost something in the translation. She didn't find anything funny about people spreading rumors about her husband being gay. She thought under the circumstances it hit a little too close to home.

Finally freed from the halo, Sandy let the twinkle of love in her eyes meet the returned look in Robert's eyes. She stroked his face and thought how wonderful it was to see his big brown eyes so full of life. She sat mesmerized by them for a moment and then the spell was broken by the sound of Cara's voice.

"Well, guys, it's been fun but I need to piss like a race horse, about to die for a cigarette and need to get back home to Buster."

Robert looked at Cara and couldn't resist a dig. The woman made him feel alive.

"You know, cigarettes cause cancer and death. They also make you look old, wrinkled and they dry out your skin."

Cara shot back without hesitation,

"Oh yeah? Well bein' homo makes people wish you were dead and that really dries out the skin! I bet your butt won't ever be the same after what happened. They didn't bother with the KY, did they?"

Sandy was appalled by the laughter she heard. How could they make jokes about what happened? How could they think any of it was funny?

Cara kissed Avery and Robert goodbye and asked Sandy to walk to the elevators with her. She knew that Sandy didn't understand the dynamics of the conversation she'd walked in on and she wanted to explain. She guided Sandy toward the door and felt like she was pushing Old Blue towards the water hose for a bath. She didn't realize how hard it was to move a mass that didn't want to be moved.

Cara waited until they were far enough away from the door and then stopped to face Sandy.

"Hon, let me explain. When they wheeled Robert into that room the two of them couldn't even look at each other. It was like they each had a chunk of shame sittin' on 'em so big that it blocked out that they'd been friends. Robert blamed himself for what happened for bein' gay and Avery blamed himself for what happened for bein' straight and takin' Robert to a hell hole. They need to rise above the pain, little girl. They need to laugh about what happened or the pain of it will injure innards the bat never touched."

Sandy thought she would never get used to Cara making sense. It was like being in a sci-fi movie called The Body Snatchers Meet Mr. Rogers! She knew her mama was right but doubted she would ever be able to laugh about any of it.

Sandy hugged her mama as the elevator doors opened and was surprised to see Morris Foley step out as Cara stepped in. He nodded to Cara and then acknowledged Sandy.

"Hi, Sandy. I hear Avery feels like making a statement. I figured he would come around once the pain was replaced by anger."

It was the first Sandy heard about Avery wanting to talk to the police about what happened. She wondered what had changed his mind? For some reason she didn't feel as happy as she thought she would about Avery naming his attackers.

She followed Morris back toward Avery's room. She wasn't sure she wanted to listen to what would be said once they got back in the room. Seeing the results of a vicious act and listening to a blow by blow description of it were two different things. Somehow it seemed to Sandy that hearing Robert and Avery talk about the incident would make it more real. She felt fear about the wheels being set in motion to identify, find, arrest and indict the attackers.

When she and Morris entered the room, Robert and Avery were talking but stopped as soon as they saw that Morris was with her. It was evident that Morris had no idea Robert would be included in the interview and his greeting showed his surprise.

"Man, I didn't expect to see you again, ever. You were lookin' at death or it sure seemed it was lookin' at you the last time I saw you. By the way, I'm Officer Morris Foley. I was the officer on the scene that night. Real glad to see you made such a speedy recovery."

It wasn't that Morris didn't mean his words in a sincere manner, it was more that the others in the room knew the situation made him feel uncomfortable. He'd witnessed an incredibly debasing act perpetrated against Robert. He tried hard not to let his own morals, even prejudices, influence his work but it was a fact that Robert was a gay man. His sexual preference had been the reason behind the attack and there were many people in town who thought he got what he deserved. Hell, there were many on the police force who thought that by being gay he'd asked for it.

Morris pulled out his notepad and then asked if both men wanted to give a statement.

"I can take statements from both of you but they have to be given independently from each other. Mr. Laningham, were you wanting to make a statement, too?"

Robert looked at Avery. It was what they had been talking about before Sandy and Morris came in. Robert had suggested to Avery that if he alone gave a statement then any threats of reprisal would come to him instead of to Avery, Sandy and Tommy. It was something that worried him greatly. He smiled to himself. Avery had told him to speak English and use words a body could understand! He decided it would be best if he talked to Morris first and give Avery a chance to talk things out with Sandy.

"If you will wheel me back to my room, Officer Foley, we can talk in there."

Avery shot Robert an appreciative look as Morris stepped in behind the wheelchair to take him to his room across the hall. He smiled at Avery and winked at Sandy. He knew that telling his side of the story would certainly buy them enough time to sort out what they wanted to do.

As the door shut behind Robert and Morris, Sandy went to Avery and hugged him. She felt so torn by what she wanted to happen to the men who'd hurt him and the fear of what would happen to her family if she got her wish. She felt Avery try to pull away from her hug and thought she was hurting him. She moved her head back so she could see his face and realized she wasn't hurting him but keeping him from saying what he needed to say. Taking his left hand in hers, she sat back down in the chair she'd pushed between the two beds and waited to hear what Avery had to say.

"Sandy . . . darlin' . . . the thing is . . . what happens if I don't say nothin' about what happened and the bastards who did this think I did anyway? Robert's gonna talk, Sandy. He's gonna nail them to the wall and use them to decorate the gay man's hall of shame. He told me he was. He ain't gonna run scared on this and I think I'll feel like shit if I do!"

Sandy sat back in the chair and let go of Avery's hand. She wanted to think about things without feeling the warmth of Avery clasped to her heart. She'd never thought much about the philosophical issues of justice. She'd always thought that it did no good to protest the wrongs done in life because, as Cara had always said,. "there weren't no changin' it." She tried to weigh the pros and cons of Avery testifying against the JCCL because that was what he'd be doing. It wasn't just the men that had hurt him. It was their neighbors, people at the grocery store, police officers, and probably city officials as well. She knew their life would change but she also knew it already had. She looked at Avery and said the only thing she could.

"You do what you need to, Avery. I wish the bastards hadn't reached out and touched us so we could just ignore them like we always have but that ain't the truth of things now. I love you, Avery, and I'll stand by you no matter what."

Morris Foley sat writing feverishly as Robert recalled the events leading up to the attack. He had to stop Robert several times to ask what certain words meant. He studied the man before him. He watched his hand gestures and listened to the timbre of his voice. He wasn't sure what he expected but Robert Laningham was not what Morris imagined a gay man to be. He hated himself for expecting Robert to not be a real man. He'd grown up with the same prejudices most people in that area of Texas had and letting go of over twenty years of preconceived ideas was hard.

Morris shifted uncomfortably in his chair as Robert described the scene in the bathroom with Leo. He'd spent many a night in Liars and could almost smell the urinals as Robert spoke about the conversation he had with Leo. When Robert said that it was in the bathroom that he realized where he knew Leo from, Morris wondered why it took a place where men's dicks were exposed for him to remember. No matter how hard he tried to block such thoughts, they kept making hits on his judgment. He stopped Robert to ask a few questions and to clear his mind of the intruding prejudices.

"Mr. Laningham, you said you thought Leo looked familiar when you sat at the table and that he actually asked you if the two of you had met before, right?"

Robert nodded and added that he'd felt uncomfortable with Leo from the very start.

"Yes, I have that down here. Now, when the two of you were in the bathroom, did Leo threaten you in any way? Did he let on that he knew you were . . . well, that . . ."

"That I am gay? No, it wasn't like that. I just knew he knew."

Morris bit the end of his pen and wished like hell the interview was over. He knew he would feel different taking Avery's statement. He decided to just let Robert continue without interruption. It was almost two o'clock and his shift ended at three. He wanted a cold beer, a hot shower and to think about having his daughter, Sarah, for Christmas.

It was two thirty by the time Robert got to the end of his story or at least the part he remembered. Morris thanked him for his statement, rose from the chair and shook Robert's hand. He expected the hand to feel limp and noncommital in its grasp but was surprised by the firmness of its shake.

Morris went across the hall, knocked on Avery's door and entered feeling the weight of Robert's pain in his heart. He'd decided that Avery's statement could wait until tomorrow. He had to get back to the station and type up Robert's version of what happened that night. He hated that it was so late and that his fellow officers would all be around when he was doing it. There were ten on the force who had rumored affiliation with the JCCL and four of those worked his shift.

Sandy stood up when Morris entered the room. She'd told Avery she didn't want to stay while he talked about what happened. She said she would go visit with Robert while Morris talked to him. She started to leave but Morris stopped her.

"It's almost time for shift change and I need to go type up this report. Would it be okay with you guys if I come back tomorrow morning for Avery's statement?"

Avery felt let down. He'd been geared up to kick ass and give names. He looked at Sandy and saw the relief in her eyes. He hated that all of this was so hard for her. He told Morris tomorrow would be fine. It wasn't like an evening and a night would change anything. He shook Morris' hand and waited until he left before speaking to Sandy.

"Darlin', you look exhausted. Why don't you go on home to your mama's. Tommy should be home from school just about the time you get there."

Sandy hated that she hadn't had more time to spend with Robert but she had to admit she felt more tired than she had in her life. The day had just been too much for her and she was ready to get away from sadness.

She bent down and gave Avery the first passionate kiss her heart had felt since he'd been hurt. Seeing the disappointment in his face over not giving his statement made her realize she had unconsciously blamed him for what had happened to him. She saw him as a victim for the first time and it made her heart ache for him. She wasn't sure why she'd felt more compassion for Robert but she thought it was probably due to Avery's association with the men who had hurt him. Guilt by association, as if what had happened to him he'd somehow contributed to by knowing the people in the first place. She hated herself for her feelings but couldn't deny them. She told Avery she would come back in the morning and opened the heavy wood door. She felt she was walking into the next part of her life.

CHAPTER THIRTY-FIVE

Christmas was a week away and Cara had promised Tommy that when he came home from school they would go buy a Christmas tree. She had an old artificial tree in one of the closets in the hall but it was an aluminum tree from back in the seventies. She remembered the nights she would come home drunk and the strobe would be on. She thought the damn tree was dancing around the room taunting her. She remembered hearing voices saying, "If you hadn't smoked and drank every penny away, maybe Sandy could have that doll she wanted. If you'd stay home at night maybe your daughter wouldn't be raped by her dad!" Christmas had never meant much more than a hang over and wishes that weren't fulfilled. This was the first Christmas in her life that actually meant something to her.

She was back in the bedroom when she heard the front door open. She knew it wasn't Buster because he'd gone to the hardware store and wouldn't be back till dinner. He was Tim the Tool Man, Bob Villa and the Gadget Guru all rolled into one man. She started down the hall and was met by Sandy. Her daughter's appearance made her catch her breath.

"Good God, Sandy, did you jog all the way home? You look plum wore out! Come on into the kitchen and let me fix you a cup of coffee."

Sandy sat at the kitchen table and stared at the salt and pepper shakers. Her mind felt heavier than her body. She didn't know why but she felt like turning to her mama for answers to the questions in her heart.

"Mama?"

Cara turned away from fighting with separating the coffee filters and looked at her daughter.

"Yes, darlin?"

"Mama? Is it wrong to hate something so bad that you just wish it dead rather than havin' to deal with it? I mean if the problem is a person, is it ever all right to just wish someone would die?"

Cara finally freed the filter from its hold on the pack and placed it in the holder. She measured out three heaping tablespoons of coffee and put the basket into the coffee maker. As she was running the water to fill the carafe, she tried to answer Sandy's question.

"Well, sweetheart, I wished someone dead for a time. When I realized what your daddy was doin' to you I wanted him to be struck down without mercy. I mostly did because he weren't human but the same sick animal my daddy was. I realized if he should be struck down, then so should I. I lived, though, and what I done to myself was worse than anything death could have done to me. Who you lookin' to take out with your thoughts? Me?"

Cara's laughter was half tease and half fear of what Sandy's answer would be. She knew if her daughter wished her dead there was plenty of reason for it. She knew that most of what an adult gets in life they earned by deed or omission.

Sandy looked pensive and concerned as Cara came to sit at the table with her. She played with the packets of Sweet N Low Cara put down. She half expected her mama to tell her to quit fidgeting and calm herself. She felt very childlike and thought it ironic since she'd never felt like a child when she was one.

She studied Cara's face. She'd never dared really looked at it before. She was afraid that it would start to change into a monster's face. As a child that is what she thought her mama was, one of those monsters who lived in a human body. There was never a day when she wasn't getting drunk, drunk, or suffering from a hangover from being drunk.

Sandy looked at the milk and remembered a time when she was ten. She'd picked up the carton and poured some into her cereal. She remembered it tasting like whiskey and she'd gagged from the taste. Her mama had slapped her twice, once for wasting her hangover remedy and a second time for gagging at the table. The slaps didn't hurt nearly as much as the words that followed her hand. She recalled the sting of them as if they'd been said yesterday.

"You stupid little bitch pig! Always the selfish one, ain't ya? Got to feed that ugly face of yours! Well, missy, that's the last of the milk and what's in it is a hell of a lot more important to me than you are!"

Cara could tell by Sandy's expression that sour thoughts were running through her mind. She didn't know whether the shit in her head had been stuff flushed recently or old stuff that had gotten lodged in the pipes along the way. If there was one thing she'd learned, it was not to ask a question of Sandy she didn't feel like hearing the answer to. She wanted to cheer Sandy up and thought maybe getting a Christmas tree with her and Tommy would do it.

"Hey, sweet girl, Tommy'll be home any minute. I promised him we'd go buy a Christmas tree. Wanna come with us?"

Sandy looked up from the table and thought how strange it was to hear things like that come out of her mama's mouth. She hated herself for the feelings of jealousy that swirled in her heart but couldn't help it. It wasn't that she didn't want Tommy to reap the benefits of a sober Cara, it was that she wished the little girl she'd once been had been important enough to have the same chance. She was so tired but couldn't resist the pull of having such an experience with her mama.

"That sounds like fun, Mama. Do I have time for a hot bath first? I'm feeling really dirty and spent."

"Sure darlin'. I'm sure Tommy'll want a snack or something before we go, so take your time. Sandy?"

"Yes, Mama?"

During the course of their conversation, Cara had felt words scratching at the door to be let out of her heart. She'd ignored them because she hadn't wanted to open a can of worms. She knew she had to begin to heal the huge gap she'd rutted out between her and Sandy.

"Sandy, it ain't no secret that I loved my whiskey more than I loved most things in life. J.D. and I had a relationship that was a powerful thing. I ain't trying to excuse it, just tellin' you the truth of it. I stole every important moment from the real world to be in the world it offered me. What I'm tryin' to say is . . . Sandy it weren't you I hated all them years, it was myself."

Sandy's sigh was one of tired resignation and so was her answer.

"I know, Mama. We'll have to talk about it someday. Right now all I want is a hot bath."

Sandy let the warmth of the water wash over her as she closed her eyes to the world. Her tears were quiet ones. Little trickles of pain leaking out as if there was a safety valve on her heart to prevent a flood. The soap felt smooth against her skin and the wash cloth felt soft and warm. It was the closest thing to comfort she'd felt in a long time. She laid her head back and wondered why her mama had opened up about her years of drinking? She hoped like hell that the sober Cara wasn't psychic and able to read her thoughts. She imagined it was more likely sober guilt eating at her. There was way too much pain and anger to wash away with words but maybe time and forgiveness could at least make some kind of relationship possible.

Sandy was very nearly asleep when she heard the knock on the bathroom door. She thought maybe Tommy had just come in and was desperate to pee but then she heard Cara's voice.

"Sandy, Avery's on the phone. He sounds upset, darlin'. Want me to take a message?"

"No, Mama. Tell him I'll be there in a minute."

Sandy dried off as best she could and wrapped her robe around her shivering body. She shook as much from the cold as she did with fear about what catastrophe she would have to face now. She knew Avery wouldn't just call to say hi when she'd just left him.

Cara was talking to Avery when Sandy came into the living

room. She was telling Avery to calm down. She looked at Sandy with a look that said she couldn't make sense out of what Avery was saying and handed Sandy the phone.

Cara heard Sandy yell into the phone.

"Damn it, Avery, slow down! I can't understand what you're sayin'! Now, who's kicking you out?"

Cara watched as Sandy's face went from maternal irritation to disbelief and fear.

"What the hell, Avery? It's got a million dollar cap and you ain't even been in the hospital long enough to use that up! Hold on, Avery, just hold on. I just got out of the tub. Let me get dressed and I'll be there soon as I can. We'll get this shit straightened out!" She turned to Cara, "Mama, you and Tommy'll have to get a tree without me."

Sandy started back down the hall and Cara was at her heels saying her name over and over. Sandy ignored Cara's questions completely. Not to be ignored, Cara followed Sandy into the bedroom.

"God damn it, Sandy, are you going to tell me what the hell is going on?"

Sandy grabbed a bra out of her suitcase and laid out some panties on the bed. Cara found her eyes drawn for a moment to how huge her daughter's underwear was but then turned her attention back to why Avery had been so upset.

"Sandy! Did that telephone call make you deaf? I want to know what the fuck is goin' on!"

"They're kicking Avery out of the hospital, Mama! The sons of bitches say his insurance's been terminated and that they ain't no charity hospital!"

Cara just shook her head and walked out of the bedroom. She went back into the kitchen and positioned the step stool in front of the stove to reach the cabinet above it. She couldn't see into the cabinet but she knew her fingers would know when it touched what her mind was searching for and her heart needed. Her fingers tingled when she felt the familiar smoothness of the glass and the clink of a bottle that was more than half full. She brought the bottle of Jack Daniels down, opened a cabinet to her right and took out a huge tumbler. The screw cap was harder to open than she anticipated. She guessed that infrequent use made the top fit tighter on the neck. She brought the bottle over to where she kept the dish towels and was still trying to unscrew the cap when Sandy walked in. Cara looked up to see her daughter standing in front of her, anger playing on her face like the shine of the noonday Texas sun. She almost wanted to shield her face from the intensity of the glare.

"Sandy . . . this . . . well . . ."

"Shut up, Mama. You think I care if you get fallin' down drunk and disappoint every god damn person who needs you right now? Well, I don't! I gotta go, Mama. I can't be wastin' my time on you when real people need me!"

Sandy was gone before Cara could even open her mouth to speak. She brought the bottle over to the kitchen table and sat so hard in the chair that her tail bone hurt. She heard the screen door open and thought Sandy had come back. She looked up to see it wasn't Sandy at all but Tommy. He dropped his book bag on the kitchen counter. She watched as excitement left him and disappointment made his mouth turn down at the corners. He stared at the bottle and said,

"Guess we'll get the Christmas tree another day, Grandma. Mama told me to never go no where with a stranger, a bad person, or you, when you're drunk."

Cara watched as he turned around and walked back towards the front door. She heard the screen door shut and slumped in the chair, dish rag still in hand. She ran her fingers along the length of the bottle and felt the saliva in her mouth thicken in anticipation. She got up from the chair and walked out to the porch.

Tommy was sitting in a wicker rocker that had been half eaten away by age and weather. His legs were drawn into his chest and his eyes were fixed toward the yard. She noticed that his jaw was working like it was chewing on all the anger he felt but wasn't allowed to vent. She kneeled down in front of him and took his hands in hers. Her voice was soft and full of understanding.

"Tommy, your grandma ain't drunk. I promise I didn't even have a sip. I ain't gonna lie to you, honey, I was wantin' one but I didn't have a drop. We can go get that tree, darlin'. You can get in the car with me. Tommy, you're safe with me."

Tommy looked at his grandma's eyes to see if she was telling him the truth. He knew what her drunk eyes looked like. His mama thought he didn't know things but he was smart. He used to think his mama was stupid when she told him his grandma was sick or that his daddy was too tired to walk right. He knew sickness and imbalance came out of a can or bottle and so did harsh words and whippings. He hated when adults lied to him about things. It made him feel like he was invisible to them, like he didn't have a brain or eyes that worked. He peered into his grandma's eyes because he always knew that the truth lived there. Her eyes didn't have red stripes but he wanted to make sure.

"Grandma, open your mouth and blow."

Cara smiled. She opened her mouth and blew almost directly in Tommy's nose. She laughed outright at his reaction and his words.

"Oh yuck, Grandma, you been eatin' tuna fish!"

He put his hands over his nose, stuck out his tongue and crossed his eyes.

"We can get that tree now, Grandma, but we need to stop for ice cream first 'cause I need to get the taste of your tuna out of my nose!"

Cara hugged Tommy and asked him to come inside with her. She took the bottle of Jack Daniels off the table and went to the sink. She picked up the dish towel and unscrewed the lid. The sound of the J.D. glugging down the sink actually made her feel physically sick but when she saw the look in Tommy's eyes, she found a new thrill. She tipped the bottle until the last drop was gone and ceremoniously threw it into the trash. She looked at Tommy and said,

"Let's go get us a Christmas tree!"

Sandy stormed through the automatic doors at the entrance of the hospital. She marched through the lobby and straight into one of the offices where patient accounts were handled. There was an older couple seated in the two chairs and they looked fearful of her. Sandy asked them where the representative was and they both just pointed towards a room where the whir of a copy machine could be heard. She walked to the inside door and stuck her head through. The woman at the copy machine looked up and sounded like a snotty, over-confident little bitch.

"Ma'am, you are not allowed back here. I am currently helping other people. Please sign the book outside the offices and wait your turn."

Sandy felt her face go bright red but from anger not embarrassment. She took in a deep breath and spoke as calmly as she could.

"I don't really care who you are helping right now. This piece of shit hospital is about to release my husband because some idiot said his insurance was terminated! I don't have time for bullshit hospital red tape! I need you, or someone, to take care of this immediately!"

The woman was not moved by Sandy's demanding attitude. She stood her ground and with impatience mixed with anger in her voice, she sternly said,

"Ma'am, if you do not do as I asked, I will have security escort you to a private area until the police come to take you to jail. We have a way of doing things here and you will abide by our procedures like everyone else!"

Sandy was beside herself. She decided to go up to Avery's floor and see if she could get someplace with the nurses and doctors rather than waiting for a bureaucrat to actually care about a person. She got into the elevator and thought maybe she'd been too hard on her mama. Maybe all the alcoholics and drug addicts in the world had the answer. A person couldn't care about going insane if the brain was too anesthetized to recognize reality. She wished she was home getting drunk with her mother.

Sandy opened the door to Avery's room and was glad to see a doctor already there. Avery had been crying and it made Sandy's heart sink to the bottom of her toes. For the first time, she felt like maybe it wasn't the hospital's mistake but something else. She stood listening to the conversation.

"Mrs. Anderson, I was just telling your husband that technically there is little risk in him going home now as long as he does no more there than he did here. He would need to be monitored for any signs of unusual swelling, sudden fever, or other symptoms associated with infection but time is his greatest healer now. I explained that he has to wear the halo for another three weeks and that if after that time he comes back to me, I will remove it at no cost to your family. I've had the nurse gather some dressings and such for you to bring home and she'll return in a moment to show you how to care for his head wound. I'm truly sorry about the circumstances behind his release but there is really nothing I can do. Now if the two of you will excuse me, I'll go see what's keeping that nurse."

Sandy stood staring at Avery. She wondered how life had become what it was for them. What happened to the days when having money for cheese and beer was their biggest concern? She asked what she thought was a logical question.

"Avery, have you called the insurance company? Did you ask them why this was happening?"

She couldn't help but be angry with his response.

"Sandy, *they* called the hospital! Are you stupid or something?"

She swallowed the urge to strike out at him. She told herself he was ill, afraid and under enormous stress. She took two deep breaths and removed her insurance card from her wallet. She walked to the night stand by Avery's bed and dialed the 1-800 customer service number.

She thought it appropriate to hear the canned recording of a woman's voice that sounded full of help but wasn't even there. She would hear the woman's voice every five minutes or so explaining how all the representatives were busy but to please stay on the line and then the space between was filled with elevator music. She was about to hang up when she heard her call finally ring through. She gave the customer service representative the identification and group number and then waited for the computer to bring up their information. A man's voice came back this time, most likely a supervisor, and was curt and to the point.

"Mrs. Anderson, your insurance was terminated as of two days ago. It is standard operating procedure for benefits to cease once employment has ended. You should be receiving information about COBRA options available to you and your family."

"Excuse me, what do you mean by employment ending?"

"Well, all I know, Mrs. Anderson, is that we got a call from Baker Diesel and Heavy Equipment saying your husband, Avery Anderson, was no longer in their employ. It says here the representative spoke to a Mr. Joe McGill."

Sandy hung up the phone and looked at Avery. How could he have been fired and not told her? She could understand him wanting to spare her more upset but sure in the hell couldn't see him keeping something like that from her. It required huge effort not to let her voice shriek with accusation as she opened her mouth to speak.

"Avery? Have there been problems at work you been scared to talk about? Somethin' you might have been afraid to tell me for fear it would push me over the edge?"

Avery looked at Sandy and could tell she was in her controlled explosion mode. He had no idea what she was talking about but knew he better be very careful how he answered.

"Sandy, darlin', you know I ain't been to work in over a week; how am I supposed to know if something happened there? What'd the insurance company say?"

"What did they say, Avery? What . . . did. . . they .. . say? Hmm. Let me see. You want their words or mine? Shit, I can't remember how they put it so I'll just tell you my way. They say your ass was fired!"

The minute she saw the look on Avery's face she realized he was as surprised as she was by the news. She felt guilt creep up and push her tongue to apologize instantly.

"Oh, Avery, I'm sorry. I thought you knew and was keeping it from me. I'm sorry I told you like I did."

It was Avery that reached for the phone then. The halo and the steel rods made it impossible for him to judge distance or turn properly so he asked Sandy to dial his work number and to hold the receiver to his ear. He was surprised to hear Joe McGill's voice after the second ring.

"Joe, this is Avery Anderson. I'm fixin' to be thrown out of the hospital because of some foul up with the god damned insurance company. They said I ain't no longer an employee and that you was the one that called. I'm sure there's just some big old mix up."

"Nope, Avery, no mix-up. George Mason come in the mornin' after you had your accident and told me he'd done drunk beer with you at Liars. You told me you had the flu. I don't 'preciate a fucker who lies to me, Avery. Hell, out of the kindness of my heart, I kept your ass on 'til you was out of danger. You ought to be thankin' me!"

"Joe . . .wait . . . don't hang up! Joe, I worked for you since I was fifteen years old! That's been goin' on eleven years! I broke my fuckin' back for you and did a damn fine job! How can you just fire me and not even tell me?"

"Hell, Avery, we been tryin' to tell you. Ain't no answer at your house and you ain't got no machine. Guess I'm tellin' you now. You're fired, Avery!"

The dial tone sounded louder to Avery than a jet taking off from the floor of his room. He motioned to Sandy because he knew he was going to throw up. They got half way to the bathroom and his body convulsed and everything but Sandy wore the contents of his stomach. Sandy decided not to try to move him any further in case he slipped and fell with all the mess. When she thought he was done, she helped him back to the bed, rang for a nurse and went to get a towel to wipe him up.

When the nurse came into the room, her irritation was obvious.

"Oh my gosh! Don't you people know how to use the bathroom or a damn call button?"

For Sandy, it was the last straw. The last thing she needed was a snooty nurse to treat Avery and her like they were nothing but trailer trash. There was Texas thunder in Sandy's voice when she spoke.

"You tight assed little bitch! How dare you talk to us like that! I suggest you turn around, call an orderly to clean up this mess and get the god damn release papers for my husband!"

Sandy heard Avery's laughter and she turned to see him trying to stuff his amusement back into his body. She laughed too because he looked like he was about to pop. There was more love in his voice when he spoke than she'd heard in awhile.

"Darlin', I swear I thought you was gonna rip that little nurse's head off like you done to that Barbie doll you got from the Salvation Army that Christmas when you was nine. I 'member you beatin' on that doll like she'd called you names and spat on you or something!"

He laughed with true affection because even as a child, Sandy had been special to his heart. The truth was he knew exactly why she'd torn that doll apart. To her, Barbie represented everything she wasn't and would never be. He sure in the hell would have taken a torch to Ken if he'd ever gotten the chance. He wondered if there was a market for Texas Trailer Trash Avery and Sandy dolls? He sure knew Sandy was a doll to him. He loved her with all his heart.

Robert had heard the yelling and asked a nurse to wheel him over to Avery's room. When the nurse opened the door he saw an orderly mopping up what looked like an explosion of peas, mashed potatoes and Jello covering almost everything in the room. Robert was quick with his usual humor.

"Oh, so that's what all the noise was. Which one of you exploded? Hmm. Oh, it must have been you, Avery, I see your brains spattered over there on the bathroom door. I know now why people call you pea brain! Hey, orderly, get a picture of this. It is good commentary on hospital cuisine!"

Sandy explained that they were releasing Avery because he'd been fired and they no longer had insurance. She watched his face as his brain tallied yet another strike against the people he loved. His heart hurt for them and he wished they could all go back in time and change the events of the past few weeks.

Sandy embraced Robert and kissed the softness of his cheeks. She pushed his chair around so that he could see Avery better and then left to go find the nurse who was supposed to teach her how to care for Avery. As soon as Sandy was out of the room Robert told Avery about an idea he'd had.

"I was thinking, Avery, do you think it's possible that they fired you because you're HIV positive? Think about it! Those bastards are bound to know after what happened. Hell, I wouldn't be surprised if everyone in town doesn't know by now. What I'm saying is if that's the case, and you can prove it, you got federal law backing you for a suit!"

The thought of everyone knowing about his illness made Avery shiver. He couldn't imagine the guys at work knowing and wondering about how he got it. Hell, they would probably think he got it from Robert. He knew Robert was waiting for him to comment on his idea. He wasn't sure what to say.

"Robert, I don't know nothin' 'bout no law or suing for rights and things. I think I'm better off to just let this go. Sandy's gonna call Celia Callier when we get back to her mama's. Ain't that some shit? We get off welfare for the first time in eight years and then gotta go right back on it!"

It bothered Robert that Avery was so accepting of the situation. He just knew he was right about why Avery had been fired. He could see the evil twinkle in George's eyes as he reported having seen Avery at Liars, the news about the beatings being spread around at work and the "accidental" slip of the tongue by one of the brother police officers about Avery being HIV positive to one of the other JCCL members. Robert would wait until things settled but he knew he wouldn't let Avery forget about his suggestion.

Sandy came back and told Avery they were bringing a wheelchair and that she would take his gear and go bring the truck to the front. She asked Robert if he wanted her to take him back to his room and he said yes. He thought maybe talking to her might plant a bug about doing some research on Avery's firing.

She brought him back into his room, hugged him and just as he was about to mention Avery having a possible lawsuit, his doctor and a nurse came into the room. Sandy kissed him goodbye and told him that she'd called Cara and they would all be staying at her trailer for awhile. Robert laughed and said something about Avery deserving a halo for living under the same roof with Cara. Sandy left but he would talk to her when the time was right. He would set the wheels in motion.

It felt weird to Avery to be outside in the world again. It looked different to him and unfamiliar. The psychologist who had talked to him warned him about cold sweats and feeling a fear that he wouldn't understand. Truth was, he hadn't understood most of what the woman talked about in the first place! He'd just nodded his head like he knew what she was saying. He was starting to think the strange flutters in his stomach had something to do with her warning.

Sandy looked over at Avery as much as she could, while still keeping her eyes on the road. She was worried about the truck greeting the road with its bad shocks and jarring him too much. She was scared to death about having the responsibility of his care but was so glad to be bringing him home with her. She'd actually been glad when Cara had suggested they all stay with her and Buster for a bit. It made her feel better knowing there were other people to help if something happened.

Sandy turned onto the road leading to their neighborhood and Avery suddenly started shrieking like a wild animal. Sandy was so frightened she almost ended up in the ditch twice before she could get the truck pulled over. Avery was frantic and yelling.

"No, don't stop! Keep going, Robert, hurry! They'll kill us! We're gonna die!"

Sandy was screaming at Avery and trying to get him to calm down. She didn't know what the hell to do. She finally decided to do what they always did in the movies, shake Avery and then slap him. She didn't dare slap his face so she slapped him hard on the left arm. To her amazement he stopped screaming and looked at her, only it was more through her than anything. His face was wet with tears and sweat and he was trembling uncontrollably. Sandy took off her sweater and put it around his shoulders. She patted his left leg while she put the truck back in gear and slowly started to move back onto the road. Her legs felt like jelly on the clutch and gas pedal but she kept telling herself she only had a few miles to go before they were home. It had never occurred to her that she would have to take him back down the road where it all happened. She felt all alone in the truck because Avery was still someplace behind them fighting for his life.

Sandy pulled into the grass and told Avery to wait until she could go get Buster to help her bring him in. She took all the medical supplies she'd been given and was just about knocked over by Tommy as he came racing out the door. She tried to stop him before he got to the truck because she wanted to warn him about Avery's injuries and the way he looked but Tommy was past her in a flash. Buster and her mama came out of the house too and they watched for a moment as Tommy crawled in through the driver's side door. They all laughed when they heard him exclaim,

"Hey cool, daddy! You look like one of those robots in the movies. Can you pick up television pictures in your brain like them?"

Cara took the bundle out of Sandy's arms so she and Buster could help Avery into the house. Sandy thought Buster looked like he was about to cry when he saw Avery's bruised and swollen head. Buster was a good man and certainly better than her mama deserved. They walked Avery toward the house, one on each side. Tommy followed behind and asked his daddy if he knew his hospital dress didn't have a back to it?

Buster and Sandy both almost sat with Avery as they slowly lowered him to the couch. Cara ran to get something for him to put his feet on and a blanket to put over him. They'd given him two fresh hospital gowns but she knew he didn't want his butt hanging out at her house. Actually that was something she probably wanted less than he did.

Sandy told Tommy to go outside for a little while because his daddy needed to rest. She explained that the ride home had made him real tired. She motioned for her mama to follow her into the bedroom. Cara helped her carry the bandages and salves, and followed her down the hall.

"Mama, I didn't want to say anything in front of Avery but he just freaked out in the truck and nearly caused me to have a wreck! He went wild, Mama! What will I do if he stays like that?"

"Darlin, hold on a minute. The poor man just traveled down the same road where he got his brains beat out, what there was of them, anyway."

Cara stopped to see if her humor registered with Sandy and calmed her any. She was glad to see her shoulders relax a little and a smile cross her lips.

"Anyway, he's gotta heal inside and out and that takes time, little girl. Alls we can do is be there for him and try to make him feel safe with us."

Sandy nodded. She knew her mama was right. It was just that she'd been so worried about his physical injuries and hadn't much thought about how hurt he was on the inside. Something told her the days and nights were going to be longer than any of them knew. She put some of the bandages on the dresser and then went into the bathroom to store the rest. When she came back into the bedroom, her mama was making some sort of body rest on the bed for Avery. Sandy put her arms around her mama from the back and squeezed gently.

"Thanks, Mama. You're really comin' through for me on this and I really do appreciate it. I don't s'pose Buster's got a cold beer in the house, does he? I sure could use one right about now."

Sandy hadn't even thought before speaking. She immediately felt bad about asking for a beer and talking about needing one. She'd, of course, seen the Jack Daniels earlier but wondered if Buster had made a pact to quit drinking too? She felt embarrassed using liquor as a means to calm down.

Cara sensed an awkwardness in the room and thought it most likely had to do with Sandy and the egg shells her daughter had set down between her and her drinking. It occurred to her that for all Sandy knew she'd spent part of the day making love to a tumbler of whiskey. She wasn't sure why but she needed Sandy to know it hadn't been that way.

"Sandy, I kinda went wild myself for a moment this afternoon. When you left out of here, I was determined to fix what was ailing me the way I always had, the only way I've known since I can remember."

Sandy interrupted her and her voice was full of contrite understanding.

"Mama, you don't got to explain. I don't need a beer, really."

Cara ignored her comment and continued.

"Now, I gotta say I probably would have drank 'til Jack and I were one and the same if Tommy hadn't come in right after you left. My point is, I didn't just put Jack away, I threw him away! Little girl, I been drinkin' longer than you've been alive so this ain't somethin' I can just leave alone like it ain't there. It's a part of me just as much as the heart that beats inside me. There's something else you should know, just 'cause I have a problem with liquor don't mean you, or anyone else, has to stop drinking around me. When you go on a diet do you tell everyone you see not to eat chocolate cake or to never ask for second helpings? Hell no you don't and it's 'cause the problem is yours and not theirs. Now come on, I'll get you that beer. Maybe if we talk real sweet to

Buster, he'll go get that Christmas tree out of the barn for us and put it up. Tommy and me bought a dandy!"

Sandy stood looking at the space she thought Cara Covington had just occupied and then pinched herself to see if she'd fallen asleep on her feet. How could it be that the mama she'd always known was such a rational person underneath? She battled hard against the resentment she felt and decided to enjoy a moment at a time. She would come to grips with her feelings when she wasn't in such need for comfort. Right now she could walk into the other room and feel the warmth of the family she'd only dreamed of before.

Sandy went into the living room and sat next to Avery. Cara was scolding Tommy for opening all the boxes of decorations they'd bought before Buster even brought the tree in. She listened to her mama's voice as if she was hearing it for the first time.

"Now Tommy, we're gonna lose or break half the stuff before Buster even gets the tree in the door. I know you're excited but we got do this methodical like. I tell you what, you be the organizer. What goes on the tree first?"

Tommy rolled his eyes as if like a slip, his grandma's ignorance was showing. He sighed and plopped down in front of her on his knees. He positioned the packages on the floor and with great care in explanation said,

"Grandma, you see, the lights has to go on first 'cause they are the background for everything else. It would be dumb to put on the decorations and then have the lights on the outside! Gosh, don't you know nothin' 'bout Christmas?"

Cara looked at him and could never tell him what the truth about that was. No, she'd never known a Christmas, an Easter, a Halloween, or even her birthday. No day had been special when she was growing up. To her, moments were special. The times she was alone walking home from school, or the moment her daddy would get up and leave her room. There came the moments when she was fourteen and she would be able to sneak out to be with other men who would buy her liquor so she didn't care what they did to her. Those were the special moments in Cara's life, not holidays. She smiled at Tommy and felt glad he had something to hold onto besides the pain other people put in his heart. Her words to him were sincere.

"Tommy, I'm makin' it your job to teach your old grandma about Christmas. It'll be like homework. Every evening you gotta tell me somethin' special about the holiday. Okay?"

Tommy's grin filled her heart and the sight of Buster coming through the door with the tree made her realize Tommy had already taught her the first lesson. The smell of Christmas is not in the nose but in the heart.

Avery was watching as they all gathered around the tree and ohed and ahed. He felt bad about taking Sandy away from the excitement but his head hurt so bad he thought only a guillotine would ease the pain. He tried not to be too loud when he spoke but they all turned anyway.

"Sandy? I think I need to go on to bed now."

Sandy looked at Buster and he was immediately by her side to help Avery up, leaving Cara and Tommy to hold the tree. They tried once to raise him off the couch and had no luck. The second time Avery was more ready and used his legs to help propel his huge body. They walked each on one side until they got to the door leading into the hall. Sandy made sure Buster had a firm grip on Avery and then moved so that she was through the door. She noticed that Avery placed his feet down without thought to where they were going. She hoped it was merely the pain of the headache and not some problem with the signals getting to his brain.

They got him to the bedroom and eased him down on the makeshift incline that Cara had made for him. Sandy was amazed when Avery sighed and sunk into the bed's comfort. Cara could be resourceful, as well as kind. Would wonders never cease?

Sandy told Buster to apologize to her mama because she felt she needed to stay with Avery until he was sleep. She thought that maybe she would lay next to him for just a bit until he started snoring and then she would go back and help with the tree.

Sandy awoke to the sound of Avery's moaning. She felt disoriented, not knowing where she was, what day it was, or even how long she'd been wherever she was. There was enough light in the room from the security lamps outside to see Avery's face, once her eyes adjusted. She realized that he was sleeping soundly, just in pain or dreaming. She got up because her bladder felt as if it would burst any minute. As she peed, she kept hearing music that had almost the same pitch as her urine hitting the water below. She wondered if the phrase tinkling had come from such an experience. The sound intrigued her, so rather than go back into the bedroom, she went into the living room.

As she walked down the hall, the smell of the Christmas tree met her first and then the smell of cinnamon made her nostrils flare with delight. She came to the hallway door and saw the glow of the Christmas tree lights. She looked beyond the tree and saw her mama in the kitchen. She seemed to be talking to herself while spooning something from a bowl onto something else on the counter. Sandy walked towards Cara with a stealth that would surprise anyone. Her words were the softest of whispers.

"Mama? Are you all right? What are you doing?"

Cara jumped so high, Sandy feared she would hit her head on the low ceiling of the trailer. She watched her mama grab her chest and listened to the puff of words that came from her mouth.

"Oh gosh, Sandy, you scared the pee out of me!"

Sandy looked at the kitchen table and saw the bottle of Jack Daniels sitting ready for the next tip of the bottle. She felt her heart beating in her feet but was careful in her choice of words.

"Mama? Can I help you spoon those cookies? What kind are they? Here, let me at least light the oven for you. I just love the smell of cinnamon, don't you?"

She was amazed at how fragile her mother felt as she steered her toward one of the kitchen chairs. It wasn't the first time that Sandy had felt maternal toward her mama but it certainly was the first time the feelings were not accompanied by anger and hatred.

Cara turned loose-fitting eyes to her daughter and stirred her words better than she had the cookie dough.

"Want to know the funny thing about bein' up alone lookin' at the first Christmas tree ya ever had? Makes ya wish ya could forget the years ya didn't have one. Hey, sounds like I shoulda used that rolling pin on my tongue instead of on those cookies! Hell, I didn't even drink that much. I wanted to but the first taste went right to my brain and started doing the god damn Macarena in my head and you know how much I hate that damn song!"

Sandy lit a match and positioned it to light the pilot. She smiled at the thought of Jack Daniels doing the Macarena in her mama's brain. She didn't exactly know why but there was a comfort in Cara's sliding back a little. It was more familiar, almost normal, to Sandy and so little had felt normal in her life lately. She sat in a chair across from her mother and was surprised to see tears streaming down her face. Sandy covered her mama's hands with her own and lovingly tried to soothe Cara with her voice.

"It's okay, Mama. I know what you feel like. My attachment ain't to Jack Daniels but it's an addiction just the same. You know that feelin' you got right now? It's the same one I get when I tell myself I ain't ever gonna eat another cookie and then I see the bag in cupboard and think maybe just one. It don't take long before the whole bag is gone and I'm hung over from the sugar. I hate myself inside, Mama, just like you do right now. I know your heart. It's why I get so angry, Mama. When I scream at you I'm really screaming at myself."

Cara nodded. She wasn't nearly as drunk as she sounded. She'd actually only had a few shots but it was late, she was tired and they'd been one right after the other. What she found amusing was that she hated the taste. The whiskey tasted bitter on her tongue and she'd realized something after the third shot went down. She always drank to block the bitter residue life left on her but the past days of being sober showed her that sometimes when life is at its most bitter, the living of it is the sweetest.

Cara rose from the table to check the cookies. The smell made her mouth water and the glands in her neck get that squeezed feeling. She placed the sheet on the counter and carefully guided the spatula under each cookie to slide it onto a platter. She put another batch into the oven, then brought the platter of cookies to the table.

She was about to continue the conversation with Sandy when she saw Sandy's hand reach around the platter for the biggest cookie. It seemed she wasn't even aware as she brought the cookie up and let her nose inhale the baked cinnamon smell. She held the cookie so close to her nose that Cara was sure if she looked there would be tiny granules of sugar in her daughter's nostrils. Without an ounce of judgment, Cara stopped Sandy's hand from going near her mouth with the cookie. She took the cookie in her left hand and with her right, moved the shot glass in front of Sandy. Her words were filled with decisive truths.

"Darlin, I got an idea. How 'bout I eat this cookie and you take my next drink. It's a cinch the sweetness of the cookie won't make me want more and the bitterness of the drink will make you want less. We'll manage to kill two birds with one stone by tradin' weaknesses. Sandy girl, life's been fuckin' us ever since we've known it. I think it's 'bout damn time we quit doin' things to fuck ourselves!"

Sandy smiled as she picked up the bottle to pour a shot. It was three in the morning and as she held the glass to Cara and Cara held the cookie to her, they toasted the coming of Christmas. The tinkling music was playing Oh Holy Night and as Cara took a bite from the cookie, she said,

"Hey, little girl, maybe now I can quit calling that song Oh Holy Shit!"

Sandy laughed and it felt really good. She knew that there had been an understanding reached at the table and that it was okay that neither her nor her mother stood on ceremony about such things. For them life was never simple but the seeing of it was, even when the living of it wasn't. She downed the rest of the whiskey, grimaced at the taste and feel of it, and said good night to Cara. She walked back toward the bedroom and heard the clunk of the cookie as it hit the bottom of the garbage can. She would sleep well and knew her mama would, too.

Avery woke to the sound of Sandy yelling at Tommy to be quiet. He wondered how come it was people did things that made no sense. Whatever Tommy had been doing hadn't wakened him but Sandy's booming at him about being too loud sure had. He tried to swing his legs around so he could go pee. As he got his right leg to cooperate and was working on getting his left one to follow, when Sandy came in and yelled at him.

"What the hell are you doing? You want to fall and end up hurting your head again? I swear Avery Anderson, we ain't got no insurance and you'd just have to lay on the floor and bleed to death right here in front of everyone! Now, what do you need? I'll do it for you."

Avery gave her his best smart ass look, the one she hated and then laughed at her reaction.

"Okay, babe, you go on in the bathroom and pee for me okay?"

Raising his hospital gown, he added,

"You may want to take this along for the ride!"

Just as he exposed himself, Cara came into the room to see what all the commotion was about. Avery thought she was going to keel over from laughing. She grabbed hold of the door jam and tried to stop laughing long enough to speak.

"Hey, Avery, I'd be showin' that around too if I were you. It's the only good head you got left! Course, it's pretty near the same color as the one attached to your neck, all purple like!"

The three of them stood laughing so hard they brought Buster and Tommy running, wanting to see what was so damn funny. Buster looked at them and felt the infectious pull of their laughter. He looked at Cara, still standing in the doorway, and asked,

"Have ya'll lost your minds? What in the hell is so damn funny?"

Cara turned to him and replied with a perfectly straight face.

"No, we ain't lost our minds. We were talking about how purple Avery's head is."

Buster didn't understand. He thought it was mean to make fun of Avery's injuries. He shook his head and walked back to the living room. He heard the laughter continue as he went outside to do his chores. He was convinced he was living with a bunch of looney tunes.

Tommy jumped on the bed and started chanting.

"Daddy is a purple head. Daddy is a purple head."

Sandy shooed everyone out of the room and took Avery's arm to help him to the bathroom. She positioned him in front of the toilet and stepped back to wait for him to go. She couldn't see his face but she knew he wanted to speak.

"Hey, darlin, aren't ya gonna come hold it for me? In the hospital that little nurse, Kathie, did. The only thing was, she must have thought it had to be primed before it worked, 'cause she kept a pumping it back and forth. Man, I sure liked that little nurse!"

He didn't see the snap with the towel coming but he sure felt it on his bare ass. He thought how wonderful it felt to be home and that if nothing else, he had a real appreciation for the warmth of his family.

Morris Foley felt strange about going to Cara's to take Avery's statement. He'd never been on the right side of the woman, if she even had one. He had been surprised when he found out Avery had been released from the hospital and flabbergasted when he found out they were all staying with Cara. Maybe he'd misjudged her and she was a nicer person than he thought. He wasn't the type to judge a book by its cover but the Cara he'd known had been naked with her pages flapping in the wind for everyone to see. She had showed her butt in public too many times for there to be too many wrong ideas about her.

He pulled into the yard and saw Buster walking towards the barn. He nodded to him and thought when Buster nodded back it was with a stiffness, like he was afraid his head would fall off his neck. He didn't know much about the man but figured he couldn't be too bright if he chose Caustic Cara over Caramel Candy. Morris shook his head and knocked on the door.

Cara greeted Morris with almost cordial civility. She told him that Avery was staying in the room second door on the right and to just go on back. He walked down the hall and heard Sandy's voice and Avery's laughter. Just as he neared the second door, he almost collided with Avery as Sandy helped him out of the bathroom. Morris was as embarrassed as Avery was surprised to meet him in the hall.

"Morris! I thought Cara was talkin' to Buster. I had no idea you were here. I guess you came to talk about what happened?"

Morris nodded and mouthed a hello to Sandy.

Avery suggested they would be more comfortable talking in the living room and asked Sandy if she could go back into the bedroom and get him a blanket. As if on cue, Morris took Avery's arm and guided him down the hall towards the hall door. He felt a little hostility in Sandy's welcome and the gesture was one to reassure her that he was not there to cause pain but to help.

Cara asked if any of them would like some coffee and placed a plate of cookies on the end table next to Avery. As she filled the carafe, she watched the expression on Sandy's face as she placed a blanket over Avery. A picture of a protective mother hen came to mind as Sandy tucked the blanket around him. She felt the tension in her daughter's shoulders as if it were her own and thought how strange to feel that connected to her. She realized, that for Sandy, Avery's statement made the whole ordeal real. It would set the wheels in motion for justice and she knew Sandy feared such a thing didn't exist in their world. Perhaps she was afraid it would be the final link in a chain of disappointments and one that would make her completely lose faith in life.

Morris let Avery speak without interruption. He was afraid if he said anything he would color Avery's recollection by interjecting things Robert had said. He wrote down three names and then added two with question marks by them. He had been conducting a little side investigation on George and Leo but he hadn't included them at all in the report he'd typed. Arrest warrants had been issued on Spike, Sponge and Harry but he knew finding them would be more difficult than just knocking on their front doors.

Morris felt he must have been telegraphing his thoughts because Sandy asked him what was being done to find the men. He knew no matter what he said, she would feel "not enough" was the answer. He wondered if his incredible uneasiness with the case was because of the hostility he felt coming from the victims and their families, or because he knew that it was likely that the perpetrators had been tipped off by his own co-workers concerning imminent arrest. There were literally thousands of places the three could be hiding. He also knew that wherever they were they had police protection.

Morris finished his coffee and thanked Avery for making his job easy. Everyone in the room knew it was a lie but he said it to try and make them understand he was on their side. He didn't want them to think he was like some of the others on the force. He rose to leave and Sandy surprised him by accompanying him to the front door. As he opened the screen, he could almost feel the heat of her breath on the back of his neck as she whispered,

"Find them, Morris. Find them and put them away!"

Sandy walked through the living room in a huff and muttered something about cleaning the bedroom. Cara looked at Avery and thought he looked like a heap of sorrow that had been left to melt into oblivion. She went to the couch and sat next to him. She patted his leg and spoke like a true mother-in-law.

"Give her time, Avery. She has what they call internal injuries. The only way she can keep from going off completely is to carry anger around in her furnace. She ain't mad at you. She's just mad at the whole god damned world. The thing that happened didn't just cripple you all up; it made her head damaged, too. Just love her like you've always done and she'll come around."

Avery nodded. He knew Cara was right but he felt so responsible for everything that had happened. He should have known better than to take Robert to Liars in the first place. He should have been honest and said that homosexuals weren't considered patrons at a place like that but were on the menu as fair game! It was his fault. It was all his fault!

Sandy pulled the covers up on the bed and placed the pillows just as Cara had the day before. Her head hurt from clenching her teeth and working her jaw. She could not shake the powerful need to hurt back. She'd never felt anything inside her like the hatred she felt for the men who hurt Avery and Robert. She couldn't believe that the memory of her father grunting and rutting over her didn't fill her heart with as much venom as imagining those men on that road that night with her husband and her friend. She'd seen stories on the news about family members of victims walking into court and killing the defendant; she understood now why they did.

Sandy stood at the dresser putting away socks and underwear and didn't hear Cara come into the room. She continued to bundle socks and talk to herself. When Cara spoke, Sandy lurched forward into the dresser.

"God damn, Mama, why don't you make a noise when you come into a room? You just about gave me a heart attack!"

Cara apologized but went on to say what she'd come to say in spite of Sandy's agitation.

"Sit down, Sandy. I got somethin' to say about Morris' visit."

Sandy turned and without putting her anger in her words, she aimed for a direct hit.

"Mama, first it ain't none of your concern and second, I ain't in no mood to talk about it right now!"

Sandy's answer was fuel to Cara's fire and the blaze was hot.

"Bull shit! It sure in the hell is my business when I got your whole family livin' under my roof! You think you're the only one feelin' the pain of all this? Guess again, little girl. Now Sandy, we've come a long way since all this mess happened but you're way out of line on this one, missy! You just left your husband sittin' on that couch feelin' like he's responsible for takin' your world and turnin' it to dust. That ain't fair, Sandy!"

Sandy sat on the bed next to her mama and sighed so deeply four plants could have lived off the carbon dioxide she exhaled. She stared at the wall for a moment as if to get the words right in her head.

"Mama, I know it ain't Avery's fault. There's an anger inside me right now that makes me want to strike out and hurt someone. I ain't used to feelin' that way and I don't know how to keep it from coming out. One minute I think I'm gettin' a handle on it and then the next it hits me like a tidal wave. There also ain't no controlling what sets it off. I been friends with Morris Foley my whole life and just now I wanted to punch his lights out!"

Cara had an evil smile on her face. More than once was the time she'd wanted to smack Morris around. She was almost positive he'd felt the same about her though. She patted her daughter's leg and left her with the only solution she had at the moment.

"Darlin', I ain't tellin' you to stuff your anger like a kid stuffs a bra. I'm just sayin' that Avery ain't the one to leave your anger with. It hurts him deeper than most. He's beatin' himself up over all this."

Sandy sighed again and simply said,
"I know, Mama."

CHAPTER THIRTY-SIX

Robert was half asleep when he heard a knock at his door. He assumed it was Sandy or Cara so he said "come in" without reservation. He was about to make some smart ass comment about the sick and their need of rest when his mouth dropped too far to utter any words.

Maurice had the tan of a man who'd spent hours on the sunny slopes skiing his heart out. His blonde hair was bleached from roots to ends and his teeth looked whiter than snow itself as he smiled. He stood just inside the door a moment to get used to seeing Robert all bruised and battered. When he spoke, his words sounded like honey.

"Hi, Robert. I was in the neighborhood and I thought I would pop in and say hello."

Robert couldn't speak. He felt joy, anger, confusion and pain all at the same time. He knew anything that came out of his mouth would sound stupid.

"Maurice, what the hell are you doing here? I mean . . . hi!"

He hated the feeling he had in the pit of his heart. It was that kind of excitement that betrayed his resolve to hate Maurice with the totality of his being. He didn't want to be happy to see him and he didn't want to be sucked in by his looks but he was and he was.

Maurice moved into the room fully and sat on the edge of the bed rather than in one of the chairs. He had tears in his eyes as he looked at Robert's battered face and head. He felt an overwhelming desire to touch the bruises and trace the outline of Robert's lips with his fingers. He felt so sorry, so sad for his one time lover and forever friend. He wasn't sure how to brooch the reason for his visit but decided truth would work better than anything.

"Robert, before you get the wrong idea, Charles is with me. He's waiting in the lobby for me. We flew into Houston last night to do some shopping and to attend a Gay Rights Gala in River Oaks. We argued a bit about me coming to see you, but I told him it was my duty as your friend."

Robert rankled at his words. He felt the veins in his neck pulse against his skin. He decided he'd been a victim enough and it was time to cut loose and cut deep.

"How white of you, Maurice. I realize slumming is not something you enjoy doing. God knows, the stench of your whoring past is stuck so far up Charles' butt that he walks with both legs out to the side. I don't need your sympathy. I don't need your guilt. But mostly, Maurice, I don't need your shit! Get over yourself, get fucked and get out, you bitch!"

The look on Maurice's face was worth more to Robert than any grand prize in the contest of life. Maurice had been shocked, shamed, and slammed all in one fell swoop. He rose without a word and was out the door in a matter of seconds.

Robert felt like dancing on the bed! He had a lightness to him that had nothing to do with his slight build. He knew at that moment that he was going to be okay and that life lived in him again. He whispered to himself the infamous line from Poltergeist II with a personal slant . . .

"I'm baaaccckkk!!!"

He was basking in the strength he felt when his doctor came into the room. He was actually glad to see him because they'd been discussing the possibility of his release. He thought if Avery had been well enough to go home, then perhaps he was too. He planned to lobby on his own behalf and show the doctor just how great he felt by getting up on his own to go pee. He felt a little like a child who was being potty trained and had to show his mommy that he made wee wee.

It was agreed that if Robert could find someone to stay with him then he would be released the following day. His disappointment was evident because he had no idea whom he could ask. The only people he considered his friends were Sandy, Avery and Cara and their plates were full. He would rather die than have his mother fly in and she was the only other option he had. He rested his head against the pillow and wondered how much a private nurse would cost and whether his insurance would pick up part of the tab for one.

Sandy decided she needed to get out for awhile. She was glad when her mama said she thought it was a good idea, too. Cara told her she and Avery would be fine and that she might even talk him into playing a couple hands of Gin with her if he felt up to it. Sandy kissed Avery and headed out the door. She wanted to get a card for Robert and bring it by the hospital.

It seemed every card Sandy picked up was over five dollars and she wondered when cards had gotten so damned expensive. She was worried about money and knew that even if Avery still had a job, it would be a long time before he was well enough to work. She finally found a two dollar card and went to the register. There was a sign posted near the cigarette cases that said ACCEPTING APPLICATIONS. She paid for the card and asked the checker for an application. She didn't have to be educated to wait on people and if she did, then Avery and Tommy had made sure she'd earned her degree.

When Sandy walked into Robert's room he was beaming. She thought he looked happier than he'd ever looked before. She couldn't help but tease him a little about the goofy grin on his face.

"Hmm. I see they have you back on drugs again. What is it this time? . . . crack?"

He laughed and patted the bed next to him. She sat and waited to hear about what had made him so happy.

He scooted over a bit to give her more room and then started to relay the events of the morning in the order of their importance to him.

"Well, I talked with the doc this morning and if I can find someone to help me out, I can get out of this place tomorrow! I have a call into my insurance company about home health care but no one's called me back yet. Then, just before you came up, I got a call from Morris Foley and they arrested Spike a half hour ago! They doubt he'll tell where the others are but they feel like if they found him they'll find the others too. I know this is wrong, but I hope they put him in a cell with some great big bubba butt brother like some of the guys I met at the seedier bars. He'll find out what it feels like to have something stuck so far up his butt he'll feel it in his throat!"

Sandy was shocked at the anger in Robert. He'd seemingly been so together and strong she hadn't realized how deeply hurt he'd really been. She'd just heard what he really carried in his heart and she felt guilty for not seeing it before. Just as she was about to comfort him and apologize for being blind to his pain, he became animated like she'd never seen him.

"Sandy, girl, I saved the best news for last. You will never guess who came by to see me today!"

He clapped his hands together in pure excitement and kept telling her to guess, guess, guess. She laughed because he looked like Tommy when something wonderful happened at school. She tried to imagine what on earth would make him so filled with joy. She couldn't think of anything and finally just shrugged with her hands opened and out. She could tell he was preparing one of his pithy, dramatic explanations.

"Well, the doc had just left and I'd made the call to the insurance company. Anyway, there was a knock at the door and I just figured it was you or Cara so I said come in. Sandy, it was Maurice!! Oh my gosh, I about fell out of this bed. I mean, I hear nothing in all this time and then when I finally do hear, I get that mean little note that I'm sure Charles typed up about using Maurice's name as next of kin. No, I'm sorry about your accident, sorry about being such a dick, or even a get well soon! I swear, when I saw him standing there at the door I was just more surprised than I can say. He looked good, honey! His hair was all bleached and his skin was all tanned. He was downright yummy looking! Well . . . he starts in about how, before I get the wrong idea, Charles is with him and is waiting in the lobby. Then the bitch has the nerve to say they argued a little about him coming to see me. Sandy, the whore had the nerve to tell me he felt it was his duty. Well, let me tell you, it might have been his duty but I slammed his ass and kicked real booty! I told him to take his sorry ass and get the fuck out!"

Sandy was rolling with laughter. She had tears streaming down her face and her mouth hurt from the exercise. Robert's explanation had gone from swishy to being down with the home boys theatrics. She had been begging him to stop because she really felt like she was getting way too sore from laughing. She loved him more at that moment than she thought possible to love another human being.

She took one of the tissues off the night stand, dabbed her eyes and caught her breath. Robert's mood changed and he got serious. She really didn't know what to expect from him next and she liked it that way. His voice was back to normal when he spoke.

"Sandy? Did Avery mention the possibility of bringing suit against the company he worked for and the owners? I told him I thought that his HIV virus was the real reason he was let go and that if he could prove it, federal law was on his side."

Sandy looked at Robert and he knew Avery hadn't said a word. He wanted to tell her what he thought and why. He knew if Avery wouldn't listen Sandy probably would. He thought the best approach would be to make her want to bleed the bastards dry.

Robert hit a sore spot with Sandy. A trial would publicize Avery's condition and that was the last thing her family needed. She hated herself for thinking it but there was shame related to HIV and even if it was ignorant to call it the gay disease, that was how Avery had contracted it. She thought Avery would rather die than have everyone know about his past. Robert didn't understand what it was like to grow up in an area where a person was born five minutes from where they live as an adult. She knew he meant well but she couldn't even consider any more pain right now. She was still thinking on how to answer him when he did it for her.

"You think it's a bad idea just like he did? God damn it, Sandy, we got to fight against discrimination. Why in the world do you think they put laws of protection in place? What would happen if we all just laid down and told the world to run over us?"

Sandy stopped him before he got too far up on his soap box.

"Robert, you gotta think of me and Avery for a minute. First, all I got to fight for is the very life of my family. What do you think our lives would be like if on every news channel and in every paper there were headlines about how Avery Anderson done sued his company for firing him when they found out he had HIV? How could we face anyone in this town ever again? I'm scared enough about prosecuting the men that beat ya'll up. I swear three of the checkers at the Quickly Seven glared at me so hard yesterday when I went to get Mama's cigarettes that I looked for stab wounds after. Our world ain't like yours. We got a son, each other; we got family to consider."

Sandy hated herself the minute the words came out of her mouth. They didn't sound like she meant them and she desperately wanted to take them back. She looked at Robert's face and saw a wall go up that had never been there before. His voice was quiet but obviously controlled.

"Yeah, that's right, Sandy. I forgot; I'm just a reactive queer wanting to change the world and shake things up. It's much better to let discrimination beat us down and place us deeper in the hole society dug for us. Why fight anything? They're right. I'm a fucking faggot and you're nothing but poor white trailer trash!"

Sandy couldn't believe how the mood of the room had changed. She needed another tissue but this time the tears weren't from laughter. She'd just hurt the best friend she'd had in her life and he'd hurt her by not understanding the tremendous fear her heart felt. She thought she was very close to breaking down completely, so she got up and walked towards the door. She told Robert she needed to go down the hall to the bathroom.

Sandy walked to the nurses station instead and explained that she'd recently had blood tests done at the hospital after a miscarriage and needed to know where to go to get the results. The nurse told her she remembered her and that she would have to either speak to Dr. Sethler or get the results from her family physician. The nurse added that Dr. Sethler was on duty and she could have him paged if Sandy wanted. Sandy nodded and waited at the far end of the counter.

Dr. Sethler came up and shook Sandy's hand. He said he'd forwarded the results of her AIDS test to her private physician but he had her file with him and would be happy to discuss the results with her. He asked her to follow him to a more private area and Sandy wasn't sure her legs would work they were shaking so badly.

They went into an area reserved for family members receiving tragic news and her mind went immediately to Virginia. She imagined sitting behind the glass walls to hear that a loved one had died and then to be outside the walls seeing the actions of grief without hearing its sounds. She sat and drew in a deep breath. Dr. Sethler looked at her file and then turned his eyes to her. He wore glasses and as many people in their mid-forties do, he looked over the rims to see her.

She knew he wanted to be sure of what he would tell her but she wished he would just hurry and give her the news. He had that doctor sternness to his voice when he spoke.

"Mrs. Anderson, your test came back negative for the virus."

Sandy gasped and felt like floating to the ceiling. Dr. Sethler was quick to bring her back down.

"Please don't misunderstand, Mrs. Anderson. This test came back negative but you will have to continue to be tested every three months for a year. Some doctors say less time is needed but I like to err on the side of too much than too little with HIV. You are never to have unprotected sex with your husband again and please be very careful when handling anything that contains his bodily fluids. Do you understand?"

Sandy nodded and thanked the him. She walked back towards Robert's room ready to apologize and then make a beeline for home and Avery. She knocked on Robert's door and heard a barely audible "come in."

She opened the door and stuck the card through before she poked her head in. She put an exaggerated pout on her lips and mouthed the words, I am so sorry, followed by, I love you!

Robert begrudgingly crooked his finger and waved her in. She came around to the left side of his bed, hugged him, kissed him and handed him the card. He opened it and on the front it had a little boy and girl hand in hand. He read the verse.

> If friendship could be measured in feet
> You'd span the world twice over complete
> If love is the question then you are the answer
> If friendship's a ballet then you are a dancer
> I wonder how I lived life before you were there
> Just stopping by to say how much I do care

The card was signed, loving you Simply Sandy! It was Robert's turn with the tissue and he wanted to wait until he had just the right words.

"Sandy, I owe you an apology. I can't expect you to throw yourself into a world you've never been a part of. I get so angry about things and I have a blind side when it comes to social causes. You and Avery have to make your own decisions about things. I was just trying to help, Sandy, I really was."

"I know, Robert. I have to tell you something. I lied to you just now. I didn't go to the bathroom. I went to find out if the results of my AIDS test had come in. They have."

She watched as Robert's eyebrows arched in surprise and then knitted together with the wrinkles in his forehead. He looked like he wanted to know but didn't.

Sandy wanted to go home so she didn't prolong the suspense.

"It came back negative this time, Robert. I'm okay for now!"

Robert forgot about the halo on his head and hit Sandy square in the face with it when he hugged her. He laughed and she heard the same playful, loving tone in his voice when he spoke.

"Here you give me good news and I bash you in the face with my halo! Oh Sandy, I just can't tell you how happy I am that you tested negative! I know we can't bank on just one test but considering how long you and Avery have been together, it's a really good sign. Are you going to have Tommy tested?"

Sandy shifted uncomfortably. She'd been battling over whether or not to test him or wait to see if she was clear. She knew that drawing blood would scare him and he wouldn't understand why it was necessary. She told Robert the only thing of which she was sure.

"I don't know yet, Robert. I guess I'll have to talk to Avery about it."

Robert nodded but wondered how Sandy could even consider not getting Tommy tested. He felt she was being ignorant but didn't pursue the conversation further. They'd already had their disagreement for the day and he wouldn't open that can of worms again. He knew he was being overly sensitive about it all but he'd seen the reality of the monster too many times.

Sandy was about to leave and then she stopped and came back to the side of his bed. He could literally see her mind working. It made him want to laugh out loud. He wondered if she knew what she looked like when she mulled something over in her brain? He tilted his head to the right side and let out a slow,

"Yes?"

Sandy laughed and sat back down next to him.

"Is it that easy to see when my mind gets to workin'? Mama always did say I was clear headed but I thought she was payin' me a compliment. Robert? What would you think about coming to stay with us at Mama's? Now, before you call for the orderlies to have me thrown out, just listen a minute. You could stay in the room with Avery and I could sleep in the other room with Tommy. Mama and I could make sure you both are took care of without havin' to divide our time or drive anywhere to do it. It's coming on Christmas and we could just have our own little family. I know Mama would love it. Hell, I'd love it. She'd have someone besides me to tease and devil!"

Robert was both appalled by and in love with the idea. He couldn't imagine actually living with the likes of Cara and her crew but at the same time thought it could be the most fun he'd ever had. While he liked Avery, the thought of sharing a bed with him was almost repugnant. He promised her he would give it careful thought. He watched Sandy walk out the door and knew he'd probably agree to her plan. Hell, staying there would be a lot better than hiring a nurse.

CHAPTER THIRTY-SEVEN

Buster called Cara into the bedroom. He'd been trying out the new post hole digger he'd bought and smelled like a summer sidewalk egg on a bed of winter lettuce. He stunk to high heaven but not a drop of sweat was visible. Cara told him as much when she came into the room to see what he needed.

"My gosh, Buster, the sun shits on you no matter what time of year it is. I sure in the hell hope you didn't call me back here to fool around because if you did I'd have to go find cow shit to improve the smell in here!"

Buster was never offended by the truth and he knew Cara always spoke it. He talked while he gathered clean clothes to take into the bathroom with him.

"Darlin', I been thinkin'. Christmas is in a week and I got a couple of thousand saved in a Christmas account at the bank. Avery, Sandy and Tommy been havin' such a rough time and I thought maybe you and me could go get that money and give them a real Christmas. It ain't like it would put me back any."

Cara looked at Buster with his beer belly straining against his overalls and grease stains on his shirt and thought he was just about the finest man she'd ever seen in her life. She hugged him to her and whispered that she thought that would be just fine. His smile could've lit the Christmas tree all by itself and as he picked up his clothes to head for the bathroom, she said what she never had.

"I love you, Buster."

He just nodded and replied,

"I know you do."

Cara smiled and hugged herself. She was feeling what life felt like for the first time and she liked its natural warmth. She'd never realized how cold being a drunk made the outside even as it warmed the inside of a body. She heard Sandy's voice coming from Avery's room and went to see if her outing had made her feel better. She stuck her head in the door and came in on the tail end of a conversation she just had to ask about.

"Excuse me, girlie, did I just hear you right? Did you say you asked Robert to come stay here when he gets out of the hospital? Did I miss something? When did this become your house?"

Sandy didn't let her mama's tone damper her enthusiasm. She didn't think she was serious anyway. She explained it to her as she had to Robert and to Avery.

"Think about it, Mama. It makes sense. Robert is like family and we wouldn't have to be dividin' our time up between the care of him and Avery. We can kill two birds with one stone kinda."

Cara held her hand up for Sandy to stop. She had some say in things.

"Sandy, I know you've got a heart as big as Houston but did you give any thought about what it would look like bringing Robert here to mend? Talk about killing things and casting stones, I could sure see a few throwed through our windows in the middle of the night with notes on 'em. They'd read something like, fuck you, faggot lovers! I love the boy; you know that, but ain't no hidin' that he's queer. Hell, after what happened, the whole town knows and I ain't had a one shake my hand to congratulate me about bein' his friend. Think about Tommy if you can't think of anything else."

Sandy was shocked and angry. She decided she wasn't in the mood to fight so she just told her mama how it was going to be.

"I'm sorry you feel that way, Mama. We got plenty of room in our trailer and me, Tommy, Avery and Robert can just stay there startin' tomorrow. I appreciate all you've done to help us but, Mama, Robert needs a family and we're all he's got."

Cara looked at her daughter and then at Avery. She just couldn't resist asking Avery what he thought of Sandy's idea.

"So big boy, what do you think of this plan? You gonna feel good about opening your home to all the hatred and talk?"

Avery sat as straight as he could on the bed and thought carefully about what he was going to say.

"Cara, Robert is one of the best people I know. Hell, when those men came at us he was on Harry like a wildcat, even as small as he is. He literally went to bat for me and I think I'd do just about anything for him. If Sandy says he needs a place to stay, then he's welcomed in my home."

Cara just shook her head. She didn't think either one of them knew what they were in for but she decided that if they were willing to risk the wrath of the town, then she'd stand by them.

"Well, looks like I'm out voted here. I can't have my daughter carin' for her brood and takin' in strays to boot. Robert can stay here if he wants, Sandy, but when the shit hits the fan don't be surprised when the walls get dirty!"

The phone rang and as Cara went to answer it she heard Sandy talking to Avery with excited anticipation. She put the receiver down on the counter and walked back to the bedroom.

"Sandy, it's Morris Foley. He wants to talk to you."

Every time Sandy noticed her mama staring at her she would turn to face the opposite direction. She didn't want her mama to know what this conversation was about after the discussion they'd just had. Morris told her they'd arrested Harry and he was squealing like a pig. He wanted to warn her about what he'd heard guys saying at the station. She tried not to shudder at his words when he said he'd heard one of the officers say, "The JCCL don't miss no targets and the Andersons and Covingtons may be skeet now but when we're done with them they'll be nothin' but skeet shit."

Sandy hung up the phone and tried to gather her composure. She was shaking internally and hoped it wasn't visible on the outside. Her mama asked what Morris wanted and she passed the conversation off as inconsequential.

"Oh, he just told me they arrested Harry. Seems he's talkin' more than they thought he would."

Cara didn't need to be a psychologist to recognize silent signals. She knew her daughter too well not too notice how she'd tried to protect her conversation with Morris. She knew Morris said a lot more to Sandy than she was letting on and she imagined what he'd said wasn't good news.

Sandy walked back towards the bedroom and thought maybe Morris had been exaggerating. She had no doubt the men on the force talked about the case but she thought it improbable that such bold threats had been made against her family. She decided to keep things to herself because until something actually happened, it was only talk.

Avery looked strange and distant when Sandy came into the room. She sat next to him and ran her fingers along the base of his neck in gentle massage.

"You got one of them headaches, darlin'? Want me to go get you some of them pills that knock you on your ass so you can get some sleep?"

Avery's eyes narrowed and anger lit the corners. He placed his hands on hers to stop her kneading action and asked what Morris had wanted.

"Oh, I almost forgot. He just wanted to tell me about Harry singin' in jail. Seems we're gonna have a real good case against those guys. He feels sure . . ."

Avery interrupted her and she saw the bones in his jaw working against his skin as if to break free.

"Sandy, I heard what Morris said. I got up to pee but Buster was still takin' a shower so I went on into your mama's bedroom and picked up the extension. I was gonna ask Morris about somethin'. I heard him, Sandy! I heard what they're sayin' down at the station!"

Sandy placed her hands between the two front bars of Avery's halo and turned his face toward hers. She saw the fear in his eyes but more than that she saw the guilt of a man who thought he'd wreaked havoc on his family. She wasn't as sorry he heard Morris as she was sad he took responsibility for such things being said.

She was going to try and calm Avery's fears the same way she'd calmed her own but Cara's excited voice stopped her.

"Sandy! Get in here! Hurry!"

Sandy told Avery she would be right back and was irritated as she walked down the hall to the living room.

"What the hell, Mama? I was talking to Avery!"

Cara put her fingers to her lips, took the remote to turn up the television and patted the couch next to her.

"You need to see this, little girl. It's about one of those guys that done beat up Robert and Avery. They just interrupted my story with what they call breaking news."

Sandy sat next to her mother and turned her attention to the graphics swirling around in melodramatic fashion on the television screen. The local news anchor looked somber and his voice took command of the air waves as he said,

"There has evidently been a murder at the Harris County Jail. Harry Johnson was being held on two counts of felonious assault and battery in the county jail and was evidently stabbed to death this afternoon in his cell. A Harris County Sheriff's Department spokesperson said that Johnson was found in his bunk where he'd apparently been stabbed four times in the chest. The spokesperson said a guard went to get Johnson for an afternoon meeting with the district attorney to discuss making a deal with the prosecutor's office and saw Johnson lying in a pool of blood. Sources say that Johnson has known ties to the Jacinto Corners Control League and that he was killed to keep him from testifying about JCCL activities. We will bring you more on this story in our five o'clock broadcast. We now return to our regular programming."

Sandy suddenly felt violently ill. Everything she thought about Morris exaggerating no longer held up and she felt real fear. She looked at her mama and knew that there were going to be a lot of words between them before the full story hit the five o'clock news. She got up from the couch and told Cara that she would tell Avery.

The hallway felt cold as Sandy tried to think of what she would say to Avery. She couldn't get the image of Harry Johnson lying dead out of her head. She played the scene over and over in her mind. She wanted to be glad he was dead but she couldn't. The kind of hatred that lived in the hearts of the people like Harry had no place in hers. The very things that made her different from them kept her from feeling that their lives meant less than her own.

Sandy stood in the doorway of the bedroom and stared at Avery who was sleeping soundly. She was relieved she had time to think before she had to tell him about Harry. She didn't really want to sit in the living room with her mama and listen to her go on about how Robert's being there would just make things worse, so she went out to sit on the porch. Tommy would be getting off the bus soon and she thought they could spend a little time together having some fun. She needed to listen to his laughter and hear his excitement about Christmas. It dawned on her that with all that had happened she hadn't even asked him what he hoped Santa would bring him. For her as a mother, Christmases of the past were the only times she ever felt close to her son. His excitement had always been contagious and his belief that the world was brighter that time of year had always lightened Sandy's heart. She was thinking about last Christmas when she heard the bus pull up to the corner.

Sandy saw Tommy running and thought something looked different about him. She rose from the chair and stepped out into the yard. As he came closer, she ran out to meet him. He was crying and he flew into her arms. He was sobbing and talking at the same time and nothing he said made sense. She brought him up to the porch and sat him in the wicker rocker. Wiping the tears from his face she told him to take some deep breaths and then tell her what was wrong. Tommy's voice put pain and heart break in the air like a puff of smoke.

"Oh Mama, somethin' terrible happened in school today. My best friend at school, Jessica Johnson, well her daddy got kill't today. Her mama came up to the school and got her. We was at recess and I saw her goin' to her car just cryin' and cryin'."

Tommy started crying all over and Sandy felt a lump in her throat the size of a softball. She'd barely thought of Harry Johnson as human let alone as a father. She thought of Avery sleeping soundly and how if Harry would have had his way, Avery's sleep would have been permanent. It was hard to even feel anger about the situation with Tommy so devastated and the thought of a family mourning the loss of a husband, father, brother and son. Sandy was confused by what she felt. She wanted the men who hurt Avery and Robert to pay for what they did, but now she wondered what the cost to all of them would be.

Cara had heard Tommy and came out to the porch to offer him comfort. She had a glass of milk and three cinnamon cookies for him. She put the snack down on the plastic table to the right side of his chair and sat on the porch railing across from him.

"Hey there, little frog, I heard you talkin' to your mama. I sure am sorry to hear about your friend's daddy."

Tommy looked at his grandma and then at his mama. He hadn't even told them the worst of it and they already looked real sad for him. He felt an uneasiness in them that had nothing to with his tears or pain for his friend. He wondered if their being uncomfortable had anything to do with what the other kids were saying. He decided the best thing to do was to ask.

"Mama? Toby Moore said we was the reason Jessica's daddy got dead. He said daddy and Uncle Robert put him in jail and bad men got him. Is that true, Mama? Did Daddy help kill my friend's daddy?"

Sandy was floored by the honesty of his question and shocked by the conversations that eight-year-olds had with each other. She'd seen shows on Jerry Springer where JCCL members brought their children up from an early age spouting the beliefs of the organization but she had no idea just how freely such things were talked about in their homes. She looked at her mama and was at a total loss as to what to say to Tommy. She had not one answer for him; hell, she didn't have any answers for herself.

Cara stepped in and took over the conversation. She picked

Tommy up off the rocker, sat and then brought him onto her lap. She rocked and talked.

"Listen to your grandma, little frog. There are all kinds of people in this world, some good and some not so good. Sometimes there are people who hate other people because they ain't exactly like them. They think them other people aren't as good and shouldn't be allowed to walk down the same streets and such. You know how them kids at school call you Trailer Trash Tommy? Well, wonder if they didn't just call you that but beat you up because you live in a trailer and your name is Tommy? That wouldn't be fair, would it?"

Cara felt her grandson's head brush against her blouse as he said his silent no. She hoped like hell she was making sense. She tilted her head down so she could see his face and continued.

"Some of those kids don't even know you. They ain't never spent a minute of time with you to see how smart and fun you are but they hate you just the same. That's kinda what happened here, little frog. You see, the people that beat up your daddy and Robert are like those kids at school. Your little friend's daddy was one of those people, Tommy. He was in jail for hurting your daddy but your daddy didn't kill him, darlin'. He got killed because the same people that hated your daddy and Uncle Robert decided they hated her daddy, too."

Tommy picked up the glass of milk and took a long drink. He looked up at his grandma and then over at his mama.

"Grandma, it don't matter who kill't him; he still ain't gonna be able to kiss Jessica good night anymore."

Cara just sighed and rocked her grandson. He'd said the truth of things. She looked at Sandy and saw the tears running down her daughter's face. She thought if people truly wanted to know what was important in life, they should ask a child. Good night kisses were the same no matter what color they were or if they were flavored with hatred or love. The porch became a place of quiet contemplation and mourning and even Old Blue seemed to ponder the events of the day.

CHAPTER THIRTY-EIGHT

Robert awoke in a cold sweat. He looked up to see the nurse Avery called Sour Puss staring at him with wild eyes. He had no idea how long she'd been there or why she was even in his room. He waited for her to speak and when she continued to do nothing but stare, he addressed her.

"Is there something I can do for you? Is there a problem?"

When her mouth moved to speak, the words sounded like they'd come out of the darkness of a cavern.

"I just wanted to stare at a live queer so I can make a comparison when you're a dead one. I think you faggots are like the cats. Them fur balls look better as road carpet!"

Robert reached for the buzzer. He wanted her out of his room and out of the hospital. She continued talking as he kept his finger on the buzzer.

"They killed Harry in jail today and just like the bible says... an eye for an eye, boy. You and that fat assed prick of a friend of yours are gonna be next. You best watch your back, you homo!"

She was out the door before anyone got to his room. When a nurse finally did come in, she was irritated.

"Mr. Laningham, we have a lot of patients and riding the buzzer doesn't bring us here any faster! Now what is your problem?"

Robert was shaking with anger and he tried not to explode but knew he was not in control as he spoke.

"You want to know what the fuck the problem is? The problem is that this hospital hires hate mongering bitches who threaten lives rather than help to save them! I want that woman fired and I want her arrested for criminal threats on my life!"

The nurse looked at him as though he'd lost his mind and he

wanted to slap the shit out of her. He was positive she knew who he was talking about because there was no way she hadn't seen the woman leave his room. He decided the nurse was not the person he should talk to and asked her to have an orderly wheel him downstairs. He told her he'd just gotten upset and was probably going stir crazy being cooped up in his room all the time. He didn't want her having any say over whether or not he was okay to be in control of himself. He noticed her posture relax a little and a fake understanding smile form on her lips.

"Sure, Mr. Laningham, that's totally understandable. I'd start seeing and hearing monsters, too, if I had to spend so many hours in a room like this."

Robert told the orderly he needed to go to the administration office. He made up a story about needing to find out about home health care options, since he was being released soon. He told the orderly he'd have someone call when he was done.

Robert looked at the woman who came into the office to help him. She was an attractive woman and wore a suit he recognized as a Calvin Klein design. She smiled and introduced herself as Marion Weber and her accent had no hint of Texas in it and he felt relieved. He hated to admit it but he had become wary of people and didn't want to tell a Sour Puss clone what had happened. The woman started to talk about home health care and Robert stopped her.

"Excuse me, I just used home health care as a reason to get down here to talk to someone about something going on in this hospital. I don't mean to sound cloak and dagger but this is of extreme importance and I am not sure who I can trust."

Ms. Weber looked a little shocked but had a gleam of interest in her eyes. She sat behind her desk and readied herself for what she was sure would be an interesting story. It certainly wouldn't be the first time she'd heard a wild tale about the hospital.

Robert started with the Sour Puss incident with Avery and then continued with his own encounter with her. He demanded that she be arrested and removed from the hospital immediately.

He made a point that if it wasn't handled he would call the local papers and television stations and be sure the place was filled with reporters and cameras. Ms. Weber assured him such tactics would not be necessary. She made a call and then stepped out to have the orderly take Robert back to his room. She shook his hand and told him not to worry, things would be handled.

Robert felt a sense of relief. He wished Sandy could understand the importance of taking action rather than just accepting things the way they were. He knew it was a risk to shake the conscience of the world but it was the only way to facilitate change. When he talked to his gay friends about becoming involved, he normally used the civil rights issues of the Sixties as an example but Sandy didn't know enough history to feel the impact of that argument.

The orderly helped Robert back into his bed and as he wheeled the chair back out the door, a well dressed man walked into the room. Robert's breath was literally taken away by the looks of the man. He was tall, had wavy dark brown hair and eyes as green as fresh mown summer grass. Robert hoped the gentleman had the right room and reason to stay for awhile.

With hand extended, the man introduced himself.

"Mr. Laningham, I am Steve Colbert, head of hospital security. Ms. Weber told me of your allegations. I would like your permission to get real time evidence of the nurse's threats and action toward you. Do you know her name, by the way?"

Robert smiled and decided to test the waters a bit. He felt an extreme attraction to the man standing before him and his flirty side was emerging, whether appropriate or not.

"Well, I do remember seeing the name Linda. Hell, I'm sure it has to be something like Linda Lou, or Linda Bob Faye, or any number of combinations thereof."

He saw a smile light Steve's face, though his professional self tried to stifle it. Robert could not tear his eyes from the incredible beauty of him. He felt something stirring in his heart that he'd not felt since meeting Maurice. He didn't even care if he was being premature about things. If Steve wasn't gay, then at least his dreams would be filled with nice images.

Steve set up a scenario whereby he hoped to catch this Linda in the act. He told Robert that he would be assigned to her as a patient for the morning's shift. Since he was supposed to be released tomorrow, Steve would come in as his lover to pick him up. He told Robert that he felt sure seeing the two of them together engaged in loving conversation would prompt her to expose herself for what she was, a card carrying, hate filled monster.

Robert thought the plan sounded wonderful. If play acting made Steve and him lovers, then he was ready for an Academy Award performance. He shook Steve's hand again, thanked him and told him he'd be ready for tomorrow morning.

Robert laid his head back after Steve left and thought how good it was to feel human again. He'd just been going through the motions long before Maurice left and could fault no one but himself. It had been easier to live with Maurice than to venture out into the world again to face the rejections, the bull shit and the traumas. In a way, he was glad that trauma had been brought to him because now life meant something to him and he wanted to drink it in. He closed his eyes and pictured Steve's gorgeous face as he drifted off to sleep. He didn't need to watch the news; he was making it.

CHAPTER THIRTY-NINE

Sandy and Cara took their coffee and went into the living room. They both wanted to watch the five o'clock report from the jail. Buster sat in his recliner watching the two as they huddled together on the couch. He heard Tommy's laughter coming from the bedroom as he and Avery played Candyland together. He couldn't help but feel it was the most unlikely picture of Cara's family he could ever imagine. He thought about the Christmas present he'd bought Cara when she thought he'd been out buying nothing but big boy toys. He felt good about the warmth of the gift. He hoped it gave her as much hope as it had given him when he purchased it. He knew that if nothing else, this Christmas would be memorable.

The smell of chili filled the house as the voice of the news anchor used sensationalist terms to describe Harry's murder in jail. Cara hit Sandy's leg as the TV showed a reporter in Jacinto Corners interviewing Morris Foley. She seemed excited to see someone she knew on television but Sandy was left with a sick feeling in the pit of her stomach. Cara laughed and had to comment on the way Morris looked.

"Don't Morris look like his damn hat's been fittin' too tight and it done made part of his head slide to one side? I'll tell you another thing. They sure don't lie when they say them cameras put weight on ya. Morris ain't no bigger around than Avery's thigh and he purt near looks like a full grown man!"

Sandy didn't feel like making fun of Morris and she really didn't feel like watching any more of the news. She got up and went back to the bedroom to see who was winning at Candyland. She thought it was so sweet of Avery to make Tommy feel better after his upsetting day at school. She knew part of Tommy's pain had been the thought that his own daddy could have died. In his eight year old mind the bad men had been after him too. In Sandy's mind, they still were.

Cara called everyone to dinner and Sandy told Avery she would bring him a plate and a glass of iced tea. She told Tommy to go wash his hands and she went back into the living room. Buster was already at the table shoveling chili and rice into his mouth with his right hand and taking bites of cornbread with his left. Sandy hadn't had much of an appetite since she'd lost the baby. Depression had been good for her diet. She thought it was too bad that she felt like she was losing everything else along with her fat.

Sandy made Avery a bowl of chili and brought it to him. She curled up on the bed next to him and said not so much to him but to herself,

"I didn't know Harry Johnson had kids. The people that killed him were his friends. I wonder how they kill their enemies? We're their enemies now."

Avery put his bowl on the night stand and put his arms around Sandy. He didn't know how to make her feel better. He felt the same fear she did but there was no stopping what had started. He had a gnawing at his center that the worst was yet to come. He would never tell Sandy but he'd heard the guys talk at work. They told stories about visits to the south side of town where the blacks lived and unspeakable things were written on their cars and houses. His thoughts were interrupted by the screech of tires and the yelp of a dog. Sandy jumped off the bed and ran into the living room. She recognized the cry as Old Blue's.

Tommy met her in the hallway looking frightened and Sandy told him to go into the bedroom with his daddy and not to come out. She didn't mean to scare him even more than he already was but she couldn't contain the terror in her own heart. She was almost to the living room door when she heard Cara's voice from outside.

"Oh god damn, Buster! They done run over Blue! Is he dead?"

Sandy stood frozen at the front door. She saw Cara standing in the yard too afraid to approach the part of the grass where Buster was standing over Blue. She watched as Buster picked the dog up and rushed past Cara and towards the porch. He yelled for Sandy to call the police. She told her legs to move but she seemed rooted to the floor. Buster was tying something around Blue's right leg. He was shouting orders to Cara. He told her to get the keys to the Bonneville because they had to get Blue to a vet. He looked up to see Sandy still standing at the door. He shocked her into movement.

"God damn it, Sandy! I said call the police. It was Old Blue this time but it could be Tommy next!"

Sandy didn't think it was right to call 911 so she called the non-emergency number. She told the dispatcher what happened and asked for a patrolman to be sent as soon as possible. She hung up the phone and went to the bedroom to be with Avery and Tommy.

Tommy was near hysterics and Avery was having no luck calming him down. Sandy took him in her arms and held him tight as she whispered in his ear.

"It's okay, baby. Blue ain't dead. Grandma and Buster are gonna take him to the vet and I promise the doc will help Blue as much as he can. It's okay, Tommy. It's gonna be okay."

She rocked back and forth on the bed and wished she believed her own words. What Buster had yelled settled in her heart as she clutched Tommy in her arms. She kept repeating in her mind that next time it could be Tommy. She would see these people in hell before they touched her family again.

Sandy heard a car pull up into the yard and carefully laid Tommy down next to Avery. He'd finally fallen asleep and she decided to let him just sleep in bed with his daddy. Avery caught her by the arm and whispered that Buster kept a gun in the house. She went into the living room, opened the cabinet above the television and took down Buster's .45. She checked to make sure it was loaded and then looked through the blinds to see who'd driven up into the yard. She saw the lights of the police car and two officers walking towards the porch. She placed the gun back into the cabinet and opened the front door. She stood on legs of rubber waiting for them to come up on the porch.

She asked the officers to come inside and as they sat on the couch she explained what had happened. The officer taking down the report had a smart ass smirk on his face and his partner was stifling a laugh. Sandy felt rage choking at her throat. She wanted to lash out and slap the shit out of both of them. She tried to control the anger in her voice but was so close to the edge she felt herself spilling over.

"I'm glad you both find this so god damn funny! I guess runnin' over a dog ain't high on your list of emergencies. Maybe you bastards would prefer if it'd been my son! Well, if you don't find out who did this to my mama's dog then maybe next time it'll be one of us and you can do a real report!"

The officers looked down at the floor like children being scolded for talking out of turn. The one who had been writing looked at Sandy and as if lightning had struck him, realized who she was. He felt terrible for making light of her situation. He spoke softly to her.

"Mrs. Anderson, I'm truly sorry. I didn't realize the circumstances surrounding the dog being run over. I do now. We'll make a report and make sure we put an extra patrol out here for you the rest of the night."

Sandy felt some of the tension leave her body. She had no idea who to trust and knew that talking the way she had left her open for reprisals from the very people who were supposed to protect her. She just wanted it all to be over. She shut and locked the door behind the officers and went to lay on the couch until her mama and Buster got home. She was more tired than she'd ever been in her life and more alone than she'd ever wanted to be.

Buster tried to comfort Cara on the drive home. He felt so

helpless as she quietly sobbed into her hands. He knew that her tears weren't for Blue but for Sandy, Tommy and Avery. The vet had told them that he would have to keep Old Blue for a few days but that dogs were amazing when it came to coping with broken legs.

Buster stroked Cara's arm and knew if she wasn't yelling about what happened, it was living deep in her heart and festering in the place of her quiet pain. He always worried when she didn't rant and rave about things because the more she swallowed, the more full she became and the more she was apt to want to dull the ache.

Buster helped Cara out of the car. She looked so tiny to him, almost like a child with an old face. He helped her up to the porch and put his key in the lock. He hoped that everyone was asleep so there would be no more talk of what had happened. He'd always felt like he was good at protecting what was his but all the shit that had happened made him feel like Custer surrounded by Indians. He knew enough about skinhead groups and the JCCL to know that they could be found at every level of society. They weren't always wearing cowboy boots or waving Confederate flags. Sometimes they wore suits and called themselves businessmen and powerful.

CHAPTER FORTY

Robert woke at five and felt excited about the day. He would get to spend time with Steve, put away a nurse that didn't deserve to breathe the same air as good ones and got to leave the world of the sick and infirm. He'd had a dream about staying at Cara's and ending up dressing and talking like Buster by the time he was well enough to go back home on his own. He was smiling to himself when a nurse came in to take his blood pressure before shift change. He couldn't wait to give Sour Puss what she had coming to her.

The nurse finished and the orderly brought in his breakfast. He opened the lid and almost gagged at the sight of the gritty eggs and greasy bacon. He sure wouldn't miss the stuff they called food. He wasn't so sure breakfasts at Cara's would be any better. He doubted she used egg substitutes or turkey bacon or anything that wasn't filled with fat and cholesterol.

Robert put the lid back over his eggs and pushed the tray table aside. He was trying to get out of bed to go pee when Steve came into the room. He was half off the bed with one leg swung over the side and his hospital gown bunched up around his waist. Startled, he grabbed for the sheet to cover himself. He noticed Steve's eyes dart away in the way people's do when they feel more embarrassed for someone else than they do for themselves. Robert tried to make the mood in the room a little less awkward.

"Morning. I haven't quite got the hang of how to do that yet. I'm not used to wearing a backless dress!"

He wanted to kick himself the minute the words left his mouth. How stupid did that sound? He wished he hadn't used the word "hang" while he'd had his balls and penis bouncing off the white of a sheet!

Steve laughed and there was a real kindness in his eyes.

"Hey, don't worry about your less than graceful exit from bed. Trust me, I've seen worse, much worse."

Robert wasn't at all sure that was a compliment. He wished he didn't have to look at Steve because he felt a boyish giddiness that was accompanied by equally immature actions and words. He watched as Steve walked across the room and dragged one of the chairs up to sit beside the bed. He smiled and Robert felt his heart melt.

"I figure if we're supposed to be lovers, then I ought to at least be holding your hand when Linda Monroe walks in. That's her name by the way...Monroe. Boy, would she make our idol Marilyn want a name change!"

His laughter danced around the room and then zipped into Robert's hope chest in his heart. He thought Steve's reference to Marilyn Monroe was significant and his use of the word "our" even more so. People who thought all gay men were obvious were simply uneducated. Robert had more than once gotten signals crossed and ended up embarrassing himself and dodging fists. He would wait until the signals were clear before showing overt interest.

He felt the warmth of Steve's right hand envelope him as their fingers clasped together. He got lost in the sensations that radiated from his touch and willed himself to think of all the attention as a calculated mission and nothing more. He wanted to ignore the naturalness with which Steve reached for him and the little pulsating squeezes he kept feeling. He told himself it was play acting. He was carrying on a full conversation in his own head when Steve placed a gentle kiss on his lips and whispered to him.

"We'll get through this."

Robert wondered if his gasp was as loud on the outside as it was in his mind? He looked at Steve with question in his eyes. Just as he was about to ask if Steve believed in dress rehearsals, he felt the soft lips again and an urgent pushing of a warm tongue. Robert opened to him. As if on cue, the door opened and Linda Monroe walked in.

It all made sense to Robert, then. Steve knew exactly what her schedule would be and that his room would be her first order of the day. The first kiss had been a rehearsal for a carefully timed second.

Linda's voice dripped with disgust and hatred.

"Son of a bitch! Look, you faggot, I told that other friend of yours we didn't allow no conjugal visits and I'm tellin' you! Shit, if I'd known I was gonna walk in on two homos makin' out, I'd sure in the fuck not eaten any eggs for breakfast! You . . . visiting faggot, get on out of here while I do what I gotta do to your boyfriend!"

Steve rose as if to leave and then opened the door to the two armed security guards waiting outside. He did not address Linda Monroe at all. His orders were direct, simple and unambiguous.

"Officers, please escort this employee to her locker to gather her things and then escort her off hospital property. She has just been fired!"

The officers went to her, one on each side and walked her out of the room. Steve shut the door behind them and Linda could be heard cussing all the way down the hall. He smiled at Robert, shook his hand, thanked him for his help in cleaning up the shit in the hospital and left.

Robert couldn't hide his disappointment. He hadn't wanted it to end at all and to have it end so soon made his heart fill with loneliness. He made himself a promise as he rose out of bed to prepare his things for release. He was going to stop waiting for other people to bring him happiness. He would walk out of the hospital with new awareness, new hope and a new zest for life.

As Robert stuffed the tissue that cost him nine dollars a box into his bag, a nurse came in with a huge bouquet of flowers. She placed them on the night stand and told him his release papers were being processed. He zipped the bag and went to see who sent the flowers. He dipped his nose into the array of roses, babies breath, daisies and tulips. The colors made him almost sorry they had been cut from their stalks. He picked up the attached card and sat on the bed to read it.

Robert turned the small envelope to its back to see if anything was written there. The back was blank and as he opened the tiny flap, he thought perhaps Maurice had sent them. He took the stiff card from its case and read the hand written words.

"You are an incredible kisser. Steve"

Robert didn't care who heard his whoop! He wanted to skip around the room but could only do it verbally. His head was still spinning when Sandy came into the room. He greeted her with a smile that couldn't be denied. She played right into his mood.

"Hey there! Are you just happy to see me or did some good lookin' male nurse just give you a sponge bath?"

She leaned into him to sniff as if she expected to smell soap mixed with sex. She loved that Robert made her forget the pain in life and made her feel normal. She watched as he bent to pick up his suitcase and was reminded of reality. Robert looked crippled and bent. More absentmindedly than consciously, she talked about the crippling of Blue.

"They ran over Blue last night, Robert. He'll be okay but we won't."

Robert stopped putting his things together and looked at Sandy. He had a strange vision in his head. He remembered the ditch and thought that's how he must have looked, like a dog that had been hit and crawled into the ditch to die. He turned to Sandy and said,

"Better Blue than Tommy, Sandy. It's gonna get worse. I had Sour Puss fired today. She's Leo's wife and you know what that means."

Sandy just rounded her shoulders in defeat. They were going to end up on the evening news. She was sure someone would be sticking a microphone in Tommy's face asking what it felt like to watch his entire family murdered. She tried to imagine the kind of people who could run over a dog on purpose.

Robert thought life had an out of control feel to it. It didn't snow in East Texas but they all had fallen into a massive snowball and were tumbling downhill. Their arms and legs were flailing about and each move seemed to strike at the very nerves of each other. He knew they wouldn't stop mangling themselves and each other until at least one of them got their feet on the ground and could stop the motion. He knew that his release from the hospital would help. They would all be together and at least appear as a united front.

A nurse came into the room to tell Robert he had been released. She placed a packet of medical supplies on the bed, much like the one Avery had been given, and explained how to care for himself. She said an orderly was on his way and that he could leave as soon as he was ready.

Sandy smiled and touched his shoulder. She had an evil glint in her eyes when she spoke.

"Well, you got any last words before entering the Cara Zone? You ain't never gonna be the same, you know?"

She hugged him and was out the door to go bring the truck around front. Robert would never have told Sandy but in a way he felt that staying with Cara for a while would bring him home. She was so like his mother in so many ways, except that he liked her. He didn't see her from the same perspective Sandy did. Unlike his mother, Cara had a seed of love planted in her heart. She cared more than she ever let on and was not so self involved that she thought she *was* the world rather than in it.

Robert had his back turned to the door when it opened and he told the orderly he would be ready to go in just a minute. He was surprised when he turned around to see Steve standing behind a wheel chair and smiling like the Cheshire cat. His heart skipped a beat and the hue of his already bruised face deepened with the rush of excitement. He didn't want his voice to crack with juvenile anticipation when he spoke so he coughed before saying anything.

"Have you been demoted? Wow, Linda had more pull around here than I thought!"

Robert loved the sound of Steve's laugh. There wasn't much about the man he didn't want to know more about. No matter how much he cautioned himself about jumping in with both feet, he was too smitten to heed his own words. He took his bag and walked to the wheel chair. Steve came around and took the bag from him while he maneuvered into the chair. He hoped the elevator took its time going down so he could muster the nerve to give Steve his phone number, address and underwear size!

The nurses said their goodbyes as Steve wheeled him down the hall and when the elevator doors opened Robert was glad to see it was empty. There seemed to be an awkward silence between them and it made him fear he'd misinterpreted Steve's card. He suddenly thought perhaps the flowers and card had been meant as a joke. He decided it would be best to act as if that was the intent all along. He would make a joke out of the whole thing.

"Well, Steve, I guess it was worth having to kiss a frog to get rid of the wart that was on this hospital's ass! I hope it is something you won't have to experience again any time soon!"

He couldn't see Steve's face but he imagined he was smiling and feeling relieved. He felt a hand on his shoulder and gentle pressure and then he heard Steve's quiet voice caress his heart.

"Robert, I was hoping I would experience kissing you again and much more. If I seem aloof it's because I'm wishing just that and I shouldn't be. I'm in a relationship and until I met you I never gave straying a thought. My feelings for you confuse me."

Robert felt both pleased and saddened. He wanted to pursue a relationship but would never cross the line and break up a stable relationship. He'd had it done to him and he respected himself way too much to be a home wrecker. Fidelity was something he cherished. He would say goodbye to Steve and live off "what ifs" again.

As the elevator approached the first floor, Steve came around to the front of the wheel chair and bent to give Robert a gentle kiss. It was a sweet corner-of-the-mouth kiss and Robert knew he'd made his choice. Like himself, Steve would go home wishing for things he wouldn't have.

The automatic doors gave way to the warmth of the Texas sun and a smiling Sandy ready to be the friend Robert needed. He couldn't help feel he was starting life over and that it would be the biggest adventure he'd ever been on. Steve helped him into the truck and gently squeezed his hand in goodbye.

Pulling away from the hospital, Robert's mood was reflective. When he'd come out as gay he'd felt like he had done his own DNA testing to prove his identity. It was as if he'd stamped himself with the words . . . NOT DEFECTIVE—JUST GAY! His mother had gone into her usual hysteria, crying and asking him why he'd done it to her? She soon let anger take over and told him how he would burn in hell for his crimes against God and nature. He'd laughed in her face. He'd said he was sure heaven was a lovely place if it accepted people like her. He thought his mother would be to heaven what landfills were to the earth, accepted, but full of garbage. He'd actually been happy with her reaction because to have her approve of him would have been too confusing and made him doubt his own reality. He'd never felt any ties with her, just tied to her because of birth.

As Sandy turned on to the road leading home, she looked at Robert anticipating a reaction. She tried to read the look on his face but it was like he wasn't even in the truck with her. She patted his hand, thinking his mind was deep in the memory of that night. She started to ask if he was okay but knew if he wanted to talk he would.

She maneuvered the truck into the grass next to the Bonneville and noticed Buster's truck was gone. She would have to rely on Cara's help to get Robert inside and that meant putting up with her mouth, too. She worried that Cara would be in a bad mood after what happened with Blue. Sandy knew Robert's being there was not what her mama wanted in the first place.

Cara came flying out of the house and looked as angry as a

hornet. She came up to the passenger side door to help Sandy with Robert and said the last thing Sandy expected her to say.

"Hi, darlin', welcome to the nut house. We're all cracked but with you here we can start on the healin' now."

Sandy could hear the controlled anger in her mama's voice but she also knew it wasn't directed toward Robert. Her words to him had been sincere. She also knew whatever was wrong was not up for discussion until Robert was safely inside and settled. Her mama's signals were clear and her humor kicked in at times of stress. Sandy almost lost her grip on Robert from laughing when Cara expressed her take on Robert sharing a room with Avery.

"Well, homo boy, I can sure tell you that if sleepin' in a room with Avery don't make you want to go straight, then there ain't no hope for you. I swear, you see that fat ass naked just once and you'll be thinkin' of them programs they once did with criminal kids. Oh hell, what was that show called? Oh yeah, Scared Straight!"

The three walked into the house laughing and as they steered Robert toward the bedroom, the phone rang. Sandy said she would answer it if Cara could handle Robert and her mama almost screamed "no". The phone rang four more times and then stopped. They got Robert settled in the room with Avery and Cara told them to talk amongst themselves while she and Sandy went to fix lunch. Sandy started to protest but the look in her mama's eyes told her not to.

Cara went into the kitchen, slammed the bread onto the counter and opened the refrigerator door so hard it hit the front of the counter abutting it. Sandy took the luncheon meat out of her mama's hand and they both sat at the kitchen table to make the sandwiches. She waited for her mama to calm down enough to speak.

"They been callin' all fuckin' day! They speak sometimes and other times just breathe heavy into the phone. Buster went on up to the police station and then he's gonna go pick up Tommy at school. We can't be havin' Tommy ridin' a bus no more. Them phone calls made me change my mind about Robert bein' here, girlie. Those fuckers ain't gonna tell me who or what to be! I'm Cara Covington and will be to the day I die!"

Sandy absentmindedly made circles on the bread with the knife and mayonnaise. There was only one part of the whole mess that scared her and it was Tommy being hurt. She didn't think they would harm a child but when they got together in a group and then got to drinking, she wasn't so sure of what they'd do. She spoke what was in her heart.

"Mama, you don't think they'd really hurt Tommy, do you? He's only eight years old and don't have no control over everything that's happenin'."

Cara put two sandwiches together on a plate for Avery and enough potato chips to feed four people. She thought about a bunch of drunk, hate filled people and what liquor mixed with vengeance was capable of. She sure didn't want to take a chance on what they might do and told Sandy as much.

"Sandy, we ain't talkin' about normal people here. They done run over a defenseless dog and probably see any offspring of yours and Avery's as less than Old Blue. I don't trust the fuckers no farther than their dicks reach and, girlie, that ain't very damn far!"

Sandy just shook her head and laughed. Her mama's explanation was the beauty of her. She put life into understandable terms. She saw it from the eyes of a person who'd known and been at the bottom. Cara made sense much of the time and while that scared some people, it made Sandy proud.

Sandy took the sandwiches into the bedroom and just about spilled everything from the tray at the sight of Robert and Avery sitting on the queen size bed together. With their halos almost touching, they were involved in a game of Candyland. Her voice was filled with a lightness when she spoke.

"Okay, boys, put the game aside so you can eat your lunch. If you're real good and eat everything, I'll bring you some milk and cookies for desert!"

Avery rolled his eyes but Robert jumped right in.

"Aw Mommy, I just landed on gum drops and Avery is stuck

in the fudge! I was about to roll again and move way ahead of him. You know I like to lick my suckers before eating them! That's what makes winning in the end so much fun!"

Sandy could tell that having Robert in the house was going to be like having another child. She placed the sandwiches between them and went back to the kitchen to have lunch with her mama. She wanted to finish the conversation they'd started.

Cara had made her a sandwich but Sandy wasn't hungry. She put Sweet N Low in her iced tea and said exactly what was on her mind.

"Mama, do you wish Avery and Robert hadn't started all of this? I'm sorry we drug you into this and I'm so sorry they hurt Blue."

Cara took a bite of her sandwich, seemingly chewing on what Sandy said. She drank some tea and then took another bite as if she needed to push down the first thoughts that came to her mind in answer. When she did answer, her voice was sure and exact.

"Sandy darlin', I lived here my entire life and I lived with these people as a part of it. I even went to some of their meetins' with my daddy when I was a girl. I grew up with hate livin' in my heart. I believed what my daddy told me about the niggers, the spics, the dirty Jews, and the queers. Hell, when a body thinks of them in those terms they sound every bit as awful as what people say. It weren't until I met Ella Mae that I got a flavor for the truth of things. I loved that woman, Sandy, and she was blacker than the night. She had a laugh and voice that could lift me right up from the depths of hell and make me feel special. It come to me after she helped me bury my baby that her skin was black but her heart was pure gold. Ya see, I realized it ain't never gonna be what a person is on the outside that makes 'em good or bad; it's what's on the inside. My daddy was the nigger. His heart was black and he was bad. So, no darlin', I ain't sorry 'bout all this. Those people hate for the sake of hating. Them people don't know who the fuck their messin' with cause when I hate, I hate for a reason! Cara Covington don't get scared, she gets pissed!"

Sandy felt in awe of her mama. It was as if she was seeing her as a person for the first time in the twenty-five years she'd been her daughter. No matter what the situation lately, her mama had been there for her and offered support.

Resentment still tweaked at Sandy's heart for all the years she'd lost this woman to booze and men but she wanted to work through that to be free to love her. It amazed her to think of Cara as loveable. For some reason, sitting there with a sandwich in front her reminded her of a time in second grade. The teacher had asked the children what their parents did and when Sandy answered that her mother drank, all the other children laughed. She remembered the teacher's red face and how she moved on without asking about her father. Sandy thought if her first answer had made the teacher's face red, then her answer about her dad would have made her faint. She looked at Cara slowly chewing on another bite of sandwich and felt a softening of the all walls she'd built as a child. It was time to let go of the Cara she'd grown up with and take a chance with the one sitting in front of her. Cara's voice jolted her out of her thoughts.

"You ain't hungry again? Hell, girl, you get skinnier than me and you're gonna have a cat fight on your hands. I ain't havin' no young, good lookin' daughter takin' no attention from my ass!"

Sandy was trying to think of a good come back but Tommy and Buster walked in before she could.

Tommy threw his book bag down in exaggerated exhaustion and stuck his tongue out. His voice was raspy and he slumped with his arms forward like he'd been walking in the desert for days.

"Starving . . . need food! Thirsty . . . need coke!"

Cara got up from the table to get a coke from the frig and Sandy pushed her plate toward Tommy's side of the table. He opened the top piece of bread, held his nose and then protested.

"Bologna? That's nigger shit, not food!"

It happened so fast it was more instinctive than calculated: Sandy's hand slapped his arm so hard the sandwich flew into the living room. Tommy sat staring at her too stunned to cry or speak. Cara came around to Tommy's side and suggested that when he did speak he apologize immediately. She went into the living room to pick up the sandwich. She knew Sandy was trying to gain control before she said anything to him. Buster decided it was safer to be in the bedroom with Avery and Robert. He didn't like angry Covington women. They were scary! Tommy started to get up to go with him and Sandy's voice stopped him cold.

"Where did you hear someone calling bologna that?"

He swung his legs under the table and acted like he didn't hear her. He put his elbows on the table, put his head in his hands and started humming. He looked at his grandma and addressed her.

"Hey, Grandma, can I have some cookies and watch cartoons?"

Sandy looked at Cara as if Buster had picked up the wrong child from school. She reached across the table, grabbed his hands away from his head, told him to sit up and answer her. With a look of defiance, he brought his right hand back up under his head and said,

"I learned it at school. It's the truth too 'cause some sixth graders said it. They also told me you love niggers and queers more than you love me!"

Tommy's voice was loud, angry and filled with hate. He hadn't seen Robert in the hall heading for the bathroom but sure enough felt the hand of a man on his shoulder. He flinched because at first he thought it was his daddy coming to slap him for yelling at his mama. He was relieved to look up and see Robert standing behind him. Robert asked Sandy's permission to take Tommy into his room to talk. Sandy, still reeling from what Tommy had said, just nodded.

Tommy walked to his room with Robert and wondered if he was going to get a spanking. He thought since Robert seemed to get around better than his dad maybe he'd been given the honors. Robert sat on the bed and told Tommy to come sit next to him. There was no trace of anger in his voice when he spoke.

"Tommy, do you like me?"

Tommy looked at him as if he'd lost his mind. He shook his head in an up and down motion and rolled his eyes in a silly manner. He decided maybe it wasn't good enough and spoke what he meant.

"Yep, you're cool. You like to do fun things and let me eat pizza for breakfast!"

"Well, that's good 'cause I like you too and think you're pretty cool. You know what though, what you said in the kitchen just now wasn't cool at all. It was stupid and mean. Tommy, do you know what a queer is?"

Again Tommy shook his head in the affirmative.

"Yep, it's a bad man that hurts people and little kids."

Robert had come out to many people in his life but he'd never tried to explain himself to an eight year old before. Part of him feared that he would lose something by telling him but with all that had happened and would still happen, it was time for honesty. He turned toward Tommy and tried to find the easiest way to say it.

"You know what, Tommy? Those kids that told you those things today? Well, they'd call me a queer and in a way they'd be right. Queer isn't the right word to use but it's what I am. The proper word is homosexual or gay and we aren't bad people, just different."

Robert decided to wait to see if Tommy had any questions before going into any detail about what different meant. Tommy's confusion showed on his face and Robert hoped when his little friend did speak it would be with the same affection that had been there before. He was just about to ask him if he understood, when Tommy spoke up.

"I didn't mean to call nobody nothin' bad. See, we was at recess and the older kids were there too. They were playin' kick ball and let some of the kids in my class play. They wouldn't let me play and they said that stuff to me. I was just mad 'cause it seemed my mama was the reason they didn't let me. I'm sorry."

Robert hugged Tommy and told him he thought the apology belonged in the kitchen with his mama. Tommy nodded and ran out the door. He heard Sandy and Tommy talking in the kitchen and felt such a sadness about things. He tried to imagine children no older than twelve already hating so deeply, so completely. He thought it absurd to worry about polluting the air when so often we polluted the minds of our children. Robert got up, straightened the bedspread and went to his room to take a pill to sleep. He was tired.

Sandy, Cara, Buster and Tommy sat watching television and they all looked at each other when they heard the knock on the door. Buster looked toward the cabinet where he kept the gun, gave a knowing look to Cara and went to the door. He didn't recognize the woman standing on the porch. He wasn't rude but he wasn't friendly, either.

"May I help you? If you're selling something we don't want it."

Celia Callier looked at Buster and thought he looked swollen by the sun. He had that kind of puffy body that said he was vine ripened. She was afraid he was going to shut the door on her so she introduced herself.

"My name is Celia Callier. I am Avery and Sandy's case worker. Sandy left a message saying she would be here. I tried to call all day but the phone was either busy or no one answered."

Buster still wasn't sure about letting her into the house so he turned and called for Sandy.

Sandy felt an immediate response to seeing Celia standing at the front door. To Sandy, the woman was a reminder of everything that had been wrong with her life. She hated that she needed her help again. She felt as if her grave had been dug and there was no way out of misery of a live death. She backed away from the door so Celia could enter.

Sandy introduced her to Cara and Buster and then asked if they could go into the kitchen to talk. Cara told Tommy it was time to do homework and asked Buster if he'd help her put some things away in the bedroom. Sandy watched as the living room was cleared of ears and mouths with questions. Celia was the first to speak.

"Mrs. Anderson . . . Sandy, I heard about your husband's accident. I'm truly sorry."

Sandy thought her choice of words was strange. As much as she needed the woman's help, her pride could not let the occasion slide to set her straight.

"Accident? You make it sound like he had a wreck or fell from a ladder. Ms. Callier, my husband and Robert were brutally beaten by some monsters in this town. They hunted them down like animals and didn't show them as much mercy as they would have a deer or duck! The bastards purt near killed them and ruined our lives."

Celia sat staring at a different Sandy than the one she'd known before. There was a strength to her and none of the visible signs of apologizing for being alive. She'd pitied and disliked the woman she used to see but the woman before her now had potential for being respected. She wanted to make sure Sandy understood she knew the circumstances of Avery's injuries.

"Oh, I am fully aware of the events surrounding Avery's beating. I read the papers and listen to the news. Mrs. Anderson, I also know about the people with whom you are dealing. I'm sure I don't have to tell you that they are terrorists and capable of unspeakable things. I think it is a good thing that you have all your family with you."

Sandy didn't want to trust Celia Callier any more than she wanted to depend on her but she was grateful there wasn't the obvious judgment in her eyes.

"Ms. Callier, I appreciate your warnings and no, you don't have to tell me to watch my back. We'll get through this but what I worry about mostly is that Avery lost his job. It's a long story and I ain't gonna get into right now but I need to do whatever is necessary to get back on assistance. That's why I called you."

Celia riffled through some papers in her brief case and laid what looked like an application out on the table. Sandy watched as Celia the person became Ms. Callier, the state employee.

"Well, if Avery was fired, he will be eligible for unemployment. His company might contest it and if they are successful we will have to take a different track but for now I'll leave you the subsidized income forms to fill out. It will be the same as before only I've added an application for Medicaid as well. Fill all these out and bring them by my office so we can get the ball rolling. It won't take as long as it did the first time because we already know your circumstances."

Sandy rose to walk Celia to the door. She closed and locked it behind her and turned her thoughts to Tommy. She needed to have a serious talk with him and perhaps be more honest about things than she'd thought she would have to. She had trouble explaining hate and prejudice when it was something she didn't understand herself. She went to Tommy's room and sat next to him on the bed, where he was doing math homework. He looked up and wondered if he was in trouble again.

"Look, Mama, I'm learnin' goes intos. It's where you take a number and another number and see how many times the first number goes into the second. Ain't that cool?"

Sandy smiled at him. He would be a smart person if the world let him. She knew it wasn't just the other children that tried to keep him in his place; the teachers sometimes projected their prejudices on him too. They looked at him as not being as privileged and consequently not as bright as other students. She thought sometimes as much as things change they stay the same. She didn't want their perceptions to color his world and was why she would be honest with him.

"Tommy, I need you to take a break so we can talk. I've been thinking about the things you said and I think I know why you said them."

Tommy'd had a feeling his apology wouldn't be enough to completely be out of trouble with his mama. He often felt angry at her about things and really didn't know why. He felt like his parents were walls that kept blocking his entrance to the world. When he would feel the anger rising up in him it would mix with guilt and make him want to crawl out of his body. He wished he could do just that as he waited for his mama to speak.

"Tommy, the kids that have been saying things about me and your daddy . . . well, they ain't right about things. It's kinda like when Old Blue growls at Charlie. He hates Charlie 'cause Charlie is a cat, plain and simple. It ain't 'cause Charlie's ever done nothin' to him or hurt him; it's cause of how Charlie looks. Old Blue don't see a heart that beats, or legs that walk. He just sees what he thinks is an enemy. There are people like that, too, Tommy. Them kids have parents that taught them to be like Old Blue and to growl at people 'cause they look different or act different. It's wrong, Tommy, and very hurtful. I know Robert talked to you about his being gay. Did you understand what he was sayin'?"

Tommy shrugged and then his eyes lit up and he answered.

"Did he mean he was happy and funny?"

Sandy laughed.

"Well, in a way that's part of it but he was trying to tell you he's special, different. You know how I love your daddy and he loves me? Well, when your Uncle Robert loves someone in that way, it's another man. What I want you to know is that there ain't no right or wrong when it comes to lovin' a person. Love is love and it don't matter what kind of face it wears."

She looked at his eyes to see if her words made sense to him. He sat with his hand on his chin and his fingers drumming at his lips. She could tell that he was thinking about what she said and trying to process her words. She saw his eyebrows arch upward and then heard the wisdom of understanding in his eight year old voice.

"I know what you mean, Mama. George and I was talkin' about this when we was playin' soldiers. See, George told me I was his best friend 'cause nobody ever played with him 'cept me. He said I was like his brother or somethin'. George told me he loved me,

Mama, and I said it back to him. I had to, Mama, 'cause don't nobody else love George and he needs someone to."

Sandy hugged Tommy. He did understand and it made her feel she'd done something right with him somewhere, if not by action then by example. She kissed him and told him to finish his goes intos and then get his bath. She was almost through the door when she heard him say,

"Mama, why do I have to take a bath so soon? We ain't even had supper yet. 'Sides it's Friday and I ain't got school 'til after Christmas! I don't got to be clean for nothin!"

She turned to give him a stern look but his words made the thought melt away.

"Know what, Mama? I love you as much as I love George. Not 'cause no else loves you, just 'cause I do!"

Sandy went across the hall to check on Avery and Robert. They had been talking but stopped when she came into the room.

"Okay, guys, what are two plottin' on now? You gonna start bettin' on Candyland or gonna wait 'til we're all asleep and play strip Candyland?"

Robert looked appalled by the suggestion but Avery laughed and put his arms around her. His voice was loving and a little too throaty for a man as sick as he was.

"Now, darlin, you know when I get naked I got to have you as my reason. Boy, I tell ya, when this halo comes off, I'm gonna get off!"

Sandy mockingly thumped at his head and wondered if his opened display made Robert feel uncomfortable. She didn't have to wonder for long.

"Hey, Avery, I have an idea. I'll go in the living room and watch television with Cara and you and Sandy can grab a quickie. You may as well get some use out of your one good head! Sure in the hell ain't no halo around that one!"

It was Sandy who was embarrassed this time. Somehow talking about sex seemed wrong. She'd always been passionate with Avery but she'd never been the type to discuss what they shared with anyone. She'd always been mortified when her mama would come over and talk about the things she'd done with men. When her mama talked about sex it seemed dirty and Sandy had grown up with enough dirt. She looked at Robert and Avery and they were still giggling about the little joke. She decided to leave them to their little boy camp-out silliness.

Sandy walked back into the living room to see Cara putting the finishing touches to the mashed potatoes. She never remembered her mama cooking. She'd always either cooked her own dinner or eaten cold cereal if there was nothing else in the house.

Cara turned and saw Sandy staring at her.

"You look like you done seen a ghost. What are the boys doing? I was thinkin' Buster usually eats his supper sittin' in the recliner and, well, I always drank mine, so why don't you and the boys have your dinner at the table together? It might be nice for Tommy to have the whole family around."

There had been something gnawing at Sandy from the bottom of her heart. She'd felt it well up over and over but stuffed it back down without acknowledging it. She felt alone. In her eyes, everyone was acting as if life was great and they were all one big happy family. She decided she needed air and walked out the door without answering her mama.

Cara helped Buster get Robert and Avery to the table and then excused herself. She went out on the porch to find Sandy rocking back and forth in a chair, staring at the Texas sunset. She went to sit in a lawn chair next to her and felt more than the chill in the air.

"Supper's ready. The boys are already eatin'. You best go now if you want anything to be left."

"I'm not hungry, Mama, thanks anyway. The sunset is a pretty one tonight, ain't it?"

Cara looked at the intense oranges and purples of the Texas sky. She'd never noticed the art work of the Mother Nature much or if she had its beauty had been distorted. Everything looked much clearer now. She knew Sandy didn't really want to talk sunsets though.

"Yeah, looks like God was in an orange mood tonight. What kind of mood you in, darlin'?"

Sandy turned her head away to answer.

"I ain't in no mood, Mama. I'm just fine."

Cara scooted her chair around to face Sandy squarely. The air felt thin and crisp outside but she knew that the air in her daughter's lungs was misted with pain. She tried again to get her to open up.

"Sandy, you ain't never been no kind of liar. Your eyes give you away and your shoulders round the bend of your mood way before the train carrying your thoughts get there. I can tell you're chewin' yourself up about somethin' or lettin' somethin' chew you up."

Sandy stretched her legs out in front of her and felt tiny tears edge up in the corners of her eyes. She feared the dam would break if she gave it even the slightest opening with her mouth. She strained against herself to keep the torrent of emotions in check.

"Mama, I really don't know what's wrong. Everything I guess. I really don't feel like talkin'. I just came out here to watch the sun go down and be by myself for a time."

Cara rose and figured she couldn't force Sandy to talk. She was about to go back in when from out of the blue she heard a question that sent a chill all the way to her bones.

"Mama, did you ever love me?"

Cara sat back down with a thud. She felt as if a mirror had been placed in front of her and the time to look at herself had come. She'd been happy to be involved with everyone else of late and not have to examine herself at all. She tried to pass over the question with an easy answer.

"Of course, I loved you; you're my baby girl!"

Her answer was exactly what Sandy had expected from her. She got up from her chair, sighed heavily, kissed her mama on the forehead and said before going in.

"Sure you did, Mama. What was I thinking?"

The silence of early evening fell around Cara on the porch.

The huge orange ball that was the sun was low in the Texas sky and she felt her heart sinking with it. Solace for her lately had been having to focus on other people. It was the thing that kept her away from Jack Daniels. She didn't need a shrink to tell her that self destruction happens when self is the only person you have to live with and a body doesn't like the living arrangements. She hadn't had time to miss being numbed by booze when she was busy being numbed by activity. Sitting alone on the porch with Sandy in her heart, she missed the courage liquor had given her to ignore who she was and had been. It was like after a funeral when everyone leaves and the reality of death is the only thing that surrounds a survivor. She heard laughter coming from inside the house and decided it was time to go in. For now it was easier to pretend to be the matriarch than to be admit she was only a fairy tale.

Cara walked in to total mayhem. There were mashed potatoes on the table, the walls and on the floor. Everyone, including Sandy, was laughing so hard that they couldn't even answer her when she asked what in the hell was going on. It was Buster who finally caught his breath enough to speak.

"Well, darlin, it seems that Avery ain't that coordinated with that halo on his head. He tried to maneuver a big fork of mashed potatoes into his mouth and the fork hit one of the rods and the tater's ended up on Tommy's head. Then Robert, thinkin' Avery was startin' a food fight, flung a fork of them at Avery. Well, Tommy bein' a kid joined in and a food fight was in full swing!"

Cara shook her head and tried to hide the smile her lips formed. She went to the cabinet to get the 409 and some paper towels. She wasn't sure where to start but wondered if 409 would hurt Tommy's hair. She thought all three of them looked like eight-year-olds and ignored their laughter as she wiped the mashed potatoes off the floor under their chairs. She would never let any of them know how happy she was to be picking up their mess instead of trying to understand the mess that had been her life. She looked up from between their chairs and spoke like a mother of misbehaving children.

"Well, I hope you boys know that 'cause of this, ain't a one of you gettin' any of that cherry pie I made for dessert! That shit stains and I ain't takin' any chances!"

Avery stopped laughing. He suddenly felt very tired. He'd noticed that since the beating he just hadn't had any strength. He got up from his chair and grabbed the back of it to steady himself. He felt hands on his shoulders and knew that Buster had come to help him. He leaned into the strength of the body behind him and slowly turned to walk away from the table.

Cara stopped scrubbing for a moment to look at Sandy. She saw unspoken fear in her daughter's eyes. She realized she'd put Avery's HIV on the back burner of her mind but the look on Sandy's face brought it back to her. It suddenly dawned on her that she'd taken no extra care in washing dishes or doing clothes. She knew the thought was selfish but if thinking about protecting the others in the family was selfish, then selfish she would be.

Sandy followed Buster and Avery into the bedroom. Once Buster helped settle Avery into bed he left the room. Sandy lay down next to Avery and stroked his left arm and put her head on his chest. She spoke in whispers to him.

"Don't you go gettin' sick, Avery Anderson. I need the warmth of you around me to get through life."

She positioned her neck so she could see his face. The tears in his eyes scared her more than she'd ever been scared. His voice was soft and devoid of fear when he spoke.

"Sandy, I think I need to see about gettin' some medication. I ain't sure what's goin' on in my body but I do know it ain't the outside injuries makin' me feel this way. I ain't said nothin' 'cause I know that shit is expensive and we can't afford it. I been a burden my whole life. I ain't gonna be a burden to you and Tommy."

"Shut up, Avery Anderson! Just shut the hell up! You gave me my heart and soul and I ain't lettin' nothin' take you away from me! You can just stop talkin' that way right now or I'll go in the kitchen and get some of that cherry pie and slap your ass with it!"

Avery laughed and hugged Sandy to him. She made him entertain wonderful thoughts and he felt compelled to express them to her.

"Darlin', you go get that pie and I'll take off this gown and you can take my cherry a second time!"

Sandy reached up and placed a sensual, rather than sexual, kiss to Avery's lips. She was so filled with love for him. She'd never known what love was about until she'd met him and the thought of losing it was incomprehensible to her. She would do whatever was necessary to have every moment she could with the only person who'd shown her she had a heart.

Robert walked in on what he thought was a tender moment and felt the red of embarrassment creep up his neck and into his face. He wished he'd known what he saw displayed before him. People always assumed his being gay was about sex but it wasn't. His heart wanted no less than other couples shared. He felt a deep longing for it, seeing Avery and Sandy in such a sweet embrace. His thoughts went to Steve and the hope he'd felt in an elevator. His thoughts were a dichotomy. He both wanted and feared the realness of love. If there was one thing his mother had taught him, it was that love could be unconditional but people seldom were. He backed out of the door way and went back into the living room.

Cara looked up from a television crossword puzzle she was doing and asked Robert for one of the answers.

"Hey, Robert, give me some of that college brain of yours. What's a four letter word for walkway? I know lots of four letter words but they don't fit too good in this puzzle. I cheat on these things anyway but I ain't ready to throw in the towel just yet."

Robert realized he took things for granted. He couldn't imagine not being able to scan his mind to find a word with four letters that meant walkway. He wondered if the want of education was born into a person's soul? His mother had been as mentally thick as a football player's neck but he'd had a thirst for knowledge. He didn't know what it was that made some people simply follow their circumstances like a lemming to a cliff and others veer off to take a different path. He smiled as he thought, yes, Cara, if you were in my mind you would know the word. He spoke to her more from the middle of his thoughts rather than from the middle of the room.

"Path, Cara. That's the four letter word you're likely looking for."

She moved her pencil carefully along the paper to see if the word made sense with the others and decided he was right.

"Well, I'll be damned if it don't make sense out of the rest that's wrote here. What kind of person uses the word path? Why don't people just call a thing what it is?"

She put the pencil down on the coffee table, straightened her posture and pursed her lips in high brow snob fashion. The words that came out of her mouth were almost English accent perfect.

"I say old chap, good fuckin' word but why don't they just say road!"

Robert laughed and thought Cara to be one of the most charming people he'd ever met! She was harsh, worn, base and everything she looked to be but all those things made her wonderful too. He was surprised when she suddenly turned serious and asked him to sit with her for a minute.

"Robert, do you know what's eatin' at Sandy? I realize she's got bees in her bush and worry up her butt but it ain't the obvious things that seem to be botherin' her."

Robert had sensed it too and he thought he knew what it was. He'd seen the hollow look in Sandy's eyes in his own and he couldn't tell Cara that she was the trouble with Sandy. How could he tell her that the little girl that Sandy never got to be still haunted her heart? He no more wanted to hurt Cara than she'd ever set out to hurt Sandy. He chose his words carefully.

"Cara, I just think Sandy is too hurt to be a part of life right now. Give her time to settle things out in her heart and mind."

Cara picked the crossword puzzle up again but wasn't so sure Robert was right. Sometimes she caught herself thinking of him as one of Sandy's girlfriends. She watched him over the top of the page as he went into the kitchen to get some water. She eyed him as he reached into the cabinet for a glass and wondered how it came to be that men could be interested in men and women in women. It was inconceivable to her ever to have feelings for someone of her own sex. She shook her head and read the clue to twenty-six down.

The noise was deafening and Sandy instinctively jumped on top of Avery to protect him. The screech of tires could be heard and then the pounding of feet as Cara, Buster, and Robert came running into the room. Tommy came into the hall screaming, naked and still dripping from his bath. Buster stopped him before he came into the room because glass had been blown everywhere. He guided him back to the bathroom and shut the door.

Cara checked Sandy and Avery for blood while Robert cautiously opened the drapes to look out the window. He asked Cara to go get Buster and to not let Tommy in the room. She'd found no blood on either Sandy or Avery but when she started toward the door she gasped at the size of the hole in the wall just feet from where they'd been lying. She turned to Robert and said,

"They ain't playin'; are they? That hole looks big enough to have come from an elephant gun!"

Robert tried to stop shaking long enough to help Sandy off the bed. He had never seen anyone look so pale in his life. She dabbed at a scratch caused by Avery's halo and asked Robert if he could get a clean pair of underwear out of the top drawer for Avery. Her voice sounded more pitiful than anything he'd ever heard.

"They beat the shit out of him once and now they've scared the piss out of him. I'm gonna take Avery, Mama, and Tommy over to our trailer. I'll drop them off and then come on back here. If you wanna go too you'll be safe there."

Sandy went to take care of Tommy and pushed past Cara as she came in with a dust pan and broom. Cara asked Avery if he could go sit in the living room while she got all the glass up and changed the sheets. She saw him wince and she felt sorry that mentioning the bed linens had embarrassed him. She had a fleeting thought of that night in Sandy's trailer when she had to change Tommy's bed. Sadness sat in her heart and made her feel tired.

Morris Foley pulled up along with the other two cars dispatched on the call. He could see the blown-out window and knew the shot was intended as more than a warning. He aimed his flashlight toward the street to look for shell casings. He knew only one shot had hit but wanted to be sure it had been the only one fired. He saw the tire tracks and moved his light along their path. His experience told him the vehicle had most likely been a heavy truck of some kind. There was little they could discern from the tracks since looking for a heavy truck in East Texas was like trying to find a blade of grass in a meadow. He joined the other officers inside and listened as one of them asked Cara if she by chance saw who shot at the house. He readied himself for her answer and smiled because the officer obviously didn't know much about Cara Covington.

"Oh yeah, here lately me and Buster make a game out of it. I take the first shift starin' out the window to watch and wait for people to drive by to terrorize us. We got this point system worked out. Runnin' over my flower beds is five points, runnin' over my dog is ten, shootin' a hole in my wall counts for fifteen, shootin' a hole in my loved ones is twenty, and shootin' a hole in me is worth one hundred points and the grand prize! Ya see, them fuckers know that this old bitch is just crazy enough to run outside naked, offer them a taste of me and then pull an AK47 out my ass and blow their balls off!"

Morris wondered if the red of the officer's face matched the red of his ass? He could tell the officer was about to make a fatal error by responding in kind to Cara's attitude so he stepped in to wrap things up.

"I found a bullet casing out front and we've called an expert in to check out the tire tracks. You know we ain't gonna come up with much but we'll cover the bases anyway. I doubt they'll be back tonight but maybe it'd be best to get the young un and the others out of the house for the night."

Cara narrowed her eyes. The deep wrinkles in her face folded over each other and her thin lips drew taut as if to make her words line up with her thoughts.

"Now, Morris, you know damn well I probably screwed the brains out of some of these asses and I know they ain't nothin' but pricks dipped in dumb sauce. Trust me, a woman can't be scared of no man once she done seen him naked. These fuckers may carry guns in their hands but the pee shooters between their legs is the only brains they got and, darlin', I ain't about to run scared. You might be right about Sandy and the others but I ain't leavin' my home to go hide from no men whose dicks are so small they can't pee in the toilet without standin' in it."

Morris thought that Cara was more like a man than she would want to be. She had a bravado and macho style that could rival any gun toting bastard he knew. As she shut the door behind them, he wondered if her bite was really as mean as her bark. He thought that it was probably worse.

Everyone gathered in the living room except Tommy. Sandy started talking about going back to the trailer and Robert thought he had a much better idea.

"Sandy, your trailer is only a few miles down the road. How about we all go to my place? These people don't know where I live and plus it's safer than a trailer anyway. We have a gated entrance and no one can get through without a code."

Cara spoke before Sandy ever had a chance.

"Now that sounds like a good plan. Ya'll were talkin' about going to stay with homo boy before all this happened and so it won't be no different than you planned in the first place. There's only one thing I'm gonna ask and that's ya'll come back here for Christmas Eve. I ain't gonna let no god damn chicken bastards keep me from havin' Christmas with my family!"

Sandy looked at Avery to see if his face showed any objections. She saw relief and knew that Robert's was where they would go. She went in to the bedroom to pack a few belongings for them and the medical supplies and then went in to wake Tommy.

Buster took Avery and Robert in his truck and Cara rode with Tommy and Sandy in Avery's truck. Sandy could see Buster turn his head toward any oncoming lights to try and see around the glare to the approaching vehicle. She knew as well as he did that the shooters could have anticipated their leaving the house and be lying in wait. She knew that one carefully aimed shot could mean both trucks of people could be done away with handily. She was happy when they got off the dark roads and into the well lit streets of Jacinto Corners. There was noise and traffic and life seemed to go on without a thought to what they'd been through. Somehow, it made her feel safe, like the world hadn't really changed at all.

Cara stared out the window at the rows of neatly cared for condos and watched as the big iron gate opened to let them through. She had never known the feel of plush carpet under her bare feet or the smell of a room whose insulation stayed dry in the rain. She had never lived in a house that wasn't crusted with the dirt of her family's past sitting on every surface.

Robert handed Sandy the keys to the front door and the moment it was opened, Tommy ran through the house like he owned it. Robert apologized for the mess and lack of furniture and then laughed himself silly at Cara's expression. He waited for her words to follow her mind's lead.

"Oh lord, I can just see it now!"

Cara flailed her arms and swished her hips way out as she walked into the kitchen. She took a rotten banana out of a fruit basket and and put her left hand up to her mouth. In an exaggerated voice of desperation and hysteria, she said,

"Oh Avery, dahlin', I just feel in a tizzy about ruinin' your breakfast! Will you ever forgive me for letting your banana get all mushy? If only I could suck it and make it come back to life!"

Robert laughed the hardest at her queenly impression of him. It didn't matter that he had never in his life been a flitting fairy, her portrayal was as endearing as anything he'd ever seen.

"Oh Cara, I swear you could be a stand up comic. I could take you around to the gay bars and you could dazzle them with your country flavored humor."

Cara squinted at Robert and he knew she was thinking on a come back. She was quicker than anyone he'd met when it came to word play.

"I tell you what, honey, you put me in with a room full of homos and I'll have them clapping with their dicks instead of trying to grab each other's! Darlin', I don't just eat homemade country gravy with bacon, I douche with it! I am one tasty bitch!"

Buster told Cara that they needed to go so everyone could get a decent night's sleep. Cara kissed Robert and then pecked at Avery's cheek. She started to walk with Sandy to the door and stopped. She put her arms around Sandy's neck and gently kissed her cheek. She focused her eyes right into Sandy's and willed her to feel loved rather than saying it. She slipped her arm around Buster and was through the door before Sandy could say a word.

Sandy made a pallet on the floor for her and Tommy and then went to check on Avery. He looked so strange lying in Robert's bed with the white eyelet lace bedspread moving with his enormous stomach as he snored. Tommy had fallen asleep next to him and she was about to lift him out of the bed when she felt Robert's hand stop her. He shook his head and held his finger up to his lips. She followed him back down the hall and he waited to speak until they were in the living room.

"Let Tommy sleep with his daddy. I can stay out here on the couch. I've been resting so much I feel like my butt has callouses. I made some coffee. Do you want a cup? I figured we could sit for awhile and talk."

Sandy thought the idea was a wonderful one. It would give her a chance to feel like things were normal again. She'd missed her fun conversations with Robert. She went to the kitchen to pour some coffee for them.

Sandy didn't fit so well on the small love seat but she felt she could fit into Robert's world. She'd felt smothered by feelings of jealousy and rejection more each day and she'd feared a blow up.

It had always been hard to be around her mama but seeing what she'd missed out on was too hard. She was sure he didn't want to hear what was holding her mind hostage. She watched as he sipped his coffee and could tell he wanted to talk about something he feared would upset her.

"Sandy, Cara asked me something tonight. Just before all hell broke loose she asked me what was wrong with you? I know what it is that's bothering you, sweetheart. I know where the pain comes from. I know it's hard to see your mama care about things when you never had her heart, her time, or her motherhood. I see your eyes when she talks to Tommy. I see the jealousy and pain of what you missed out on. I see it and understand it, Sandy."

He saw the tears well in her eyes and he put his cup down and stroked the side of her face. He saw words spill out onto her cheeks but knew her tongue was too tied to her heart to speak. He continued to pull out the words she couldn't say.

"You hate feeling envious of your own eight year old son and torn because you want him to have that which you never had. You tell yourself it's great that he has a chance to feel the love of his grandmother even if she was never a grand mother to you or any mother at all but each kind word she gives him makes you feel like a lost child. You want to hurt Cara the way she hurt you. You don't want to love her because for so many years she didn't love you."

He saw it start as a small quake in her shoulders and then felt the roaring tremble of her body as she collapsed into tears. To him her tears were from the ground up, the inside out and the most pitiful he'd ever heard. He hadn't meant to hurt her but to validate what he knew was in her soul. He knew she'd felt the pull of the past and present. He'd known that pull himself a thousand times.

He was disappointed when she rose and whispered,

"I can't talk about this, Robert. I love you for trying to help but I am just too tired and raw to do this now. I'm going to bed. I'll see you in the morning."

Robert watched as Sandy went down the hall. He reached over to turn out the lamp on the end table and sat in the darkness wishing he felt like he was at home. He thought about the truths he knew about life. He thought the number one truth was that people were only disappointed in life when they had expectations of others rather than expectations of themselves. He'd learned a long time ago that parents were mere humans, most friends were temporary connections of equal vision from different perspectives and that lovers were most often growth spurts of the heart.

Robert put his feet up on the couch and positioned the pillows behind his head to support his halo. He drifted off, thinking that as bent as his mom's halo would be, maybe she deserved to have it for herself anyway. He knew she'd worn pain and tonight his house was filled with it.

CHAPTER FORTY-ONE

Cara woke excited about Christmas shopping but too cold to move her body out of bed in any kind of hurry. She could hear Buster in the kitchen rattling around with pots and pans and knew he was making his morning oatmeal. She smiled and stretched under the warmth of the blanket. He had a thing about regular bowel movements and Cara knew how full of shit he was so she guessed oatmeal was a fair remedy. She stretched again and decided her bladder wouldn't allow anymore time to stay warm.

She hated the feel of the cold porcelain under her butt. It was a lonely feeling, hard and empty. She thought about the times she'd gone in after one of Buster's visits and felt that the smell he left behind was worth the warmth of the lid. She could handle the continuous spray of air freshener more than the lonely feeling.

She decided to take a bath before getting her coffee. Sometimes a person traded off warmth on the inside for warmth on the outside. She was getting outside warmth from baths and Buster instead of strangers, and her inside warmth came from coffee instead of whiskey. As she let the stream of hot water make clouds of steam rise from her body, she hoped she could generate warmth with some sort of regularity, too. She'd been trying with all the people in her life but had to admit the hardest for her to warm to was Sandy.

Cara lit a cigarette and sunk deep into the tub. She watched the patterns of the cigarette smoke meld with the rising steam. Her vision was clouded by thoughts of Sandy on the porch looking much like a little girl who'd lost her puppy and only friend. The truth of it was Cara knew what was wrong with Sandy. She had always been her daughter's biggest problem. Sandy was the hardest truth for her to face and that was the reason warming up to her was so damn hard. They seemed to bounce of each other like a chain reaction car wreck. It was Cara's guilt meeting with Sandy's sorrow that kept them apart. The buffer had to be honesty but both of them knew that once out, it could never be stuffed back in and it could break even the dysfunctional bond they shared. There were many things she didn't remember about Sandy's childhood and the things she did remember scared her out of filling in any blanks.

Cara raised out of the tub and shifted her thinking to buying presents for Tommy. She wanted to give him the best Christmas he'd ever had. She and Buster had discussed a new bike and perhaps getting him a pair of roller blades. She hadn't discussed anything with Sandy about gifts but she knew he had so little it wouldn't be difficult finding things to make his eyes light up.

Buster came in to shave and told her she needed to get her skinny ass in gear because traffic was going to be a nightmare. He looked at Cara wrapped in a towel and had a real urge to remove her from it. There had been so much going on and so many people around they'd not had much time alone. He was amazed at the change in their sex life since she'd stopped drinking. He'd never had the heart to tell her that the only reason he'd wanted sex so seldom before was because making love to a drunk Cara was like riding a bull, quick, rough and painful. She made him feel too much like her empty whiskey bottles, a lot of rattle but nothing warm left inside.

She slapped his ass as she walked out of the bathroom naked, clothes in hand and headed for the kitchen for coffee. He smiled and thought he'd unwrap her as a present when they got home. The feeling of being loved made him happy. He ran the razor over his chin and thought about how happy Cara made him.

Sandy woke up with every bone in her body aching. She didn't have the build for sleeping on the floor. She heard Tommy and Robert talking in the kitchen and went to check on Avery before going in to the bathroom. She was startled when she saw an empty bed. She didn't think Robert was stable enough to be helping Avery around.

Sandy sat on the toilet and marveled at the cleanliness and organization of Robert's things. It amazed her that he hadn't been there in well over a week but everything still sparkled. She knew it was a reflection of who he was on the inside. He'd taken what was handed him and made the best of it rather than wallowing in the filth of it all.

She walked into the living room and saw Avery sitting in front of the television with Tommy and Robert in the kitchen preparing breakfast. Robert looked over his shoulder and tried to talk above the sound of the mixer.

"The cereal was stale, the bread was moldy but I found some just-add-water pancake mix and I have syrup. One lump or two?"

Sandy was confused. He had just been talking about pancakes and the question seemed to come from outer space.

"What? You mean in my coffee? I don't use sugar, remember?"

Robert laughed and turned off the mixer.

"I meant in your pancakes, silly! I suck at making these things. Morris used to tell me that where he grew up they called them flap jacks but when I made them they were more like crap jacks!"

Everyone in the room laughed and Sandy thought it felt so right for them all to be together. She felt the tension leave her shoulders and her breathing slowed. There was no denying that her mama had a really negative affect on her nervous system. She also knew it was a mutual thing which made one play off the other even more.

They ate the crap jacks with lots of butter and syrup and no one was the wiser for the lumps. Robert went to read his stack of mail and Avery said he was going to go back to lie down. Sandy finished clearing the table and silently worried about Avery. She couldn't help but wonder if the way he was feeling of late had more to do with his emotional state rather than the HIV. She needed to talk to Robert the next time they were alone to find out how to get help for Avery.

By the time she finished the dishes and went exploring with Tommy around the condo grounds, it was well after one before she was ready to go to the grocery store. Robert had given her a hundred dollar bill and a list of things he wanted. He'd told her to buy whatever she wanted for her family with the rest.

She was glad she'd asked Tommy to go with her. She told him to put the two sacks he carried down and open the front door. She had three in her arms and two more in the truck and was surprised to see Cara at the door to help her. She came out to take the packages from Sandy and to whisper that Tommy couldn't go near Buster's truck but as soon as they got the groceries inside she wanted Sandy to come see.

Sandy had no idea why it rankled her to see Cara standing beside her putting things into the refrigerator. She was humming and seemed too excited for words. Robert, Tommy and Buster were in front of the television watching a science fiction thriller on cable and Sandy watched as Cara went around the couch to sit by Tommy. She could have sworn the woman's voice that came out of her mama's mouth was from someone else's long dead grandmother.

"Oh Tommy, my little sweetie, just wait until you see what me and Buster got you for Christmas. You're gonna start callin' your old grandma Santa!"

Sandy slammed a can of peas into the cabinet and then crumpled the sack loud enough to cause everyone to turn towards her. She hadn't meant to be obvious and certainly didn't want to call attention to her childish antics. She heard her mama's sugary sweet voice again.

"Sandy, darlin', you okay in there? Sorry I didn't finish helping you put that stuff away. I guess I was just overcome with excitement and the holiday spirit!"

Sandy felt like she was going to throw up right in the middle of the kitchen floor. She wondered if she was the only one who noticed how sickening Cara's enthusiasm was? Maybe it was genuine but it was a side of her mama she'd never seen and it made every nerve in her body stand at attention. She jerked around to finish putting the groceries away and before she knew it Cara was beside her.

"Come on, Sandy, let that wait until later. Come on out to the truck with me."

Sandy looked at Robert to rescue her but knew that he wouldn't say a word. She followed Cara out the front door and gasped as they walked up to Buster's dually parked across the way. It was literally loaded with packages.

"Mama, what the hell did y'all do, rob a toy store?"

Cara laughed and told her that Buster was worse than her about shopping.

"I ain't gonna show you everything but looky here in the back. We got Tommy the neatest bike and a pair of roller blades, too. Oh yeah, we bought one of them Sony Play Stations for him and some video games. Did you know those games cost sixty damn dollars a piece?"

Sandy backed away from the truck. She felt like the world had just crashed and was sitting directly on her chest. Cara came around to her to see if she was okay and saw the wildest look in her daughter's eyes she'd ever seen. When Sandy finally found her voice, it was a cross between a hiss and a guttural roar.

"You ain't doin' this, Mama. You ain't buyin' forgiveness through Tommy. It ain't gonna happen, Mama, not this Christmas or any god damn Christmas 'til the day you die!"

Cara couldn't speak as Sandy ran back towards Robert's house. She stood trembling from her head to her toes in the parking lot, just staring at where Sandy had been. She tried to get her legs to move and would take a small step and stop. She grabbed the side of the truck and decided to give up trying.

Sandy flew through the living room without a word and slammed the door to the bedroom where she'd slept. Buster looked at Robert and then went out to see about Cara. Sandy hadn't shut the front door so he could see Cara standing by the truck looking like a statue set for demolition. She swayed slightly back and forth but stood rigid otherwise. He went to her and held her before taking her back inside.

It was Robert who suggested that he, Buster and Tommy go into town and get ice cream. The three got up and Robert motioned for Buster to take Avery's keys off the counter and to take Tommy on outside. As soon as he thought Tommy was out of ear shot, Robert bent to Cara and took her hands in his. His voice was loving but firm.

"Go talk to her, Cara. Nothing will ever be right between you two unless you both share the hurt in your hearts. I know you're scared to hear it but you need to hear it, Cara. Sandy has a right to be angry."

Cara heard the front door shut and Sandy's open. She knew that Sandy thought it had been her and Buster that had left. She looked like she'd seen the boogie man when she saw Cara sitting on the couch. She started to turn back towards the hall but Cara called out to her.

"Sandy, don't keep running away. You got things in your heart to tell me. I ain't been ready to hear you and I ain't ready now but we ain't got a chance otherwise."

Sandy paced up and down in front of the couch. She had so much anger churning in her and it propelled her feet on the carpet. She went to the kitchen to see if Robert had any liquor. She found a bottle of really old whiskey and poured a shot in a glass. She picked up the bottle, her glass and went to face her mother.

Sandy poured another shot and put the bottle down in front of her on the coffee table. She needed to smooth the anger and the whiskey helped it slide down far enough to facilitate an opening in her heart to speak. She thought it ironic that in order for them to come together her mama had to be whiskey free and she had to have the freedom whiskey offered.

"Mama, I always had an excuse to hide my heart because you were always sicker than what you made me. Since you been off the booze I've been seein' someone I don't know and yet do know.

You've become the person I longed for my whole life, Mama. You are the tears on my pillow all those nights as a child that turned into dreams of happiness and love. I see you with Tommy and my heart becomes eight again. I remember nights I cried for you, Mama! Those nights you was either out drinkin' or too drunk to know I was alive."

Sandy stopped to see the stone Cara's face had become. She waited for the words that she knew were going to come. Not even the new Cara disappointed her.

"Sandy, I ain't gonna apologize another time for my drinkin'. I done it before I ever had you and it was more a part of me than you. I didn't stop for you when you was conceived and it ain't because of you I ain't drinkin' now. I don't know why in the fuck you got to keep bringing this shit up!"

Sandy wiped away her tears and let her anger return for strength. She was not going to let her mama beg off the pain she'd caused. She was not going to let Cara's guilt dictate her feelings anymore. Cara had to stand in front of her firing squad and she had all the rifles pointed at her mother's head but her words were aimed at her mother's heart.

Cara put her hands over her ears and shook her head. Sandy grabbed her mama's hand away and yelled into her head.

"You listen to me, Mama!! God damn it, Cara Covington, it ain't about what you want to hear! It's about what I feel! You made me mute my entire life by stayin' too drunk to hear! You can hear now and I have to speak! Mama, the first night Daddy came into my room, I know you heard my screams. He started kissing me and saying how soft I felt. He told me how my lips were plump like my body. I loved him, Mama, he was my daddy! I trusted him more than I trusted you because he was there for me when you weren't! Mama, I was Tommy's age! The only present your drunkin' ass ever gave me was my daddy's dick in my vagina!"

Sandy saw Cara break. She saw it as clearly as if her mother had been picked up and broken in half by the force of her own life. She heard the pitiful sobbing and felt the trembling of another childhood lost to the shortcomings of being born of human parents. She didn't know why, but she reached out to comfort her mama. She put her arms around the tiny shaking child that was the woman who bore her and yet not once in life had taken responsibility for giving birth.

Cara finally looked into her daughter's eyes. Her lips trembled and her heart bled into her voice. Her words were soft but had an edge of poignancy and meaning.

"Sandy, get me my purse. I bought you somethin' today that came from money I stuck aside more than twenty years ago. It weren't a lot to begin with but time and interest made it enough to buy you somethin' nice. I wanted to give it to you for Christmas but I think it'll mean more to you now."

Sandy reached over to get the faux Gucci bag off the floor. She felt the fake bag fit her fake mother. She handed the purse to Cara and waited for her life to magically appear out of the bag.

Cara fished around in the purse. Her tears didn't let her distinguish the feel of her cigarette case from the gift she'd bought Sandy. She finally felt the velvet of the box and brought it up to the surface along with the huge lump in her throat. She knew there could be no words so she just thrust the box at Sandy as if it burned her fingers to give.

Sandy turned the box in her hand. She wondered if it contained the emptiness that had been the common bond between mother and child. She eased the ribbon from around it from the corners and took a deep breath before opening the lid.

Inside lay the most perfect emerald and diamond ring she'd ever seen. There was a tiny card pressed into the top of the lid and with trembling fingers, Sandy opened the paper. The note simply said:

From the day you were born, the sparkle of your eyes made me see greener pastures. The brilliance of your smile made me see coal turned to diamonds. Look to this ring for the answer to your question.

Sandy turned the ring in her hand and looked at the band to

see an inscription. The tiny engraved letter read:

I love you, Sandy, Mama.

Her arms simply followed her heart as she hugged Cara. It felt like both the first and last time for them to ever touch. She had to be the bigger heart in it all but she had to make sure her mama knew the ring couldn't fix it all and certainly not over night. She put the ring on her finger and then turned to take her mother on a brief walk through the heart of an abandoned child.

"The ring is so special, Mama, but it can't fix things right away. You raped me as surely as daddy did and it's gonna take time to let that go. As long as you were drinkin' you was still lost to me and all the shit you put me through still made sense. I never saw you as a person, Mama, just a bottle of booze. I need to learn to see you as somethin' I ain't never known, sober. It'll take time to stop bein' mad for what you weren't. I never liked you, Mama, and I never wanted to."

Cara sat staring at the coffee table. She knew what Sandy said was true but she was angry. She didn't know why Sandy couldn't just know how sorry she was and get over the past. She decided it was better to just say nothing and let time speak for her. Her main responsibility was to herself and staying on the road to making herself whole. She knew people saw drinking as a disease of a physical nature but it was more a disease of hearts. Her heart had never been her own so how could Sandy expect her to give it to anyone? Cara turned her eyes to the bottle sitting on the table and knew it held the secrets of her soul but not the answer to her life, not anymore.

Sandy rose from the couch and thanked her mama again before going to check on Avery. She wondered if he'd heard the conversation she'd had with her mama. She knew he'd seen it coming. They'd talked about their respective upbringing at length and cried with each other about the tremendous loneliness that came from being abandoned by parents who never physically left.

Avery looked up as Sandy walked in to the room, his eyes brimming with tears. He saw the frightened look on her face and tried to speak but his words were too choked to be coherent. He straightened against the pillows and cleared his throat of the pain that blocked it.

"Let me see it, Sandy. I wanna see your mama's bridge from the past to your future."

Sandy sat on the bed and showed Avery the ring. She took it off and turned it so he could see the inscription. Her voice was filled with determined anguish when she spoke.

"It's a precious thing, Avery, but it ain't good enough. A person can't erase a lifetime of neglect, abuse and rape with just want to and a ring."

Avery wanted to step carefully but he knew he had to march right in.

"Sandy, we gonna tell Tommy that, too? Do we tell him that there ain't no excuse for the way we treated him and he should hate us for what our hearts told us to do? We ain't been good to him, Sandy. I was layin' here thinkin' when I heard you talkin' to your mama about the ring. You member that pinwheel he wanted for his birthday? We told our son that beer was more important to us than he was. I done took my belt to him so many fuckin' times just for bein' what he is, a kid. I always felt I'd come from my mama's bowels instead of her vagina. She musta told me a million times that I weren't nothin' but shit. How come I done made Tommy feel like shit, too? Sandy, I need to go see my own mama. I need to see if I can forgive her so I can forgive myself for what I been to Tommy."

Sandy rubbed Avery's chest. She recognized the incredible need in his eyes and in his voice. She understood the want to be connected not only to the world but to one's self. Consequences was a word that had more meaning to those who never understood it than to anyone who lived its definition. She spoke softly to the little boy inside him as if the ring had given her back the voice of a little girl.

"Darlin, tomorrow is Sunday and if you're up to it, I'd be

happy to drive you to the nursing home. Avery, are you sure it's what you want?"

Avery looked at his hands and turned them over palm to back. He thought of how he'd had the dirt and grime of life under his fingernails since birth. His were the hands of the working class poor. Trailer trash was only two steps away from the hated blacks and one step away from the welfare garbage. He'd never made the distinction and never called blacks anything but friends and never once asked a neighbor where their food came from or how their rent was paid, but the world he grew up in sure did. In his mind, most of the people he knew were better than him because they had a mama waiting at home to ask them how their day went or to just sit in the same world with them and share space. It wasn't ever about money to him. For him, being rich meant having things that money couldn't buy and he'd grown up poorer than anyone else he knew. He wanted to find pocket change to put a jingle in his life and leave the emeralds and diamonds to those who had mothers who cared.

"Yes, Sandy, I'm sure. I gotta know and the only way I will is if I go see her. Baby, my mama sat around the house in a robe all day smokin' cigarettes, drinkin' coffee, and watchin' television until it was time to go out to the bars to pick up men. She didn't have a sense of humor like Cara and she beat the shit out of me if I even looked at her. I raised my brothers and sisters not 'cause she told me to but 'cause she wouldn't. Sandy, my mama didn't have alcohol for an excuse, she was just a poor excuse for a human being. I didn't never know why she did things. I never knew a thing about her. When my daddy would come home he'd beat the hell out of her for what he thought she'd been doin' and then beat the shit out of me for lettin' her."

Avery wiped at his nose and Sandy reached for a tissue. She'd always been so involved in her own crap with Cara she'd forgotten that Avery had a mother, too. She had to admit that there had never been a time when Cara had just abandoned her. There may have been times she'd come up for open house or something at school drunk, dressed like a hooker and on the make for every man in sight but she'd come just the same. There were the times like her third grade Christmas party when she'd thought she would die from embarrassment. Her mama had been drunk when the room mother asked her to help out and even drunker when she attended. A smile crossed her lips as she recalled that her mama brought all her Avon castaways as a little girl present for the gift exchange. She'd made reindeer cookies that looked like they'd been doing psychedelic drugs. The icing colors all ran together and the candy beads she put on as eyes and noses were just dropped any place like in a Picasso painting.

Avery's voice jolted her out of her thoughts.

"Where'd you go, darlin'?"

Sandy stretched out on the bed next to Avery and rested her head on his chest. She shut her eyes and listened to the sound of his heart. She spoke more to it than to his mind.

"I was just thinkin' I had it luckier than you and here you are bein' a finer human than me. You have such a forgivin' soul and I just let mine get mean over what I thought I shoulda got from life."

"Sandy, there ain't no good in any of it. All I meant was at least your mama made some kind of effort and is really tryin' now. My mama had kids as a by-product of sex like she was some kind of processing plant for hormones and the babies was the rejects of the factory. You told your mama once that she'd placed the garbage of life in your room 'cause she couldn't stand the stench. Well, to my mama, we were the garbage of life. I don't want to make Tommy smell like garbage or be garbage. I love that boy, Sandy, and he needs to know it."

Avery's words struck her hard. She never even questioned Tommy's love for them. She'd never seen herself as abusive until she and Avery started talking about it. She could no more make up to Tommy the things she'd done than Cara could take back and do over her childhood years. It occurred to her that abuse was not perpetrated by degrees but by method. In the mind of a child, love was simply caring enough not to abuse. It dawned on Sandy that pain was pain and the heart processed it the same no matter how it was inflicted. Life was not a Richter Scale but a barometer reflecting the warmth others gave. They'd done to Tommy what had been done to them.

Sandy stroked Avery's face and touched his cheek with a kiss. She understood his need to see his mother and realized that part of what had been wrong in her own life was keeping Cara an arm's length away with her anger. In a sense, she'd continued her mama's abuse by holding on to it in her own heart and letting it beat her all over again and prevent a real relationship with her son.

She heard the front door open and Tommy's excited voice asking for her. He came bounding into the bedroom and she never thought she'd seen eyes that twinkled more. His words were breathy puffs of wonder when he spoke.

"Oh Mama, Daddy, y'all won't never guess what I got y'all for Christmas! Uncle Robert and Buster told me I could buy whatever I wanted and I got the bestest stuff!"

Sandy looked up at Avery and smiled. It wasn't too late for Tommy and maybe it wasn't even too late for them. She could tell that Avery was tired so she put her arm around Tommy and led him out of the room, explaining his daddy needed to rest. Before shutting the door, she turned to Avery and whispered,

"We'll take you home to your mama tomorrow, Avery. You rest now."

Sandy helped Buster load the packages in the truck and when Cara came out the front door she walked towards her. She opened her arms and hugged her with real tenderness. She placed a light kiss on her mama's cheek and directed her eyes to the one's she'd spent a lifetime avoiding.

"Mama, I don't hate you and I never did. I'm tryin' as hard as I can to let go of the old Cara. Don't give up on me, okay?"

Cara nodded and smiled. She couldn't fault Sandy for the anger, the sadness or the feeling of tremendous loss she had inside. As a mother she'd been making pain deposits in her daughter like a bank and resentment was her natural dividend. She waved and blew Sandy a kiss as Buster waited for the big iron gates to open and let them out of the lot.

Sandy decided that sandwiches and chips would be a good supper. It had been a long day and everyone seemed more than ready to put an end to it without much fanfare. She'd had to reprimand Tommy constantly since he'd come home from shopping. She knew he was over tired from all the excitement but she also knew she couldn't let him get away with being a brat. As she stood cutting tomatoes, she thought she understood how and why people get confused about the difference between discipline and abuse. She'd instinctively swatted his legs only moments before for standing on the back of Robert's couch and proclaiming in a loud voice that HE WAS HUNGRY! She noticed that Robert hadn't said a word to him and seemingly thought he was being humorous. It made her believe that the line between tolerance and intolerance was drawn by the harshness of a person's heart.

Sandy was bringing Avery his sandwiches when she heard the phone and Robert's voice calling her. She went back to the living room and sat on the couch to take the call, since Robert and Tommy were eating at the table near the kitchen phone. She wasn't particularly surprised to hear Celia Callier's voice.

"Ms. Anderson, this is Celia Callier. I'm afraid there's been some kind of problem with your application this time. Why didn't you tell me that your husband had tested positive for HIV and that he was currently involved in a homosexual relationship?"

Sandy nearly dropped the receiver as her entire body went limp with disbelief. Getting her mouth to close together enough to form words was almost as big an effort as finding words to say.

"Ms. Callier, I have no idea where you're gettin' your information but it just ain't true. I mean part of it is, Avery did test positive but he ain't havin' no relationship with a man!"

"Well, Ms. Anderson, the bureau seems to think so and there has even been talk of a hearing as to whether or not you and your husband are fit to have Tommy in your home. I will do what I can on this end and I mainly called to let you know there won't be any money issued until all this is settled. Ms. Anderson, for what it's worth, I'm really sorry about all this. You should be hearing from me in a few days."

Sandy just held the phone in her lap and sat looking stunned. Robert told Tommy to put his plate in the sink and to go get his bath. He was glad when Tommy didn't give him any argument and went down the hall without hesitation. He went to Sandy and picked up the receiver and put it back on the cradle. He sat next to her on the couch and told her to tell him the bad news.

"There's a problem with the public assistance. It seems they done found out about Avery's disease and think he's havin' an affair with you. They don't want to give us no money and are even thinkin' of taking us to court to see if Tommy should be taken away."

Robert was as stunned as his dear friend. His whole body trembled with anger at the incredible conclusions people jumped to about everything they didn't understand. He was so glad he'd decided on his Christmas surprise for them.

"Sandy, it's gonna be okay. Trust me and believe that it is. I'm here for you and just let the bastards try to take Tommy away."

Sandy wanted to believe Robert but she was finding it hard to have faith in anything. She didn't want to hurt his feelings but reality was coming at her full force. She tried hard to find words that didn't diminish the sincerity of Robert's offer of support.

"Robert, I know you'll be here to support us emotionally but, darlin, we can't live on carin' and love. You ain't worked in weeks either and between givin' me that hundred dollars for groceries and the Christmas shopping you did today, I imagine you're pretty strapped for money too."

She bent to kiss Robert on the cheek and then rose from the couch and disappeared down the hall to go check on Tommy. She stood at the bathroom door and listened to Tommy singing in the bathtub. She laughed at his rendition of Rudolph The Red Nosed Reindeer because it was the one about a grandmother being run over by a train and he didn't really know the words. She opened the door and laughed so loud at the sight of Tommy with his arms up in the air as if singing an operatic aria. He turned to her and smiled. There was such magic in Tommy's face in that moment. He was full of soap and had water dripping from the top of his head, making suds sideburns down both sides of his head. She couldn't help but feel that for him everything had to be okay. She left him to his fun and went in to talk to Avery.

When Sandy walked into the bedroom, she at first thought Avery was sleeping but then recognized the shaking of his shoulders. She went to him immediately and held him to her. She had no idea what was wrong and asked if he was in pain. He shook his head no and tried to speak.

"I been listenin' to Tommy in the bathroom and feelin' my heart break with each chorus of that silly song. Darlin', I done let you and him down and I just can't let loose of it. I'm supposed to be the one who protects you and here I am layin' up in bed, a useless piece of shit that ain't nothin' but a drain on everyone. Tomorrow is Christmas Eve and I just realized the best thing I could give you and Tommy is a divorce from me!"

His shoulders quaked as his tears spilled his sorrow. Sandy touched, stroked and patted him and fought back her own tears. She took a deep breath and slapped his thigh. She wasn't going to let him get away with any wallowing.

"God damn it, Avery, I ain't got time for pity parties. You need to pull yourself together and do it now. That was Ms. Callier on the phone and there's a problem with us gettin' assistance. You got to quit feelin' sorry about everything and get angry enough to fight. I can't keep battlin' alone, Avery. I need you and Tommy needs you!"

Avery looked at her and felt a twinge of anger but at her, not the world. He felt he had a right to a pity party. Everything that had happened had emasculated him and made him feel as useless as he was physically. He wanted a new life for Christmas and he knew he wouldn't even get a new day! He wasn't in the mood to tread lightly so he let his words tumble.

"Sandy, within the last month I done found out I got HIV, had the life beat out of me, lost my job and now ain't even good enough to be a welfare. You got any idea how that makes me feel? It's like a little boy who just struck out at home plate for the third time and he knows his teammates don't want him joinin' them for pizza after the game."

She'd heard enough and this time was not delicate in any way with her response.

"Shut up, Avery. You talk about how all this has affected you, well, there was somethin' I didn't tell you about Ms. Callier's conversation with me. It ain't only the assistance that may be kept from us. They done found out about your HIV and think you're havin' an affair with Robert and are talkin' about havin' a hearin' to see whether or not we're fit to keep Tommy. You didn't mention it in your list of poor me's but I done lost one baby this month, Avery, and I sure in the fuck ain't losin' another! You just feel as sorry for yourself as you want 'cause I've had enough. I can't take this shit anymore!"

Avery was about to speak but Sandy was up and out of the room before he could say anything. She walked to the kitchen counter, grabbed her keys and told Robert she'd be back later. She didn't give him time for questions either and slammed the door on her way out.

Sandy drove towards the mall and then turned in the opposite direction. She was going to go someplace where life was lively and decorated. She pulled into the parking lot at Liars and sat for a moment wondering if it was really where she wanted to be. She whispered to herself as she took the keys out of the ignition.

"Sandy, if you're gonna be a bear, might as well be a grizzly!"

She could hear the whoops and hollers before she even opened the door and felt her mood lift slightly. The place was all lit up and a woman, with nothing but garland wrapped around her, was dancing on the bar. Sandy understood then why there'd been so much whooping going on. The woman had breasts the size of watermelons and the garland did little to cover them.

Sandy sat at the bar and ordered a light beer. She hadn't looked around at the crowd because other than the waitress, Candy, she really didn't know any of the people. She'd only taken a few sips when she heard a voice she thought she recognized. She turned to look at a small group of people sitting at a table near the center of the room and indeed saw a familiar face.

Sandy decided to finish her beer and then go to the mall as she'd started to do in the first place. She was watching the woman with balloon breasts continue to act like a drunken fool when she felt someone behind her. She turned and stared right into the face of Linda Monroe. Sandy knew Linda had been drinking for quite awhile because she swayed back and forth and reeked of beer as if it was coming from her pores. Just as Sandy was about to turn back around, pay for her beer and leave, the beer barrel spoke.

"You's that bitch, married to that fuckin' faggot who's fuckin' that faggot that got me fired! I done kicked your whore mama's sorry ass with words in the hospital but you're gonna get the real deal, bitch!"

Sandy had heard enough. She had never fought anyone in her life and she was not about to let scum drag her into one. She put three dollars on the bar and slid off the stool to the right of Linda. She stepped down fully on the floor and it was then she felt Linda's arms come up to block her from leaving.

She had no idea where the voice came from. It was lower and more primal than anything that had ever come from her body and it was accompanied by the strength of ten men as she yelled, "NO" and pushed Linda away. She'd only meant it to get Linda out of her path but it sent the woman flying over two tables into a third. She'd seen Leo and George get up when Linda had thrown up her block. She thought they'd just wanted to have a good vantage point for the show but when they saw what happened they came toward her. She only had seconds to react but without thought, Sandy picked up a chair from one of the tables and held it out like a lion tamer warding off snarling cats. She kept her eyes on the two men and started to back toward the door but felt arms go around her from behind. She started to whirl around fighting but heard Morris Foley's voice before she could turn.

"Sandy, it's okay. Put the chair down!"

The rage in Sandy made her want to ignore Morris and beat the men that had hurt and terrorized her family but the person she was made her do as Morris asked. She turned to explain what had happened and saw Morris move around to the side of her so he could keep his eyes on the others. Linda had gotten up and was standing with Leo and George with a confidence that made Sandy want to slap her.

"Ain't no need in talkin' to that bitch, Morris Foley. Ain't gonna get nothin' out of that faggot fuckin' piece of trash 'cept shit!

Sandy started to respond but Morris took complete command of the situation.

"Not another word out of anyone unless I ask them to speak!"

Morris motioned for Candy to come over and took her aside. They spoke for a few minutes and then three more officers came in looking like attitudinal punks. They were the kind of policemen that made Sandy think of steroids and spouse abuse. Morris spoke to the officers and then turned to her. She was afraid he was going to arrest her and started to move away.

He moved into her and whispered so that the others couldn't hear.

"I want you to leave now, Sandy. Go home to your family where you belong."

She quietly thanked Morris as he moved to where the other officers were standing and heard Morris' voice as she opened the door. "Assume the position" were the words she heard and as she glanced back she saw Linda, George, and Leo spread out over the tables and cops behind them ready with cuffs. She smiled and said to the air,

"That's what you get for disturbing my piece!"

Sandy got in the truck and felt like Rocky, for some reason.

She had a bouncy feel that made her want to hear the song Eye of the Tiger. She couldn't wait to tell Robert and Avery about her experience. She knew her mama would blow a gasket and think she was lying. She drove back home humming the tune from Rocky.

Cara and Buster sat snuggling on the couch looking at the Christmas tree and all the packages under it. She ran her hand along the inside of his thigh and rested her head against his shoulder. She'd gotten more satisfaction from just feeling him next to her than she'd ever gotten from any man being inside her. She felt Buster move to get up and she looked to see if she was making him uncomfortable. He smiled down at her and took something out of his shirt pocket. His voice had the most soothing tone Cara thought she'd ever heard.

"Cara, darlin', I been ponderin' over whether to give this to you tonight or wait 'til tomorrow evening when everyone is here. I'm thinkin' it's somethin' I'd rather do in private so would you mind Christmas a little early?"

She didn't know why but fear struck at her heart. She had a feeling about the box in Buster's hand and why he wanted to give it to her in private. She'd seen him looking at little medals at the mall for people who'd accomplished certain things in life and she'd known he thought she deserved one for not drinking. She hadn't told him about that night with Sandy in the kitchen and the guilt of not deserving recognition was creeping in. She was about to tell him about the incident when he rose from the couch and knelt in front of her. She could feel the red of embarrassment creeping into her face as he started to speak.

"Cara, there was a time when bein' with you was like livin' on a roller coaster without no restraints. I'd love your humor one minute and hate your acid cruelty the next. The nights I'd spend alone in the bed I missed you and the nights you were here but drunk I'd wish you gone. We done takin' the ride and while I know you ain't never gonna be a ride without bumps, you're sure a ride I take great joy in. I ain't asked but one other person this in my whole life but, Cara Covington, would you marry me?"

She felt her mouth drop open as he opened the lid to the box and displayed a beautiful marquee diamond and wedding band. Her hands were shaking as she reached out to see if the ring was real or if it was some kind of weird awake dream. She looked at Buster and saw as many tears in his eyes as she felt in her own. She wanted to be sure he understood what he was in for before she answered him.

"Buster, I ain't never had any kind of proposal that meant anything decent in my whole life. I ain't never loved a man I ever been with but you and you know I ain't always good at it. I ain't never gonna be like Bessie Mae and I'll always want to run away from a problem before facing it. I'll try every day I'm alive to be the best I can but I'll always be Cara."

She felt his fingers on her lips and a shushing sound come from his.

"I know all that, darlin, it's why I asked. So does that mean yes, Cara?"

He placed the ring on her finger as she nodded and kept trying to wipe away tears that came faster than her fingers could wipe them.

Sandy could hear the television and hoped Tommy was already asleep so she could tell Robert and Avery about her adventure. She didn't understand the rush the experience had given her but she did know it had gotten rid of most of her hostility when she pushed Linda and took a stance against George and Leo.

She immediately saw two halos jutting above the back of the couch and then heard Tommy's squeal of delight because she was home.

"Hey Mama, Grandma's been callin' every two seconds! Daddy finally told her to just get her old ass over here!"

Sandy started to say something about Tommy's choice of words but decided to let it slide. She was sure it was exactly what Avery had said and Tommy was just repeating. She bent to kiss Avery and he grabbed her, making her fall onto the couch with him. She laughed and waited for him to ask her where she'd been. Hell, she wanted someone to ask! It was Robert who gave her an opportunity.

"So did you go jog around the mall to work off all that steam, Miss Talk To The Butt As It Leaves? Didn't your mama teach you not to slam doors, young lady?"

His playful attitude made her decide to tell the story even though Tommy was there. As she relayed the events as they happened, she would reach out and hit both Avery and Robert for laughing. She almost sent Robert to his room when he exclaimed,

"I can just see the headlines! Sumo Sandy lets loose on Linda at Liars!"

Both men were in hysterics when the door bell rang. Sandy walked to the entry and then turned and shot them both the finger before answering the door. She dodged a pillow thrown by Robert just as she opened the door and it hit Cara square in the face.

Sandy couldn't help it, she laughed so hard when she saw the look on Cara's face she couldn't even move out of the way to let her in. She felt her mama's skinny hands poking at her to move and she backed away, laughing and holding her sides. She looked up as Buster came through the door and for some reason hadn't expected him. She suddenly felt sobered and thought something was wrong.

"Mama, I'm sorry. Is everything okay? They didn't do somethin' else to your house did they?"

Cara shook her head and felt a little awkward about barging in to tell her daughter that she was engaged. She'd given no thought at all to what Sandy would think or feel and recent events made her think perhaps she should have. She steered Buster toward the couch and she settled on one of the folding chairs. She really wanted to sit next to Buster but with Avery and Sandy on the couch there wasn't room for her. She looked at them all and realized they were all waiting to hear whatever news had made it so urgent for her to talk to them. Her voice was shaky when she started but gathered the excitement of her heart almost immediately.

"Sandy, it's really you that needs to know what I gotta say and it's why I kept callin'. I hope what I'm gonna tell you makes you more happy than anything but I'll understand if you feel a little strange about it."

Sandy was getting impatient. She wasn't trying to be mean but she hated it when her mama danced around things instead of just saying them.

"Get on with it, Mama. We're family here and if there's one thing we know it's how to handle problems thrown our way!"

Cara drew a deep breath and just blurted it out.

"Buster and I are gettin' married!"

If the couch had been a seesaw, Buster would have been launched like a rocket as fast as both Sandy and Avery came off it and over to where she sat. Their chatter and hugs made her happier than she'd ever imagined being. She really felt the connection of a family for the first time in her life. It dawned on her that through all the sad events they'd all become engaged, engaged in each other's lives.

Robert sat back and felt he was seeing magic. His thoughts went back to the first time he'd met them all together and how they seemed to him to be people placed together by mistake and happenstance. He was amazed to see a family before him now. To him, it seemed that all their trials and all their dashed dreams had become the very cement that rooted them together. They were the reverse concussion of a bomb. They'd started out fragmented and time was the super glue that brought them all back together.

CHAPTER FORTY-TWO

Avery sat on the edge of the bed to put his pants on. He'd have Sandy button his shirt and put his socks on for him. It wasn't so much the halo that made dressing difficult as it was the combination of the halo and his weight. Bending down had always been a problem and now even bending his head was impossible. He got his jeans zipped and went to the top drawer where Sandy had said she put his wallet. He sat back down and opened the secret compartment where most people hid money but where he'd hidden his heart.

He carried his mama in his wallet because he'd never been able to carry her in his heart. The picture was worn, cracked and had a surreal look to it. She had been beautiful, tall and thin with long thick brown hair. He'd never noticed it but even in the picture her eyes seemed devoid of emotion and warmth. He guessed it had been taken when she was around twenty and as beautiful as she was, she looked like life had left just a shell behind.

He rubbed his thumb over the top of it as if he could make it whole again. He'd wished all his life that he'd had a healing touch, not so much to make things as if they hadn't existed but to make the fact that they did less painful. He put the picture back into his wallet and got up to have breakfast with the others.

He walked in to the living room and saw Tommy wrapped in a blanket on the couch next to Robert, where they watched Woody Woodpecker. Sandy turned as he walked into the kitchen to get a cup of coffee and asked if he was okay. He wondered if she knew the fear in his heart. He was almost certain she did.

He moved the eggs and bacon around on the plate with his fork but couldn't bring himself to actually eat them. He hadn't liked them when he was a boy and for some reason he didn't like them now. He thought it was amazing that the worst thing about being rejected by a mother was the incredible need to apologize for being who you were. It wasn't so much that he'd done something wrong but more that he'd been wrong from the very beginning. He'd never felt like he'd fit in his own skin and thought that was why he'd always tried to outgrow it.

Sandy sensed Avery's fear and took his plate off the table and stroked his back. She felt the heaviness of his heart as he rose to go finish getting ready. She scraped the eggs into the garbage and turned to ask Robert something.

"Robert, I need to go help Avery get ready. Do you think you and Tommy could get these dishes done?"

Robert nodded. He'd been thinking all morning about being in Avery's place and how it felt. He'd always had some kind of contact with his mother, so it wasn't the same. He thought how some people thought hatred was the antithesis of love but they were wrong. It was indifference that broke the souls of mankind and it was Avery's mother's indifference that had been the monster in his life. He hoped Avery found himself even if he didn't find a mother at the nursing home.

The nursing home was a buzz of activity. Christmas music could be heard from not only the public address system but from the day room where Silent Night was being plunked out on the piano by someone's great grandchild. The nurses and attendants all wore Santa hats and sported necklaces with Christmas bulbs hanging from them. There were jingle bell sounds and laughter in every hallway. Avery went up to the desk and told the nurse that he was looking for Mabel Anderson. He watched as she typed the name into the computer. She looked up at Avery and asked,

"Excuse me, sir, but may I ask why you wish to see her?"

Avery looked at Sandy. He wondered that himself but gave the nurse the answer that had been given him since his birth.

"She's my mother or at least, I'm her son."

The nurse excused herself and went towards one of the offices behind her. She knocked at a door and then disappeared for a few minutes. She came back out and asked that Sandy and Avery follow her so the director of the home could talk to them.

The director was a huge woman who wore too much make up, too much perfume and earrings the size of hubcaps. She motioned for them to sit down and opened a file sitting on the desk in front of her. Her words seemed to drip with insincere concern as she spoke.

"Mr. Anderson, your mother is no longer with us. Mabel always led us to believe that she had no next of kin. She told us that you visited her because you had been a neighbor boy who'd brought her wild flowers that you'd picked on the way home from school. She said your own mother was neglectful and so she would have you in for milk and cookies after school. She said she loved you in order to make up for what your own mother never gave you. We never questioned her story, I'm sorry. She was admitted here by the state and we just didn't know any different. Mr. Anderson, your mother died last week from heart failure and complications due to diabetes."

Avery didn't say a word but rose from the chair, walked through the reception area and out to the grounds faster than Sandy had ever seen him move. By the time she got outside, she saw him sitting on a bench under the biggest oak tree she'd ever seen. He had his hands over his face and she thought he was crying. She sat next to him and hugged him as best she could. Her words were filled with tears.

"Oh god, Avery, I am just so sorry."

His answer shocked her and she lifted her head to look at him.

"Don't be, Sandy, I'm not sorry at all. What that woman said in there tells me that mama couldn't let people know the truth of things. She made herself out to be what she never was, a caring, giving person. Don't you see, Sandy, it meant she felt guilt. It meant she cared about what she never was to me! I have my answer, darlin' and it's the one I wanted!"

Sandy sat staring at two squirrels running down a tree. She didn't understand Avery's feelings completely but it made sense that in life his mama had been dead to him but in her death there had been a spark of life. She was thinking about the incredible irony in that when Avery spoke again.

"Let's go home, darlin', it's Christmas Eve and we got a family waiting."

Robert got the last of the pies and cookies and told Sandy he thought they had everything they needed for a night at Cara's and Christmas dinner. Tommy was bouncing off the walls and telling everyone to hurry. Sandy checked through the house one more time as everyone piled out of the door and felt she was leaving one home to go be in another.

Cara repositioned the beers in the fridge so she could put the turkey she'd just seasoned in until it was ready for cooking. She stirred the egg nog and lined the bottles of booze up on the counter. She watched Buster as he put another Christmas CD in and thought how very strange everything felt. She felt like a six year old who'd just been given her first bike without training wheels. She knew how it was supposed to work but wasn't quite sure she had the momentum and balance to ride along without falling.

She felt a rush of excitement when she heard the familiar sound of Sandy's truck pull into the yard. She heard Old Blue's greeting and thought he would probably show Tommy the huge rawhide bone before letting him come inside. Cara looked at the ring on her finger, looked at Buster as he went to the door and felt the pedals of life firmly under her capable feet.

As Cara turned out the lights in the living room she thought how strange and wonderful the evening had been. No one got drunk, no one argued and everyone laughed and had fun as if the night was a prelude to the future. She'd never been a religious person and she realized that the celebration of Christmas was about the birth of spirit in humans. It was the coming together of past and present to facilitate warmth in the future. She walked down the hall and loved the sound of snoring and breathing that filled her house. She loved the magic of having life fill her heart. As she crawled into bed next to Buster, Cara Covington felt love, was loved and knew that was the miracle of truly being born again.

Sandy felt small hands trying to lift her eyelids and her first thought was to slap them away but then remembered it was Christmas morning. She opened her eyes to see Tommy's smiling face not an inch from hers. She laughed and turned to look at the clock. She turned back to Tommy and whispered,

"Tommy, it's three in the morning. Are you really thinkin' about gettin' your grandma up now?"

He stood up on the bed and nodded. He explained himself in the simplest of terms.

"Mama, it's Christmas! Kids are s'posed to wake everyone up early!"

She knew he was right and made a deal with him. She told him she would go put some coffee on and he could go wake up his daddy and Robert. She explained the best way she could why it was better to wait to wake up his grandma.

"See, if you wake up Daddy and Robert first, then it will give the coffee time to brew and grandma won't forget it's Christmas and act like it's Halloween!"

Tommy was off like a shot to his daddy's room and as she passed the door on her way to the kitchen she heard him explaining to Avery why he got to be the first one woken up. She saw that Cara had set everything out for the coffee before she'd gone to bed so she simply poured the water and turned on the pot. She was taking eggs from the refrigerator when she felt arms around her. She straightened up thinking it was Tommy and saw Cara standing behind her with a huge grin on her face.

"Merry Christmas, little girl."

Sandy folded into her mother's arms and held her tight. They were interrupted by an impatient Tommy screaming it was present time, not hug time. They went into the living room and thought Tommy was going to have a heart attack when Buster went out the door.

"Hey, where is Buster going? We ain't never gonna get to open presents!"

Sandy handed him his stocking so he wouldn't feel so agitated about having to wait. He zipped past the apple and orange, briefly looked at the candy and nuts, and then fished for the toys he knew were at the bottom.

"Oh cool! Hot wheel cars! Look Mama, here's a sports car like the one you told daddy he'd be too fat to drive!"

Tommy was turned towards them and away from the front door when Buster wheeled in the bike. He was chattering away about the cars and then suddenly noticed no one was looking at him but past him. He turned and screamed at the top of his lungs.

"Oh my gosh! Is that mine? Oh wow, oh gee! That's the coolest bike I've ever seen!"

Cara sat by the tree so she could hand out the presents. She let Tommy spend time looking at his bike and handed Avery a present. She had a gleam in her eye as she winked at Sandy. Everyone watched as Avery tore away the paper. Inside he found a framed adoption certificate. It had his name on it and it said that as of December Twenty-Fifth, Nineteen-Hundred And Ninety Seven, Avery Anderson was officially the son of Ms. Cara Covington. It went on to say that if not by birth or blood then surely by life they would be mother and son always. Avery couldn't find words but his tears and hug said more to her than anything he could ever say.

Afraid she was going to cry, Cara handed Robert a present that was sure to be the laugh of the day. She moved in close to watch him open it. As he tore away the paper a stunned silence fell around the room. He held up the billy club for everyone to see and then read the attached note.

"Thought you might want to keep this close at hand. The

next time some jerk tries to hurt you for what you are, homo boy, just take this little thing and tell them to blow it out their ass!"

Their laughter was loud enough to be heard all the way into town. Cara went back to the tree and handed Avery and Robert three more presents each and then nodded to Buster to go get Sandy's. She brought out two other presents and handed one to Tommy and the other to Sandy. Tommy opened his first and showed everyone his bike helmet. Sandy opened hers and just sat looking at the bike helmet. She was about to say thanks but she was too big for Tommy's bike when Buster came through the door with a woman's bike with a huge red ribbon.

Robert handed out his presents to everyone except Sandy and Avery. He went to his room and took the last gift from his overnight bag. He came back into the living room feeling it was the one thing he could give them that no one else could right now. He watched as she unwrapped the small package. It was a checkbook and he saw the confusion in their faces. He felt he'd truly found a way to make use of the only good thing he'd ever gotten from his parents.

He heard both Sandy and Avery gasp when she opened the book and they saw not only their name on the account but the balance as well. He knew he needed to explain the gift but felt they knew why he'd given it.

"Sandy, Avery, when I was sixteen my real father died. I never really knew him and it seems he felt guilty about that before his death. He'd evidently become very wealthy through the development of land that had been in his family for generations. Anyway, he set up a trust fund for me. I've used a little of the money at times but I worked and lived mainly off of what I made at the store. I can't think of a better reason to use that money than to help the people who have truly become my family. I sure love you guys a lot more than the feelings that went with it as a gift to me!"

Complete silence fell in the room as each person felt the magnitude of giving. It was Cara who broke the spell and did it like only she could.

"So, homo boy, just how rich are you? You got any need for a mama to go with the brother and sister you just adopted?"

Cara's humor had not given Sandy or Avery an opportunity to deny Robert his chance to give. Conversation filled the room as Tommy showed Robert his Nintendo games and roller blades. Buster asked Tommy what he wanted to do first, try out the skates or the bike? Sandy suggested no matter what that he try out the helmet before either of the others.

Sandy started to pick things up while Cara was busy readying the turkey for the oven. Buster, Tommy, and Avery were outside with his bike. Sandy went into the kitchen to open the oven door so Cara could put the bird in. As soon as the bird was safely on the shelf, she hugged her mama like there was no tomorrow and every day would be today.

Cara took Sandy's right hand and led her to the couch. She sat with her and showed her the things that lived in her heart.

"You see, darlin, lives go unanswered because people look for meaning in other people and other things. It ain't till a body finds their own center that they know what kind of chocolate they are. I couldn't be a mama to you until I was a person to myself and the same holds true for every relationship a person has in life. It wasn't never about what I wasn't to you, Sandy, it was about what I couldn't be to myself. We all got bikes for Christmas, Sandy. Life is a bike and we're all pedaling through trying to avoid the potholes and clinging for dear life when we hit them. I love you, baby girl, always have, always will."

The End

Made in the USA
Lexington, KY
27 May 2016